DEAL WITH THE DEVIL

DEAL WITH THE DEVIL
The Withrow Chronicles
Book III

Michael G. Williams

Falstaff Books

Cover Design by Natania Barron

Print Formatting by Susan H. Roddey, Clicking Keys
www.clickingkeys.com

ISBN: 978-1-946926-11-1

For more information on this or other Falstaff Books publications, visit www.FalstaffBooks.com.

Published by Falstaff Books
Charlotte, North Carolina
Printed in U.S.A

To Kelly Jo for her dedication to living a life of meaning and experience.

To Josh for his endless generosity in kindness, companionship, creativity and joy.

To Kat for her ceaseless enthusiasm to make, to do and to try the new and interesting.

To Brian for his immeasurable endurance, friendship and many hugs.

To Mike for his humor, intelligence and constant encouragement.

To Corwin for his boundless creativity and humor as a storyteller.

To all my other sisters and brothers in St. Anthony Hall and my brothers in Mu Beta Psi for their devotion to art, letters and expression.

A Bit of Background

If you haven't read *Perishables* or *Tooth & Nail*, the first and second books of The Withrow Chronicles, it might help to know that Withrow Surrett is a vampire lord who lives in suburbia. He would probably object to that description but it's accurate, like it or not. Withrow has asserted personal authority over the vampires of North Carolina but spends his nights trying to go unnoticed by the state's many mortals. In *Perishables* he battles the zombie apocalypse twice: once at a meeting of his neighborhood association and again six years later at a discount store. In the latter instance he allies himself with an exceptionally resourceful employee named Jennifer McCordy who is a fellow veteran zombie combatant. *Tooth & Nail* features Withrow fighting a bunch of redneck vampires in the area where he grew up: Asheville, North Carolina. With the assistance of Roderick, his psychopathic cousin and fellow vampire, Withrow learns that there was a vampire conflict of some sort in the past though he doesn't know when or why. Withrow also develops his Last Gasp, an ability each vampire manifests (sometimes uniquely) once there is no one left in the mortal population who knew that vampire when they were alive. In Withrow's case, it's referred to as *hindsight*: the power to pick out one topic from a victim's life and learn everything there is to know about that topic. Unfortunately, it requires the victim's death.

Better yet, why not read *Perishables* and *Tooth & Nail* yourself?

Chapter 1

Ann Fletcher was out on patrol in the 800 block of Dupree Street when she opened and closed her first case as a vigilante hero.

It was approximately ten o'clock on an October night just beginning to get crisp around the edges. Ann still had another mile and a half of streets to hike before she finished her usual route. That was a lot of ground to cover in a suburban setting: lots of short segments of heavy shadows, lots of cross streets where people paid only glancing attention to stop signs, lots of uneven ground. It seemed especially far in the dispirited, better-days-seen sort of suburbia she'd adopted as her turf. There were few unbroken sidewalks and plenty of uncertainty about the future glancing out of a too-certain past as she trod them. Ann told herself it didn't bother her, though. She told herself she was used to it or that it couldn't be as bad as a hundred other situations she'd seen before. That word landed with a clank and a thud insider her own head: *before.*

Ann's shrink called these "meditation walks" and had prescribed them to her when she refused psychoactive medication to treat what he called depression and she called being bored as all hell. She had to play a certain amount of patty-cake, though, to keep her appointments going at the VA hospital. So, she manned up and went out for walks every other night after she finished her shift at Durham Tech. Ann got herself psyched for them by joining her Neighborhood Watch and treating them as a short shift of guard duty more than as exercise or meditation. It wasn't like she could just not do it and then lie to her doctor. Lying wasted everybody's time and she had come to see time as the most precious thing she had left.

Ann walked by herself as always. She kept her hair cropped very close still and tucked it out of sight under a ball cap. She was wearing dark blue jeans and lace-up boots and a black fleece. The cap kept her dark-skinned face and her narrowed, attentive eyes shielded from the glare of what few streetlights worked in these neighborhoods. She could see plenty, though. For instance, she noticed the door of 812 Dupree was ajar. It was a little old bungalow from the 1930's or 1940's, maintained but worn, recently painted a pink that couldn't conceal its slightly sagging roofline. The lights were off inside but the flickering sodium bulb at the corner revealed all she needed to know: there was a problem in that house and she was very likely the only person in the world who had noticed.

Ann showed neither hesitated nor even considered calling 911. With the care and caution of her years of training she slipped over the rail on the end of the front porch, under and past a dark front window and right up to the front door. She strained to listen and heard the clinking of metal on something else – a different metal or a very hard wood or something. There were clanks and scrapes and something jingling. Ann knew all too well what looting sounded like. She figured it was probably a burglar. She knew the people at this house had been out of town. The box at the end of the drive leaned a little to one side when the mail built up; a dog that had barked at her every night had been absent the last three; the flickering blue glow of a TV hadn't come from inside. Ann had noted all of these on her mental map of life in the shabbier parts of Durham, south of the freeway. This particular burglar presented no risk of harm to a family that wasn't home but Ann couldn't stand the thought of someone just stealing out of convenience. She felt there was a scale by which iterations of a given criminal act could be judged worse the more petty, random and unfocused they became. A personal vendetta was something Ann could understand and appreciate; bad luck roulette and pure opportunism were *not*.

She snuck the door more widely open, slipped past it and set it back as precisely where it had been as she could manage. She started silent roll steps forward up the stairs that led to the small second story. There was probably a bedroom in the back, standard with this type of floor plan, and the wobbly streak of a flashlight being bounced around from up there. As Ann climbed the steps she would test each with a hand first, almost on all fours: it distributed her weight and let her detect loose boards before stepping on them. She was up to the top in no time at all without a creak or a pop to give her away. Ann stepped into the bedroom (immediately filed in her memory: lots of dingy whites and faded colors on aged quilts, a grandmother or the aging mother of adult children who lived at home; strong impressions of maternity, dust and routine use of enough rose water skin lotion to leave a little of the scent behind in her bed) and saw a young light-skinned guy in a pair of sweat pants, running shoes and a Philadelphia Eagles sweatshirt. He was going through the jewelry on the top of the dresser to separate out costume jewelry and sweep the valuable stuff into a pillowcase. Her first thought was that the Eagles' logo was far too reflective to work on a stealth suit.

"Put down the jewelry, put your hands on your head and kneel." Her voice was a confident alto, forced lower than its natural range with a gruff aggression she had acquired from years of use. The guy looked at her, threw the flashlight at her – she dodged – and then he threw a small wooden rocking chair, sized for a child and holding a rag doll, through the thin, brittle glass of an old window before leaping out after it. Ann had the hair's-breadth slice of a second for which she was trained to decide yes or no on giving pursuit.

She dove out after him.

The window had shattered unevenly but the burglar had cleaned out most of the edges himself. He had survived the drop without apparent injury to his legs and was running across the back yard. Ann leapt far enough out the window to overshoot the debris on the ground, rolled on the side of her subordinate arm and came up in a crouch. The guy was trying to climb the fence to the next yard and doing a surprisingly quick job of it: he was over before Ann could catch up to him and she found herself slowed down by the surprising flexibility of the aging wood of the fence. It was almost spongy to the touch and could only barely support her weight; she was surprised it didn't disintegrate under the other guy but maybe he got luckier with which boards he grabbed. It occurred to her that she could just kick the fence down but that would be another cost to the homeowner. She got over the fence in time to see him swerve to the right and then the left to run around the side of the house. Ann was off and after him, running in slow, measured, easy strides, preemptively taking breaths timed for maximum oxygen and heart rate regulation. She wasn't at the absolute peak of fitness as she had been when she was deployed but she was as close as she could stay and still hold down a day job. She could easily run a couple of blocks without breaking a sweat or being noticeably out of breath.

Around the side of the house Ann went, onto Fleetwood: a dead-end with no traffic. When Eagles went across the street his feet were pounding hard. He wasn't used to this kind of exertion. The running shoes were all talk. Ann was deer-fleet as she bounded after him and every now and then his head turned and he checked to see that, yes, he was still being chased by a shadow that wasn't ever supposed to be there in the first place. She didn't bother crying out to him to stop; he'd missed his first opportunity and that was the only one she'd give him.

Directly across Fleetwood was a paint-chipped A-frame house that was up a couple of cement steps, elevated above the street. The sides of the house were dark but the living room was lighted and he stomped up the steps, across the yard and through the front door. Ann heard the door bang against the wall of the entryway and a woman's scream before she followed him through the door in a long stride. An old woman was staring and her husband was going for the mantle; he wouldn't make it to the old rifle before both she and her quarry were gone. Hell, they could have *walked* through here and beaten him to it. Eagles and then Ann flew out the door at the back of the kitchen and around an empty and weather-beaten above ground pool she figured they'd gotten for the grandkids in the spring of some more optimistic year. Eagles pushed through a high hedge that was patchy with holes; she did the same.

Another kitchen, another house of faded and aged people screaming in fear, just like the last one but in reverse. They shot, one after the other, down the front steps and into another street, across a line of pseudo-woods separating the back of a city park from the sidewalk. In the artificially open clearing, by the moonlight, she could see that he had dropped his sack of jewelry somewhere. That was no problem: he'd just saved her from having to get fingerprints on it when she caught him. They ran fast and free across close-cropped grass that had been mown to within a millimeter of its life as autumn bent closer to winter, before the frost came and dew got heavy and the groundcover stopped growing altogether. She could hear her target breathing hard, his lungs rattling deep in his chest. He was probably a smoker. This would be over soon.

Eagles surprised her by vaulting the chain link fence around the large yard of a small house someone was using as a daycare. Plastic jungle gyms from a lousy discount store and a small herd of those toy cars a toddler can sit in and push around with their feet were scattered about the place. The guy tried hilariously to pick one up and lob it backwards but it was nowhere near Ann when it came down far short. All that turning of momentum backwards just slowed him down even more. Among the several topics she imagined he had failed in school was clearly physics. She was closing the gap between them and he only had seconds left. Finally he hit the other side of the yard, went over the fence at a run and into the open garage of a low brick ranch with Christmas lights already up. These were people who took their holiday celebration seriously: multicolored icicle lights along the front gutters and electric candles in every window. Ann heard more screaming. Time to shut this guy down.

She ran in after him, past the power tools of a previous decade and a number of rather skillfully crafted birdhouses, into a laundry room and then a den where two kids were shouting their lungs out. There was an older woman brandishing a frying pan – a real cast iron frying pan, which Ann allowed herself to admire – and a big man with rough hands was blocking the burglar's exit down a hall towards whatever door or window he hoped to find. All of the people who lived here were making sounds but none of them was *saying* anything intelligible. The burglar was frozen in the chaos so Ann took her chance while she had it: one hand on his right bicep, the other on the back of his neck, she levered the burglar around and slammed his head against a wall paneled in fake pine boards. The guy's face broke through and he made some muffled cry before she yanked his right arm back and around. She heard something rip and snap; maybe his bone, maybe his shoulder, whatever, she was here to cause injuries not to diagnose them.

Ann yanked him back out of the wall by that disabled arm, blood flecking the boards as she flexed his body against his will. She twisted him around and swept one foot up to kick him in the right kneecap. Something audibly snapped before he went down in a shrieking heap. Ann dropped to one knee by his right side, rolled him onto his stomach, yanked both wrists behind him and pinned them with her weight. She stuffed a throw pillow into his mouth to shut him up. It bore a machine-stitched message of incongruous good cheer.

Everyone was still screaming so Ann looked from each to the next in slow, serious succession. Eye contact can either excite or calm civilians and she was using it to assert authority. She wanted them to know they could let go of their fear of being out of control in the sudden chaos. The man stared in silence and the woman continued to brandish that well-seasoned frying pan but they all fell silent after a few stunned seconds. Ann looked back down and studied the burglar long enough to make sure he wasn't trying to muster meth-strength or something. He had that slight mothball smell but she guessed it was from production rather than consumption. She let her eyes flick over again to the man of the house. They locked gazes for a long second. He turned, finally, to the woman: "Call 911, Dora." He was a huge slab of beef: tall, with skin the color of toffee and what hair he had left turning gray. Dora was a little younger but not much; too young to be a grandmother, though. They must have been kids when they got together. They'd made a happy little life together. His birdhouses revealed a soul that could see the value in doing something well for another's enjoyment. Dora lowered the frying pan. She was wearing a pink housecoat with fuchsia roses sewn down the front like a priest's vestment. She swept into the kitchen and Ann heard a phone pick up.

There was absolutely no way Ann would be able to explain this to the police. There was just no way. This was everything a cop fears in a neighborhood watch. This was going to be way too Trayvon Martin for anybody's tastes. Ann shook her head at the man, once to each side, with a hard look that communicated urgency. She heard Dora say, "Yes, I need the police. I'm at..." The guy hadn't been quick enough to say something. The street address was out. The police would come. Ann had broken almost as many laws as this burglar had. She had stopped him, though. He was a criminal; she wasn't; but she wasn't sure the police would recognize the distinction. There would be an awful lot of questions.

Ann yanked an old lamp off a table, ripped the cord out of the wall socket and then pulled the other end free of the lamp's base in one tug, her arms flexing. Her whole body sang out in joy for this chance to run and chase and *fight* again. Lifting weights and going jogging and taking long walks were not the same as action. They were less than methadone to a heroin addict, less than any other substitute she could think of for any other act. They were like hearing someone describe a porno. This chase had been the real thing.

Ann tied the guy's wrist in a knot not even a boy scout could recognize or undo and yanked the pillow out of his mouth; no good stealing from these people in the course of preventing the theft from some others. Ann hefted the burglar over one shoulder, held him by his feet, stood up and tested her weight: she could move with the guy like this. She thought about his Eagles logo and wrenched to twist him around to one side, then over, so that the insignia was on the inside of the fold she had made of him over her shoulder. It wouldn't be comfortable for him but it would be harder for him to fight and she didn't much care.

Even as the guy who lived there cried out for her to stop, Ann ran back out through the laundry room and the workshop garage, into the street and across it and back into the park. On her way through she grabbed a used shopping bag from Target and in the darkest corner of a copse of trees she turned it into a gag around the guy's mouth. He could still breathe but he couldn't vocalize. Then she set off to cut through dark neighborhoods and onto the American Tobacco Trail, a bike and jogging path that was technically closed at night. Once on it she turned towards downtown and the Durham Bulls Athletic Park.

Twenty minutes later, Ann had trussed the guy up in a couple of extension cords she found at the ballpark and tied him to the front of the huge motorized Snorting Bull overlooking the stadium. It was lighted at all times and accessible from a restaurant patio behind it. The Bull was built for a movie but stuck around. During games it announced victories and home runs: its eyes would light up, the tail would wag and smoke would come out of its nose. The front read, in plain white letters, HIT BULL WIN STEAK. This was the most obvious public place Ann could think of on short notice and it was right on the trail. She figured, what the hell, if she wanted the guy to be found she might as well shine a literal spotlight on him.

Ann worked fast and was lucky: it took the cops even less time to notice the guy hanging there than she'd imagined. While a couple of police officers were interviewing Clyde and Dora Hanford about the anonymous melee that had burst into their home off South Alston Avenue, many of their colleagues were swarming the DBAP. When they realized the place was otherwise empty they just stood around while a fire truck brought down the apparent kidnapping victim on hand. When he was conscious, the burglar was only too happy to confess to his crimes if it kept him away from the lunatic who'd put him up there. The next day a writer in the *Herald-Sun* made an allusion to the repeating logo found on the shopping bag Ann had fashioned into a gag and to the sign from which the burglar had been displayed for police to find: he dubbed the anonymous vigilante "The Bull's Eye". It was a joke, but it stuck. Durham, North Carolina, also known as the Bull City, had its first superhero.

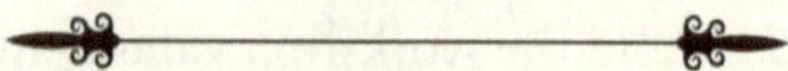

Ann went home and slept well for the first time in many months. She did not bother to linger over old photos of herself in Delta Force days as she often did. She simply walked in, changed clothes and went to bed. The silence of the house usually kept her awake for a while after she tried to close her eyes but this time it couldn't get its hooks in.

Her therapist was very glad to hear she wanted to make her "meditation walks" a nightly practice.

Chapter 2

A couple of other vampires and I were watching the local youth ballet perform *Dracula* in hypnotic slow motion when a perfectly pleasant autumn broke out in a war. It started with a scent: the faint but distinctly sickly sweet bloodstench of a fellow predator – another vampire, one I didn't recognize – in an auditorium I'd expected to hold only humankind. One sniff sent the hairs on the back of my neck straight to standing and I groaned to myself. I was still thoroughly spoiled then: I'd gone out with some friends to enjoy a little culture. I didn't want to endure politics instead.

The ballet performance was good but not great. To be honest, that's one of the things I liked best about it. At human speeds of perception it probably looked fine enough, maybe a little rickety in the way of every event ever staged for parental benefit. I'm a vampire, though, so I was watching everything happen at a fraction of real time courtesy of my predator eyes. Ground to a supernaturally slow pace, that same ballet performance took on a poetry improved by its imperfections. A child – a teen, but gods: a child! – donned the mantle of that classic monster skillfully but not infallibly and I loved every second of it. The best art speaks to something universal and at the same time to something deeply felt and *personal*: Faulkner's tales of familial claustrophobia, a lasting pop song, painted landscapes that snare the viewer's mind by arranging colors and textures into somewhere familiar they've never been. These kids were doing the same with the archetypes of predator and prey.

The teenager in the title role was depicting a character we'd all seen a hundred times, sure, but he was also showing us *himself* as a monster: how it would look one day when *he* would stalk one or another type of prey. That probably didn't occur to the average mom and dad in the audience but there were children on stage hunting and fearing and slaying one another to the applause of those who loved them and it was important – it was *art* – not just because of the skill or the time they'd invested in it but because they too would one day face monsters and chase each other and eventually they would maybe even kill or be killed. These kids were dancing the nightmares that kept them awake into the gray hours and so too their own uneasy society. In wide arcs and graceful swoops – and trembling embraces and slightly staggered tempos – their frail vitality contrasted the inevitability of mortality and I reveled in that contrast.

They weren't actually moving in slow motion, but I was seeing them that way. Speeding ourselves up so that the world around us slows down is a vampire specialty. It's a useful trick when you're swooping down off a fire escape onto the back of unsuspecting prey, of course, but we use it for other stuff all the time. Sometimes, in the end, I find it fails to improve an experience. I had thought there would be a satisfying perversion in attending the performance of a stage illusionist and using supernatural powers to observe as he palmed the coin, privately forcing a demonstration of the *absence* of magic behind the trick. It held some pleasure, yes, but it also felt like finding the Christmas presents early: sneaky, fun and just a little disappointing. The pleasure of revelation fades into a shadow of regret. You learn it's possible to scratch an itch so hard it breaks the skin.

Used purely as an enhancement of the spectator experience, the best targets are any circumstances in which physical strength, agility or speed must be exploited to create the illusion of delicacy. A curveball thrown with full force looks like the nimblest of insects at hyper speed. I've known or heard about vampires who would sit and watch spiders spin webs because, dangerously close though that might be to living the stereotype, it afforded them an opportunity to meditate on the patience with which one might plan and execute some plot or vendetta. It is a different thing to watch someone dribble a ball down the court in the blink of an eye than it is to watch that same athlete use all the big muscles of the arms and legs and back in concert with all the little muscles and tendons around ankles and wrist and fingers and eyes to control a ball in a spontaneous and self-updating zigzag down the court. I don't know the first thing about basketball – I mean, honestly, it's just a game – but I respect how beautiful all that thoughtless self-control is when not just seen but *examined*.

That's all to say I was sitting stock still in the first balcony of an historic Jazz Age theatre in downtown Durham, North Carolina, when that smell of another vampire was carried to me from the orchestra level by a slight updraft: the simple physics of body heat in a venue with over a thousand seats.

As I mentioned, I was with colleagues. I was sitting with two vampires: Seth and Beth, whom I tend to regard as the rhyming opposites. After all the business with the Transylvanian I'd decreed that we all had to go out and be sociable with one another sometimes. I'd been convinced by my cousin Roderick – to whom I'd handed control of the city of Asheville, four hours to the west – of the value in choosing to stay a part of the world, to generally do things *people* do. So, we'd gone to see the ballet because I got a chuckle out of the thought of vampires having a social outing to see *Dracula* and just about every bloodsucker loves to watch mortals dance.

We gazed with slack faces as performers whirled and twisted their joints so that parts of their bodies could snap into a specific posture on more or less the right beat. There was a small orchestra droning in long, humming tones across my warped perception as I watched. The magic of dance is that the human body is a collection of curved shapes, all stuck together, and these kids could stretch and bend those arcs into wholly new geometries that were fascinatingly alien to their form.

Beth is a dancer by trade. She runs a strip club, which I'm sure some people would try to wall off behind caveats, but bodies in motion are bodies in motion. She was sitting in entranced fascination. Beth was in fantastic physical shape when she got turned into one of us but she has the least interesting face in human history. That forgettable mug sits in front of mouse-brown hair she pulls back in a limp ponytail. Beth tends to tuck her dancer's body away under layered sweatshirts and dresses the size and shape of a flour sack. I don't criticize her for this or question her reasons for doing so. We all hide ourselves from the world in some way and a woman in our culture has at least ten times the reasons of any man.

Seth looks like a young '80s punk: all badly bleached mohawk, sinewy limbs and blank gaze in leather and studs. He has slightly olive skin and I have no idea what ethnicity he might be or how old he really is. Beth turned up ignorant of everything but fangs just a few years ago so I'm pretty sure she's extremely new to this stuff but Seth has eyes as old as time and then some. He looks like a kid with a bad case of Small Dog Complex (chief symptom: bark without ceasing) but in fact he is quiet and wise in a way few of us are. I used to think he would one day be gunning for my job – I'm in charge of the whole state with a couple of exceptions – but now I think he'd do anything to stay out of the spotlight.

I'm a huge fat-ass and I like the balcony of that particular theatre because the seats feel bigger and the tiered rows have more legroom. I was dressed chiefly in black, but that's because that's what I always wear. Under my black overcoat I had on a white and silver checkerboard shirt and pants so dark gray they were black in most light. I had on old jump boots I'd about worn out, but not quite, and the big mop of wavy black hair on my forehead was flopping over in a fashion regrettably close to being back in style. I'd liked being something of an anachronism, but no such luck anymore. At least I was sitting in a balcony once forced on African-Americans as a form of institutionalized insult. I need to feel a little bit like an outcast, all the time, everywhere, or I never quite know what to do with myself.

We were staring in silent fascination but that scent of unknown vampire from the orchestra level nearly snapped me out of my meditation hard enough to push me back to normal speed. I leaned forward very slowly and started flicking my eyes around the seats below us. I didn't immediately see anyone or anything of interest so I glanced to either side and saw that Beth still seemed to be lost in the moment; that's how we refer to it sometimes when we really zone out watching something. Seth's eyes were also crawling all over the audience. He and I locked gazes for a fraction of a second and he gave me a curt nod: he had likewise detected it and failed to recognize the source.

I leaned forward – extremely slowly, just in case that would camouflage me amongst all the other fractional movements going on in any given instant of human perception – and looked across more of the floor. Seth did the same. Beth still didn't seem to have noticed or cared, and though Seth and I sat there gawking as hard as we could no one seemed to do anything out of the ordinary.

The odds were, and we both knew this, that the other vampire in the audience was probably sitting very still and watching the performance as we had – or, perhaps, that he didn't have the ability to dilate time like most of us do and so he was sitting there watching it as a human would. I'd pity him a little if that were the case but we all wind up with such a weird grab bag of powers he probably had something to make up for it. Shit happens.

The problem for me was purely that I didn't recognize him. That meant he was new in town or that he'd *better* be. Hopefully he was just a tourist – maybe he'd even come in just for this one show – because if he wasn't then he and I had to have a conversation and those talks were rarely fun for anyone. Sometimes people would ask around, call ahead, make themselves easy to notice or otherwise try to be polite, but not always. Vampires have worked out a system of subtle signs they can leave in public to indicate they're new in town and looking to connect to whatever the local social scene might be. It's not entirely unlike the hobo signs of an earlier era and from time to time I've wondered if they somehow got the idea from us. Sign use isn't totally universal but they're the common etiquette in major East Coast urban centers these nights. I hadn't noticed any of them around lately but on the other hand Durham is both in my turf and not where I spend most of my time.

Sure, I'm in charge of the vampires of North Carolina, but it's a big state. When I say I'm in charge I don't mean I'm so conceited I think I can actually know everything going on in all places at all times. What I mean is I reserve the right to find out what's going on in any given place at any given time. There are vampires I more or less trust as my proxies in two towns: my nutso cousin Roderick up the mountain in Asheville and an ally named Sara who nests in Greensboro. There are also a couple of places where none of us ever dares go, especially the city of Charlotte. Besides those, though, I have no hesitation telling someone that North Carolina is mine. Where I *live*, on the other hand, is Raleigh. Though it is only twenty minutes from Durham by any number of highways, Raleigh is big and it's where the vampires in my part of the state are concentrated. Durham used to be a really run-down town with horrible city and county governments and too much crime, too much sprawl, too little to give a shit about, but in the last few decades it's really pulled itself together. That's a lot of why I started coming to shows in Durham on occasion instead of sticking strictly to Raleigh: Durham is just as nice a place to hang out as anywhere else.

If it appealed to me, though, it could just as easily appeal to others. I knew I needed to spend more time in Durham and in Chapel Hill than I'd been doing in order to create moments just like this: opportunities to find out things I needed to know. I wasn't exactly on patrol, per se, but I wasn't exactly not on patrol, either. That didn't make me any happier about having my reverie broken by the appearance of a strange vampire but were I really honest with myself I'd admit I'd come here in hope – and fear – of exactly this.

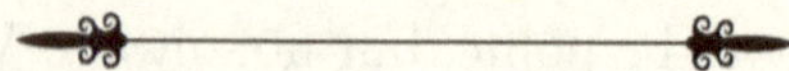

I immediately started thinking of this unknown vampire as a trespasser. My knee jerk reaction was to view them as at best a rude guest and at worst an invader. My experience with the Transylvanian, an ancient vampire who'd tried to set up his own little sphere of influence in the mountains around Asheville the year before, had made me wary and touchy and territorial all over again, just like I'd been right after I stole the crown from the last state-wide boss. My inability to spot this interloper started to grate on me after not very much time at all, so I turned off the slow-mo and let time rush into the chronological vacuum created whenever I use it. There's this weird kind of hiss and pop sound and then, boom, everyone goes from sounding like they're very far away and under water to sounding normal again. It was just in time for the movement going on right then to wrap up and the applause to start as the house lights came on. It was intermission. I turned to Seth and said, "Sorry, but I just can't sit here and enjoy myself anymore. Time to go to work."

Beth had rejoined the here and now, too, and was completely oblivious to what was going on. "She's very beautiful," Beth said in a kind of dreamy exhalation. I looked over, followed her gaze to the dance floor – empty now, curtain descending – and Beth went on. "If we turned her she could dance forever." She sounded like she was high on the good stuff and I half smiled and half sighed.

"No dice," I said. "Remember that." I held up a finger and caught her eye by waving it in front of her and then used it to drag her vision back to me. "Remember. Seriously. No turning anyone."

"I know," she said. She sounded a little closer to the here and now – not that she ever got closer than spitting distance from it most nights – but her voice was a little sad. "Still, it's a pretty thought."

I dipped my forehead towards the stage. "No," and I put one hand lightly on Beth's shoulder as I said this, "It's that *she* was a pretty thought." I smiled at Beth as I stood and turned around to walk down the aisle. Seth's face – always so still and emotionless – was so blank it spoke volumes. Beth always seems one misstep away from going on a permanent mental vacation and I wondered how many vampires of that sort Seth had seen in his unknown and unknowable years.

Intermission was a chance to go get some popcorn and a beer and I am never one to turn down fresh movie theater popcorn or a cold one. My maker taught me to eat after she turned me. It's not something most vampires can still do. I mean, sure, they could put food in their mouth and chew it and make it go down their esophagus but they would eject it again pretty much immediately. My sire knows how useful it is to fit in amongst the living. Agatha made me sit and eat little nibbles of soft, bland, inoffensive things in the nights and weeks immediately following my turning. That was decades ago now and let me be the first one to tell you that there was plenty of boring white pap around to practice on in the 1940's. If someone had asked me back then to describe Indian food, for instance, I would have thought they meant Wild West type Indians. There wasn't a tremendous amount of variety back then. I was enthusiastic to learn to eat, though, because I had never been one to shy away from the plate when I was among the living and I had no intention of giving up one iota of pleasure in the ever after, either.

I went downstairs to the lobby's concession stand, bellied up to the counter and ordered my food. Popcorn and beer in hand, I walked outside to a courtyard of bricks and paving stones and concrete hell. I settled in on a bench of shaped and shapeless cement conceived in some war crime of urban planning. This place had been designed during Durham's bad old days. The landscape was constructed from the bits and pieces lying around some hack's pale excuse for an imagination: obstructing curves and prickly shrubs and all the creature comforts of a cargo container. I started eating popcorn one puffed kernel at a time, slowly but steadily, as I watched the throng of smokers and their friends and anyone else who'd walked outside during the break. I wasn't sure exactly for what I was looking but I figured I'd know when I saw it. Sure enough, a few moments later I felt that *tingle*.

You know what it is: that sense of being watched. So many narratives hinge on that moment of intuition that it has taken on an air of being a trope but the fact is it happens sometimes and we all know it even though it scares us not to know why. I once read a theory that it has to do with low-grade, subconscious telepathy given off by the watcher's brain and picked up by that of the watched, but that seems a little far-fetched to me and I say that as a pretty far-fetched thing in the world. I've also heard a theory that it has to do with subharmonic sounds or something people generate that tip one another off to their presence. I don't know what it is, but I felt it and it's not the sort of thing a vampire feels very often. When we do, well, we know it right away. It made me think of Z Day, the first Steeplechase Event: the night zombies rose out of an abandoned graveyard next to my neighborhood. That tingle had been what I felt whenever their attention turned to me: the certain knowledge something predatory was sizing me up.

I tried not to react, at least not visibly. You don't survive your first sixty-odd years or so by being jumpy or quick to overreact. Instead, I sat there and ate my popcorn and drank my beer and as I felt those creepy crawly eye tingles on the back of my neck I focused instead on how I could turn around and look without giving away that my watcher had blown his cover. After all, I figured there could only be one person who would be trying to spy on me: the interloper, who had undoubtedly smelled me in the lobby when he also came out at intermission.

Hell, it was half of why I went to get a snack: to give them a chance to notice and present themselves. Well, okay, maybe a third of why.

I had almost decided I wouldn't need a reason to turn around – I was going to finish my popcorn and the intermission was going to be over – when I heard Seth call my name from across the plaza.

"Withrow!" Seth didn't sound angry or agitated, just letting me know he was on the approach. I appreciated that. Seth is very conscious of boundaries and of politeness and that carries a tremendous amount of weight with our kind. Still, the part of me that was once a mortal man wanted to jump out of my skin. I turned around and looked across the plaza perhaps over-much, as though not sure exactly where or who had called out to me. Under the black studded leather Seth was dressed in anonymous gray slacks grown careworn and a slightly undersized t-shirt that made him look like a scrawny guy trying too hard to look tough. That was probably some twisted and over-complicated form of camouflage for him. I'd seen him fight; he could have killed everyone in the building, half of them before they'd known what was happening.

I started to say something in response, something generic and innocuous and forgettable, when the spidey senses all of a sudden just... went blank. The interloper who had been staring at me, watching me, probably scoping me out as a potential threat, was apparently no longer interested. I left my mouth hanging open and scanned the periphery of the crowd – teenagers sneaking sips of something from hip flasks, their boyfriends with cigarettes, little kids running around – but I didn't see anything out of the ordinary. I even stood up and got real obvious with my looking, but no, not a single ping on the old radar. The intruder was gone.

Seth didn't bother to ask what was going on. He just stood there and scanned the crowd, eyes moving methodically from one face to another. "Was he out here?"

"Yeah." I clucked my tongue at nothing, scolding myself halfheartedly. "He was watching me. But the moment you called my name he took off."

Seth made a little hrmph noise from deep down in his sculpted – and extremely attractive, I had to admit – chest. Too bad he didn't roll that way; not that there's much point to it for vampires, but sometimes the coffin's a little lonely on a cold night. *Anyway*, he didn't like that the interloper had studied me and then taken off once he heard my name. "Possible follower of the Transylvanian?"

I drew a breath, considered my answer and then shook my head. "Nah. I think Roderick's probably cleaned them up sufficiently that there wouldn't be anyone left to care that much." That had been the mission I'd given my cousin: destroy anyone left from the Transylvanian's budding enterprise.

"Could be someone who wants to make a name for himself locally," Seth went on. He shrugged. "Play the mystery man, sneak around, brag about how he got away with it. That's, like, Rep Building 101 when you're new in town."

I glanced over at him and smiled a little. "Voice of experience?"

Seth allowed one corner of his lips to curl upwards for half a second. "Just thinking out loud."

"Sure," I chuckled. I didn't give a shit how many other vampires Seth had toppled in his day. He was my second in command and he was apparently perfectly comfortable there. If he decided to turn on me I would never see him coming, and we both knew it, so there was no point sitting around being paranoid. "Anyway," I said, with nothing to follow it. I drained the last of the beer in my bottle and chucked my popcorn bag in the trash. "Enjoy the second act."

"You going after him?"

"The scent is fresh," I said, and I hopped relatively lightly down from my bench, all three hundred fifty pounds of me. "And daylight's not getting any farther away."

"I'll tell Beth you said goodnight."

"Thanks," I smiled, genuinely fond of both of them and able to show it in some small way for once. "But I doubt she'll notice I'm gone. She's more checked out than usual." I didn't feel paternal towards Beth but she lived on my turf and I liked her and I wanted to make sure she never went off the deep end and did something bad.

"Well, she comes and goes," Seth murmured.

"I know," I said, "Let's hope she always comes back." I held out my right hand and Seth, with only the minimum necessary amount of hesitation, took it and pumped it once up and down before letting go.

"It's been a long time since we've had trouble right around home," he said, voice low. "I hope we don't have it again anytime soon." The scent of a new vampire had spooked him more than I would have guessed. To me it was an annoyance; to Seth it was a cause for genuine worry. I wondered again about that phrase I'd heard in the memories of the Transylvanian: "the last war". I wondered when it was and how much of it Seth had seen. For some reason, however, it didn't even occur to me to ask.

"Don't worry," I said instead, shaking my head. "I doubt he's one of Bob's and if he is then we'll just kill him, too."

Bob had been the boss of North Carolina before me, and a right bastard, and the third in a long line of Bob's stretching back as far as anyone remembered. I got the gig for myself by taking the last Bob out; then his chauffeur and all of his spawn; then I burned down the house they'd lived in. After that I put out the word I was king of the hill and anybody who disagreed could come talk to me but they might want to bring every friend they had. No one took me up on it.

I would have been only too glad to dust every single vampire who was loyal to that self-satisfied old ball of crap. I killed him on the side of an abandoned stretch of dark road because I wanted him to know who'd done it and I wanted him to die alone. Plenty of people referred to it as "Withrow's coup" but in my heart of hearts I considered it a successful slave rebellion. We had been expected to kowtow and suck it up and give Bob all the best hunting rights and ask his permission to zip up our pants every time we took a piss. I'd tolerated more than my share of that by the time I'd been in Raleigh for forty years.

Once I was sure no one was aiming for an open confrontation I set about the business of killing every vampire I could get my hands on who had any relation to Bob the Third. After I'd run out of them I started going after the maybes and the kindas and then I'd simply started killing off possible mortal relatives of the last. There weren't any little Boblings left to pop up and make a bid for revenge. I spent years making sure of that.

I'd killed so many of Bob's line I wasn't sure I could tell Seth – another vampire, my second in command – how many without sounding a little crazy. He'd never know the miles I put on my old Firebird just chasing rumors about self-important little pipsqueaks who happened to be named Robert or Rob or Bob or Bobby and how many whimpering little lives I'd ended just to make sure there was no chance any of them would ever turn out to be related to the Raleigh Bobs of old.

Seth studied me as I let all that run through my head and I wondered if he were telepathic. That would be a shitty thing to find out the hard way, I said to myself, and then I realized if he were telepathic then he'd just heard that, too. Even though he didn't show any sign of anything, I couldn't resist letting myself laugh a little, just once, which got something like quizzical uncertainty out of him. That's the way it is with us: always playing the weird little angles against one another, even against the ones we almost sort of think of as our friends.

"Anyway," I said, "I'm going to go look for him. See you around."

"Later," Seth mumbled, and he strolled back inside as I moseyed down the sidewalk and around a corner into darkness, nostrils wide, trying to find a hunter in the streets of night.

Chapter 3

Durham started out as a tobacco town. When I was alive it was the place Chesterfields were made. You probably don't remember Chesterfields, but they were a major brand when I was a kid. I remember the slogan: "Blow some my way." These days I don't even know if they're still around. Plenty of vampires smoke – not exactly a big risk of cancer when you're dead – but lately it's gotten so damned inconvenient. It used to be a great way to remember to breathe or to cover for not having misty breath on cold nights, that kind of thing, but now it's just not as useful because you can't do it any damned where you like. I guess that's for the best. I don't have any special love for carcinogens in the food chain. I gave up the cover of smoking years ago when they started outlawing it in bars. All the good brands are gone anyway.

I set off up the hill on Morgan Street, headed northwest through downtown. Durham is a small city of huge old cigarette factories and tobacco warehouses, some renovated and turned into condos and others sitting there waiting for a second career to arrive while they crumble in slow silence. There are more of the latter than the former and the empty ones are the tallest by far: huge slabs of brick and concrete standing mute in one another's shadows. They're skyscrapers compared to the rest of the two- to four-story buildings that make up Durham's downtown. Durham is not a real metropolis. It is not some expanse of cloud-clawing glass and steel. Durham is just a town, but a town with a lot of history and a lot of money and a couple of huge, renowned universities sitting behind miles of low rock walls in opposite corners of town.

The tobacco company that made Chesterfields and the college that turned into Duke were both started by the same people. Duke does a ton of medical research now, so Durham is called the City of Medicine. A city of medicine framed in tobacco buildings is just about right in a lot of ways as an emblem of the South, of North Carolina, of the twentieth century. The other big institution is North Carolina Central, a major historically black university and one of the very best law schools in the southeast. Squatting all around it are blocks upon blocks of lower- and middle-income African-American neighborhoods white people tend to lump together, entirely inaccurately, as the "ghetto".

Morgan Street met Main Street at the top of the hill. The scent of the interloper seemed to turn right down Main, towards the part of town that catered to Duke: a bunch of great restaurants and a record store and a gas station or two. I sighed and stuffed my hands into my pockets. Colleges are like vampire flypaper. They seem like such a great place to crash. The bars and tiny rock clubs and countless parties that pile up around them like suckling pigs look like the easy pickings we're all always happy to find, but it's a false allure.

Going that direction meant walking down a shadowy street framed by overhanging tunnels between abandoned factory buildings. Chutes just big enough for a man to crawl along connected all the buildings to one another, four or five stories above the sidewalk. I imagined carts full of Chesterfields being rolled from one end to the other, a team of men hunched over in a too-small space shoving it along toward their counterparts at the other end. The recipients would be waiting to empty it into some great machine, everyone's mind on the carton of free smokes they got at the end of the day to hand around to their friends.

It didn't bother me even a little to consider that the intruder might be waiting for me in those shadows. I like being able to be direct about things, even if it means walking into an ambush.

The old Liggett Meyer factory was two blocks long and two blocks wide with a giant quadrate cross of street and alleyways at its center. I strolled down it, listening to my own boots clack against the brickwork of the sidewalk, hoping like hell I'd hear the scuff of another's shoes coming out of the darkness to attack. There was no better place for it in all of downtown: quiet, dark, abandoned, feared. There were condominiums nearby in what used to be warehouse space but they had a couple of buildings shielding them from the complex industrial corpse I was navigating at the moment. Two people – or two vampires – could fight and scratch and holler all night without a respectable soul so much as rolling over in their sleep.

One step, and then another, and then a dozen more; I crossed the intersection after pausing to gaze into the deepest shadows with a vampire's piercing eyes. Nothing. I didn't see a thing. There weren't even rats down those alleys because there weren't any people around anymore to leave trash for them to eat.

With a few more steps I was back in the light. There were people all over the damn place. The sensory crush of mortals and food coming from the restaurants around Brightleaf Square was too much for me to be able to dissect in search of one specific scent. I walked on past them, nose alert, but the fish-fry place alone was enough to scrub the air of any useful trail I could follow. It was like trying to find a fingerprint under three coats of paint. I gave up bothering. There was only one really notable thing on up this street anyway: Duke University and its false promise of easy co-ed prey.

The reason colleges and universities are such terrible places for vampires these days are manifold, but I'll run them down briefly. First and foremost is the Internet. Once upon a time a vampire who had been turned at the right age could spend decades in the isolated ecosystems prone to formation around a college. Live near campus, go to parties and make new friends every four years; lather, rinse, repeat. The high churn in student populations meant one could have the best of both anonymity and identity: a persona one maintained believably and which was then forgotten by countless generations of students on a four-year cycle.

No more of that these nights. Now everyone stays in contact forever with old chums. I guess a really dedicated vampire could maintain online identities for each of their various cover stories, recycling them every few years, but it's already too much work trying to maintain one false identity in the real world without the Internet getting involved. Every twenty or thirty years we're up to our belly buttons in transfers of property, fictional heirs, supporting legends, mortal paperwork, birth certificates, death certificates and on and on and on, and it all has to be done again just as fast. Trying to do the social media stuff on top of all that – changing names, setting up new accounts, untagging all those party photos and blocking everyone we used to know – is just crazy. Jesus, I hadn't thought of it before, but were we all setting ourselves up for trouble by avoiding social media now? In thirty years, would it be suspicious not to have a whole online life already documented? The fixers – vampires and cooperative mortals who get paid to do the heavy lifting on that stuff – were going to make a million bucks.

Reason number two to avoid a college campus is the modern obsession with cameras. Every kid on every college campus has a camera built into a phone. Roderick is the one who explained this part to me: they take pictures all the time and post them willy-nilly and *bang*, the wrong picture is everywhere and nowhere. Anybody can find it and nobody can make it go away. Then there are all the cameras owned by the school itself. You don't need too many instances of shootings or muggings or lawsuits to convince the Board of Trustees pervasive surveillance cameras might be cheaper than paying out when someone's precious snowflake gets shot up by their crazy ex.

So, despite being covered in nubile men and women quite comfortable making out with a total stranger and waking up the next morning feeling drained, remembering nothing, cameras and paranoia and social media have conspired to make a college one of the most dangerous places available to vampires. If they only knew the favor the powers that be have done themselves.

Two blocks later I was standing right next to the campus of Duke University. I'd hoped I'd get the scent back by the time I got away from the fish-fry but no such luck. I could smell nothing but crisp autumn air and willing teens. I sighed and ambled off down the gravel path that bordered Duke's campus. I was just killing time by then: no point in trying to hoof it back to the theatre for the rest of the second act and no target left to track, so why not enjoy a walk while I had the chance? It was a lovely evening, and even though I knew better than to feed on a college campus it was still fun to window shop.

Mainly, I think I just wanted some time alone. Vampires have plenty of that, of course, but now that I knew there was a stranger in town who seemed to be avoiding me, I knew I probably had a problem to solve. If there was new trouble to be had, the moment of respite I could take now was going to be all on its own over the next little while.

Duke's campus contained huge swaths of protected forest extending long fingers of green all over any map of the town. That was all called Duke Forest, of course, because if rich people are good at anything it's putting granddad's name on everything in sight. Some of the forest's acreage wasn't anywhere near the university campus but enough of it was contiguous that a walk from one end of Duke to the other – from East Campus to West – could take me through a huge chunk of lonely and quiet and delightfully dark places. I set off at my usual plodding trudge, slipping past a few of the freshman dorms and the world's ritziest steam plant.

Eventually I walked under a highway overpass and the forest started to really open up around me. The street tunneled between trees to connect the two halves of the campus map. It was a curving road with two lanes, a generous sidewalk and a handful of dim street lamps but basically no man-made structures: just woods and more woods. A footpath ran uphill to the left, towards some rundown housing overvalued by virtue of its proximity to campus. A university bus went past me at one point, all moaning engine and groaning shocks. Otherwise, no one at all saw me and I saw no one else. There was no one around to see or be seen on a chilly Friday night.

As I emerged onto West Campus I strolled by some old houses the school had bought from earlier generations of faculty. Elaborate, expansive homes had been converted into offices for small programs, strangely isolated from the rest of campus: little islands of administrivia in someone else's fairy-story woods. There was an office for "graduate life" (whatever that meant) over here and an environmental studies program over there, all trying to turn the ersatz dining rooms of old money into a place to store paperclips and printer toner. They were lighted like snow globes in a dark curio cabinet, fighting against the shadows with fluorescents and keycard locks. Not all of them were in use. Some of them stood out for being so quiet, so empty, so devoid of signage.

On a couple I noticed the signs out front were blank and the interiors were completely dark. A disused building, especially one that looks like a house, has a special aura of emptiness it gives off. I live in suburbia and the housing crash of the mid-aughts of the twenty-first century produced more than a few in my neighborhood. They gape at passersby like a corpse in a ditch. Someday a psychologist or an anthropologist or something like that is going to figure out why they stand out so much. Science will gin up some mundane explanation involving a small detail we don't realize we have the capacity to parse. Until then I like to think of it as a malevolent psychic aura detected by some mystic antenna the average human being has forgotten they have. The world is a lot more fun with a little magic left in it.

The autumn night was beautiful and I was taking my time and enjoying myself. My anxiety over the intruder was dissolving. Maybe he just didn't know what he was doing. Maybe he was new. Maybe his maker got killed right after turning him – it happens more than we like to admit. Maybe he's just plain dumb. Maybe I would find him and it would all work out. Maybe he would try to challenge me and I could get rid of him in a fashion so messy no one would try that again for fifty years. There were a lot of ways this could turn out OK and I was running over them in my mind, playing out scenarios in which I drove him off, killed him, made an ally of him, welcomed him as a subordinate or a peer. I fanned out all the possible happy outcomes in the hand of imagination and waved mental fingers over them, spoiled for choice.

Of course, that's when I just barely detected his scent again.

I stopped dead in the street, closed my eyes, opened my ears and took slow, deep, even breaths. I pushed my senses out as far as I could strain them – out across trees and shrubs and humming power lines and leaves just thinking about turning brown – and I couldn't find anything but that one faint trace of a vampire I didn't recognize. I wasn't even entirely sure it had been tonight. I was certain he'd been here, though, and it was the closest I had to a clue so I stood there and sniffed for all I was worth.

The trail – the faint echo of the impression of the *ghost* of a trail, but you don't wind up in charge of a state by being lousy at this stuff – led off the same way I was already going and, I suspected, right into the large, beautiful and civilian-packed Sarah P. Duke Gardens. It's a massive botanical space full of rolling lawns and jogging paths and, at other times, Saturday afternoon play groups, amateur photographers and self-guided tours. It was the sort of landmark where it would be a very, *very* stupid idea for anyone to hunt or live or otherwise risk discovery. Vampires stay out of huge, beloved, public spaces for the same reason hookers stay off of Main Street. I sighed and shook my head to myself, fluttering my eyes open again. He had to be a kid, I figured. He probably had no idea what he was doing.

At least a couple of major campus thoroughfares curved around the outer edges of Yet Another Duke This or That. I walked down the side of one until the scent took a sharp right onto a gravel path and disappeared into the darkness. I followed the faint, old olfactory impression and was surprised to detect a faint aroma of human blood underneath it. I was led along by that harmonious mix of vampire and victim, like a cartoon cat dragged nose-first by the scent of a fresh-baked pie, past a storybook babbling brook and around the side of an old hexagonal snack bar at a snail's pace. I was moving slowly so I could keep my ears and eyes open for anything that might start or jump or otherwise take off running.

It turned out to be just the squirrels and me though, and whatever other tiny things ran around the Gardens at night. I didn't see or hear or smell any sign of any life form higher than a rabbit. I was a little surprised there weren't some drunken teenagers out in the bushes at this hour, but I was sticking to the main paths as my respective quarries had done. Eventually I meandered across a long, beautiful and entirely out of place Japanese bridge over one end of a large pond, up an abrupt little bit of steps and was deposited in what looked like a street through the ugly part of an industrial park.

Across from me were the business ends of a couple of random stone buildings and the mechanical detritus they'd tried to sweep out of donors' view: HVAC systems and dumpsters and whatnot. There was an ambulance outside one of the buildings, parked between a loading dock and the largest stand-alone air conditioning unit I had ever seen, and I figured that to be the campus infirmary or whatever colleges call such things these days. I crossed the street, weaved between traffic barriers designed to keep the hoi polloi from intruding on the parking spaces of the tenured, and up some steps that emptied, much to my ignorant surprise, onto a quad that looked like it could be on any Ivy League campus anytime in the last century: trimmed hedges, stone walkways, neatly mown lawns and memorial benches on which no one ever sat.

Collectively they were bordered by buildings of almost identical and slightly antiquated design: more huge gray and occasionally beige rocks set together with mortar, windows tall and narrow and shielded from the elements by being set far back into the stone facades. I couldn't imagine it was ever very bright in there during the day, but of course I wasn't in any hurry to find out. Some were clearly more modern than others – the stone was lighter in color, from fewer decades of accumulated pollution no amount of pressure washing could ever really remove – and over the huge banks of double doors on the largest building of all, the one to the right, the one out beside of which there was an ambulance parked, a sign cleared its throat and tastefully proclaimed: DUKE HOSPITAL – SOUTH ENTRANCE in restrained letters.

"Good gods," I muttered. They had an entrance to the hospital – half or more of the reason for that whole "City of Medicine" title – right there on one of the main quads of the campus. The trail of scent went directly up to those doors and, I presumed, through them and beyond. I chuckled a little. The intruder, whoever he was, had pulled a standard vampire trick: he'd gone to where there are plenty of blood bags and made off with a few and that was what I smelled. Maybe he was smarter than I'd thought.

Maybe we wouldn't have any trouble after all.

I let out a long breath, relaxed a little and then had another look around. I'd lived in Raleigh for years but I'd rarely if ever come to Duke to just walk around. It wasn't something I did much. I tended to stay around home or go downtown, like most of us do. Durham is just minutes away but it has always been kind of devoid of vampires and I've never really known why. Some towns are like that: they just aren't attractive to us. At some point Durham had become that way and we'd stayed mostly out of it ever since.

I decided to walk towards the huge bell tower not too far off, figuring it was probably the "chapel" I'd heard about: a cathedral built by Protestants and given a modest name suggesting they were a little embarrassed to find themselves putting on airs. There wasn't anyone on the quad except for the occasional distant footfall of someone leaving an office late. I didn't even hear the burble of student parties in the offing. I'd figured any Friday night on a college campus would be rocking and rolling.

I marveled at how beautiful and dark and still the campus seemed to be. Here there was peace and quiet and it deepened the closer I got to the chapel. A structure like that imposes its own order on a place, its own set of rules, and people follow them without even realizing they're there. I passed by a long, low, wide set building with a sign out front reading Perkins Library. I couldn't help but notice something unusual: a door propped open with a rock and, in something I later decided was a sign of psychological symmetry to the other subject of this tale, a propped door was nothing if not an invitation to investigate.

I noticed that the sign on the door said that the library was open 24 hours but then, taped to its inside glass pane, a second sign made out of typewriter paper read FALL BREAK HOURS and showed that, actually, there weren't any. The library was closed from Thursday afternoon through Sunday morning on the assumption everyone would be out of town.

That must be why I hadn't seen anyone and didn't hear any parties.

The sign only made me even more curious as to why the front door of the undergraduate library would be so haphazardly open. I shook out a coat sleeve and used it to cover my palm and fingers. I pulled the door very slowly open, slipped through and brought it back to rest against its makeshift doorstop behind me without a sound.

Inside, in the distance, I could hear something interesting: a dull thud, with a light echo, repeating very slowly.

THUD.

THUD.

THUD.

Then I heard the voice of a young man say, "Damn it! Why won't you break! Damn it, damn it, damn it! Damned coated glass!" I arced both eyebrows towards the sky, rolled onto my toes and started creeping slowly and quietly towards the middle of the main floor.

From around the side of a reference desk I could see the back of a twenty-something guy wearing the standard college apparel: blue jeans, black tennis shoes, a t-shirt in the dark blue that is Duke's main school color. He had tawny, close-cropped hair that had been trimmed with clippers into that not-a-crew-cut crew cut a lot of the kids were wearing. I couldn't see his face but I could hear in his voice that he was just desperate to get into the huge glass display case in front of him. It was a rectangle larger than a man, the sort of structure you'd see protecting a delicate sculpture in a museum. I couldn't see what was in it; just that whatever it was, it was lighted from below. I mentally clucked my tongue; a thief stealing from a University library is either really dumb or really smart. On the one hand, there's plenty of security around; on the other, they want something of academic value so badly they'll pick a lock and try to smash a glass case to get at it.

The kid turned around so I could see him in profile for a moment: good looks, strong jaw, but a meanness in his expression that spoke of something really terrible having happened to him or maybe just of the lack of anything really good. It was the look of someone who's pissed off, not someone merely desperate or greedy. It also gave me a chance to see what was in the display case and it was a little surprising: a blue and silver devil costume made of something that looked improbably like satin. The Duke mascot is The Blue Devil, a horned cartoon devil in a blue and white outfit, and the mascot is a guy in one of those big, foam bodysuits with the oversized head: a cartoon in three dimensions wearing a goofy expression.

This devil costume was nothing like that. It was elegant. It was theatrical. It was trim and slim and it would take an athlete to wear it. On the right body it would complement their physique in the same fashion as a tailored shirt or a frock coat. There was an informational pedestal outside the case, standing on the floor, but I couldn't read it from there.

The kid picked up a wooden library chair with surprising ease and hefted it sideways, measuring its weight in his hands, lining up for a swing. "I wish I could wait," he said. I had the absurd impression he was addressing the devil costume itself. "I wish I could do this with my own hands, but it hasn't been long enough. No matter. I'll use the tools available to me, however rough they are."

He swung the chair and the glass splintered inside its thin protective anti-shatter sheath. It wasn't safety-coated, as he'd complained. It was bulletproof glass just like Bob had in every window of the Lincoln Towncar I'd cracked open the night he died. I knew exactly what it looked like when someone shattered that kind of glass. This kid had just managed to spider web it with the leg of a chair. The chair split apart from the force of the impact.

This kid was *strong*.

He then reared back and punched the splintered glass in the very center of the web of fractures, unshielded, and a hole opened up like a mouth ringed in jagged teeth. The kid started tearing at the edges of that hole with his bare hands, expanding it and knocking out other sections until finally he was standing in front of the suit with nothing between him and it. I could hear the smile in his voice when he spoke to it again. "I cannot wait to show the world *El Diablo Azul*."

He paused, seemed to be thinking about something and added, "Maybe... I am El Diablo and I welcome you to hell?" He said it again a couple of times, with minor variations: "Welcome to Purgatory? No. No. Get a load of your devil now?" He laughed at that, then paused and clucked his tongue. "No, just, 'I am... El Diablo!' Yeah. That works." He reached forward and lifted the mannequin wearing the costume from the case, set it aside, and started to take off his own clothes.

Never a dull night, I guess. Not that I objected. The kid was pretty ripped.

That's when the smell of his blood hit me.

He'd sliced open one of his knuckles – only one, which was itself shocking – when he punched out the glass. The aroma had eventually wafted this far and the smell of it was like, gods, I'm not sure how to describe it to you. Take all your favorite smells: baking bread, pumpkin spice, the cologne of your best friend, autumn leaves, spring flowers, jasmine, mint, curing tobacco, a charcoal grill, a fresh orange, rain, pine sap, sweat after sex. Roll them all up, not into one smell but into one *experience* of smell, one emotional response to all those things at once.

I'm a vampire. I love the smell of blood, yes, but this blood was something else. This blood was indescribably special. This wasn't a perfume sample on a paper card in a fashion magazine. This was being at the factory, suspended over a great big vat.

I smelled the blood of this blond-ginger, athletic, whiny, under-dressed for the weather kid and in it I could detect life and youth and vigor and agency and desire and anger and hope. What I didn't smell was fear. Vampires are good at smelling fear, of course, and I didn't detect a bit of it. Well, maybe a little, just around the edges, just around the part of him that as a small child was told we do not steal, no matter what. It was hiding from the rest of him, though, or he'd beaten it down. The rest of him was just power and a want to *exercise* that power and I wanted something, too: I wanted that blood and I wasn't even especially hungry that night.

I realized my fangs had dropped and I was salivating. Normally we try so hard to be more discreet and restrained. It was like getting a boner in the middle of dessert.

The kid had stripped down by this point and realized his hand was bleeding. Licking the blood off – oh, Jesus Hambone Christ in the merry month of May, did he have to linger over it like that? - he walked off and out of sight in exactly as casual a fashion as one might expect of a beautiful young person who thinks he is alone and knows his body is perfect. I was trying to fight my fangs back into my face and thinking about baseball wasn't helping any.

I realized this was my chance to read the marker next to the display. Figuring I would hear his return way before he'd see my escape, I sprang up from behind the reference desk and shot across the room. The small rectangle of brown plastic read, in white beveled letters:

MACHINE-SEWN SATIN AND COTTON
C. 1952

The suit itself was a kind of foppish dark blue top. The waist was tapered, the chest built for deep breaths and the shoulders broad. The fabric was shiny and I wasn't entirely sure I bought it was real satin: maybe sateen instead. It had a silver-white oxford collar and puffy sleeves that came to tight cuffs of white. The whole thing looked custom tailored to fit one person and one person alone, presumably the person who was the mascot during that era. The pants were a reverse of the design: mostly white but with beautiful blue fire running up the legs, like the mascot's calves were being consumed by sapphire flames. They shimmered in the light. They begged the wearer to run and to be seen running.

To the eyes of a vampire who'd only ever lived in the era of mass-produced garments this was one of the most beautiful pieces of clothing I'd seen. There were no shoes but there was a matching dark blue cowl with holes for eyes and a slightly beaked nose. It was topped by big, plush devil horns. It was, I had to say, a damned good-looking suit and it probably looked great on a guy with the right physique. The kid trying to steal it fit the bill.

I heard the bathroom door open in the distance so I shot back around to behind the reference desk and then under it. Bare feet padded back up to the display case. I peeked over in time to see the kid slide the shirt off the mannequin with a reverence bordering on the religious. He wasn't just stealing a uniform here, or a historical object of interest to a certain limited set of aged alumni. He was literally donning a new persona. That was what all that El Diablo stuff clearly had been about.

It was a lot like I imagined it would be watching someone get turned into a vampire.

Spying on him in secret, I felt dirty and voyeuristic and I couldn't even have begun to look away. It didn't hurt that he still smelled like a million bucks.

The kid slipped the blouse over his head and down his perfectly sculpted bare chest until it rested flawlessly along his waist. He gently tested the fit of the trousers, just on one leg, to make sure he wouldn't do anything bad to the fabric or the stitching by putting them on. I was surprised the outfit's component parts had held up this well, but a bunch of grad students probably fought for the chance to spend each semester curating them. Maybe there was some modern stitch work under there, where no one would notice, to keep the seams together.

The trousers seemed to withstand his initial probing so he very, very tentatively slid the other leg into them and then pulled the elastic waistband up around his midsection. Christ, the outfit *did* look like it was made for him. It fit him almost perfectly. I could tell it had been tailored for someone else, but the fact it had been tailored at all and yet it fit him this well was noteworthy. The shirt and trousers both fit him better than anything sold in any store ever would.

He lifted the cowl and gazed at it, eye to eye. His breathing was very shallow.

I thought he might have something to say, another slogan to try on for size, something, but he surprised me: he slipped the cowl on without a word. He did so almost hurriedly, like he knew doing it – putting on the actual mask — was a line he wouldn't be able to un-cross once he'd done it and he was afraid he'd lose his nerve. The cowl went on with just as perfect a fit as the rest. He toyed with the way it sat on his head for a moment, tied the chin straps under his jaw and wobbled his head around to make sure it would stay put. It did, and he let out a breath I don't think he realized he'd been holding.

It's worth noting I don't love a thief but neither do I hate one. Glass houses and all that, and I know it. I've certainly trespassed more times than I could possibly begin to count. This kid smelled like sleeping late on a Monday morning and despite the cameras, despite the Twitters or whatever, the appetite at the core of my being wanted to step up to the ice cream cone and take a lick. That was extremely worrying in light of having just found out a stranger was on my turf and visiting the hospital next door when he wanted a snack. Even though I knew I was going beyond what I would normally do, and was way over the line into bad ideas, I stood up and cleared my throat. Apparently what I aim to spend forever doing is introducing myself to the absolute worst choice of mortals I can make in any given situation.

The kid was tying the laces of a pair of black leather jump boots, squatting down with his back to me, and when he heard me he stood and turned to face me in one long, graceful movement that was not what I expected. He was an athlete and he moved with confidence but the way he stood and turned was beyond human capability. He moved with a ripple of leonine elegance, and the suit! I marveled again at how great it looked on him. I could see his musculature shift under the fabric. He was actually a little bigger, a little better built, than the person for whom the clothes were made and it made them work even better by modern fashions.

I drew a breath and spoke. "Listen, I don't know what all you're trying to be about with this, but you're in real danger." I let a hand sweep take in him and the busted display case and the opposite thumb jutted towards the propped open front door. "There are some electronics that just came on a few seconds ago. I would guess those are a silent alarm, from the door being propped open for some predetermined period of time. That's pretty common with physical security systems. More importantly, though, there's this, um." I struggled to find a way to phrase it emphatically but discreetly. "There's this really bad dude who's around. He's just, you know, around? Somewhere? I'm not sure where. Anyway, he's probably really, really interested in you for reasons I shouldn't bother to explain and you wouldn't believe anyway, and all that's to say -"

A disturbingly serene smile broke out on that part of his face visible under the nosepiece of the cowl. It made me slow down and peter out but he interrupted outright before I ran out of steam. "The Bull's Eye? I know. A bad dude, indeed." He gave this snorting little laugh, a kind of a strangled guffaw. I think he hoped it would be menacing or maybe indicate that the topic was but a trifle to him, I don't know, but he pointed at me and did that finger-like-a-gun thing of used car salesman and other psychopaths. He went on, saying, "But do you know who's a much, much badder dude?" He grinned now. "Me. In fact, I'm the worst of them all. I'm –" His voice caught for a second. "I'm El Diablo and I am going to destroy this school, this town and The Bull's Eye with them if he gets in my way!" Then El Diablo, without irony, lifted his chin and gave me an honest-to-gods villain laugh, like something out of a Hanna-Barbera cartoon, before growing abruptly serious. "But who are you? A campus cop?" His face got a lot less friendly. "One of the fenced-in pigs come to shut me down? Some dressed down security guard?" He was snarling the words now and his face had grown grim. His hands were flexing open and shut. He wanted to use them on something. I wasn't scared of him, of course, but I didn't want to hurt him either.

"Now, listen kid, I ain't nobody's cop so just take it easy." There are a lot of little tricks of body language one can use to calm someone else down and they mostly involve broadcasting calmness on one's own part. People don't chill out when someone shouts at them to chill out. They relax when they see others relaxing. I stuck my left hand into my pocket as I gestured with the right: my hand out, flat, palm down. It was a pose of ease, a gesture that is neither commanding nor supplicating. I've had decades to practice this, and I know what works.

"I said... *I. AM. EL. DIABLO.*" Then the kid – El Diablo – went from standing still to an open sprint much faster than most of the humans in the world and maybe some of the newer, weaker vampires. He shot past me in the blink of an eye and was out the door.

My mouth was still open. OK, so the body language *usually* works but not always.

As I stared at the space where he'd been when he disappeared from sight, a third presence made itself known. A rumbling bass voice said, "Wow. Don't see that every day."

I turned around, very slowly, expecting the interloper to be standing there. Instead there was a guy who would have been extremely handsome if he weren't covered in blue scales like an exotic fish. His eyes were the color of honey if it could go bad and he had little black horns with very sharp tips erupting from the flesh on his forehead. "I'm Ross," he said. His voice was apple butter and dark chocolate. The weird scales stopped mattering. He was gorgeous. His voice reached right down into my stomach and chased butterflies. "I bet you're Withrow."

I started to ask something real smart, I'm sure, but he waggled a finger. "No, no," he interrupted. "No questions just yet. First we meet-cute, then we get to know each other."

I blinked.

He lifted one hand, snapped his fingers and was gone in a puff of yellow smoke.

I walked nearly an hour to get back to my car, drove back to Raleigh and pretended it had never happened just as hard as I possibly could.

Chapter 4

The Bull's Eye was on patrol on a new route when she found The House.

Ann read the stories about her ridiculous exploits on that one lucky night of neighborhood patrol and never looked back. The next time she went out she thought of herself as The Bull's Eye without consciously deciding about it. The identity was a full-body disguise so natural she didn't even need to spend time adapting to it. Everything shifted into place for her when she put that name on. Even her walk changed a little. It was as close to an experience of magical transmogrification as she was ever likely to experience.

Ann had felt dead inside for so long. When she went out as The Bull's Eye she could feel her soul breathe.

Ann told herself she had taken to that identity because it sounded good and she needed something other than her life as a janitor at Durham Technical Community College, something more like the blank slate of a completely new identity. She'd gone out every night since catching the burglar and busted up a couple of other smallish crimes: she chased off a car thief, for instance, then left a note of sorts under the windshield wiper. On the slip of paper were three concentric circles drawn in red marker to make sure she got the credit. The paper was only too happy to emphasize that detail. Ann later learned the car's owner had offered the note for sale to the newspaper and a couple of local stations as though they would pay for something on which she'd doodled.

She bought herself some new clothes for patrol: black cargo pants, a black cap, a black head wrap to hide her shoulder-length hair and black fleece tops that were reversible so that she could turn them inside out and they would be various extravagant colors: easy to see and hard to square with a description given by a witness. She could, in seconds, go from a panther stalking the night to being any other woman out for a walk, if needed, and that was exactly what she wanted.

The House was just a normal, two-story structure in the mill town style: wider than it was deep with white clapboard siding, a metal roof and a satellite dish bolted to the railing on the front porch, pointed at an unlikely angle. There were a few thousand just like it scattered around Durham's oldest neighborhoods, at least in the places where they hadn't been razed by highway projects or "renewal." They were historical artifacts now, but many of them were also still someone's home.

The street in question was an otherwise anonymous row of working class homes built across several eras and with varying degrees of optimism. There was absolutely nothing about The House, casually viewed at driving speed, to make it stand out as special or to distinguish it from the half a dozen others just like it dotting the surrounding blocks. The Bull's Eye had been trained to spot the little things someone might haphazardly hide. She saw things of interest where others would not: broken down cardboard moving boxes sitting by the recycling bin, for instance. They had the logo of a truck rental place on them and they were emblazoned with the words WE SELL BOXES. In a world already full of unused cardboard boxes, these people had gone and bought new ones with which to tote their junk across town – the truck rental place was local, not a chain – only to fold them back up and dispose of them again.

There were other signs of things being slightly off: windows with thick double curtains drawn shut over an additional layer of sheers and four prominent NO TRESPASSING signs posted at the edges of the front yard. Whoever had moved in was scared of the people around them. She wondered if they marked some new front line in the ongoing gentrification of neighborhoods just outside downtown or if the people who'd moved in were simply new to being upper lower class. There were certainly plenty such people in the post-recession economy: people whose jobs went away and would never return or whose industries fled somewhere less interested in a living wage. Maybe it had been a bad divorce or a sudden death. Maybe there had been a fire at the old place. Maybe a child had died. Those no-trespassing signs were sometimes the last refuge of a person who had been shocked by something and retreated into their living room — well-appointed or poorly so, white or black, invested in fantasy or indulging in it — in hopes the world outside would change to their liking without them having to get too involved.

Of course, sometimes they simply served to announce a meth lab. The Bull's Eye slowed down as she walked past it, then stopped. She dawdled and watched it casually, just giving it the once over.

One of the curtains inside twitched aside for about half a blink of an eye, then closed again. If she hadn't been looking at the house, Ann would have missed it.

She stood stock still for a few seconds — she had slowed between two trees, on a block where there was no working streetlight, and she was clad in the discount store equivalent of a cat suit. She should be effectively invisible to anyone inside the home — they had lights on, glass windows and no light on *her* — but someone inside had looked right at her and then hidden again.

That word stuck in her mind: *hidden*.

The first question to present itself to her was whether it would be okay for a superhero to break into someone's home on suspicion they were weird. Wanting privacy wasn't a crime. Looking out your own window wasn't a crime. Still, something about it bothered her. Something she couldn't quite name was needling the back of her neck. She knew from her training and her years of service that one should listen to the Spidey senses when they go off. The gut is almost always right. She would never know the number of soldiers she'd interviewed who said they just knew not to take a certain path, to stop, to swerve. She knew many more who had not listened to that little voice and lived to regret it.

The Bull's Eye found herself frustrated by the certainty she had no excuse to act on what her gut was telling her: that something on the house was wrong. She wanted to find out what. It was not a desire or a curiosity; it was a calling.

Well, she told herself, those people had just moved. Maybe someone should welcome them to the neighborhood. There was no law against looking out a window and there was no law against knocking on a door. She weighed the possible outcomes — angry, shotgun-toting neighbor answers vs. no one answers, to describe very briefly the ends of a broad spectrum of results — and decided it was worth the risk of initiating some dialogue.

The Bull's Eye stepped out from between the beautiful but age-gnarled, claw-fingered oaks and strode confidently across the deserted street, across the yard, onto the front walk, up the two wooden steps of the whitewashed front porch and right up to a white front door. She pressed the glowing orange button of the doorbell. A harmless and generic chime sounded inside, two thirds of a major chord, and then she heard the doorknob move and was only a little surprised she hadn't also heard footsteps.

It was as though whoever was about to answer had been standing there waiting for her to ring.

The door opened slowly, tentatively, and on the other side of the screen door was a tall and very thin boy. Ann had worked around plenty of kids his age when she was in the army and she knew he was technically a man but she thought of them as boys all the same. He was Caucasian with dark brown hair and thick black eyebrows in a slightly darker shade. He was clad in worn out blue jeans and a light gray sweater. He had so many bags under his eyes he needed help getting the groceries to the car. He looked like he hadn't slept in six months. The boy was gaunt and almost gray in the dim light available to her: a TV inside, a street light in the next block and The Bull's Eye's utterly human night vision. "We don't want any," he said. "We're on the Do Not Call list. Doesn't that cover this stuff, too?"

Ann blinked and said, "I'm not... Wait, I'm not selling anything." She hesitated; she hadn't done this in a long time and there was rust on all the social hinges. It shook her a little. "I'm... the welcome wagon." She cleared her throat. "Neighborhood watch. You know. Just coming by to say hello, see if I could help with anything."

The guy had only opened the door about the width of his own nose. He stood there, with most of a solid wooden door between them and she could tell he was absolutely terrified. "OK," he finally replied. "But we're fine." He closed the door without another word. Ann heard it lock again, and again, and again. The kid had three different deadbolts on his side and he'd thrown them all after just that little interaction.

Ann stared at the door, at the space where he'd been when she spoke to him, and shrugged. Definitely gentrification. She didn't have any other immediate conclusions about them. Something still struck her as off but it could easily enough be dismissed as paranoia after recent events. She had spent two days "sick" from work, waiting for the cops to show up and arrest her. She had watched every newscast, in rotation, for anything other than what she got: positive buzz from every station's usual motley crew of people on the street. Nobody quite knew what to think about her but nobody liked burglars, either. She was certainly the lesser of two evils in that one specific circumstance, which is better than she had thought it would be. The car thief thing had sealed the deal. People loved her on the six o'clock news. That made her nervous more than reassured her. If the media loves anything more than a narrative it's a chance to flip that narrative into a twist ending. If they liked her now they would hate her in six months no matter what happened.

That was neither here nor there, though. The Bull's Eye had gotten a twinge of intuition, had acted and had found nothing strange. Time to move on: there were plenty more blocks to walk in the dark of this one particular night.

She was halfway down the front steps when the door unlocked and the guy called out to her, only he was in different clothes: khakis and a Duke University t-shirt and some of those ridiculous rubber shoes everyone was wearing at the time. She turned and then did a double take at the instantaneous costume change. "Please don't go," the boy said. "My brother's just having one of those days."

"Twins." She didn't realize that was out loud until she heard herself saying it. Ann got her hand halfway to her mouth to cover it before deciding it wasn't worth the effort. "Sorry. I... I didn't expect that. I was explaining to your brother that I'm from the neighborhood watch. I just wanted to say hi, check in, see if you need anything."

"No," he said, and though he didn't look as bad as his brother he also seemed to be running on something less than a full tank. "No, I think we're fine. Thanks for stopping by." He paused, hesitating in a doorway he'd opened farther than his brother but, Ann noticed, not all the way. He seemed to want to say something else but nothing was coming out.

"What's your name?" Ann knew the polite thing would have been to introduce herself but she hadn't thought this through that far. She was suited up for patrol. Giving people her name might not be the smartest idea if they put two and two together. She didn't even know if these parts had a neighborhood watch.

The boy opened his mouth to answer, stopped, closed his mouth and, face as blank as a new sheet of typing paper, closed the door on her. He locked all the same deadbolts behind it and turned off the light in the front hall so that now she was shut out, locked out and in the dark. She could hear him pad away in his stupid shoes but there was no conversation or commentary from inside. The brothers both simply settled back their quiet little exile amongst the downtrodden as though she had never knocked.

The Bull's Eye couldn't believe she'd just been cold-shouldered by weird twin brothers who were, in their own way, utterly out of place in a neighborhood she would patrol. Her curiosity was piqued. It was beyond piqued: it was halfway to pissed off. She could find out more about them another time, she told herself. It would just require finding the right people to ask, and for that she'd have to come back tomorrow.

The next day was one of those bright October days when the temperature is just fine but the light is all too sharp, like glass that's cracked and going to shatter in the next little gust of wind. I don't see those days anymore myself but I remember them from many years ago.

The Bull's Eye had thought about The House the rest of that night and all of the next morning and decided there was something more going on than a couple of white dudes moving into the neighborhood to flip a house. She was off from her job on Saturdays, so she got up early and walked her usual route, dressed this time in one of the reversed fleeces so that she looked more "normal" in her own mind: blue jeans, bright pink fleece, white tennis shoes. She wanted to wear the plain black ball cap because, honestly, she couldn't imagine going on patrol without it but this time she wore a blue and white and orange Durham Bulls hat instead.

What The Bull's Eye had pondered the night before was that everywhere you go, whether it's a street in Durham or a village halfway up some gods-forsaken mountain in Afghanistan, the kids are the ones who know what's really happening. They always know the most because they're curious about everything and they're always watching. Kids like the new and the different but it's possible to cross a line into being so different they detect you as a threat. That had made The Bull's Eye's job hard sometimes in Afghanistan, in Iraq and in other places she'd sworn never to name, but in the context of that one neighborhood she hoped she was in the sweet spot of trustworthy and being an outsider. She was an African-American woman who could look like anyone else the average Durham kid had seen a hundred million times. The guys about whom she wanted to know more, on the other hand, didn't look or talk or act the way those kids had learned to expect of their neighbors.

The Bull's Eye knew she wasn't guaranteed to get anywhere with the neighborhood kids. She might look like them and the other people they knew, sure, but these were kids who had been raised in the simmering cultural war zone of a neighborhood continually unsure whether it was going to climb back out of the economic trenches or tumble over into being an explicitly "bad" block. That meant becoming someone they would associate with trust rather than nosy questions.

There was a small park – a little slide and a sandbox and a couple of benches – a couple of blocks away from The House. The Bull's Eye put on the disguise of Ann and sat in that park for a couple of daylight hours, reading a paperback and looking at her phone. A few kids were there pretty much continuously, but larger packs came through for a few minutes at a time every once in a while. She didn't bother to approach any of them; she was just making sure they had seen her before.

The next day she did the same thing, and by the two-hour mark she figured she had established herself as enough of a presence to be allowed to approach one. He wasn't having any of it, though, and took off as soon as she walked up and opened her mouth. She blinked, and stared after him. She'd gotten that reaction before, sure, but in places where no one spoke English. She wasn't sure what to do at that point. Having a Pashtun kid run off when she approached was no surprise; having it happen in her hometown, on the other hand, was a confidence shaker. Her next two attempts were more hesitant and that didn't help any – she got the same lack of results: either kids who took off or kids who just pretended she wasn't there.

Finally she noticed a kid of maybe 13 or 14, just old enough to be trying to look bored at the park, and she walked up to him.

"Hey," she said.

"Hey," he replied.

"I need some information."

The kid was dressed in a generic black hoodie with an indecipherable pattern of swirling and swooping art, everyday objects with thick contrails all looping around one another across the chest. It probably had a lot of significance of some sort, but it was all just shapes to her. He was wearing black sweatpants and near-featureless black shoes from a discount chain. The shoes failed in their attempt to masquerade as a more stylish name brand. The kid squinted up at her in that sharp autumn sunlight. "You a cop?"

"Furthest thing from it," she said. She folded her arms over her chest and struck her battle-ready-soldier pose: feet apart, shoulders squared, not backing down, not taking no for an answer. Thugs in the biker bars of movies and storybooks try to intimidate their prey by leaning in close and invading personal space; good guys intimidate their prey by becoming a wall that can't be climbed or tunneled through. Goons promise a fight; heroes let the absence of threats speak volumes. "I just need a little info, that's all."

The kid looked her up and down – she had half a foot on him, and she meant business, and she wasn't a cop, and maybe he figured why the hell not do something today that he didn't do yesterday? It took him some time to work through those conclusions, but he got there. "What's in it for me?"

The Bull's Eye considered this for a moment. She had been asked that plenty of times by kids in places where talk cost lives. She'd simply bribed them in the end: every kid wants something. She wasn't sure how to appeal to or buy off a kid here at home, though. *What's in this is getting to walk home with your head held high*, she thought to herself, but she knew that didn't convert well on the local exchange. "Five bucks," she said.

The kid snorted.

"Ten."

He thought about it for a second and then said, "Let me hear your question. That way I'll know what the answer's worth."

The Bull's Eye shifted her weight and started to slip into her reflexive response – suggesting that there is no room for negotiation – but she stopped herself before she opened her mouth. She was trained to deal with hostile

46

populations but this population didn't have to be handled like the enemy. She eyed him up and down one more time and said, "It's that house." She nodded in a vague direction. "The House." She wanted to see if she would need to be more specific. She bet he would know the one she meant. She was right.

"The new guys." The kid didn't ask it, he said it. "Twenty bucks."

"Ten or nothing." She knew how this part worked. She pulled out her wallet and took ten dollars out, so he could see the money he was turning down. "Not a lot of time to decide. Plenty of other kids in the neighborhood."

He watched her hand, and then she sighed and started to put it away. "Okay," he said. "Ten."

She smiled. No reason not to be nice about it. "Deal." He held out his hand but she shook her head. "When you're all talked out."

He shrugged. She didn't care if she seemed paranoid. The Bull's Eye knew this kid would very likely never understand how someone who'd fought wars that never had names because they never officially existed would look at the world around her. "They're new. Moved in a couple months ago. Nobody ever stays very long in that house, but they've stayed the longest of anybody. Two white dudes, and we don't get a lot of that. Weird, too. They're twins. Nobody wants to talk to them and they don't want to talk to nobody, either." He shrugged again. It was the resting state of the teen male.

"Why doesn't anyone want to talk to them?"

"Like I said: they're weird."

"What's weird about them?"

The kid was visibly uncomfortable. Whatever it was, he didn't want to say. The Bull's Eye folded the bill and lowered it. "Sounds like you're a long way from talked out."

He opened his mouth again and looked away for a second, then back. "They're all... they're like cigarette ash. They look gray in their skin. They look like something's eaten at them, all the time. Every family that moves in there looks that way, one by one, and then they go away again, but these guys got that way and then just stayed sick. My mom says there's radon in the house. Says there's radiation in the basement making them sick. My grandma says the place is cursed *and* got radon in it. All the kids know those guys aren't okay, and nobody wants to catch what they got. There's a sickness to them, and they don't seem to know or care, so we just leave 'em alone."

The Bull's Eye knew the sound of a meth house when she heard it. She hadn't smelled it when she was there, though, and a meth house stinks to high heaven. "Do they ever have company? Maybe a lot of people coming by at night for just a few minutes?"

"Hell no," the kid said. "They ain't some crack house. Nobody ever comes and nobody ever leaves and they just sit in there in the dark. Sometimes they watch TV, most times they don't. No friends, no visitors, no parties, no nothing."

"They sound like pretty ideal neighbors." She smirked a little, but she knew she was feeling something that jibed with what the kid had said: a wrongness way down in her gut when they answered that door.

"There's something bad about that place. We don't go there, the little kids don't go there, nobody will go trick or treat there on Halloween, nobody goes there to sell candy bars for school or none of that shit." He shook his head. "There's something wrong with that house and if those guys stick around then there must be something wrong with them, too. It just makes sense. Most of the people who move in there seem nice or whatever, but then they leave again real fast. These guys weren't cool when they got here and they haven't gotten any better since."

"What wasn't cool about them when they got here?" That part surprised her just a little. The notion of a house that turns its occupants sick or bad wasn't necessarily anything new – the doomed manse, the cursed hut or the haunted cabin are not new concepts – but this business about them being unusual when they got here was at odds with the gentrification theory and went nicely with her sense there was something deeper going on. She looked up and the sun was high overhead. She had hours of warm autumn light left but she knew the night would arrive soon enough. Something about seeing that ashen skin and those sunken eyes in darkness made the back of her brain itch.

The kid looked away and kicked a rock. "They were... it was like they were hiding in there. We'd see them peek out the curtains sometimes. I mean, we went and looked at the place, you always go look at a place when somebody new moves in, and they would peek out. They had to see us but they never said hey. They'd just close back up and not look again for a real long time. It didn't seem like it was 'cause they were white, though. It seemed like they were afraid of something else. They didn't look scared of us. They looked like they'd been scared before they got here." He rolled his shoulders. "I don't know what to say."

"Do they ever go out?"

"Once in a while." He shrugged. "Just once in a while they go somewhere together and they're gone for a couple of hours before hey come back, but that's it. The kids say they're going grocery shopping but I seen them one time. They bring back huge bags from the store, like lots of bags, more than two people need."

The Bull's Eye knew how questioning someone worked, so she circled back to a point she'd visited already once before. "And they never have visitors?"

He started to say something else but stopped himself. "It's... No. No visitors. They're just weird."

"Tell me what you were about to say." The Bull's Eye didn't hesitate to press the moment. She held out the money, out of his reach but where he could see it. "Whatever you were about to say, whatever you're afraid to tell me, that's what I am willing to pay to hear. The thing you choose to hide at the last moment is the truth someone will be looking to find." She looked deep into his eyes. "Remember that."

He blinked at her, not getting it, not seeming to understand, but he spoke. He whispered, like he was worried someone would hear them on an empty street next to an empty park. "Some of the kids say that if they stay up late and watch out their window they see a man in an old coat come walking down the middle of the street." The kid licked his lips, suddenly chapped in the autumn air. "He's not on the sidewalk, just walking out in the street. There's never any traffic when he does it, and everything gets real quiet. He always goes straight to that house, nowhere else. He lets himself in and he's in there for a while then he leaves again. I never saw it, so I can't say, but the kids who claim they've seen him say he's the boogeyman." The kid's eyes weren't on the money and they weren't on The Bull's Eye. They were far off, in a memory of something he'd seen but couldn't own, something so scary when he witnessed it he now attributed it to others, to nameless kids up and down the street. "He wasn't alone, though. He had a bunch of little kids with him, all in hoodies. Like, all in the same kind of hoodie. They stand on the sidewalk while he's in there like they're his bodyguards or something. They just stand there and if anyone looks at them too long they make like they're going to walk over to you." He drew a thin breath. "They all have the darkest eyes…"

He abruptly remembered who and how old he was and tried to shake it off by forcing a chuckle but it faltered in his throat and he fell back into hurried gusts of speech. "The little kids say the man's real bad. They're real scared when they see him. They say sometimes he looks up at them – like, they can be in their room with the lights out in the middle of the night and he's out there in the street and he looks right at them. They say he can feel them looking and when he looks back they can feel it, too. They say it feels cold." The kid shuddered suddenly, drew a breath and said, "I want my ten bucks."

"You earned it." The Bull's Eye handed the money over. "Thanks, kid. What's your name?"

"That costs extra." He paused before asking, "You're The Bull's Eye, ain't you?"

She smirked. "Have a nice afternoon." She crossed her arms to indicate she wasn't going anywhere and thus was not the one who should walk away now they had concluded their business. The money disappeared into the kid's outfit somewhere. He started to say something else but closed his mouth, turned around and walked away and around a corner.

She smiled to herself: The Bull's Eye had just worked a connection on the street. *Damn*, she thought to herself. *Bad-ass.*

Too bad everything she'd learned bothered her so damned much.

Chapter 5

I'd spent a week debating whether to tell Roderick about my encounter with El Diablo and with Ross, the blue-skinned guy with devil horns. My uncertainty stemmed from all manner of sources: a little fear of ridicule for having an experience so strange, a little shame over having taken so long to bring it up, a little embarrassment over how I'd reacted to El Diablo when he was just some naked hot guy and I'd found myself playing the part of voyeur.

I was mostly worried about this Ross guy, though, and how Roderick might react to that part of the story. Ross was clearly a demon: the horns and the weird skin and the disappearing in a flash are a dead giveaway. At least, that's how it seemed to me. Polite society might call the walking dead "Steeplechasers" but we all knew they were zombies and a guy with horns and weird skin disappearing in a puff of smoke was surely a demon if ever one there was.

I am not a religious person, I should say. That's true for lots of reasons, not just for the distaste with which I regard the notion of someone going to the trouble of becoming a vampire only to spend eternity feeling guilty about it. I mostly rejected religion as a mortal because I was force-fed so much of it as a boy. My experiences as a vampire simply affirmed my atheism. I have seen too many lives gutter and go out like a candle in a cold wind to believe there is a god somewhere who gives a damn or would do anything if they did. If the gods were ever real they must surely have wandered off millennia ago in search of a drink big enough to make them forget the things they have seen. Heaven as the destination of what humans have ever been truly good would be the loneliest place in the universe.

That there is no Heaven, though, does not mean there is no Hell or nothing like it. I wouldn't have dared hazard a guess regarding where demons come from. I was only willing to entertain their possibility because of the circumstances in which I discovered my cousin Roderick amongst the vampires of Seattle in the first place. I originally went out there at the request of my maker, Agatha, to satisfy a favor from one of her allies, who had been asked by a friend to provide an assist, and so on and so forth. That's how things work in the bizarre professional network that is freelance immortality. It's not uncommon for us to do time acting as our makers' fixers in one arena or another and it's not uncommon for the ones who like to climb local ladders to barter their available resources for favors and prestige. For a while – several decades – I was Agatha's best source of violence on demand. I wasn't a great diplomat but I was perfectly happy to make a buck running questionable goods around in a fast car or putting my fist through the face of someone who almost certainly had it coming anyway.

When I killed off the last of the Bobs and declared myself the boss of North Carolina, though, that was that. I'd established my own territory. I couldn't be Agatha's errand boy anymore. We still passed news back and forth and spoke once in a great while but I'd had to cut those apron strings or the vampires around me never would have respected what I only grudgingly will admit is my authority over them. It isn't that I love the idea of giving orders, but damned if I'm going to let anyone *else* give them to *me*.

The trouble in Seattle turned out to have a demon in the middle of it and Roderick not too far removed. It ended ugly: blood and ash all over, and plenty of politics to boot since I helped put a new boss in place when we wrapped up the deal. Roderick had reacted to the presence of a demon with undisguised enthusiasm for its destruction. I had zero worry Roderick would hear there was a demon in town and come roaring up to sit in its lap and learn some new tricks. No, I was worried Roderick would show up with a Gatling gun under one arm and two priests under the other. He is not the subtlest vampire I've ever met and he's the one Agatha tried to adopt to be her new source of hot and cold running murder. Telling Roderick there was a demon in Durham would be a little like lighting a torch in front of Smokey the Bear.

I was most worried about the way the demon seemed interested in me. Ross had said, "First we meet-cute," and I didn't know what that meant but I didn't like the implication of a second step in whatever literally diabolical plot he was unfolding. A demon just being around wasn't necessarily a big deal in my book. A demon noticing me, though, could be very, very bad. That I'd reacted by thinking he was hot was worst of all.

I'd spent the intervening nights chasing myself in tighter and tighter circles. Finally I was sick of hearing myself fail to get anywhere. I said to hell with it and called up Roderick to ask for help.

Whereas I'm a great big lump of lard with a bad attitude from the 1940's, Roderick is a bird-chested little 1960's go-go boy with vinyl boots, a permanent smirk and a plastic outfit for every occasion. He's also, I strongly suspect, a complete psychopath. On the one hand, we're all crazy: we attack mortals and drink their blood to survive. On the other hand, any mortal who eats a fast food hamburger is a little crazy in the eyes of their well-meaning vegan friends, aren't they? It's all relative.

Roderick is my cousin in the traditional biological sense as well as being a vampire. We are each other's last un-living relatives. Every other soul in our family, to our knowledge, is dead and buried and long forgotten. I don't even remember most of them. I suppose a photograph of my immediate family would look like any other gathering of antiquated strangers. I haven't got any photographs by which to check.

"Cousin." Roderick picked up on the second ring and answered just as smooth as you please, as though he'd been sitting by the phone waiting for my call.

"Cousin," I replied. "I need to tell you about something and I need you to offer me your honest opinion without judging me."

"Withrow," he breathed, all heartfelt concern. "Of course. What is wrong?"

"It's… I… Okay, here's the deal," I said. I cleared my throat. Smiles was curled up next to the ottoman where I'd crossed my ankles. He could tell I felt uncomfortable. He sat up, circled around and nudged my knees with his forehead in order to get a scratch behind the ears. "I just need to tell you something that happened. And see what you think. Without you telling me I'm crazy and without you strongly overreacting." I hesitated. "And I need you not to tell anyone." By "anyone" I meant Agatha. I still didn't really know how much he spoke to her. In theory he had turned down her job offer in favor of being given dominion over Asheville by me.

"Do go on." Roderick tends to jump straight to the point and he wanted me to do the same. "You have my word. I will honor whatever restrictions you place on this conversation and I will contain any outbursts of emotion. Now, dear cousin, please, *dish*." The thing is, psycho or not, I have a lot of respect for someone who will state their terms and get down to business and Roderick is exactly that. Just these few short sentences between us had me feeling a little more like I was on an even keel. Roderick's whole thing about being more socially connected really did have some substance to it.

"OK, so, it's like this." I told Roderick about seeing El Diablo and about Ross and, with a lot of hemming and hawing, I mentioned that Ross had been powerfully attractive.

"So what did you do after?" Roderick's tone was entirely calm. Surprisingly calm. Diametric-opposite-of-my-expectations calm. Dangerously calm.

"I walked across town and drove home." I shrugged to myself. Smiles panted happily for a moment, then climbed up onto the couch and tried to sit in my lap. Even a lap as generous as mine is too small for a hundred fifty pounds of supernaturally enhanced Doberman but that never stops Smiles from trying.

"And then what?"

I opened my mouth, drew a long breath and held it. And then what, indeed? "I tried to pretend it didn't happen."

"Withrow!" Roderick's tone was a sharp rebuke. "Withrow Calhoun Alvison Surrett!" I blinked at hearing my full name for the first time in decades. "You will never fix anything by sitting around thinking it to death."

"Neither," I replied, with my dander just a little bit up, "Will I ever find the guy. I'll never find either of them! One of them moved as fast as a vampire and the other seemed to teleport, so explain to me how I'm supposed to find either one of them to do anything?"

That shut him up for just a second, but only a second. When Roderick spoke again his voice was silky smooth again. "Cousin," he said. "I apologize. You are clearly deeply bothered by this, and I shouldn't have been so quick to judge."

I still felt a little sulky, but I allowed as how I appreciated him saying so.

"Now," he said, "Let's think this through. One of them is a human with superhuman abilities. You're certain he wasn't a vampire?"

"He didn't smell like a vampire. He smelled like a human but…" I waved my free hand around in the air, invisible to Roderick but a part of how I talk nonetheless. "He smelled extra human. You know how blood…" I trailed off. This sort of stuff was another form of dirty talk in vampire circles. For the ultimate transgressions against god and man, we sure could be prudes about things from time to time. Blood and our impassioned pursuit of it weren't something we often discussed and talking about it with my cousin seemed yet another dimension of the perversion of having a cousin who's a vampire to begin with.

"It smells like life," Roderick said. I was glad he'd done me the favor of breaking spades on that. The phrasing was perfect. Blood, to us, doesn't just smell like mom cooking eggs on a Sunday morning. It smells like every time you've ever smelled eggs and bacon and pancakes and steak and fresh coffee and birthday cake. Blood smells like the future and the past and the vital energy of every breath of the person from whom it bleeds. It smells like potential. It smells like fate waiting to happen.

"Yeah. But he smelled like lots of lives. Two or three or maybe half a dozen of them. He smelled like distilled, reduced, ultra-concentrated life. He was the strong stuff. High-test. I can't compare it to normal human blood. I could only compare him to a legion of humans with open veins."

"Fascinating," Roderick breathed. "And the blue guy, you are also sure he was not a vampire? Maybe he was a vampire in elaborate stage makeup?"

"Nah," I said. "He was a figment of my imagination or he was an honest to gods demon. I can't really think he was anything else."

"Technically he may call himself a devil, it all depends and I do not really know the difference, but anyway, he will not be hard to find." Roderick announced his knowledge of this and dismissed the same in one smooth breath.

"How so? Do they have a section in the yellow pages?"

Roderick sighed quietly. "Please tell me you do not use an actual phone book."

"Roderick," I spoke very slowly, "Tell me how to find a demon. Devil. Whatever. No distractions. They are trouble and one of them seems interested in me."

"On that we are in total agreement," Roderick said. "Demons are to be eliminated at every opportunity, especially those who have taken an interest in one. If he made himself attractive to you then he most definitely has plans for you.

The 'first we meet-cute' is extremely worrisome." He sighed, clucked his tongue. "He must be found and destroyed. We can either try all the usual arcane stuff – you know, get some Satanist teenagers to summon it up for you by a human sacrifice, though those are supposed to be extremely hit or miss – or you can turn the tables and lure him in ahead of schedule. Waiting for him to approach you again is not an option. You cannot permit him to play out whatever game he has in mind for you." Roderick sounded genuinely concerned, shading into angry, but very businesslike all the same. I had caught the 'we' back there, too. He went on. "Demons hunt, just like we do, but they take a lot longer to finish off their prey. We hunt and feed like a cat: there is a target, we chase it, we toy with it a little and we are done. Devils hunt like drug dealers. They find targets but they do not just harvest them the once: they cultivate them. They find someone who is primed to become a victim and take advantage of their vulnerability."

"In Seattle, it seemed like that demon just wanted to watch vampires hunt each other instead of humans. Is that all they ever want? Don't tell me there's some bullshit about selling one's soul. That's just a fairy tale." I tried to sound disgusted instead of just a little bit afraid.

'Mostly they give the person something they think they need and then help that person make all the wrong choices until it is too late. I do not know if the souls thing is for real, but I doubt it. I think they just take pleasure in seeing people suffer: the ones their 'clients' harm and then the clients themselves when karma catches up. In Seattle, they got to turn monsters against one another with all sorts of delicious ancillary effects: murder and mayhem and public fear." Roderick paused, and we sat in silence for a moment, each of us remembering a series of awful events I won't bother to relate here. After a few seconds, Roderick cleared his throat and spoke again. "Anyway, we need to make you seem desperate."

"Oh, good grief." I nearly hung up the phone. "How do we do that, exactly?"

"Usually," Roderick said, just matter-of-fact, "If a vampire wants to get a demon to notice them they have to find a really desperate human being and drain them. You know how you pick up some of the emotional state of the person when you drink their blood?"

An honest answer stuck in my throat. Draining someone completely wasn't something I did very often for reasons of trying to go unnoticed and not make a huge mess out of things. There are vampires who find their personal Last Gasp so pleasurable or useful they do it all the time, but not me. Mine is useful, to be sure: I get to pick one topic from that person's personal history and learn everything they knew about it and then some, including maybe some things they never had the chance to know in their own right. Whereas I gain access to information about my victim, Roderick cuts off access to information about them. He erases them from reality. The world forgets they ever existed. I shudder to think through some of the implications of that or how easy it would be to abuse.

I knew what Roderick meant about the emotional states thing, though. I've always quietly assumed it's something to do with hormones in the blood or the like: some biochemical process our bodies still follow despite our state of suspended necrosis. Vampires get all kinds of superstitious about blood the same way one culture after another has done about food over the millennia. We all quietly believed there to be some psychic imprint left when we drank. I'd only ever consumed the blood of the living when they were unconscious or terrified so I hadn't enjoyed a lot of variety in emotional states to sample. I always felt jumpy and hyper-alert after but had always assumed that had more to do with having just assaulted someone in a dark alley or behind a truck stop and less to do with the emotional state of the person whose blood I'd consumed.

"So, if I eat a really desperate person I can, what, smell desperate?"

"To a demon, sure. I think 'smell' is just a metaphor, but it works."

"In exactly what context did you learn that?" I shuddered to think this had become the focus of Roderick's attentions in the time since Seattle had gone down. Yes, the world is full of terrifying things but the point of being a vampire is not to linger over unanswerable questions of why and how. We become what we are so we can instead walk on by without giving a damn.

"Seattle was just a field trip for you, Cousin." Again, Roderick remained just as calm and conversational as a weather report. "For me, it was my home. I watched half a dozen vampires try to use that demon against one another and every single one of them died. Most of them died because you killed them. Not all of them, though." He chuckled darkly. "Not all of them. I took care of my share when you were gone. After all, I still needed to bed down every morning with some surety I would wake up again. I hunted the devil's disciples for months after you left. I introduced each one of them to the death they thought to avoid. I studied their practices in the process. Demon-worshippers are always happy to describe their methods. They all think they are the one person who can outsmart a devil. They are eager to brag." I could hear the smile.

I paused. My cousin, demon hunter? I couldn't even begin to work on that. Instead, I changed the subject. "What's a 'meet-cute'?"

"It is a term from screenwriting." Roderick had the patient tone of an instructor dealing with a bright but somewhat limited student. "It is when two people meet in some unlikely or inconvenient circumstance and it complicates their eventual romantic relationship."

I choked on some combination of laughter and surprise. "Romantic relationship? Let's just set aside for a moment the fact he is a demon."

Roderick interrupted: "A demon to whom you were attracted."

I went on. "Whatever. Setting that aside, you might not have heard, cousin, but I'm a vampire. The plumbing shut down decades ago."

Roderick sounded mildly confused for a moment. "Cousin…" He paused and asked with tremendous delicacy, "Have you not done any dating since you were turned?"

"Of course not," I said. "I'm dead. We're all dead. Hell, that was half of what I wanted to get away from."

"Oh, Cousin." Roderick sounded like he'd just heard a year's worth of bad news. "Oh, my stars. You have to do something about that. We cannot let Ross latch onto any actual desperation you really do feel. I am on my way. I will be there tomorrow night."

"Why?" I was sputtering now, shifting around in agitation so Smiles had to jump up and stand at the other end of the couch, looking this way and that, on the watch for whatever trouble had me wound up.

"That is why he seemed so attractive to you, cousin. He must already know. Oh, my precious ducklings of doom, you must do nothing. Have all your calls held. Put out the word you will be busy for the next few nights. I am coming down there," Roderick said, "And we are getting you a date."

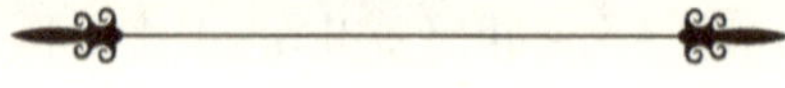

It was good to feel like the cavalry might be about to ride in. On the other hand, it was terrifying to think Roderick was the cavalry. Even if he did know what to do about Ross, I was still left to study over the problem of El Diablo.

El Diablo's declaration he would destroy Duke and take down The Bull's Eye if necessary was not exactly what I had expected. When I saw him stealing some historical artifact I figured, you know, pirates from the Ebay Islands or something. I hadn't figured on some weird personal vendetta or ambitions of general villainy.

Honestly, the scariest thing about El Diablo was his absolutely delectable aroma. His blood was like fang Viagra and that was going to cause trouble sooner or later. If he were just some guy who seemed particularly ripe for getting turned into a snack, well, whatever; that happens all the time. If he were some kind of supernatural – a blood ritualist of some sort, or gods help us a shapeshifter, both of which do exist and about which I know less than next to nothing – it could create a lot of problems. He would eventually wind up on the wrong side of the bite from a vampire in my town and then blam, more politics. Somebody was going to blow their cover out of desperation to get to him or, worse, they were going to get to him and he was going to blow them to pieces. Neither of these were okay options for me. You don't wind up in charge by doing nothing and you don't stay there by doing nothing. You stay there by solving problems, in part out of the infinite kindness of your own dead heart and in part because when you solve problems you show people what might happen to them if they become a problem for you: namely, you'll solve *them*.

I reflected on Roderick's claim that demons can "smell" desperation. El Diablo sure had looked like he was desperate to get into that case. He'd looked ready to beat that glass in with his own skull if he had to. Had that drawn the demon – Ross – to the library in the first place? Had Ross given the kid the idea? If there was a devil running around and a kid who suddenly seemed to have a bunch of superpowers – a vampire knows superpowers when we see them – it seemed logical enough to associate them in some way. If he were trying to screw with vampires, perhaps in revenge for a couple of us having been wrapped up in screwing with a demon a few years ago, turning loose a sack of vampire catnip in the middle of town would be a great way to do it.

While I let that thought ripen a little, I flipped to the late news and saw they were jawing about a carjacking in Durham. The talking head reading from the teleprompter had the sort of unlikely hair that made him look like he was running for county commissioner in 1987: perfectly sculpted and combed, just the right shade of salt and pepper, framing his face like a NASCAR helmet. I turned to that channel in the middle of his report, but what I caught ran like this:

"...at which point the cab driver was able to find a payphone and call police. The taxi in question was driven across town on Main Street, onto East Campus and then onto a residential lawn. The carjacker appears to have attempted to use it as a battering ram to destroy the historic Stagg Pavilion, also known as the East Campus Gazebo, built in 1902. Upon exiting the vehicle, apparently unharmed, the carjacker was described by witnesses as being dressed in an elaborate costume, possibly the same 1950's mascot uniform stolen from Perkins Library last weekend during Duke University's fall break. The assailant shouted that he was 'El Diablo', which is Spanish for 'the Devil', before escaping on foot. Durham and Duke University police are actively investigating and urge anyone with information about this incident to call Crime Stoppers.

"In other news, the Durham vigilante known popularly as The Bull's Eye has been credited with interrupting a gas station robbery on South Alston Avenue, across downtown from the carjacking, at approximately the same time. Police refused to comment but a witness to the crime described for us a black-clad figure she said disarmed the robber and knocked him unconscious using martial arts before fleeing the scene. Durham Police have repeated their invitation to The Bull's Eye to come forward."

The image cut to a uniform addressing someone slightly off-camera: "We want to repeat that The Bull's Eye is advised to come forward. All of Durham is inspired by his or her example but they are not a trained professional and may bring harm on themselves or another inadvertently."

The uniform zoomed out and spun, in the magic of video editing technologies, to become a young African-American woman in a suit addressing the same cameras. "The District Attorney's office may be forced to issue charges against this vigilante for having broken many of the same laws as the persons whose crimes they've interrupted. Our door is always open, however, to discussion with the so-called Bull's Eye and we want to remind him – or her – that we have the same goals of a peaceful and safe city for all our residents." A reporter said something muffled by the distance from the microphone and whatever poor assistant DA they'd dragged out in front of the cameras smiled a little. "I can't comment on whether or not we would trade clemency for The Bull's Eye's testimony at some of the trials of the criminals she or he has caught, but as I say, we're always open to conversation." The camera cut back to the newsreader. "And now, the weather tomorrow, tonight. Sam?"

I paused the TV – I don't know how people did anything before DVRs, another innovation to which Roderick introduced me – and sighed heavily. It was bad enough the newspapers were abuzz with Durham having a superhero; now it had a villain, too, and one every vampire in the Triangle would cut off a hand to get at once they got a whiff of that incredible blood.

I realized with some embarrassment that my fangs had dropped just remembering it.

The obvious thing to do would be to warn my colleagues away from him; simply put out the word that he was crazy and off-limits. Of course, if I just announced that with no reason someone would say I did it because I wanted him for myself. It would be like putting him front and center in the clearance section at ÜberBargains: everyone would want a piece of that and at yesterday's prices. If I were to dissuade my constituents from pursuing him like hounds after the hare I would have to be able to tell them why and it couldn't be some bullshit reason I'd made up. Too many of us can tell when someone is lying or when they aren't sure they're telling the truth. I had to be certain if I was going to convince Old Shoe, for instance. Old Shoe can spot a lie through a lead door.

Even if everyone stayed away from him, I reflected, it might be smartest to track him down and kill him anyway. The fact is, vampires do not last long in circumstances that keep mortals awake and alert and afraid, on the lookout for the odd and unusual. We tend to be an odd and unusual lot and our ability to pass in society is in most cases uncertain at best. That's part of why I've never actually met anyone incredibly old: current conventional wisdom says the vast majority of us don't really manage the transition from one era to the next with what you might call finesse. We wind up anachronisms and the idiosyncrasies of our behaviors give off some subtle vibe of the weird. Sooner or later there are mortals with torches and pitchforks and bundles of garlic and holy water. I couldn't have that, and I couldn't have some mortal paragon of athleticism with a bone to pick against Duke or The Bull's Eye or anybody else running around keeping both the hens and the foxes psychologically off-balance. It doesn't take very many cars jacked or purses snatched or dead kids in the bathrooms of dance clubs for people to go into panic mode and walk around with the pepper spray in their hand rather than in their pocketbook.

I was, of course, curious to find out exactly what made him so appetizing. It would be good to know if it could happen to someone else. If this marked some new environmental factor or something else that might recur in the general population and screw with vampires' already shaky ability to mix with the herd, better to find out sooner rather than later.

The last thing I knew needed seeing to, but I didn't really want to discuss with myself just yet, was this: if El Diablo qualified as unacceptably weird and noticeable, was the same true of a hero? I admired The Bull's Eye's gumption for being willing to do something in her neighborhood, for her people. I admired this in large measure because I found myself doing the same for mine sometimes. On the other hand, if carjackings and purse-snatchers made people a little too vigilant, I had to wonder to myself if a pseudo-hero would do the same.

An uncomfortable truth is that vampires thrive in a setting in which people are just a little bit downtrodden or just a little more comfortable than is good for them. Perfect and alert awareness and involvement in their community was bad for us. Having them just to either side of that was preferred. I didn't enjoy acknowledging it but the truth is we all rely on someone else's unhappiness, somewhere, somehow. For most people it's the two dollar a day anguish and psychic violence of the sweatshop products they line up to buy down at ÜberBargains. For me and mine it is the cheap, certain fear that there are monsters out there in the dark, every night, just waiting. It keeps most people out of the alleys and off the back roads so we can hunt the few who refuse to listen.

I couldn't solve a damned thing just sitting on my ass watching the TV news, though. If Roderick was coming and we were going on a hunt in Durham then I needed to make preparations to relocate temporarily.

Before I left, I walked out onto the porch and texted Old Shoe. Like I said, he's a Raleigh vampire who can smell a lie from across the street and down the block. I told him I needed to see him at the usual place. He texted back: he'd see me there in ten minutes. I loaded Smiles into the back seat of my old '76 Firebird, opened the t-tops and drove around the clock face that is the network of highways encircling Raleigh and referred to commonly as the Beltline. In Raleigh's northwest quadrant, squeezed behind a gas station and pressed against an embankment with a dead end street at the top, stood a tiny graveyard. I couldn't help but wonder if any Steeplechasers had emerged from its forgotten graves on Z day, some seven years before. I doubted it. This was a family plot no longer remembered by the family who'd put it here. The city maintained it haphazardly in their absence. It was dark enough and private enough for Old Shoe to feel comfortable emerging from the sewers he called home. As the local enforcer of some standards of normalcy and secrecy, I was awfully glad he took that much consideration given his appearance.

Smiles and I stood around the graveyard for a minute or two after we arrived, the frame of the Firebird pinging as it cooled. Eventually there was the sound of boots on an iron ladder somewhere below and a manhole cover lifted out of the ground and slid aside. Old Shoe climbed out, not bothering to knock dust or cobwebs from the maintenance worker jumpsuit he always wore. It was stained fourteen different shades of muck and smelled like a year's worth of used diapers. Old Shoe is a repulsive piece of work: skull halfway caved in, a snaggletooth snarling smile frozen in a rictus of fangs and gapped teeth, exposed muscle and bone down the back of his head and a nose broken in so many places it looked like modern art. I've never asked how he got that way but we get stuck however we are when we get turned. The obvious answer was that his maker had turned him about five seconds after he'd been dragged half a mile by the dump truck that hit him. In my opinion it was an act of cruelty to "save" him in that shape but I wasn't there and I'd never know what went through his maker's mind. Old Shoe never seemed inclined to comment on it and neither would I as long as he knew to stay out of sight. He'd picked up the nickname based on how he smells most of the time and it was so long ago no one was left who'd known him by anything else.

Smiles has never quite been at ease with Old Shoe. It's like he can sense the injuries as a kind of sickness. He always stands between us with his ears up and his eyes half-lidded. He looks like he's daring Old Shoe to make a move. I can't imagine anything less likely to occur.

"Evenin', boss." Old Shoe's voice is a rasp of collapsed trachea and punctured lungs. He always sounds like he's trying to whisper to me across a cancer ward. He calls me "boss" but I've never asked him to. If it were anyone else I'd object but Old Shoe is so pitiful I just let it slide. "What's shakin'?" For all I just painted him as a Picasso turned inside out, Old Shoe is the embodiment of good spirits.

"I'm going to be occupied for a few nights."

"Durham?" He chuckled. It sounded like rocks in a tin can.

"How'd you guess?"

"You're the boss. That means you go where the trouble is." He shrugged, or at least I think he did.

"Well, keep an ear to the ground for any trouble around here. Let me know if something odd goes on. I'm especially keeping an eye out for a tall guy, good looking, blue skin. Don't ask."

"Blue like those freakjobs in Kentucky, or blue like body paint or what?" Old Shoe elevated himself above some definition of "other" based on appearance without batting an eye. I nearly started to laugh, but I kept it down.

"Just blue. I said don't ask."

He rolled a cracked and crackling joint somewhere in the upper half of his torso. "You're the boss. I'll let you know if anything turns up." He paused before asking another question. "Why not tell Seth?"

"This guy isn't going to be showing up out in the open very much. You've got even odds of running into him in the shadows." I fluttered a tired breath out between my pudgy lips. "Are you done with the questions now or do I have to tell you *again* not to ask?"

Old Shoe put his hands up in front of him, placating me. "Sorry."

I nodded. 'And keep my semi-absence quiet, if you would."

"You got it. My lips are sealed."

I doubted that was physically possible with what skin he had left, but I just thanked him and departed. I like Old Shoe a lot, to be perfectly honest, but that doesn't mean I want to sit around shooting the breeze while he looks like last week's dinner.

<h1 style="text-align:center">Chapter 6</h1>

I live in a typical suburban neighborhood called London Towne. It was nearly destroyed by zombies several years ago, and yes that extra "E" *is* almost awful enough for it to deserve to be destroyed in a zombie attack. It's a good forty minutes from the campus of Duke University. Commuting back and forth to investigate the doings in my personal fiefdom wasn't impossible but it wasn't ideal. I wanted to be in Durham in order to get a sense of where the action might be concentrated. I needed a taste of which neighborhoods might be good or bad places to hunt a villain or find a hero. I wanted to press my lips against the flesh of that town and feel the thrum of its pulse.

I also wanted to be able to walk around to do my investigating. Driving through them, most places look about the same as most others. Walking around is how you get the sense of a place's character. Walking keeps you slow enough to notice the little things. Driving, you don't want to notice anything; you just want to get there and forget about the in-between.

That all added up to moving to Durham for just a little while.

Vampires who've been around for a while and managed to rub a few pennies together often are the same ones who start getting paranoid. It makes a kind of perverse sense: a bloodsucker with something to lose fears having it taken away from them. They start acquiring hidey-holes for all their junk. They start stuffing their metaphorical (and sometimes literal) socks with wads of cash and cheap property and burner phones. They build caches with a couple of hundred bucks, a fake ID, a prepaid phone and a change of clothes in every bus terminal, self-storage place and hollow log they can find. Like squirrels storing acorns for the winter, they pack away more than they'll ever remember having.

I haven't gotten there yet but I have started acquiring basic accommodations in parts of the state where I've got occasional business. I have my little house up near Asheville and I have my home in Raleigh but I've also got a cheap apartment thirty minutes from Wilmington, a basement efficiency in a student ghetto in Chapel Hill and a dilapidated log home in Durham.

The log home is the one of which I'm proudest. The others are nothing more than convenient crash pads: places I can land in an emergency without being noticed or sought. The log home, though, is a vampire's equivalent to an inflatable bounce-castle on his birthday.

Once upon a time I imagine the old house was someone's pride and joy. I've looked far enough into the history of its ownership to know it hasn't been owned by anybody special or worrisome. The last occupant died of old age and left it to relatives too far out of town to be fussed with taking care of it. I took it off their hands at an estate auction so long after the fact of their inheritance there was no one interested in buying it for all the repairs they'd have to make. I had the roof replaced and the windows fixed with that security plastic stuff to make them almost impossible to shatter. I nailed up three layers of blackout curtains around them to keep the curious from having anything to see. After that I didn't touch a single other thing.

From the outside, it looks like a home built seventy or eighty years ago out of rounded gray timbers with white chinking between them. After the roof was put on I went up there myself with the old shingles and spread them around so it looks like it's never been repaired. The yard has been almost totally reclaimed by the old pine woods in which it sits and the gutters have been clogged with leaves so long there are saplings growing out of them. On the front of the house that gutter has sagged or fallen off completely so it hangs down across the front door at an odd angle. The carport is crumpled from where a tree fell over on it. The yard is so grown up in shrubs and saplings the house is almost invisible from the road and none of the neighbors can see it so no one complains about their spoilt view. An inspector told me the house was structurally sound but unsellable, which was exactly what I wanted to hear. I didn't want to attract some real estate agent sniffing around for new prospects. I wanted it to stand as a warning to the respectable and the nice: stay away, keep moving and forget this is here.

On the inside, the house is badly dated and mostly empty. I left the last guy's couch and a pile of old photographs because it seemed a little sad to throw them away and they make the perfect sentimental defense. They give it the ambience of a ransacked grave. It's the sort of place a mortal knows to avoid. Humans have been telling their children to stay away from houses like that since they were caves.

The basement, on the other hand, is solid and sealed against both water and daylight. I've got a blast door between the cellar and the interior of the house and the exterior exit is via a tunnel I paid some guys to dig. It leads over and up to a false manhole riser in the back yard with another blast door in the way. I keep a mattress and a big tarp in the middle of the room and a few bags of sand covered in old chemical hazard labels. I want it to look like the sort of place a high school kid with any brains would think is about to blow their ass to Kingdom Come should they stumble inside. I want the truly implacably adventurous to decide it's more trouble than they bargained for and get the hell out of Dodge.

The only place from which the house is at all visible is a cycle and pedestrian path running through ten or fifteen miles of detached suburban housing. The American Tobacco Trail connects downtown Durham to its southernmost suburbs then skids off downhill into countryside, crossing country-fried waterways with old-fashioned names like Panther Creek and Nancy Branch before disappearing into dark, lush forests. While it's still up in the suburbs that trail wends between the huddled homes of people at a lot of different income levels. Every once in a while someone gets mugged on it. I imagined the sort of idiot kid who robs people in the middle of suburbia, surrounded by houses and cameras and places their victims could go for help would be a pretty good place to start looking for the most desperate human being in town. Middle class teen playing thug dress-up or aspirational loser trying to launch a career in crime: either way, I would be happy to drain them until they died if that's what this would take.

Roderick showed up the next night about five hours after sundown. He had his dog, an ancient St. Bernard named Dog who stands about as high as the middle of Roderick's spindly chest. Roderick was driving his great big gold convertible Cadillac DeVille.

I was standing out front of the log house around half past 11:00 when he pulled up. I directed him into the driveway that seemingly went nowhere and he crawled his behemoth across the grass-carpeted gravel to the little parking area out of sight between the house and the evergreen in its front yard.

Roderick was wearing a pair of shorts in a loud plaid print, penny loafers and a pink shirt like the kids wear these days. He looked just like one of them in that get-up. At a glance, he was just a skinny teenager like any other. I couldn't help but admire his ability to blend. He would have been invisible in any gay bar or shopping mall: just another blond twink in casual wear. Dog, on the other hand, was anything but invisible to the naked eye. He was two hundred pounds if he was an ounce. He looked like a normal dog hiding under a bearskin rug.

Smiles was seated by my side when they climbed out of the car – Roderick first and Dog right after him – and maintained admirable composure as Dog sniffed the ground here and there. Smiles ignores other dogs but he's never met another hellhound he likes. I could tell Roderick had been feeding his own blood to Dog because of his size and the intelligence gleaming in those deceptively sad-seeming eyes. I wondered if Smiles would be able to smell the power and presence of Roderick in Dog, who had been boarded when we went to Seattle. When we turn a canine into one of our hounds we extend a part of ourselves into them. We and they are never exactly separate as long as both are alive.

You don't even want to think what a hellhound goes through when its maker dies.

Dog eventually walked right up to Smiles, just as pretty as you please, sniffed all up around Smiles' muzzle for a minute while Smiles sat stonily still, and then licked him on the face.

After that was done, they were instantly the best of friends.

Neither Roderick nor I sighed with open relief but I could feel it in the air. "1970?" I gestured at the DeVille. I love old cars. I'd seen it in Seattle but we hadn't much talked about it.

"1971." Roderick smiled at me, pulling a leash out of a steamer trunk he had stowed in the Cadillac's back seat. He nodded towards the log house. "This place is marvelous, by the way. I would not have even seen the driveway if you were not standing down there."

I smiled. "Thanks. Need help with anything? Luggage?"

"Oh, heavens no, I will be staying downtown," Roderick said. "I have already checked in at the place on Main Street, the one that used to be a bank?" He waved a flutter of fingers to dismiss the notion of crashing here. "It is only a couple of blocks from the other end of this trail and I am, if nothing else, a man accustomed to his creature comforts."

I shrugged. "Suit yourself, but you're welcome to stay here. It's a lot darker in here than the average hotel room." I coughed. Roderick likes to push the limits. He always stays in hotels, which all in all are kind of a dumb place for a vampire to go if there are alternatives. I mean, we can always sleep in the tub but it still feels risky. Remember that the next time you see a news story of a hotel abruptly going up in flames in the middle of the afternoon: housekeeping might have simply opened the curtains in the wrong room.

Roderick smirked in response. "Cousin," he said, "The offer is appreciated but I like my freedom. It is simply how I am wired. Now, let us go and find a good place to get robbed."

Technically, the American Tobacco Trail closes at dark. All that means is the cops will scold the people who prefer to use it at night if something actually happens to them. While waiting twenty minutes for Roderick to arrive I'd already seen half a dozen joggers and dog walkers make their way along the trail behind the house. At night, to human eyes, it would be nothing more than a pitch-dark tunnel through the shadows of trees. It must have felt like it was a hundred miles from civilization, even though for most of it one or another back yard was only a few dozen feet away.

There are parts of it, though, that are genuinely remote: places where it veers away from the safety of suburbia and treks out through the middle of woods too uneven and inconvenient to be developed into anything. Roderick and I started to take Smiles and Dog with us as we walked but we worried they would scare off any potential attackers. We wanted to look utterly vulnerable and neither of our dogs would do much to contribute to that.

Instead, we strolled alone with no flashlights and chatted quietly with one another about this and that: all the wet weather we'd had that summer and how things were going in Asheville. Roderick was there as my monitor and enforcer. He'd tracked down the last of the spawn of a former enemy and bumped them off one by one. Now he kept his eyes and ears open for new trouble. He filled me in on the local politics and other gossip as we walked. I told him all about going to see the production of *Dracula* with Seth and Beth. Roderick was pleased at my social activity and fascinated by the notion of children playing at being vampires. With a darkly humorous lilt he sang, "I believe the children are our future…" and we both laughed with silly voices. It was the most relaxed I'd felt in a month.

Conversation wound around to The Bull's Eye and to El Diablo, as all conversations in Durham at that time seemed eventually to do. I suggested a vampire would make a natural super villain – strong, fast, often remorseless – when Roderick countered with something I found surprising.

"No, no, Cousin," he purred. "We make far better heroes than villains."

"Why heroes?" I chuckled at the thought of a vampire in spandex and a cape.

"For all the reasons you listed." Roderick stated this as though it were the most obvious of things: water is wet, up is thatta way, and so on. "Plus the fact we would be unexpected."

"Remorseless isn't something I think most people like in a hero."

"Tell that to the writers of *24*," Roderick mused. "In our modern age, so damnably aware of implications and privilege, so called upon not to be constant assholes to one another on the big things such as race or sex and, we discover, so terrible at it, I think we seek escape in a number of ways. One of the most common I observe in humanity's patterns is the eagerness with which they can be assholes to one another about the small things instead, as though there were a pressurized system of rudeness and insult circulating within them which must ultimately escape through one or another of the fissures in their psychic device."

"I think," I slowly replied, "You may be choosing to misremember how much we were all jerks to everybody back in the day." I shrugged. "People aren't meaner now. We just notice it more."

"Why?" Roderick's question was sincere. I noted that real curiosity about human behavior and filed it right alongside the way in which he referred to mortals as *them*. I made special note of it in my cousin because I'd started noticing it of myself.

"People have more opportunities to document," I said. "Used to be, you could just flip a guy off on the road and keep driving and never think about him again. You'd never know who he was or why he cut you off and that was okay. You could just react and let it go and you were allowed the opportunity to forget. Now you get your picture taken and somebody tweets it and the next thing you know your one moment of forgettable annoyance has gone viral. We don't get annoyed or express it any more often but we spend way more time processing it." I shrugged. "At least, that's how it seems to me. Otherwise, sure: I guess we'd make okay superheroes, too. Not being expected to be a hero may come in handy, I guess."

Roderick made a murmur of thoughtfulness. After we'd walked a few yards, he abruptly glanced at me and asked, "So, what would your superhero identity be?" The corner of his lip turned up in a twist.

I laughed and shook my head. "I have no idea. Why, what's yours?"

Roderick answered so quickly it was obvious he had thought about this long and hard. He smiled widely, lips pressed together in a thin line curved with pleasure. "'Just Dandy'," he said, with a flourished little tug of his perfectly rolled pink Oxford sleeves.

I threw back my head and laughed so hard a neighborhood dog started barking.

"I also have one for you," he said. "You would be 'Good Old Boy,' my teammate and relation."

I blinked at that. "Good Old Boy?"

Roderick shrugged and looked a little annoyed, though I wasn't sure whether it was with me or with his own suggestion of a name. "It is a work in progress. Smiles would be known as 'Gnasher' and Dog as 'El Gato'."

I scratched the side of my cheek for a moment before finally saying, "I like it, but 'gato' means cat. I think you mean 'El Perro'."

Roderick cut me a sidelong glance of disgusted pity. "Cousin," he finally sighed, "What on earth do you think is the point of a *nom de guerre*, anyway?"

We'd made our way past a small city park, along the back of an apartment complex, between two halves of a high school campus and into one of those long dark stretches of nothing when I sensed a subtle shift in Roderick's posture and I heard the unmistakable scuffing sound of someone in sneakers trying to creep across asphalt.

We were on a section where the trail was elevated above the natural topology around it: a deep, sharp valley with a line of raised ground cutting downhill through the middle. The path was narrow and elevated, like an earthen dam holding back a lake that'd gone dry. To keep people from riding their bikes off the steep sides of it, the city had put up a green chain-link safety fence. It kept them from becoming victims of gravity but it also created a bounded corridor easily cut off at either end. It had occurred to me, when I saw it from afar on our approach, that its thirty yards of fenced pavement with limited ingress and egress would make an excellent place to ambush the unsuspecting. I was reminded of the tunnel warfare of ancient cultures: long, narrow, underground paths used for offense or defense, easily mined, easily collapsed, easily turned into a deadly bottleneck. The only difference was that this was elevated above ground instead.

As we approached that bottleneck, Roderick had been saying something about a vampire who'd breezed through Asheville on his way to South Carolina. When we heard that slightly stealthy footfall he paused, smiled and said to me, slightly above the volume of conversation, "So I sent him on his way and continued with my date."

"Your date?" I raised both eyebrows. We were very carefully not reacting to the presence of a person on the trail. "Do you really date?"

"Of course, cousin," Roderick replied. "Not every meal has to be eaten straight from the box. Sometimes there is real pleasure in its preparation as well as in its enjoyment; and sometimes it might wish to be enjoyed again. Often half the pleasure of an experience is in its cultivation. Ask any gardener."

A young man of significantly less than average height stepped out from behind some shrubs ahead of us. He was built like an athlete and wore long basketball shorts, the kind that brightly shine in the light, but he was just barely five and a half feet so they hung too low on him. He cut off that exit from the fenced section of trail. Roderick and I both stopped short. The kid didn't say anything to us. He just stood there looking sullen.

Roderick put a hand to the middle of his own chest and said, "Oh, heavens," in the most sissified voice he could muster. It was easy to forget sometimes that he came straight from Southern stock despite growing up in Seattle. He was doing a crackerjack Scarlett O'Hara.

I turned and looked behind us. Two other young men – one very tall and one very muscular – stood at the other end of the fenced segment of trail, blocking our avenue of retreat. We were, they must have imagined, utterly trapped. "Cousin," I said, "We appear to be cut off."

The more muscular of the two behind us broke into a swaggering stride and started to approach. The tall guy stayed back. Muscles walked right to us, fearless as an angel in Hell, and reached up to shove my shoulder once. "Come up off the goods," he said.

"What?" I hadn't understood what he'd said. It was just words to me. It didn't resolve into anything, not even recognizable slang.

"Come up off the goods," he repeated.

"Huh?" In equal proportion to Roderick's play-acted fear, I offered stony incomprehension. I sounded like a tourist who didn't speak very good English had asked me for directions. Later, it occurred to me I may have sounded confident instead of checked out.

"Give me your stuff," he snapped. He hated me for not sounding afraid. Stepping back once, he looked me up and down, then again, then a third time. "Oh, shit," he said. "The Bull's Eye."

Dressed in black from head to toe and I was walking at night in the perfect place to be the victim of a crime of convenience: a long stretch of unattended suburban leisure trail with no lights, no emergency call boxes and no one in earshot save those people engaged in the honest sleep of the working class. "Well, hell," I said. "OK, look, it isn't – "

"Yeah," he said, and he broke into a grin. "Yeah." He drew it out long, savoring it. "I just wanted a new wallet but now I'm gonna get a new pair of goody two-shoes, too." That smirk crawled into my brain and started cutting the restraints I try to keep around the monster inside. "Now," he commanded, "Gimme all your shit."

I tried not to smile as I worked on a reply, but it didn't work. Instead, I pondered to whom else they might have done this. If they were willing to walk up and pick on the two of us with such brazen disregard then they'd done it before, perhaps many times. I wondered what I'd get if I were to kill this kid and then with the special gift of my hindsight draw out all the times he'd robbed someone like this. How many terrified old ladies and defenseless young men out jogging alone and all the other forms of innocence the human race can muster up would I see? I'm no better, I know, but vampires were all once human and humans are very good at justifying their actions. Here this guy was, young and strong as an ox, and the best thing he had to do with his time was pick on people for a few bucks and a laugh? It gnawed at me. The monster inside started to salivate.

"Or what?" My voice was a low growl but it carried far in the clammy silence of a dark autumn night.

Muscles stared at me, eyes gleaming in the starlight.

His buddy behind him, the tall one who had held position when this guy approached, looked nervous. "Just give up the goods, fatty, and we'll leave you and your boyfriend alone." He tried to sound tough but he sounded frightened.

"Yeah," Muscles said. "Just turn it over and you and the Fag Wonder here can go find a kitten in a tree to get in the papers tomorrow."

I didn't look at him. I glanced at Roderick, who winked at me before turning towards the one kid who'd stepped out first and blocked our way forward. I told myself they had sealed their fates when they insulted me. In truth, maybe the jab about my weight could have been allowed to stand, or the homophobia, but I think it was mistaking me for The Bull's Eye that did them in. Something about being taken for a hero was worse to me than being taken for a victim. I was tired of shit like this. I was tired of a "demon" and El Diablo and having to save the world from itself every now and again and I was tired of that world thanking me by assuming I was just another schlub. I stopped bothering with seeking to justify what I wanted to do.

Smiles and Dog emerged from the shadows fifty yards back from the tall guy at the rear. They made no noise because hellhounds are every bit as much the predators as the vampires who make them. We had walked without them in order to look unprotected but Smiles and Dog had followed behind, well out of sight, for a moment such as this. They knew we wanted them to approach now, so they did.

I snapped my finger by my side and Smiles growled, deep down, like the stones of the earth had begun to grind together.

I locked eyes with the would-be mugger in front of me and drilled into his mind with the force of my own power. His free will instantly buckled. Muscles was just a bully: a nobody with nothing going on upstairs. "Stay here," I ordered him, "And watch what we do to your friends."

Roderick made a noise a little like a giggle and smacked his lips before he and I broke in opposite directions. Dog and Smiles darted in as soon as we moved. Dog blew by me, running the other direction many times faster than a St. Bernard his size should be able to go. He bounded down to catch up with Roderick and the two of them sprinted and then leapt together at the short guy at the front. They were far too quick for him to comprehend or react. Dog hit the guy like a tanker truck and Roderick descended like a spider, all angles and limbs and miniscule agility.

Smiles met me halfway, with the tall guy between us. He leapt to clamp his jaws around the back of the guy's neck. Smiles planted his paws on the guy's spine and shook his head once with a thick, viscous snap of bone and spinal cord. I latched a hand over the guy's mouth to muffle the scream we both knew wouldn't have done him any good anyway as he collapsed, paralyzed and probably dying. Dropping him on his back, I wrenched his wild eyes towards me, bared my fangs and used them to tear out his throat in one go. Blood sprayed in all directions. It was like bursting a ketchup balloon.

Roderick didn't bother to cover the mouth of his victim, letting Shorty get out one long, loud shriek. It echoed across the little valley, bouncing off curtains of kudzu and pillars of old trees, and by the time it came back the guy was dying in Roderick's tiny arms. I realized abruptly I might not remember the kid in a few minutes, but Roderick dropped the guy face-first on the ground and let him bleed out onto asphalt instead. He didn't even offer this guy the mercy of being forgotten. His obituary, if he rated one, would immortalize him at best as a murdered miscreant in a nameless corner of an anonymous suburb.

I swiped my hand across my mouth with all the effect of one of those thin paper napkins you get in a sleeve of plastic silverware with your to-go box of pork barbecue. The last remaining kid, the one I'd called Muscles, the one who'd put his hand on my shoulder and pushed it once to assert his dominance over me, was trembling from head to toe in the very center of it all. True to my command, he had not looked away from me. I walked slowly towards him. He shook like a leaf, more and more violently, as I approached.

I locked eyes with him again and whispered, "Run."

He turned and started to sprint but Roderick was standing there, arms open like a bear trap waiting to be sprung, and twenty seconds later I dumped Muscles – still alive, but bleeding out and awake enough to experience the terrible certainty of his own death – over the fence and into the ravine below. Down there, among the kudzu at the bottom of a gulley where no person would likely go and no loved one would look for him, he could live out his last few seconds. I hoped he spent them staring up between vines at a dark sky and wondering why God had abandoned him.

Roderick hefted the little guy he'd taken out and dumped the corpse down into the same spot. I walked back to mine and found Smiles lapping at the cooling blood. "Stop that," I said to him. He did, but like any dog who sees a crumb swept from the floor, he mourned it. "We do not eat off the ground." I tried not to scold him too hard, though. We've all been there at one time or another, and for all the smarts and strength my blood gives him, he's ultimately still a dog.

Then I dumped the tall guy over the side of the drop-off beside his other two friends.

Roderick strolled up, belched noisily and said, "This is a great spot. I've got to remember it. No one is ever going to find them down there."

"Never say never," I replied.

"Well, they'll just blame it on El Diablo, right?" He shrugged with disregard.

That's when I realized what was perhaps the real reason why El Diablo bothered me so much: he was a convenient excuse. As long as he was around, vampires could act with a lot more impunity than before and that would be bad for everyone.

"Oh, cousin," I sighed. "Don't spread bad ideas."

"*C'est la vie*," Roderick said. "*C'est la guerre*." That's life. That's war.

We turned to walk away together and Ross was standing there with a smile on his face. "Well," he said, like the cat who caught the canary, "That's one way to get a boy's attention."

Chapter 7

Roderick stood very still behind me, but to my left, and it occurred to me he was using our relative sizes as camouflage. A photograph would suggest I was protecting my cousin from harm but I had just watched him leap through the air like he was on springs. A year before, we had fought side by side in Asheville and I had outpaced him. After what I'd just seen, I wasn't so sure anymore. He was probably the more dangerous one of the two of us, all things considered, and he was using to his advantage the probability the average person would think otherwise.

Ross looked as he had before: blue and silver skin reflecting starlight in a hundred subtle ways with sickly amber eyes that left a kind of slime on everything they touched. His expression seemed permanently fixed in the moment he appraised the world and found it lacking but only barely so. He was handsome, I guess. It's hard for me to think of the right word there. He had many of the compelling features of male beauty: a sharp jaw line, angled cheekbones, a slightly gaunt and hungry cast to his face. He was wearing a plain white tee shirt and blue jeans, just as common as could be. He could have played a bit part in any high school production of *Grease*. His skin was sleek and shiny and it was easy to find myself fascinated by the rippling colors and patterns as his skin flexed and moved.

Perhaps the word I wanted wasn't "handsome" so much as "interesting". He was interesting to watch: alien and beautiful, like a spider or a snake.

"Wait," I said, "Is that really all it takes? Three kids who push around the wrong guy, and snap, demon delivery service?" I snapped my fingers as I said the word. I tried to sound smirking and cool when I said it but it probably just sounded ungrateful.

Ross chuckled and it sounded like someone gargling butter. "Not exactly." He nodded in the direction of the ravine where we'd dumped the boys who tried to rob us. "I like your style, though."

Roderick stepped forward and, after only a moment of hesitation – one somewhere between nervous uncertainty and conscious insult on the scale of social timers – offered his hand to Ross to shake. "Hello," he purred. "My name is Roderick. Withrow is my cousin."

The flare of jealousy that lit up inside my chest was as hot and red as a superheated railroad spike. I didn't even know I liked this guy and I was instantly jealous of my cousin merely speaking to him. I clamped down on saying anything, but I wanted to: I wanted to clobber Roderick into next week right then and there just to get him out of the way. Just seeing Ross, whatever he may have been, made a part of me wake up from long sleep only to find itself in the loneliest, darkest possible pit. One little bit of attention had taken some part of the human me I thought died on the vine over half a century ago and made it sit up and pant.

Ross flicked those fool's-gold eyes at me for one electric nanosecond then took Roderick's hand, returning that precisely timed hesitation with equal ambiguity. "I'm Ross."

"No, you are not." Roderick smiled. I could see his ears lift. I had seen that smile before. It isn't a smile, it's just his features rearranging so it's easier to open his mouth wide before he bites. "Your name is not Ross. It's something complicated and dangerous and you keep it concealed from others because its knowledge would be a form of power over you."

Ross arched one eyebrow, then the other. "Withrow," he said to me, still shaking Roderick's hand, "Your cousin has seen some interesting movies." Ross paused for a moment, looking briefly puzzled, then stopped shaking Roderick's hand. He did not, however, let go of it. "Tell me," he murmured, "If names have power, why did you just tell me yours?"

Roderick's ears lifted farther. "Because it didn't matter the last time I killed one of you. I don't expect it will matter now."

This time the surprise on Ross' face was genuine, or appeared to be. I couldn't believe the things Roderick was saying to him but I felt paralyzed. If I allowed myself to move one millimeter I wasn't sure what it would be to do: to hit Ross, to hit Roderick, to throw them both over the edge of that ravine and let them catfight over the steaming corpses of our cooling kills. Ross let go of Roderick's hand and backed up a couple of steps, hands raised to show he had no aggressive intent.

"Easy, boy," he said to Roderick. Dog abruptly growled and I knew that meant Roderick was containing some equally feral response. Ross then looked at me again. "Your cousin's idea about finding the most desperate person around wouldn't work on me in a technical sense but I do notice things. I wasn't quite ready to strike things back up with you – I have a lot on my plate, it's just been that kind of month – but how about we make a deal? If you can find the most desperate person in all of Durham I will absolutely show up for another chat. I want to get to know you, I will happily admit, but right now I'm working on a big project. I'm willing to set it aside for a night or two, though, if you can in fact do that one thing."

I finally found my voice amidst confusion and conflicting reactions. "So, sacrificing the most desperate person in town wouldn't force you to show up but you want me to do it anyway? Why, for fun?"

"To a degree," Ross said. He rolled his shoulders in a shrug I found almost intoxicating to watch: every muscle and bone and tendon was visible against that magical skin. "Mostly just to see how you go about it. You learn a lot about a man by watching him solve a problem. I've never had much to do with your kind. I want to see how you think."

"You want something." Roderick spoke, but his voice was as flat and as dead as week-old road-kill. He sounded absolutely deathly cold.

"Yes," Ross said with a smile. His teeth were like a megalodon: too many and pointed in all the wrong angles. The part of me that was once a teenager thought they looked just as cool as all hell. "I want to get to know your cousin better."

"Tell me why." Roderick was trying hard to keep something in. Smiles had sat in silence by my side the whole time but Dog's growl rose up again and Roderick's fists were clenched.

Ross' tone was one of ultimate exasperation when he replied. "Because I like great big guys! OK? I'm into bears! Christ!" He turned to me and said, somewhat apologetically, "Look, mostly I came here to say nice work on those kids – they deserved it, trust me – and to chat you up. Looks like maybe that has to wait until some other time."

With that, he disappeared. There was a sound like a miniature clap like thunder and a puff of angry yellow smoke where Ross had been. Roderick stood, fists balled up, *en garde*, waiting for an attack that didn't seem to be coming. I waited long moments for him to relax. When he finally did, he ran his fingers through his hair, shook his head and proceeded to ask me about something inane and neutral as though the whole exchange had never occurred. I honored his agitation and concern by letting him do so without a word of argument.

By the time Roderick and I and our respective canines had walked all the way downtown it was nearly one in the morning. I offered to see him to his hotel but he declined.

"Oh heavens no, Cousin," he said. "I must go dancing first. Nothing like a little body heat when I'm all warm and tingly inside after a meal." He wanted to go to a massive gay club in the middle of downtown. It's called Power Company and by reputation it's the best bar in the Triangle – maybe one of the best in the southeast. I've been a couple of times but I don't much dance and I don't much like small talk with mortals so it just never really drew me as a place to go kill time on my own. I could see it fitting Roderick to a tee.

I had hours before sunrise so I decided to strike out on another walk downtown with Smiles by my side to think for a bit. My thoughts were on Ross and what he'd said; on the challenge he'd given me; and on El Diablo. It seemed obvious to do the math: one devil and one devil-themed villain make two, right? A part of me was worried my biggest current problem – a self-declared super-villain making life more dangerous and more tempting for my people – might be the huge project Ross had mentioned. It seemed only natural, didn't it? I didn't want to leap to conclusions, though, and I didn't want the idiocy of carnal attraction to keep me from doing my job. Maybe it would help to revisit the place where I'd first seen both of them. Maybe it would help to be alone with my dog for a while. Maybe I could just wander between the remaining signs of life in the middle of the night and hear myself think.

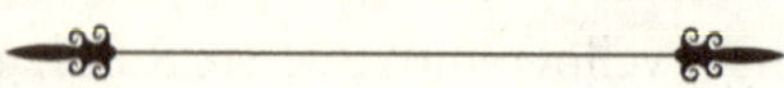

Duke's campus was not busy at half-past one on a weeknight. Still, a college is a college and kids are kids. I could hear people walking the stone paths; television sets in dorms here and there; NPR's overnight broadcast of the BBC; car doors opening and closing; cigarette lighters flicking on and off. They were all the sounds of life on a university campus. Smiles and I set off walking towards the Chapel, its tower lighted like a beacon in the night.

I didn't know exactly what I was there to find, but I knew I had to be there to find it. I figured if nothing else I might could catch a whiff of either my intruder or El Diablo. I'd first followed or found them there, hadn't I? Doing so again didn't seem so impossible. The crisp air of autumn is perfect for hunting: the scents that compete with prey are fewer and more easily distinguishable. Nobody ever mistook blood for decaying leaves or the warmth of life for the olfactory blade of a cold front somewhere high on the wind.

Smiles and I spent probably twenty or thirty minutes just meandering around between old stone buildings covered in carefully manicured ivy. Here and there we sidled past kids standing outside in old sweatshirts and jeans trying to smoke cigarettes and text at the same time. None of them spoke to me or even especially noticed me. Kids at that age are tremendously self-absorbed and to some degree I was relying on that. Eventually, the places with people in them — the dorms where fraternities with whole floors to themselves were throwing poorly-concealed keggers; the paved courts were a few kids were playing basketball in the middle of the night; the thin slices of asphalt perched over stretches of carelessly perfect forest — became the exceptions rather than the rule of my experience of campus.

I went to college, yes, but it was a different time and not a particularly happy one. I didn't like myself then and I liked everyone else even less. I had a few friends back home and fewer at school so I threw myself into my study of painting. I developed a little talent, enough that my maker noticed me, and that was that. I graduated and died almost immediately thereafter, and there I was.

The mortal life I'd had in that kind of place was jettisoned like a booster rocket: spent, useless. It was just so much dead weight holding me back from eternal night. These kids were just like the ones I had known in those days — my last *days*, in point of fact — in that they didn't pay me any mind and

I didn't want them to. I was just another pedestrian they probably couldn't even see in the darkness.

I loved it more than I can possibly tell you.

Soon enough our meanderings led Smiles and me to the edge of those Duke Gardens again – the ones through which I'd originally tracked the scent of the intruder – and in moonlight they were breathtakingly beautiful. There was a large pond and a bunch of graveled paths and trees from all over the world and all of it was just stunning when barely lighted. Everywhere the eye fell there was a huge flower that had closed for the night or another that had, in turn, opened. The whole place was lush and alive. Even as autumn approached and parts of it shed their leaves, confetti at the end of a riotous party, the place breathed vitality. I stopped short at the tree line because it would have felt almost… I don't know, I hate to say sacrilegious but that's the word that comes to mind, so I'll just say *wrong*; it would have felt wrong to go stomping out into the middle of it in my big black boots and leave prints all over everything.

I had a meditative few moments there, watching the gardens open up under the night sky, Smiles sniffing the ground around me, when I saw him: El Diablo was there, too, standing on the bright red Japanese-style arched bridge that spanned the pond in a back corner. It was a shielded little spot, shielded from view and perfect for reflection. I was probably two hundred yards away but I was sure it was El Diablo: that getup he had on was utterly unmistakable in any light.

He was sitting in the way we used to call "Indian style": legs crossed in front of him, ankles tucked under, elbows resting on the blue sateen flames that climbed his legs. He was in the full uniform, just sitting there, looking at what I assumed was his own reflection in the surface of the pond. The uniform had seen better days. Far from the pristine state it was in when I watched him steal it, it now bore stains: dark brown on the knees, the shins, the elbows, the chest. Most were probably mud but the ones across the chest bore fingerprints and I was pretty sure I smelled blood. I wondered whose.

I slipped around the edge of the tree line, up onto a dark street, around a curve and back into the trees with Smiles gliding behind me in total silence. Three minutes of slow, purposeful creeping later I was back in the trees of the gardens but I was behind El Diablo and maybe twenty yards away. I moved down, balanced preternaturally on some small, smooth stones and tiptoed up to the end of the bridge. Then I stepped onto the first footstep at the end of it – he was in its dead center – and waited to see if he would notice me. Smiles, sensing my intention, moved through darkness to cut off the other end.

It did not escape me that we were trying a close variation on the tactic of the would-be muggers from earlier that night.

"I love this place," El Diablo said. His voice was low and a little slurred: weirdly lazy, like he'd just awakened from a deep sleep. "Love*d*, I guess I should say."

So: his hearing or his vision or both were way ahead of the average human being. Not good, but in some ways it made things easier. Sometimes we think of humans as just another kind of cattle, yes, but sometimes we remember the humans we used to be and we feel something like guilt. When we're dealing with something else in the world that qualifies as "weird," the moral and ethical playing field is a lot more level. I had enough to think about from tonight already.

"It's a beautiful garden," I said. Our voices were very quiet. An unlikely pedestrian on one of the streets nearby would never have heard us. "I'd never been here until the other night but I think I'll be back. It's a really special place."

He was still staring at himself – cowl and all – in the lake surface. "I don't mean the garden," he said. "I mean the school."

"You phrased it in the past tense," I said. I took another step onto the bridge, just easing up and then leaning my weight against the railing. "But here you are."

"I'm only here in the immediate, physical sense. I'm just here to finish something. I used to be here..." He paused, and lifted his head to stare at the stars instead. "I used to come here to make things."

"And now you come here to do what?" Another step. I wanted to get closer. I wanted to get close enough to close the gap between us before he could cry out. I was telling myself I didn't know what I would do, but I knew: I would remove one of my concerns from the world. Sometimes we can't help but think destroying a thing is the easiest way to cope with it. "Did you come here to destroy things?"

He smiled, sort of: the corners of his mouth jumped around for a second, anyway, before he grew serious again. He started to turn his head towards me but then stopped for some reason. "Not things; people. Buildings. The school itself. You have no idea how I loved this place, and to think they did this to me?" His voice dropped. In a vampire that statement would have turned into a snarl. The monster inside is never very far away from us, never too distant to be heard. Something about him, about the way his social skills skittered and shuffled atop his interactions like a loose piece of paper with a roach underneath, told me he was much the same way.

"What did they do?" I took another step, then another, using the syllables of what I said to train his mind away from noticing by giving him a different sound pattern to focus on and identify. I still remember the time my maker said to me, when teaching me to hunt, that the tongue, like the pen, is also mightier than the sword: a well-said word with the former can hide the latter's unsheathing. "Did they hurt you? Did they do something to make you mad?"

"No, they said I was mad already." He smiled again.

I took one more very casual step. I was fifteen feet away and I knew that with another two steps I could be on him so fast he wouldn't realize it himself before my teeth were in.

"They took everything away from me after that. So I'm going to take away everything of *theirs*. But do you know how hard that is?" He all of a sudden had the aspect of talking to just another one of the guys, griping over a beer about the boss and his girlfriend and the crazy neighbor downstairs. "I try and I *try* to think of something really bad I can do to them and it's not that hard, but all those things? All those things make them into the victim and I can't have that. I'm just letting them win, then. No, I need to do something that will really tarnish them, something that will associate their icon with some great tragedy. I need to make people feel... *uncomfortable* when they think of this place. That would be... that would be nice." He smiled again.

"You do realize that, y'know, people realize you stole that outfit, right? I mean, nobody is going to see you do something terrible and think, 'Oh, sure, Duke did that.' On the news they talked about you stealing that outfit. The school is just desperate to have no association with you. It's impossible to know you are out there doing your thing without also knowing Duke has nothing to do with it."

El Diablo turned his head and looked at me like I was the biggest idiot in town, like he couldn't believe he had been reduced to having to explain this to me. "There are highly complicated causal relationships that happen at a quantum level. It would be impossible to explain it to some outdated hillbilly like yourself but suffice to say, there's more to the idea of sympathetic relationships than you could possibly comprehend. Perhaps like affects *like* after all. 'As above, so below' may be more scientific maxim than mere cult catchphrase: they may influence one another exactly as the ritualists claim."

I had taken one of those two final steps while he spoke and I decided when our eyes met – when I realized he also knew what I was doing – that I didn't have time for the last one. There were a few milliseconds in there in which both our eyes narrowed. My heart squeezed like a withered fist, driving blood through my black veins, and time slurred to an abrupt crawl.

Then I moved at him.

My teeth came out and I leapt forward with all my weight behind me, hands out, ready to clap one palm over El Diablo's mouth and plant the other in the middle of his chest to knock him back, neck exposed. As time slowed down for the attack I noticed with tremendous surprise that he was bringing up his right fist in what seemed, to me, to be real-time. He caught me square in the jaw and rolled as I spun into a heap in the spot where he had been. El Diablo was up in a flash and on his feet even as I was just starting to spring back up to mine. He was grinning, now, eyes little slits behind the cowl, perfectly normal human teeth bared just a bit. Smiles leapt from behind but El Diablo ducked smoothly, not even looking, and Smiles sailed overhead to land in a skitter behind me. The chainsaw motor in Smiles' chest revved once as he turned around.

"Sometimes, when I come here, I think maybe I should just give it all up," he said to me before throwing a punch I easily dodged. Any mortal speaking to me now would sound like a single being played at LP speeds. El Diablo, though, sounded almost normal. He was moving almost as fast as I did. I answered with my own punch and saw it land. He still managed to roll with it enough to tumble onto his side and then back up with a swiftness and grace no human being could possess. "Then I run into someone who reminds me what this place is like. Nice fangs! I wouldn't have guessed The Bull's Eye to be a *vampire*! That explains a lot!" Then he took off running towards the other end of the bridge and despite my vampiric reflexes and reaction times El Diablo was just ahead of Smiles and me the whole way.

"What the hell is that supposed to mean? Vampires aren't even real!" Rule number one: never let the humans find out we exist.

El Diablo didn't look back, but I could hear him: "Spare me," he yelled. "I'd love to stay and chat, but I've got some calls to make." He held up a cell phone, mashed a couple of buttons as he ran – we burst through the trees, onto a street, a car swerving with screeching tires and I just couldn't wait to hear this "witness report" on the news tomorrow night – and as the screen lit up LED-bright, phone dialing, he tossed the little device up into the air in a perfect arc such that it came back down just as I ran under it. I palmed the little device and dropped it into one of my own pockets.

"Maybe you should call the police," he cried out, his voice full. He wasn't out of breath. He was gleeful. "I hear they'd love to talk to you!"

The phone's light went off in my pocket as the call disconnected or gave up and I heard a massive explosion in the distance, then another, then a third. I stopped short at the sight of that lighted chapel tower, from the cathedral on campus, as a huge stained glass window in its steeple erupted outwards as though it had been punched by a giant fist made of fire.

That second of me slowing down was all El Diablo needed to make his escape. I stared at the place where the tower had been for just a moment or two, and when I looked around he was gone. Smiles had skidded to a stop ten feet ahead of me, trained to stick to me rather than prey unless I told him otherwise. I could hear footfalls pounding away but they echoed off the trees and the buildings, woven between car alarms going off from the explosions. I could hear people screaming somewhere far away. In all that noise I couldn't have chased that kid if I'd had two hearing aids and a head start.

Now what exactly had he meant by vampires' existence explaining a lot?

Cops and fire trucks were headed for the sites of the explosions as fast as you could say 9-1-1, so I took off at a run. Mostly people were running towards the explosions, which was roughly in the same direction as my car, and that was good for me in terms of maintaining something like discretion. Witnesses usually identify bombing perpetrators as the one person running *away* from the explosions they set off. I had no desire to stick out in anyone's memory for that same reason.

I ran alongside a few people: scared kids who wanted to see what had happened and a guy who was wearing boxer shorts, flip-flops, no shirt and an over-sized camera of some sort on a strap around his neck. He started taking pictures as soon as we rounded the corner of Perkins Library and the chapel emerged fully into view. We all kept running across a paved driveway onto a narrow street about fifty yards from the front of the chapel, right up almost to the edge of the debris field.

The stained glass from the steeple was a heap of rubble and saber-sized shards of glass on the lawn in front of the huge wooden doors of the entrance. Pulverized grit wafted in the air like smoke. The explosives up there had been no joke. They had blown the top of the tower off so hard the shockwave had turned to powder some portion of the century-old mortar holding the windows in place. There was a column of smoke coming out of the gaping wounds in the front of the tower where the windows had once been and a few stones and gargoyles teetered dangerously. We all skidded to a stop and the kid brought his camera up.

"I'm with the *Chronicle*," he panted as he started grabbing photos. I recognized it as the school newspaper. "Did anybody see what happened?"

The couple of dozen college kids standing around me all started doing one or both of two things: talking and taking video of the scene with their phones. They spread out in a wide arc around the shattered debris, taking photo upon photo even as the structure above us groaned audibly as though it might not quite have made up its mind on the question of falling down altogether. Then one of them, looking right at me, said aloud, "Are you The Bull's Eye?"

I looked down: still with the black coat and the dark colors head to toe. It's what I get for having wanted so badly to be a beatnik back in the day. Then I looked back up. The longer I stayed, the more chance they had to take my photo. I couldn't start killing them, obviously. Taking out two dozen sleep-deprived coeds wouldn't be a problem but then I'd have to deal with their phones and the camera of the Journalism major and one of them might, I dunno, tweet something while I did for the one next to them: "ACK VAMPIRE KILLING ME". There wasn't even any point to sticking around denying it. That would just be more face-time someone could post to YouTube to screw me over good and hard.

"I…" I drawled it out, long and low, then simply turned and took off running.

Smiles and I ran back through woods to emerge downtown on the other side of campus. We stepped into a bar that should only have been open another hour but had a bunch of television sets tuned to soccer games in the UK. There were a few guys sitting around watching the matches, wearing actual English football jerseys.

"Mind turning on the news?" I was addressing the bartender, who watched himself polish a glass instead of one of the games. "Something just happened over at the school."

He nodded towards a back room. "There's another TV in there. Go for it." It was a tiny space with some tables crammed into it, no one at any of them. I could smell that once upon a time the outer room had been for smoking and this had been for *non*. There was a TV mounted in a corner, tuned to some classic sports channel that was showing a bowling tournament from the 1970's. I reached up and mashed the buttons on the front until I got it over to a real channel, one of the local ones that had interrupted the late night talk shows with a news bulletin. Two bombs had gone off in the tower of the chapel but a third had also been set in the basement of the Divinity School next door. The lowest floor of the building had basically been blown out from underneath itself, causing the whole thing to collapse. To do that with just three bombs – to cleanly eject massive windows framed in stone and mortar and then collapse a building next door – took real skill. It took somebody with brains and, usually, a lot of experience. Duke had managed to piss someone off real bad and that person was really, really smart. El Diablo had also said the words, "as above, so below," a phrase I had heard before.

"Students on the scene are also reporting the event may have involved Durham's homegrown vigilante, the so-called 'Bull's Eye'. We're receiving reporting he was an overweight Caucasian male, a description which does not match some earlier reports. Copyrights or fashion trend? More analysis when we come back."

That was that: I had to find The Bull's Eye and I had to find El Diablo and I had to put them on each other's trail. The things El Diablo had said to me tonight at least gave me somewhere to start.

CHAPTER 8

The Bull's Eye had not seen the pleas by the police or the district attorney's office that she turn herself in and testify. Neither had she seen the station's discussion of whether The Bull's Eye had been misidentified in earlier reports; if she was merely one of many; or if she had simply inspired incompetent copycats. She didn't watch the news much anymore. She had patrols to do.

After the bombs went off she wondered if she had to be drastically more careful on the streets. Stopping a few muggings wasn't so bad in comparison, she knew, and her appearance was sufficiently low-profile and forgettable she didn't much need to worry about being spotted from a distance, but police patrols were up all over the part of town where Duke and those affiliated with it tended to congregate. It had not taken very many nights to realize the parts of town she favored – the dilapidated former middle class enclaves populated by less-well-off children and grandchildren of people who'd worked to make things by their own hands – were not important enough in the eyes of the law to warrant a lot of extra attention. If anything, she saw fewer cops now than she had before. They were all too busy staring at Duke's campus waiting for shrapnel to fly out of something.

This simply made her life easier. She wasn't exactly grateful for it, but she took both notice and advantage of the change in temperature on the streets. So did everyone else.

The Bull's Eye was on patrol again, as she was almost every night, but this night she had made sure to head back by The House to see if there was anything going on. Over several days she had approached more kids in that neighborhood and been able to track down confirmation that the strange visitor, on nights he visited, arrived around one in the morning. Now The Bull's Eye dressed warmly and went out on patrol and when she got to that house she kept going for a block before cutting across the street and up a string of old oaks to take up a position behind the largest one.

The strange visitor came from the same direction every night, she had been told, so she put the house between her and that end of the block. People were usually a lot more afraid of being followed than they were of being *anticipated*. Many times in her career, and in many places, The Bull's Eye had used that to her advantage when choosing an observation post.

She settled in, arms around herself, and waited for one o'clock to arrive. She decided if no one showed up by two o'clock she would leave. Sixty minutes was a long time to stand behind a tree and wait for something to happen, but she'd waited longer in less pleasant places. Last call was a pretty popular time for petty crime, too, but she could give up the hour before it to see what was going on in that house.

At five minutes past one, The Bull's Eye felt a cold tingle slither up her spine. She had learned to trust her intuition in dangerous situations. She knew that he – the neighborhood's bogeyman – had arrived and the local kids had not lied to her.

The Bull's Eye eased out from the very center of the tree she'd used as cover just a quarter of an inch at a time. Very slowly, with her cap on backwards to keep her hair from falling over her face and to keep her hat's brim from being the first thing anyone saw, she moved enough to let one eye see around the edge of the tree's trunk. A block and a half or two away, walking down the middle of the street – just as the kids had said – she saw a middle-aged man in a shirt and tie and dark pants. He was wearing a coat or a parka of some sort, but she couldn't make out more than that in the dim light and at that distance.

The guy didn't seem to notice her. He didn't seem to notice anything. He was just walking along, hands in the pockets of his trousers, though he did once – just once – stop in his tracks and turn his head. He shifted his gaze up and to the side towards a house with no lights in any windows.

The Bull's Eye saw a curtain jerk shut in a hurry. *Good God*, she thought to herself, *It's like he really can tell when they look at him.*

That was enough to make The Bull's Eye pull back so she wasn't looking directly at him anymore. She figured if his peripheral vision were that good she wasn't going to risk it. Instead she leaned around the other edge of the tree so that she could see the front door and porch of The House.

The Bull's Eye heard footsteps in the street turn into footsteps on a different surface: the sidewalk in front of their house. A few seconds later the man took two jaunting steps up onto the porch. He walked with absolute confidence and certainty. *Like he owns the place*, The Bull's Eye thought to herself, and then she made a mental note to spend some time looking into that later. From here she could see him better: nominally Caucasian but of the same statistical-average muddled features as every other Southern "white" guy who probably had a little of everything in his background. His shoes were dress shoes but in the comfortable, versatile style of all-purpose black shoes from the same sorts of chain stores where she had bought her own patrol uniform. A person working in an office could easily get away with them; a person working retail on their feet would need them to survive. No rings, no obvious signs of privilege other than the jacket... and dark sunglasses, even here, even at night.

He paused for a moment as though he might have seen something. The Bull's Eye stayed where she was, knowing if he had noticed her in his peripheral vision that her movement to hide would give her away more quickly than staying stock still and blending into the landscape. He never moved to turn towards her but in an odd way she *felt* him almost notice her, like the sweep of a radar arm on an animated display in a movie. The Bull's Eye wondered if she were simply jumpy from the stories the kids had told her. They had all been convinced he did terrible and impossible things. They told her stories straight out of science fiction, tales recognizable as variations on the sorts of urban legends the Internet ginned up out of nowhere.

Some of the kids had told The Bull's Eye they knew what *really* happened. Like the passwords and handshakes of their grandfathers' fraternal orders, they swore her to secrecy before hesitantly spilling the impossible beans: overnight disappearances, kids replaced by robots, that sort of stuff. She didn't doubt terrible things happened to the occasional kid. It was a neighborhood where as many families were on their way down as on their way up; where unknown numbers of families might be $20 from disaster at any given time. The lore a group of children weave together, whether here in suburbia or in a village in Afghanistan, becomes the mythology they use to encode the adult world around them.

A few seconds passed, then a few more, but the guy on the porch didn't do anything to acknowledge or act on that wave of awareness The Bull's Eye had felt – no, imagined – passing over her. The door to the house opened. The man stepped inside with the relaxed posture of familiarity; the door closed behind him; and the street was again exactly as it had been two minutes before.

The Bull's Eye realized she had been holding her breath.

She gave the guys inside thirty seconds to do any peeking out the blinds they might want to do before they all got settled in to complete whatever illicit deal he was there to make. After counting that half-minute off under her breath she slipped out from behind the tree and around a house three doors down from them, then into that house's back yard. From there she could close on The House from the rear, at an angle, unlikely to be detected by the occupants. If they watched a lot of TV, they would keep peeking out the front. If they were clever they'd look out the sides, too. Either way, they wouldn't see her approach.

A minute and a half later, The Bull's Eye had crept forward on rolled steps and gentle balance and was molded against the corner of The House. There was dim light coming from the front and she crouched to slide past some dark windows to get there. She'd noticed a tiny gap at the bottom when she'd been here before and they probably didn't expect anyone ever to walk up and simply look in.

The thing she kept realizing, at every turn, was how unaccustomed people in this country were to thinking about risk. Sometimes they made it too easy.

The Bull's Eye drew two deep breaths, counted to five and then raised herself to a crouch in one smooth movement, peeking in that tiny gap. In the living room she saw one of the twins – the more sallow one – sitting in front of the television. A white guy in a suit was cracking jokes on the screen, smiling real big, and she imagined the audience was eating it up as noisily as they possibly could. The kid wasn't watching. He had his hands in his face and the knuckles were wet with tears. He was sobbing, trying to stay silent, his whole body clenched like a fist as he was wracked with ragged breaths he was trying to smother.

So, the business inside – now she guessed they were hooked on heroin or meth, something that saps the capacity for joy out of people – wasn't happening in the living room.

The Bull's Eye slipped around to the back corner again and eased far enough from the exterior wall to look up and down both sides of the house that she could see from here. Nothing, just dark windows, so she risked it and ran at a half-squat to the other back corner. From there she could see the other rooms were all dark except for one. It had a mismatched set of curtains in the window and they hadn't bothered to close them. Inside, by the dim light of a night light beside a clock radio, she could see – well. She paused. This wasn't what she had expected.

The other twin and the bogeyman were making out. The visitor was kissing the neck of the twin who had been more together, healthier looking, when she visited them the first. She was a little surprised this was something so tame as an affair. The way everyone carried on was a little over the top. It was certainly more than she would have expected of having a couple of gentrifying queens move into the neighborhood. Maybe the twin in the living room was a fundamentalist who couldn't handle his brother having grown-up times with a friend. Maybe the brother who was neck-deep in a session of heavy petting was a prostitute and this guy was simply a regular john. She could come up with explanations for the anguished behavior of the kid in the living room, but either way none of it was really what she considered her beat. Hookers and gigolos live hard enough lives without getting busted for it. She would never have bound up a prostitute in zip ties and dumped her on a convenient street corner for the cops to pick up.

On the other hand, a hooker probably wouldn't have excited the kind of talk the neighborhood kids had been feeding her, either.

She kept watching, just in case something more sinister presented itself and because, to be honest, it had been a while and she was as much a latent voyeur as anyone else in the television age. The twin whose neck was being kissed didn't actually look like he was enjoying it. Rather, he looked like he was counting cracks in the ceiling while waiting for something to happen. (Definitely prostitution.) This continued for a few seconds until he grimaced and squeezed his eyes closed, the rest of his body straining uselessly against the old guy holding him down. The kid opened his eyes again for a moment before they fluttered shut with a kind of finality. He slumped in the other guy's grasp, suddenly as slack and pliant as a rag doll. The visitor noticed, pulled away for a moment while still holding the guy up from the mattress a little bit, and that's when The Bull's Eye had only her Delta Force training to thank for allowing her not to scream: blood was gushing from the kid's neck.

The bogeyman's lips were coated in it.

The older guy licked the wounded throat once and the gash was gone, like he'd just erased it with a magic wand. A little something like color returned to the kid's cheeks before he convulsed once, twice, a third time. Consciously or reflexively the kid's pale fist balled up a bit of bed cover next to him. His toes curled. The Bull's Eye realized with something not entirely unlike shame that the kid had just orgasmed in the middle of whatever anguished assault this was. The visitor dropped him onto the bed with remarkable carelessness, stood up and walked into a bathroom. He started washing his face in the sink.

Holy shit. That was all she could think. She had seen a lot in her time in the army, but that was the third or fourth craziest thing she had ever seen, *ever.* Now she understood why the brother in the living room was crying: either he was next or next time it was his turn.

Either one would be enough to make a man weep.

There were three things The Bull's Eye knew immediately about this situation: that she did not believe real vampires existed, which meant a psychopath was attacking and injuring people on her watch and she was pretty sure that wasn't okay no matter how into it the victims were by the time it was over; that she had no idea what to do about this situation, either to clarify it or to put a stop to it; and that she had to do something about it anyway. She took advantage of the visitor's time spent cleaning up to run back across the yard, confident no one would ever notice her. She had to wait until the guy was away from the house before she followed him, just in case there was a confrontation and the twins inside were in fact so into this arrangement, whatever it might be, that they would attempt to defend him from her.

The Bull's Eye slipped across the deserted late-night street and darted behind her tree from before. One hand against its trunk, the other against the middle of her chest, she tried to steady herself and her own mind against what she had seen. She had seen people do unbelievable things, senseless things, things done by an id lashing out at a world its vessel no longer could understand. She had seen people do the unthinkable to themselves, to their children, to persons they suspected of collaborating with one or another of the powers in their lives. She had spent years getting paid to be the United States' eyes and ears in situations where those sorts of moments were an ongoing problem.

What she'd seen in that house tonight had been different, though. This was in the sort of suburban neighborhood where she had let herself begin to think she was the baddest thing around. She had chased that one burglar, her very first night, out of reflex and out of anger but those feelings had morphed over time into a mission and a sense of invulnerability.

Ann had looked back on the things she had done in the guise of Sgt. Fletcher on behalf of distantly derived policy and let them make meth heads and purse-snatchers and gas station money-grabbers seem, in comparison, to be less than a real threat to her safety when she took to the street as The Bull's Eye. She had come to think nothing here could threaten her very much.

The Bull's Eye noticed someone else on the street. Glancing over, she saw there were actually two someones: two children, within the same age ranges as the others she'd interviewed in the last few days, but they were not hiding in their houses. They were standing on the sidewalk, maybe forty yards from her. They both had hooded sweatshirts on and their cowls were pulled up so she couldn't quite make out their faces. The Bull's Eye needed to get them out of here right away. This was not the time for a couple of neighborhood kids to decide to be brave. She had considered the possibility her asking around might gin up some youthful courage but she had discounted it. Now that she knew the violence of what was going on, she didn't need to have to think about these kids, too.

She'd heard nothing from the house: no front door, no screaming match, no anguished cries and no peals of laughter. Whatever was going on in there, it wasn't doing a damned thing to indicate how close it might be to over.

She decided to risk it; she had to if she wanted to get the kids off the street. The Bull's Eye sprinted in great strides from one huge old tree to the next until she was ten or fifteen feet from the two kids. They watched her approach without moving or gesturing or making a sound. Once she was within range of a whisper she pointed towards the houses nearby.

"Kids, you need to get out of here." Her voice was a harsh hiss. "Beat it. Seriously, you need to scram."

The two children in hoodies continued to stare at her, their eyes glittering. The Bull's Eye strained to see them better, because she'd noticed a disturbing trick of the interspersed light and shadow: their eyes looked completely dark. She didn't just see dark irises, though. She saw nothing but a glittering onyx void where their eyes would be, like their eyes were made of the chitin of some enormous beetle.

The Bull's Eye felt the same creeping horror she'd experienced when she looked into that bedroom window not three minutes before. Something was wrong with these kids, something beyond their eyes. There was something alien and off-putting about them, something she felt way back in the reptile brain. It told her to run from them, to run away from all of this and to keep running until she'd run so long she'd had time to forget them.

The kids moved towards her now, slow feet rising and falling in unison. A career begun with lots of marching made her recognize the way they moved as one. They were not moving quickly or even strolling. They were just barely walking, completely casually, almost entirely in silence. Little houses of all the styles marketed to lower-middle-class families for the last hundred years were stacked up all around them, practically on top of one another, all on lots above street level, every lawn in a state of care as different from the ones around it as could be imagined, and The Bull's Eye wondered if here, in the suburban jumble of a neighborhood on the skids, was where she would finally die.

The pavement was broken in places by potholes that would never be filled and the sidewalk was just as cracked and scarred. It took her less than a second to map the best running route through it and away, towards the light of the thoroughfare a few blocks from here. She could outrun any child. She just had to figure out how to move her legs again.

Her infinity of hesitation was broken when she heard a footstep behind her. A single glance back took in three more kids in hooded sweatshirts, eyes like a night sky full of unfamiliar stars, and the neighborhood bogeyman was standing in the middle of the street not twenty yards away.

"My children have seen you," he said. His voice was raspy and quiet and weak. He sounded old. He looked old and not-old. She noted his thin, grease-streaked hair; his sunken cheeks; the waddle dangling under his chin. He looked like he was very old but not all over. His hair was still dark and the flesh around his eyes was tight and firm, not in the way of cosmetic surgery but in the way of youth. He looked like a young man wearing the skin of an older one as a disguise.

It occurred to her this was not necessarily outside the realm of the possible.

"They are awaiting my command." He went on, addressing her directly, at total ease with his exposed position in the middle of the street. "I have to decide what I want them to do with you. I don't like…" He seemed to chew something bitter for a moment. "*People* in my business."

The Bull's Eye knew better than to wait for the villain to finish his soliloquy. She bolted, all her training lighting up at once, and she was halfway up the block inside three clean seconds. Tiny sneakers pounded asphalt in unison behind her.

For five blocks they ran. She reached the main thoroughfare up ahead and saw some traffic coming in each direction. Rather than slow she sped up and stitched between them like a game of Frogger on fast-forward. She wanted to use the traffic as a barrier between herself and the guy and those creepy little kids with the black eyes.

No dice: they simply ran into traffic after her. The Bull's Eye heard tires screech and horns sound as the kids threw themselves into the paths of one car and then another in their pursuit. She didn't hear any impacts, though, and moments later all she could hear was the sound of their unified footfalls again keeping pace behind her.

Keeping pace. She couldn't shake them with speed. Surely she could beat them for endurance, though. She'd run half-marathons to kill a Saturday morning. She could outlast them if she couldn't outrun them.

A perfectly preserved little Dodge hatchback from the 1980's pulled up next to her, its engine running like a Swiss watch. She could have remembered the model name if she'd tried: a friend of hers had driven that in high school. That car had been a piece of junk; junk then and junk when it was new on the lot. One day its engine simply fell out while he was driving down the road. Its motor mounts had rusted through with only sixty thousand miles on it. The Bull's Eye had no idea why all of this was coming to her now, flooding back.

The car scooted ahead, then turned to one side to block her path. The neighborhood bogeyman stepped out of the driver's side with the car between them and looked right at her as she ran up, then slowed, then sped back up to try to run around. "Did you think I would not detect you?" His voice was heavy and a little drunk sounding. His accent was Midwestern. It was the sort of accent she had heard come out of big corn fed Iowa boys. She hadn't heard it since she was in the Army. She didn't know what she had expected to hear, but it wasn't an accent so... pedestrian, with a wording so oddly stilted. "can hear a drop of blood in a bathtub from two miles away."

Our kind. Great: it wasn't just a kinky sex thing; he was definitely insane. That made things simpler.

Running hadn't worked, so it was time to change tactics. "You should raise your hands over your head," The Bull's Eye said as she stopped. Her voice was perfectly calm. She had said the same words, in half a dozen different languages, to men who were pointing guns at her in countries she couldn't remember. This was just another day at the office in some ways, even though the feet of half a dozen children skidded to a halt behind her to reinforce her awareness that she was alone and they believed themselves to be in control. "You should keep your hands there while I restrain you. If you cooperate you will not be hurt." She withdrew a set of zip-ties from one of the pockets on her cargo pants and held them up where they could be seen. "Do you understand? Nod to indicate that you understand what I am saying."

He smiled, and he had way too many teeth. Well, OK, he only had two that really stood out, but they were more than she had expected. He launched himself towards her and his mouth was open and she knew the only word for them was *fangs*. All she had time to do was drop and roll to try to trip him up by impacting his feet and shins with her body. She had to dive towards him to do so, which is not something instinct is ready to allow without extensive retraining.

The adrenaline rush came right on time, just like clockwork, so that when he pitched forward and rolled into a somersault and then stood, turning around, she was also already up and smiling. At least now he and the kids were all on one side of her, giving her a direction empty of enemies.

"You insolent…," he hissed. "I'll kill you right here on the street. When they find you in the morning you'll remind everyone – *everyone* – to respect their betters." There was a blur and something slammed into her back. She fell forward, all the wind knocked out of her, and he was standing there with his fist out. He was still grinning, but she didn't understand how he did that: how he had gone from one side of her to the other in a flash. He had simply been in one place and then another.

He raised a boot; she rolled out of the way and stood. He blurred again. This time she spun when he did so and saw him abruptly appear behind her. The Bull's Eye twisted at the same time, grabbed his arm and rotated back around to use his momentum against him. He sailed over her shoulder, forward, but turned in mid-air like he'd done it a hundred times, like they'd *practiced* this, and landed on his feet, facing her.

"…" Her lips parted to say something but her own training reminded her that he would try to take advantage of her ongoing disorientation and she dropped, sweeping a kick around her for almost the whole three hundred sixty degrees. That caught something and he was knocked off balance and fell onto his back. She let herself produce one choked guffaw as she tried to get up and moving. Whatever his deal was, he was really strong and impossibly fast and she couldn't win this fight, she knew, so she needed to do something like disable his car and call the police, anything that would get more firepower involved but there he was, right in front of her, his hand around her neck.

He lifted her off the pavement and he looked so *satisfied* when he did. She could feel his fingers digging into her throat. The Bull's Eye couldn't believe her vigilante career would end this way. She didn't give a good goddamn about her career as a janitor for Durham Tech, but this? This felt like letting someone down. This felt like losing. The children gathered behind him, staring at her with those not-eyes, their blank gazes ready to watch her die.

A car made the turn from the thoroughfare they'd crossed, down this street, and its headlights played across the darkness. LED high-beams, the kind she found so annoying every other time she had ever seen them, washed over the assembled figures and the car's brakes squealed. The bogeyman looked away – away from her and away from the car, shielding his face – and he dropped her. He simply let go and allowed her to fall into the street. Another blur of movement and he was gone. He vaulted onto one of the raised lots; she heard leaves; then silence.

The black-eyed kids stood there for another moment before scattering. The half-dozen children burst in different directions away from her, out of the light.

Feet came running up to her, from the car that had turned, and a man said, "Man, are you okay? Holy shit! I said, are you okay? 911! I'll call 'em." He struggled in his hurry to dig a phone out of a pocket. The Bull's Eye couldn't stick around and deal with that. She didn't need to get caught up in the authorities now. If she lay very still and took very slow, shallow breaths she could breathe well enough to confirm that everything was still working in her neck. She wanted to get the license plate on the old Dodge – an Omni, that's what it was called – but the headlights of that Good Samaritan were shining in her eyes and she couldn't make out the plates.

Her savior gave out a stunned "Whoah!" when she leapt to her feet. Her throat burned like hell but she was moving. The Bull's Eye ran over to the car to look at the tag and was surprised to see no plate at all on the car. She blinked. Cops could practically *smell* a beater car with no tags being driven around. It was the kind of thing she'd heard referred to as a "bust-me-mobile".

The good Samaritan got off the phone and came hobbling back towards her (she catalogued: limp favoring his right leg; probably a broken bone he'd never had properly set, several years old, he must not do anything too physical for his job or maybe he did and it pained him and he simply bore it out of necessity, she'd certainly seen that enough times in places where a misstep led to all kinds of joint problems). He said something about "them" being on their way and that obviously meant the police, so she had to go.

No time for a thank you, no time for anything like that. The Bull's Eye simply took off at a sprint, not into the darkness like her attacker but into the light, past her confused savior, back across all four lanes of Alston, and into the darkness on the *east* side of that thoroughfare so that at least there was one border of strong light between her and the bogeyman. She hoped the lights and traffic and arriving police would be enough of a wall to keep him from circling around and trying to catch back up to her.

She didn't like having to *hope* anything at all.

CHAPTER 9

The next night The Bull's Eye finished her janitorial shift at Durham Technical Community College around 10:00. She clocked out, put away her supplies and walked out of the building to go back to her house. In the unlikely event anyone looked back over the records, she wanted everything – surveillance cameras, time clock, everything – to say she was out of the building and gone for the night. So, she left and walked three of the six blocks from Durham Tech to her place.

At the end of those three blocks was an abandoned A-frame. She cut up behind it and changed clothes in the darkness of its unkempt back yard: chilly work on an October night, but necessary. She didn't want anyone to see her and she didn't want to come from any real place. If a chance observer simply thought she was a squatter living in that abandoned hovel, all the better for maintaining the secret of The Bull's Eye's real identity.

When she got back to the school she was careful to break in rather than enter using her keys. She jimmied a few windows as she worked her way to the one that she knew was unlocked. Not a lot of buildings were built with windows that opened anymore but one part of this particular wing had them: the boiler room, with its potential build-up of fumes and gasses. She slipped in through the one she had rigged, closed it behind her and picked two different locks to let herself into the back of a chemistry supply room. The Bull's Eye cut through a chemistry lecture hall, making sure to knock over an oh-so-recently emptied trash can as she went. Within thirty seconds she was striding silently down a hallway towards the library and its computer lab.

The dull blue glow of monitors visible through the window in the door was nothing unusual at this hour. The IT staff told her they were usually left on overnight. What was unusual was the way the lights flickered and shadows played out across the walls. The Bull's Eye slipped inside in silence out of habit: she found the costume had that effect on her. There were people in there with her, people who were moving around and who also had not seen her come in. She dropped to a crouch and crept forward.

Four people – a young Latino, an older Asian guy and two Caucasian women somewhere between 30 and 45 – had rearranged the tables to form a ring of computers, all of which were playing different screen savers. Both men and one of the women were sitting in the middle of the circle of electronics, legs crossed, holding hands. They swayed slightly as they murmured something. The fourth woman was tall, with slightly scraggly dark hair and an expression of impatience mingled with intent curiosity. She stood to the side with her arms crossed. The Bull's Eye could barely hear what the three in the circle were chanting. Their voices were low and slow and their words meaningless to her: not Latin, as she would have recognized that, but something which sounded equally esoteric. There were five candles between them on the floor, lighted, and their eyes were closed.

Durham was getting weirder all the time.

Questions raced around The Bull's Eye's head but the first and most pressing was to wonder where she was going to find a computer she could use if they were in here? The second was to wonder what it was they were doing? The obvious solution was to interrupt and ask them. On the one hand, no one was supposed to be here; on the other, they didn't seem to be hurting much of anything. Maybe she didn't want to hear their answers to those questions. Look what a little curiosity had gotten her last time, after all.

No, she told herself, *That is not how a hero thinks.* She was crouched no more than six or seven feet from them, in the deep shadows outside their circle of electronically-derived light, so she stood and cleared her throat to reveal herself. The eyes of the three chanters and their one observer snapped around and The Bull's Eye said in a very stern tone, through a solid black handkerchief worn around her nose and mouth like a bad man in a cowboy movie, "You folks have got some explaining to do, and then The Bull's Eye needs to use one of those computers."

The men both tried to stand up at once, fell all over each other, knocked over two of the candles and only by grace of the still-seated woman's reflexive grabbing of their hands managed not to topple two of the monitors on the desks. The Bull's Eye was across the intervening space, into the circle and on the candles in a flash, yanking them up off the floor and letting hot wax run over her fingers without so much as a murmur of surprise. They were all three trying to say something but they were talking over each other and none was making terribly good sense. The Bull's Eye put up a hand and spoke again. "Okay, it's like this: first, everybody shuts up."

They all stopped talking, pressed as close to the computer desks on the far side of the circle from her as they could get without moving the desks themselves. The woman observing them did not move or flinch or try to scuttle away. She stood there, sizing up The Bull's Eye like she was ready to square off. They each seemed to notice that about each other; they each noticed the other noticing; and they each watched one another file it away.

"Second," The Bull's Eye said, taking a moment to breathe deep, "Are you trying to rob the place?"

They men shook their heads in shocked silence and the woman seated on the floor laughed all of a sudden. The Latino guy looked to be maybe nineteen: just the barest wisp of a beard growing in, thin, good-looking if you're into kids that young. He wore dark jeans, a white tank top, black sneakers and an eyebrow piercing in the barbell style. The Asian guy – Taiwanese, she would have guessed off the bat, based on various things – was in his fifties, balding and a little overweight. He'd dressed in a Hawaiian shirt and beige cargo shorts and flip-flops. The Bull's Eye couldn't stand the resurgence of flip-flops: loud, cheap, neither shoe nor sandal. She despised them except on the occasions they slowed down someone she chased.

The woman sitting on the floor watched her with intelligent eyes. She was a little shorter than average, dressed in a cream turtleneck and jeans, and she had long, dark, naturally-curly hair she let shield a little of her face from view. The men were scared, but the woman was observant in the same wary way of the fourth who stood outside the circle.

"Okay," The Bull's Eye went on. "Third: I told you who I am. Do you recognize that name?"

They all nodded yes, though the Latino opened his mouth to make some minor point of clarification. The Bull's Eye put up one index finger to silence him before he could start. Great, that meant she was still being talked about in the media. That meant her attacker from the night before probably knew, too. *Damn.* She really needed to start watching the news.

"Finally, and only one of you answering at a time, what are you doing in here?"

The three of them looked at one another for a long moment, exchanging raised eyebrows that seemed to suggest maybe this was *your* bright idea, and finally the older Taiwanese guy spoke. His accent gave him away right off the bat. "We're engaged in a..." He cleared his throat. "Religious practice. It's endorsed by the school."

The Bull's Eye held up the candle, long since out. "I doubt somehow the school signs off on violations of the fire code so you can practice your religion. Now make some tracks in the carpet before I throw you out myself."

The Latino looked ready to start crying so she figured this wouldn't take much longer. The seated woman stood up from the floor and dusted off her hands against the thighs of her jeans as she replied. "Excuse me, but they absolutely have endorsed the practice of our religion as a recognized student group. The DTCC Techno-Pagan Society is open to all members of the campus and community who identify as techno-pagans, techno-shamans, or any other current amenable to the practice, exploration or observation of technologically enhanced spirituality." She stopped quoting a mission statement and drew a breath. "My colleagues and I are engaged in a perfectly normal ritual practice and I'm afraid you've interrupted us." She paused. "I'm Sheila."

The Bull's Eye blinked at her, then looked back and forth between the others. The standing woman with the straggly hair still watched her like a cat watches a squirrel in the yard. "OK, Sheila. The DTCC Techno-Pagan Society? OK, great, but what the hell does that mean?"

The older Taiwanese guy sniffed a little and said, "It means we're neopagans who believe technology has a role to play in ritual."

"None of that is meaningful to me. None of that is language. Scram." The Bull's Eye nodded towards the computers. "I'm not great with these and I'm going to need some room to think." She stepped out of the way so that the door was accessible.

Sheila smiled politely. "We aren't leaving. We don't want to run away from you. We wanted to bring you here, actually."

The Bull's Eye started to make a smart remark but there was something in their expressions stopping her; she couldn't say what. Instead, she asked, "How do you mean?"

Sheila jerked a thumb in the direction of the standing woman. "She hired us to summon you."

The Bull's Eye noted, just briefly, the way in which Sheila had said it as though The Bull's Eye were a genie or a ghost. She looked at the fourth woman. "And you are?"

"Jennifer McCordy." The woman's arms unfolded at last and she held out a hand to shake. Her features finally slipped out of their mask of remote disapproval and wary interest as she chuckled twice in an alto voice. "I didn't think this stuff was real. I've never been so glad to be wrong."

Roderick and I were failing to find prey we thought would be easy. I had wracked my brains on ways to find desperate people in Durham. Roderick's idea to try posting an Internet personals ad resulted in way too many responses to be useful no matter how weird or offensive he tried to make it.

"Is everyone on the Internet trying to get laid by the easiest means necessary?" I tried not to sound too disgusted or too jealous.

Roderick shrugged his shoulder at that, seated at a table in a coffee shop we'd found in a strip mall by the highway. The people who ran it seemed plenty nice but they were a little freaked out by Smiles and Dog and their matching "Service Animal In Training" vests. They didn't say anything about them, though. Everyone in town had been a little subdued since the bombs in Duke Chapel went off. People seemed to be trying to keep their tongues in check for fear they'd be next.

I was busy working on my third piece of blueberry pie. Roderick was plugging away at the keys on an impossibly bright and metallic little computer he'd pulled out of something between a handbag and a briefcase. "Yes; or sell something; or some combination of both. Or they are looking for people they knew in school. Or the combination: they want to lay the people they knew in school. Or they want to look at pictures of cats saying funny things. Or –"

I cut him off with the wave of a forkful of pie. "I get the picture."

"Of cats?"

"No."

"Your loss." He made a face as I took another bite of pie: tongue out, lips drawn back in a grimace, eyes squeezed shut. I ignored him.

We sat in silence for a few moments before curiosity overcame me. "So is that how you meet your… dates?" I felt like I was asking about a social disease.

"No," Roderick sighed. "I am too old-fashioned. I like going out and meeting people. It is easier to charm them that way and it is easier to limit one's post-tryst options for contact."

I blinked at that. "How so?"

"If I meet them online I have to give them an email address or a number they can text or something like that. If I meet them at a bar I can dump them any old place and never really give them an idea of who I am." The corners of Roderick's mouth curled up in a predatory twist.

"How…" I panned the stream of consciousness for words. "Practical?"

Roderick looked away from the screen to purse his lips with amusement. "I apologize if that seems too pragmatic. Are you worried I will never meet a nice boy this way? Are your delicate morals offended? Do we need to talk about how you are being stalked by a demon?"

I smirked back. "OK, so that can got opened, but I'm setting it aside for the moment. I just figured you were trying to get something more than feeding out of your dates. You see the same guys more than once sometimes, right? And you call them 'dates' and you go out to make them happen. I thought it was more than food to you."

Roderick looked slightly cross for a moment, his brows knit in thought. "But it is. It is the dating, itself. It is getting out and meeting people and having fun and then doing it again tomorrow or next week. Do not carry the 1940's around with you everywhere, Cousin. Live in the now. The kids these days even have a term for it: 'friends with benefits'. Not exactly a relationship, but it is two people interacting so it is a form of relationship."

"So," I said, "You're basically courting."

"Well, we are not exactly holding hands on the veranda while Mother peeks through the sheers." Roderick rolled his eyes a little.

I chuckled. "Neither were most kids who said they were 'courting' back in the day. That's what cars did for us: they gave us mobile make out rooms."

Roderick arched one eyebrow. "I have always assumed the term 'courting' meant something more formal: something parent-approved."

It was my turn to shrug. "I'm sure it did once, but parents approve of lots of idea, the words for which the kids use to mean something more. Words such as 'friends' and 'benefits' in fact."

Smiles and Dog were fast asleep at our feet, their backs to both of us, alert ears waiting for something to wake them.

Roderick let out a long sigh, his lips fluttering with frustration. "Anyway, this is not working. Online desperation-seeking, I mean. Get up. We are going dancing. Maybe we can kill two birds with one stone."

"Two birds?"

Roderick fluttered his lashes at me. "We still need to get you that date, do we not? I could practically smell the desire coming off of you in waves when that demon was buttering you up."

"I'm not desperate for a date," I growled. I paused. "But he was buttering me up. OK, let's talk about this."

"OK." Roderick lifted his hands over his head to stretch. "Here is the thing: you are a big boy. You can do whatever you like. I know better than to try to tell you what to do. If you want to flirt with a devil, that is your business and I will not make an enemy out of you over it. That said, by – aha – *virtue* of what he is, he is already an enemy of mine." I opened my mouth to interrupt with a question but Roderick shook his head: the reason for that was a conversation for another time altogether. Roderick kept speaking without pause. "Remember who and what he is. He is a machine designed to tempt and nothing more. Think of how you feel about blood, cousin: think of the hunger you feel when you see red roll down the neck of a man while fear washes off of him in delicious waves." I would have blushed if I could. This was more of the sort of talk vampires decidedly do not use with one another. Roderick smirked at my discomfort. Roderick relishes the perversions of our state. "He feels the same hunger, Cousin, but he feels it for ruin, not for blood. He will reach deep inside you, find the last human part of you, and squeeze the anguish from it like juice from a ripe tomato until you long to see the sun. He will not allow you that, though. That will be merely the beginning of the suffering he will inflict upon you and he will do it in the most subtle of possible ways."

I blinked. "I know," I murmured. I hated being wrong. I hated Roderick knowing how I'd felt when Ross had spoken to me: like a schoolboy in puppy love. I didn't know where it came from and I hadn't known it was still within me and that made it all the worse.

"No, you do not know," Roderick said. I looked at him again and his eyes met mine, as serious and sane as I had ever seen him. "You have no idea. I do. I have seen it happen and I will not permit it to happen to you. Let me be very clear: if you come under the sway of a demon I will destroy you before I let him do to you what he was made to do." He meant every word. My mouth felt suddenly dry. Roderick was much more than my silly, nelly, queeny little cousin. He was all of those things, yes, and he was a warrior as well. "I will put an end to you, hand the keys of the kingdom to your second in command and go back to Seattle secure in the knowledge I have done the right thing. Is that clear?"

"Yes." I said it, but not quickly and not with joy in my heart. I felt like I should thank him, but I will never thank a man for threatening me, no matter how good his intentions. "I won't let him do that. Did I find him attractive? Yes, I won't lie to you. I absolutely did find him…" I shrugged, waved a hand. "OK, yes, attractive, but saying that word… It's like it gets snagged on something in my brain. It's like that word isn't quite right but no one has invented a better one." I sighed. "But I think I know a little about corruption and suffering, Roderick. I won't let that happen. I am not destructively desperate for affection." I said that last word with just the tiniest hesitation, like it hurt coming out of my mouth. It did.

"Tell it to your worry lines, Cousin." Roderick stood and folded the laptop to tuck it back into his bag. "I will be unable to hear you over the sound of techno. Let us leave the boys at my hotel and get our minds off this business. Maybe you can find someone desperate tonight." The dogs stood in unison as soon as he moved. Roderick chuckled at his own words. "Oh, heavens. The subtext to a million invitations."

The inside of Power Company didn't smell like desperation. Well, it did, but it also smelled like decades of cigarettes even though no one had been able to smoke inside for years. It smelled like booze, most of it cheap, some of it very expensive. It smelled like dryer sheets and hair product and human sweat; like skin powder and Old Spice and Polo cologne; like salt and flesh and desire. Opening the door of its otherwise blank brick façade was like standing next to a burst steam pipe full of pheromones. The bar's entrance was just a plain metal door on the back of a building in a row of identically anonymous brick buildings down the middle of a city block. There was no sign and no obvious purpose for it being there. Its near-invisibility and discretion were artifacts of a time when gay bars didn't need or want to advertise themselves or their clientele.

The entryway was barely the size of a broom closet, painted solid black, with an aging queen in sloppy drag sitting behind a mesh and glass window. She wore a dark off-the-rack dress from the ÜberBargains clearance section and elbow-length gloves that matched for color but clashed for texture. Her pillbox hat had a fine black veil attached. I wondered who or what she was trying to mourn and whether it was in the booth with her. There was a metal grate in the window and a gap at the bottom for money to change hands. It was like walking up to a bank teller in a Soviet propaganda film.

"Back again, darling?" She purred at Roderick and batted her lashes in the manner of overripe schoolgirls the world over.

Roderick greeted her with a smile like a sunrise. "Miss Emilie," he crooned, "You know I cannot stay away from your..." Roderick fished around for a moment imperceptible to mortal senses. "Considerable charms."

"You shameless flirt. It'll take more than that to get you in, dear." Miss Emilie leaned close to the metal grate, her voice gravel against its stainless steel. I could smell chicken wings. "Ten buck cover for members and you'll need to sign for your guest."

I chuckled at my cousin. "Member? You've been in town less than a week and you've got a membership at the gay bar?"

Roderick waved it away with a few fingers. "North Carolina weirdness about dance clubs," he said. "It's a fig leaf of exclusivity."

Miss Emilie was quick to correct him. "It's no fig leaf," she spat. "It's for real. Nobody gets in without a membership or someone to vouch for them and we can throw out anybody we like. I'll be goddamned if I'm going to let some frat boy looking to make trouble into this place if I don't fucking feel like it."

I blinked back, stunned. Were she not another underdog out of place in the wider world I might have been a little offended at the brusque service but I always respect someone trying to defend their own turf. I remembered how precious those cramped bars and tiny dance floors of the '40s had been to those of us who sneaked in and out back alleys to find half-hidden doors with passwords required to enter. Miss Emilie looked thirty years younger than I am but twenty years older than I appear. She probably got off on getting to remind one of her juniors that things haven't always been as good as we have it now in some times and some places. I took it in stride. "Whoa," I said, "I get it."

Miss Emilie sniffed once, exchanged moneys with Roderick and held out a rubber stamp with a flourish. "Slide your hand through the slot to take the mark of the beast, boys," she said with the air of a magnanimous monarch. "Your heart's desire awaits through my humble opening."

Roderick threw me a glance that said, quite clearly, *Christ but I hope not.* As the door buzzed to indicate we could go through a hastily-installed metal detector and the blast door beyond it, I gazed with serenely frozen features at the stamp on my hand: a smeared representation of a cartoon heart with an arrow through it and the words "GET SUM".

The club itself was a three-story affair with different flavors of environment on each level. The main dance club was right there where one walked in: a couple of long bars made out of glass and metal and framed in neon served as bookends to a vast expanse of light-up floor covered in dozens of people in various states of dress all grooving together. The music sounded like someone waterboarding a chorus of robots but the patrons seemed to be into it. Some danced alone as though for some unseen audience; others for fun; and others still ground against one another in what clearly qualified as foreplay. Roderick exchanged a couple of waves with other patrons and I chuckled at the realization he was here often enough to make friends with the regulars.

I unwillingly thought of his Last Gasp, the power to make us all forget his victim ever existed, and wondered how many of them I would remember by the time he left.

Roderick had ditched the bag at his hotel and traded outfits for a tight-fitting t-shirt with a picture of a catcher's mitt and the words BOSSY BOTTOM in faded text. He writhed lithely into the crowd on the dance floor with one glance back to yell something only a vampire could have heard in all this racket: *go make a friend*. I motored off around the dance floor, then, in search of a drink and a bowl of pretzels to munch on. I didn't see it as very likely I'd actually meet someone to talk to in a place like this but I was glad to see Roderick doing something normal for once. Every time I'd taken him into public, or he me, he'd always given people a weird vibe: a slight off-centeredness radiating from the almost insectoid view with which he seemed to behold most of humankind. He loved to move among them, yes, but in the same way a cat might dive joyously into a box of happy little mice.

"Withrow Surrett," said a voice from off to my left as I bellied up to the bar. "I didn't expect to see you out."

I turned surprised eyes on Seth. He was in his usual leather punk gear but the liberty spikes he sometimes wore were smoothed down and cemented into place as a stalactite of hair draped over the right side of his face. The clothing was a little more gussied up and a little less angry than usual, too, and whereas he normally showed at best a reserved and subtle smile when pleased, he was at that moment almost grinning. "I didn't expect to be seen," I replied. We shook hands like old friends and, all things considered, I supposed we were. "Shouldn't you be tending bar at your normal joint in Raleigh?"

He rolled a shoulder at me in response. "Seems like all the action's in Durham these days."

I smirked. "Doesn't it just?" The bartender wandered by and I flagged him down. "Bourbon and Coke," I said, "Heavy on the lime. Plus whatever my friend here is getting." Seth waved it off and the bartender whisked my card into whatever holding area was set aside for open tabs.

"Gotten anywhere with either this El Diablo guy or The Bull's Eye?" Seth always knows how to get down to business.

I smiled. "That transparent, huh?"

He grimaced. "I keep thinking of all the home security systems they must sell. They're a problem for us and solving our problems is your job now. You're the boss."

"So I keep hearing," I grumbled. "You sound like Old Shoe. No, I haven't gotten anywhere. I had a run-in with El Diablo. Two of them. I couldn't bring him down either time."

Seth's eyes widened a fraction of a millimeter. "What?"

I dithered with my body language and my wording. "I ran into him once and he caught me by surprise but he moved fast. Too fast. The second time it was chance. I…" I couldn't see myself saying this to any vampires in the world other than Roderick or Seth. "He managed to run from me. I tried to take him down in a straight fight and he got away." I sighed. "Why, you looking for him, too?"

Seth took his time studying the bottled liquors on the lighted shelves behind the bar before answering. "Not out of any desire to have your job," he finally replied.

I nodded. "Good. I don't want trouble."

"Nobody does," Seth replied. He looked back and met my eyes with his. "Least of all me. I like you, Withrow, and I don't want to see anybody come along and try to knock you out of the big chair."

It was the closest to a direct oath of fealty I'd ever gotten from any vampire – anyone other than Roderick, anyway. I nodded at him after a moment, and then held out my hand. He took it and we shook again. "Thank you, Seth. I'm relieved to say I believe you."

Seth smirked. "What lives we lead," he sighed. "We rush to escape the ones we're given, and for what? So we can spend forever feeling paranoid?" He gestured at the crowded bar, the people all around us, the air full of human wants and denied desire. None of them could hear us. Our voices were low and the music loud. Vampires often spoke like this, I'd found: openly addressing secrets we'd be scared to whisper in the quiet of a mausoleum but easily expressed when surrounded by the thrum of life. Sometimes I think the smothering blanket of throbbing humanity insulates us against them and them against us and we both benefit from it. To stand like this, in a public house, and simply be a part of the world for a moment was both a good thing and a pathetic rarity. That was perhaps most of why I so appreciated Roderick coming here to be with me: the *being with me*.

I nodded at him. The drink arrived and I took a moment to sniff it: harsh and sweet and acidic from the lime. "Roderick thinks I need to find a boyfriend," I blurted out. I didn't look up. Seth did me the favor of not laughing until I did. When I chuckled, he gave one little gust of amused breath.

"Maybe you do." Seth regarded me with that half-shadowed passivity he so excelled at: something distant and reserved in his eyes suggesting Seth's brow were the roof over a deeply recessed veranda at the absolute back of which sat his hidden true self.

I stirred the cocktail with the swizzle stick and looked back at him. "You and Beth…"

He nodded. "Of course."

"How does that work?" I didn't know how to broach the subject. "I mean, do you, um." I paused. "What do you do?"

"We keep each other company," Seth said. He was holding an empty beer bottle as a prop and he gestured minutely with it to form an arc encompassing the realm of all possible answers. "It keeps me sane sometimes." He hesitated. "You've seen how she can get, too. She needs someone to watch out for her as badly as I need someone to look out for me." Another little pause. "It's more than most people get: togetherness, I mean. Remember that, Withrow. Remember the Bobs. Ask yourself where they came from. Ask yourself how they got that way."

I blinked at him. I didn't quite follow where this was going, and it showed.

Seth went on. "No," he said, correcting himself. "Let me put it this way: ask yourselves what made them that way." This seemed fraught with subtext I just wasn't getting.

"'What made them'?"

"Exactly," Seth said. "*Exactly.*"

I didn't understand, but I also had a feeling I would sooner or later if I just let it rest. We stood in silence for a couple of minutes as I took sips of my drink and savored them. The alcohol would never affect me again but I loved the taste. Seth looked around, eying the crowd in the way of bartenders everywhere, even off the clock. I was so lost in thought – uncertainties about whatever Seth was trying to say and about the notion of vampires keeping each other company and about The Bull's Eye and El Diablo and the demon Ross and my own sudden confrontations with the capacity for a kind of desire I'd long since forgotten – I didn't even notice when a tall, slender guy in beige linen shorts and a blue polo shirt strolled up and settled in next to me. Eventually our elbows bumped and I made some mumbled apology but he caught my eye and smiled.

"No need to be sorry. I hope I didn't disturb your drink." He was over six feet, with deep black skin and a jaw that could cut glass. I found myself stammering a bit. He was an extraordinarily fine specimen of a mortal. I had no idea what to say. "I don't suppose you have the time, do you?"

I stared at him, looked at my wrist – I was not wearing a watch – and said, "No, I do not."

Seth stifled something from behind me but I didn't notice it for a long time.

"Well," the guy said, "My name is Marc. Let me know if you get a watch. I might still want to know the time." He winked at me – at fat old me with my floppy hair and my big black trench coat and my beat up old boots and my unfashionable jeans – and turned to go. "I love a daddy bear."

As he strolled away I turned slowly towards Seth. "I don't know what a daddy bear is," I said, "But I would give a hundred bucks for a watch right now."

Seth smirked with one side of his mouth. "Hang on."

There was an odd metallic hum, like the dying of a gong, for just a split second. Seth looked like he'd shifted positions in a nanosecond, like a lousy edit in a movie. I stepped back in surprise and Seth – the slightly shifted-off-center Seth – held out a watch. "Here you go."

Two things occurred simultaneously to me: I had no idea what Seth's Last Gasp power was and I had no idea where he'd gotten the watch. I looked from it to him and back and then to him again. "What just happened?"

"I can explain it later. Use this moment. Right now." He put the watch into my hand and closed my fingers around it. "For fuck's sake, Withrow, go, before the guy disappears into the crowd."

I turned around, crossed the bar and tapped the guy on the shoulder. He looked at me, eyebrows raised in surprise. I held out the watch and, after working my jaw for a second, said, "Found one."

Marc smiled down at me. "Did you? So what time is it?"

I blinked. "I have no idea."

Fifteen minutes later we were making out in the bathroom. Marc tasted like vodka and sweat and thin blood. I left him passed out – but living – on the floor of the handicapped stall. When I walked outside, Seth and Roderick stood nearby. They stopped whatever conversation they were in to raise their drinks to me in a silent toast.

Chapter 10

The phrase "as above, so below" seemed like the better of the clues I had available to me regarding El Diablo. I mean, Duke University is a big place. A lot of people pass through there in a year and a lot of those people are paying big money but making precious little for their trouble. It wasn't hard to imagine a whole mess of them being pissed off at the place at any given time. They're all pretty smart, too; well, all but the *really* rich ones, I reckon. That made a hell of a haystack to start off in. It seemed like the easier thing to narrow down was that line about quantum sympathies. I didn't get all that but I recognized some of what he said it as the lingo of a physicist and some as the lingo of a modern-day ritualist. I figured there weren't that many people hanging around in the overlap area of that particular Venn diagram.

The phrase "as above, so below" is a line from a spiritual practice called "sympathetic magic." It's the theory behind sticking a pin in a voodoo doll or cursing someone using a lock of their own hair: affect something reminiscent of your target and you affect the target. An image or a component of something is supposed to have a supernatural resonance with the thing itself. Stab the doll in the arm and the person gets tennis elbow. You've seen sympathetic magic a million times in movies and on TV because it's the most visually appealing way to depict wizards and witches and all that jazz. You also see it every time you go into a Christian church, especially if it's a Catholic one: people praying to a crucifix are using sympathetic magic just the same as any witch doctor shaking a shrunken head.

It's also used by people who are into the reinvented paganism thing. It's not for me, but no significant spiritual belief system *is*. I wouldn't have a god who would take me, to be honest. I think we're in this all on our own and it's up to us to make the most of it. Every vampire agrees with me, deep down, no matter how many nights of the month they dress up like Marie Laveau or Jerry Falwell or my Aunt Myrtle and claim to tune in some higher power. Oh, sure, some vampires fall into the religion trap. I think it's a weakness, though. It's hedging a bet when they're already cheating to win. We're supposed to have successfully eliminated the after-life as a concern. Religious yahoos, on the other hand, obsessively engage in publicly performing the qualifying lap for their preferred version of the sweet-by-and-by. Bible-thumping vampires may say it's all about saving their soul or whatever other bullshit reason they can gin up to look sad, but let's get real for a second: they don't regret what they became. If they did, it would be easy to correct the mistake. Guaranteed suicide is never more than a sunrise away.

So, I don't buy into the ceremonial claptrap myself. Beyond its psychological power to shape someone's intentions and maybe ignite a little confirmation bias when they search for results of their work, I think it's just a game of dress-up. I know some people do really believe in it, though they weren't exactly physicists. They were more like really interesting librarians. Still, you start with the contacts you have, not the contacts you wish you had, and lucky me, it was a book sale weekend at the library in Chatham County.

The Book People. That's what they called themselves. I originally thought that meant they were Muslims. There's this concept in Islam of "people of the book," which is a fancy way of saying Jews & Christians are kind of special because technically they all worship the same god, but they just meant they were people who were crazy into books. There were seven of them, two men and five women, mostly older. One of them was a young Latina who told me she was the first person in her family to be literate in English. Her accent was absolutely undetectable. It was impressive. The rest of them are various shades of cracker white except for a black guy named Warren who teaches the occasional poetry class at a historically black school in Raleigh. He's a retired sports writer or something. He doesn't talk much, and I've never spent much time around them because the Book People give off kind of a weird vibe. It's like you're really seriously the hell harshing their vibe when you're speaking to them because that's time they could have spent nose-deep in a book.

They haunt book sales. I don't mean they're just there all the time, drifting around. I mean they show up at night when the venue is closed and they *do things*. I still don't really understand it, but it strikes me as a fancy form of coin flipping; the only difference is their coin is a library and it has a different face for every sentence of every book.

The Chatham County Library book sale doesn't happen at the library proper. They have it at this little Lions Club building in what I guess you'd call "downtown" Pittsboro. Pittsboro is little more than a traffic circle, an old courthouse from the 1860's that burned and collapsed a couple of years ago and a secondhand store called Beggars & Choosers reputed to be the absolute best place for fifty miles in any direction to put together a Halloween costume. Otherwise it's a slightly self-consciously folksy little place that does a lot of antiques trade and has a couple of historical markers out by the highway. Nothing much going on, but I always get the feeling that's how Pittsboro likes it. It's about 25 minutes of extremely pretty country driving from either Durham or Raleigh and whenever I go there I am a little stunned that a place so nice can exist so close to a major media market covered up in suburbs.

I'd been to that book sale before during actual business hours. It happens late enough in the fall that it's dark before the sale ends each night. I was the last customer out the door one time and that's how I noticed the Book People. They were parked down the block, trying and failing to look nonchalant. The windows of the mini-van they'd driven were tinted really damn dark, way darker in the back than I imagined would be street legal, but that stuff is no match for a vampire's eyes. I saw them sitting there watching the staff lock up behind me while I lugged three big bags of books over to my Firebird on the far side of the lot.

Let me assure you, just in case you decide to go around playing amateur burglar or otherwise finding occasions requiring stealth, pulling up to a retail establishment right before closing time and watching them lock up is a dead giveaway you're casing the joint.

I got in my car, circled the block, killed the lights and pulled around behind the book sale building to park. Unobserved, I slipped across a dewy lawn and up to the side of the building where I could peek around at the front and see what the as-yet-unknown Book People were doing.

Mostly they were standing around looking nervous while the oldest of them all, a little old lady with a stark white shock of hair that stuck out in all directions and a slightly off-kilter grin, was hunched over picking the lock. Her fingers shook but I think that might have actually helped her hit all the tumblers. I could hear the click when the door swung open and everyone let out the breath they had been holding. They piled inside, spread out and started milling around.

Vampires are nothing if not voyeurs. I peeked in a window to watch.

"Brothers and sisters." The smooth, mellow voice came from a preppy middle-aged woman. She had once-upon-a-cheerleader hair and a sweater tied around her neck by the arms, like an Izod ad from 1984. The others didn't stop milling as she spoke. She stepped up onto the end of a table to address them. "Please take a few moments to select your implements for tonight's ritual. Do not rush, and when a book speaks to you do not shy away because it isn't what you had hoped – or because it's what you feared. You will know the book as the book will know you, and when hand meets spine you will know whether the book in your hand is to be your tool for tonight's working."

I waited and watched as they walked around – some of them eyes closed and bumping into tables, others walking directly to specific sections like CRIME and CLASSICS and holding out their hands, fluttering them like nervous butterflies, then finally reaching out and jerking a book from the boxes that sat atop each table. Obviously some of them weren't thrilled with what they got but the lady had been pretty clear: the book they got was the book they were getting. They reassembled in the middle of the room but flinched as a car went by outside. They worried it was someone coming back. It wasn't. Hurriedly, raggedly, they formed a loose circle around the woman who had spoken before. She addressed them again, sounding rehearsed.

"As the world is an expression of the god and the goddess, the Lord and the Lady, the Sun and the Moon, so too are the books in our hands the expressions of their authors. Writers craft the worlds calling out to them to be created. They are the progenitors of whole realities insisting upon their own existence. As above, so below; and as below, so above. The gods on whom we call take the shapes dictated by a world in need of them, and the world they divinely fashion has the form it takes because it can take no other. The world and the divine are the hand and the glove, the glove and the hand. The cycle of creation and destruction, life and death, spring and summer and autumn and winter, is not a repetition but a moving forward, a progression, and we are the ones who witness the spin of the tire, the turn of the press, the pen stroke of the hand authoring the cycle."

There was a pause, and I could see her words had a soothing and bolstering effect on them. They all stood a little straighter and a little more solemn now. They'd forgotten all about cops and security systems and library volunteers who might forget a purse. The stooped old lady with the mad smile had her eyes closed and a sort of serenity on her face I rarely saw in sane people. The blonde lady leading them took a few seconds to look directly at each of them in turn before she spoke again. "Maria is in the East so we shall start with her. Open your book, sister, and with it light the fire of the first watchtower."

The Latina cracked her book open to a random page. She cleared her throat and I heard her read in the halting, slightly uncertain tone of one who doesn't regularly read aloud – that is to say, almost everyone in the world. "Ho, ho! Commander! It's moving! The machines are ready! Fuel, my commander! We must have fuel and nothing else!" Her voice grew in confidence and enthusiasm so that the last sentence was delivered with something like real feeling. She then stated the title with a much more reserved, subdued, almost subservient tone: "*Cement*."

The blonde woman – the priestess, I later learned, named Lorraine – turned to the younger of the two men, a forty-something white guy built like a barrel of molasses. He opened his book and read in one breath, all in a go, running the title together with the text, "The cutting-edge on even the most well-made knife is not permanent *Knife Skills Illustrated: A User's Guide*." He looked a little embarrassed by that, but Lorraine favored him with a nod that seemed to indicate maybe this was a deep truth worth hearing once or twice. She turned to a woman in her fifties who held up a thin volume and read:

"His movements have the attractiveness of the awkward man who has learned to circumvent this condition by slowing everything down. Catlike in his languid movements, with his slightly hunched shoulders, hands a little too big for his body, like he's never quite known what to do with them." She paused and then said, "*Crime*, by Irvine Welsh." Her voice was gentle and plodding and wasn't at all unlike the description she had read from the book.

Next up was a frumpy woman in her thirties. She had on blue stretchy fat pants and a shapeless sweatshirt sweater kind of thing that zipped up the front. In my mind, I immediately classified her as a recognizable variety of Bon-Bon and daytime TV addict. She held up a thick hardback and read aloud. "Windows there are none in our houses: for the light comes to us alike in our homes and out of them, by day and by night, equally at all times and in all places, whence we know not. It was in old days, with our learned men, an interesting and oft-investigated question, 'What is the origin of light?' and the solution of it has been repeatedly attempted, with no other result other than to crowd our lunatic asylums with the would-be solvers." She paused, then, "*Flatland: A Romance of Many Dimensions.*"

Lorraine smiled a little. "An excellent lesson in humility." She turned towards Warren, who opened his book and cleared his throat.

"You were either with her or you were against her. She believed that her father was not her real father; that her mother had tried to drown her in a pond when she was child; that her pulmonary specialist wanted to have sex with her; that in death she would be met by Carl Jung, the Virgin Mary, and Merlin the Magician; that she had done her work on earth and her work was good; that she was one of those who had been chosen to herald the coming new order of beautiful humanity; that in a former life she had died a water death as a Roman galley slave, shackled to the oars; that men were shits and her children were hostile; that her smoking was her business, so mind your own fucking business; that her son was an artist just like she was; that she and I should go into therapy together." He smiled a little and looked up. "*The Afterlife: A Memoir.*"

Most of them had chuckled a little at the lines about smoking and about men being shits, and Lorraine was among those who had. The Stepford Soccer Mom look concealed a human being. She flicked her eyes to the last person, the hunched little old lady, who opened her eyes and her book at the same time, eyes falling to the page. Her voice creaked out, "She kept going, her sneakers slapping the pavement, until she came to a barrier of a thousand split-open garbage bags. She crawled over it, taking the time to pick up a few interesting items, like a broken salt shaker and a soggy copy of *National Geographic,* and stuff them into her bag. Then she was over the barrier and she kept walking, the breath still rasping in her lungs and her body trembling. That had been close, she thought. The demons almost got me! But glory be to Jesus, and when he arrives in his flying saucer from the planet Jupiter I'll be there on the golden shore to kiss his hand!" She looked up. "*Swan Song*. Robert McCammon."

Lorraine bowed slightly and then turned to look at and address each of them, moving slowly, so that everyone got looked at while she spoke. "Fuel for the engine. Alienation. Insanity. A loss of sharpness. Awkwardness. Strong opinions that may or may not run counter to the facts. Jesus on a flying saucer. These are all stories that say to me that whatever we summon tonight will be able to guide those of us who might be stuck in some rut, alienated from the knowledge of how to move forward. Are there other interpretations?"

The Latina spoke, and evidently they didn't have to wait to be called on for this part. "I think whatever we summon might be, itself, alienated and stuck in a rut."

Warren nodded his head. "The thing we call on will be difficult to work with. Not of this world. It's going to have its own way of doing things and its own understanding."

"It's going to think we're crazy," the old woman said. Her eyes were crystal clear and her smile was gone. She was down to business.

The Bon-Bon addict didn't say anything, but she nodded along. Another woman didn't say a word, just shook her head and clucked her tongue.

Lorraine nodded. "You're all in agreement. Let us see. Let us call to the beyond and see what we have summoned with these words." She lifted her hands and started to say something – it sounded like Latin, but maybe not perfect textbook Catholic school Latin – and I couldn't resist.

I love a big entrance.

I stepped around with the speed of a vampire, turned the knob, opened the door and said with a great big shit-eating grin, "Don't bother asking. I'm already here."

Nobody was going to buy I was a god, but they could sense that I was something *other* and somehow that didn't scare them. We chatted for a while, playing cat and mouse over the question of my identity, and then they asked me for advice about Lorraine's work situation. I suggested she take a grad school class at night and see if being a student again suited her. It's always that kind of thing, with people like the Book People: they're a lot more interested in the nuts and bolts of everyday living – in getting useful results – than they are with pie in the sky. And that, quite frankly, makes them my kind of people.

Ever since, every once in a while, I drop in on them at a library book sale somewhere or another in the Triangle. Sometimes they ask me for advice; sometimes I participate in their little ritual; and still other times I just watch through a window and let them wonder if I was there. I suspect they think of me as their pet trickster spirit. I consider them, in turn, my pet believers. I don't believe in anything at all except myself and only sometimes at that. They, on the other hand, believe in everything, all the time, but in a very specific kind of *unified* everything: a reality held together by some weird knot of faith and the supernatural and the human mind's ability to shape the world to its own perceptions. I love talking with them about it. Warren called me their 'Q' once, which I recognized as the *Star Trek* reference it was. Vampires watch all the TV we can get our hands on, of course. There's nothing worse than running out of ways to make time pass when you're staring down the barrel of eternity.

That night they were back in the Lions Club and I didn't bother to try to sneak up on them. I parked next to their van, walked right up to the front door, made a little boot-scraping noise as I wiped the mud from my feet and knocked three times before letting myself in. They were gathered around a picture book one of them had pulled out of the kids' section of the book sale and were talking about the images it inspired in a kind of free-association game. They seemed to believe, though not in any explicit and causal way they could explain to an outsider, that wisdom could be found by a process not entirely unlike panning for gold: take the indicators of wisdom, the jettisoned meaning and attempted significance of countless writers of books and sift them, devoid of context, until the words come together to mean something to the reader. In truth it wasn't that far from the practices of Bryan Gison or how the hell ever you're supposed to spell his name. He and William S. Burroughs and a bunch of their circle used to cut up pages from magazines and try to paste them back together in some random way to discover new, unintended meanings. Burroughs wrote a whole novel that way and it's one of the hardest and most interesting things I've ever read.

When I walked in they looked up and Lorraine smiled. That was always a little disconcerting and maybe also a part of why I would follow them around and show up at random: not a lot of humans are happy to see you after they've figured out you're more than just some fat dude with a bad attitude. "Welcome, Withrow," she said. "We're divining meaning from the adventures of a hippopotamus in search of his pants."

"Story of my life," I snarked, but I was polite enough to let them finish their little exercise before demanding their attention for myself. A few minutes of quiet sideline greetings from each of them in turn, with a few scratches of Smiles behind the ears as the others worked on the storybook's arcane meanings, and then they broke out the snacks: wine and cakes, they called it, but it mostly seemed to be gas station junk food and bottled iced teas. With that done, we started chewing the fat en masse.

"Why are you allowing people to believe you are a vigilante hero?" Lorraine always knew when to ask a direct question. She would have made one hell of a Sunday School teacher.

"Are you saying I can't possibly be a hero?" I smirked a little. Smiles yawned elaborately from the floor.

Lorraine grinned with genuine pleasure. These were people who liked to banter about words and with them. "I would never suggest such a thing, but you're no public figure."

I smiled again. "I'm not trying to convince anyone of anything. Quite the contrary. Anybody who thinks I'm this Bull's Eye character is all wet. Listen," I said, "I don't mean to be rudely businesslike, but I have a specific, strange request of you." They all perked up a little. I think they'd kind of been waiting for me to show up and demand something, sometime. They seemed a little disappointed when it wasn't their souls or turning anyone's bones to molten lead or whatever they did when they did "real" magic, but hey, maybe next time. "I'm trying to find someone and he said 'as above, so below' when he was talking to me. Tall guy, athletic, pointed chin, razor-sharp nose, tawny hair, very good-looking with a..." I paused. How was I supposed to explain that he smelled like the ten most delicious samples of blood I'd tasted in my whole life, rolled up in one? "A kind of *charisma* it's hard for me to describe."

There wasn't a hint of recognition on any of their faces.

"I kind of got the feeling he might be into the same stuff y'all are, only more…" I waved my hands around, kneading my desire not to offend them like that fear was a ball of invisible dough. "Science-y. Quantum-y."

There were a few shared glances conveying something like, "Oh, *those* assholes," and I raised my eyebrows to indicate interest. Finally the oldest woman, who has never told me her name nor has anyone used it when addressing her (which tells me I'm best off not asking), spoke up. "The technopagans. There are a bunch of them around. More than one group, anyway. We can give you a couple of email addresses if you really need to get in touch with them."

I hemmed briefly, then, "That's great, and I appreciate it, but if you don't mind my saying so, y'all kind of seem to hate these guys. What gives?"

Lorraine smiled slightly. "They're fine, but the current they're tapping into is so… sterile."

"Uh-huh." I closed my mouth, but opened it again. "Okay."

Warren was already writing down the email addresses, looking at his phone to make sure he got them right.

"No emails," I said. I shook my head a little, nose crinkled, and waved it off with one hand like a bad play in football. "Directions." I've got an email account but damned if I was going to give it to someone who thought he was a magic computer witch.

They all looked at one another for a moment, hesitating.

"Have I ever hurt one of you? Any other night I would be all fun and games but I've got a situation here. Potentially one of a highly spiritual nature." I tried to sound pleading.

Apparently it worked. Very reluctantly, after a long gaze had passed between Lorraine and each of them, she gave me a street address in Durham.

The technopagan house was on a side street near one edge of Duke's campus in a neighborhood called Morehead Hill. That part of town mostly consisted of shotgun shacks with students stacked like cordwood, halal butchers operating out of random gas stations, suburban farmers with complicated trellises and abandoned brickwork churches repurposed as suspiciously niche charter schools.

I stashed the Firebird around the corner and down a block from the address Lorraine and the others had given me. Roderick had ridden with me; Smiles and Dog were stuffed into the tiny back seat like an over-full sack. We all clambered out and collected ourselves before setting off, without speaking about it, so that we'd have shadows and time on our side. I wanted to scope the place out a little before I walked right up and knocked, and I didn't really want whoever was inside to see where I came from or what I drove. Paranoid, yes, but some of these spiritual types are pretty out there. You may think of crystal-hefting hippies wearing sarongs and praying to hedgerows, but those types punch just as hard as anybody else if you piss them off bad enough, and that's *after* they throw the crystals at you. They're as liable as anyone to be assholes instead of nice, happy, Sir Hugs-a-Lot pagans. After I got to know my pet bibliomancers I read a book called *Drawing Down the Moon*. It's kind of a field guide to this stuff. Useful reading if you want to befriend them and be able to talk the lingo.

Technopagans – Lorraine said it meant they "bring their toys to the dinner table with them," and they all thought that was kind of funny but I didn't really get it – aren't common, which makes them hard to predict. The old crone of the Book People said they were nice enough kids but I was still wary.

Their place was a big, green, farmhouse-style thing: two stories, huge wrap-around front porch and about ten or twenty window-unit air conditioners. It must have been a monster in its day. It was a hundred years old, at least, yet another example of Durham's crazy patchwork of eras and styles. The siding had been painted a medium drab industrial green and the roof was done in tiles that were much darker. The effect was to camouflage it. In the eternally wan yellow light of sodium-vapor lamps it was almost impossible to see the house at all if you weren't looking for it. I imagined their neighbors drove past time and again without their eyes ever being drawn to it even once. The house blended so readily into the shadows and flora around it, chameleon-like, that it occurred to me they might have, you know, *made it* do that. Like, maybe they had witched it up somehow to make it less noticeable.

The roof over the front porch had a thick braid of cables running to it from the telephone pole out front. As I got closer I could see there were actually three thick braids of cables, as though they had dozens of telephone lines. There were also multiple satellite dishes attached to the edge of the roof that hung over the covered porch: five of them, bearing the logos of different satellite networks including one written in French and one in something that looked like Arabic.

These guys were *connected*.

Roderick pretended to be walking Dog and Smiles while I crept into the yard and skulked around the shadows at the corners of the house. I could see dim blue glows emanating from some of the rooms but not all of them. Contrastingly harsh white lights were on in the kitchen at the back. Houses like this always have a disproportionately tiny kitchen, usually because the original kitchen was in an outbuilding that's now gone. In that tiny, tacked-on cookery corral I could see a sleepy-eyed kid in his mid-20's, blond, cute in a scruffy nerd kind of way, waving a coffee grinder back and forth like a martini shaker as it whirred in its toil.

Slinking back around, I listened at the front door and could hear quiet voices. They abruptly stopped. It seemed they and I were listening to one another in silence. I had to give them credit if they'd managed to hear the quiet footfalls of a vampire outside. No reason to play cat and mouse now, so I stood upright, took and released a breath and rang the bell like a good boy. Roderick and the dogs sidled on up from the sidewalk to join me.

The doorbell chimed incongruously – something deep and bonging, like a rich lady's bell in an old movie instead of the modern electronic chirps one hears in suburbia – and there was a lot more silence punctuated by some moving around on the other side of the door. I tensed a little in case they decided to say hello with a shotgun blast.

There were a whole series of clanks and thunks as various locks were unchained, unbolted, opened and otherwise released. The door creaked open maybe an inch – far enough that we could talk, but narrow enough so human eyes probably wouldn't have been able to detect the middle-aged Asian guy who answered it. "Whaddya want?" He tried to sound gruff and instead he sounded crabby.

"Friends sent me: Lorraine and the rest of the Book People. I need your help. The thing that happened at the Chapel the other night? I saw the guy who did it and I think he might be, you know..." I waved a hand vaguely. "One of y'all. No offense."

"He's not one of us and I have no idea what you're talking about," the guy said. He started to close the door but I had one finger pressed against its center. He couldn't budge the damned thing.

"You don't seem t'understand," I drawled. "I aim to talk to you. This isn't a request, and I don't have to stay polite if I don't feel like it. El Diablo set those bombs and I think *he* thinks I'm the Bull's Eye, which I am not. So I need to find out who he is and who she is and get the two of them on each other's trail and out of my hair. I'm asking nice because my mama raised me right, but I'll only ask so many times. Is that clear?" Smiles was seated next to me but he stood up, licking his chops.

There was a lot of hesitation and confusion and fear in his eyes. Just as I decided I was going to come inside whether he liked it or not the door opened all the way and it wasn't him that did the work. Inside was an African-American woman wearing an outfit of solid black, almost all of it without labels or any other indication of where it came from, and I knew she had to be The Bull's Eye. There was no way she could be anyone else. She glared out at me from underneath the brim of her black hat and cracked her knuckles.

I smiled. "Well, that's more like it. I'm Withrow Surrett. I think we should talk."

"I couldn't agree more." The person who spoke was not The Bull's Eye. It was Jennifer McCordy, who stepped out from behind The Bull's Eye with a smile on her face. "It's been a long time, Withrow."

Well *hell*.

Chapter 11

Eventually I nodded at Jennifer. "Well," I said. My voice was flat. "Hello."

"So who or what are you?" The Bull's Eye wasn't letting me step inside, and I had no desire to push past.

"Hasn't Jennifer told you?" I smirked a little.

"No," Jennifer said from the sidelines. "I didn't know you would be here and I don't like to…" She hesitated, flipping through her mental thesaurus. "I don't like to gossip. I promised to keep my distance and I have. This is just one of those weird coincidences." She didn't sound scared or worried but neither did she sound rehearsed the way a liar might. Liars always think their calm demeanor supports the lie but it doesn't. It reveals their preparation.

I could hear Roderick smiling as he replied from down by my right shoulder. "I believe they're called 'synchronicities': two or more events unlikely to be only casually related and thus granted a semi-mystical importance."

Unlikely to be only casually related, indeed. I considered how likely Jennifer was to lie. It sounded like the truth when she said it, and Jennifer had not tried to bullshit me before. When we met she was still very much the victim of previous traumas and she didn't hide that from me. She just didn't volunteer too much too early. *Screw it,* I thought, *I'm ready to make a thing happen.*

"I'm the person a bunch of people think is *you.* I'm also the local boss for a certain subset of creatures of the night. I've somehow wound up with what ought to be *your* problem and I want to help you solve it." The Bull's Eye didn't like the sound of any part of that so I went on, not sure what to do other than to keep running off at the mouth. "Look, I'm a vampire, but the nice kind." I paused and put up a finger. "Not the annoying, self-loathing kind, though, and it's all totally different from how it works in the movies no matter which movies you think I mean."

"I've already met a vampire," she said. The Bull's Eye's voice was even in a way that suggested she was trained to keep it steady in moments of stress. "There is no nice kind. There can't be, based on what I saw."

I arched both eyebrows. "Okay. Interesting." I cleared my throat. "How about, I'm the less terrible kind?" I couldn't just leave that minor revelation on the table, though. "When did you have occasion to meet one of us?"

"A few nights ago, in a neighborhood across town. Long story." The more I listened to her clipped tones and steady voice, and the more she peeked out at me from around the brim of that hat, the more I realized she was a warrior: literally, she was trained for war, for combat. She wouldn't let me see where she was looking and she wouldn't let me draw her into conversation. She was trained to see people as foes to be defeated.

I spread my hands a little to either side. "As the boss, if someone's acting out it's my job to put a stop to it. We don't like trouble. This sounds like something I need to fix. I think it isn't so much I've got your problem after all. I think maybe we've wound up with each other's problems. Let's trade and go about our respective lives."

The Bull's Eye considered that. "You knocked on the door here and asked to speak to someone like you knew your manners." She paused. "Sort of." She turned her head just a couple of degrees. "Jennifer, do you trust him?"

Jennifer didn't hesitate. "Yes." I was a little surprised, to be honest.

The Bull's Eye considered things from under that brim. "For now I'm willing to be civil." That settled that, and without further discussion she stepped back.

Roderick put a hand on my arm to stop me from walking inside. "An invitation would be appreciated," he said to the humans. He folded his hands behind his back. Dog sat patiently beside him but Smiles just went ahead and walked inside. He isn't picky about such things. Roderick went on, "There are ways these things are done."

The Bull's Eye harrumphed. "They have to be invited," she said.

"Come in?" Jennifer sounded uncertain.

Roderick smiled and stepped over the threshold. In a voice so low only I would hear him, he murmured, "Decorum, Cousin. A little misinformation never hurt."

Walking through the old farm house, The Bull's Eye introduced me around: Sheila, Ramon and Chang, the guys she met at Durham Tech; Xi, a Taiwanese-American kid with no trace of an accent getting his doctorate at North Carolina State in Raleigh, a campus I know well; Dan, a queeny guy with an exaggerated affectation and hyper-nelly voice at UNC over in Chapel

Hill; Bob, a handsome and athletic little stud attending Duke itself. I asked why they mostly went elsewhere but lived next to Duke.

"They've got an effectively wide-open wireless network," Xi said in his perfectly Midwestern American English. "They never know what's happening on their network."

"Wide open *what* now?" asked Dan, eyebrows waggling all over the place, but he and Roderick were the only ones who laughed.

Five minutes later, The Bull's Eye and I were parked on a weird little balcony hanging uncertainly from the back bedroom on the second floor. It felt tacked on and insubstantial but it didn't give way beneath us. We had our choice of cheap folding chairs but neither of us sat. Jennifer and Roderick had faded into another room to let The Bull's Eye and me have a conversation of our own. The Bull's Eye leaned against the railing, like maybe she'd be ready to go over the side and hit the ground running if she needed to, and in all fairness I could respect that kind of thinking a lot more than easy trust. I put my back against a wall.

"So tell me about this vampire you met in your neighborhood." I pulled a little tin of mints out of the inner pocket of my trench coat and offered it to her. She didn't bite.

"No," The Bull's Eye said. "You tell me about El Diablo and why he thinks you're me. Maybe I'll like what I hear. If so, we talk about what I saw." Her arms were folded, body language plain as day. She had no interest in being out here with me but she had to be if she were going to learn anything about her *real* problem: this vampire she claimed she'd seen. Easy money said it was my interloper from the night of the ballet, of course, and they'd been in a scrap. Bully for her, going to toe-to-toe with a vampire and living.

I played patty-cake. I told her about running into El Diablo the two times I'd seen him – the theft of the mascot uniform and then seeing him again in the Duke Gardens the night of the explosions. I told her about all the kids with cameras and told her I'd simply run away rather than try to stop them. At no point did I mention Ross.

"I like your respect for the civilians." The Bull's Eye nodded when she said that. I didn't bother telling her I'd only let them live because murdering them would be too inconvenient. "Homeland Security and the FBI are all over Duke's campus now," she said. "It's in all the papers, on the news. If he wants to do something to Duke, well, he's kind of screwed himself."

"Not if he's smart," I said, "And he's smart. Took out all that stained glass like it was yesterday's trash and managed to collapse the Divinity School on itself with one bomb. He's got a beef with the school and he thinks if he tarnishes the image of the mascot he harms the institution itself via some mystical association." I shook my head. "A bunch of Deputy Dawgs with federal badges aren't going to catch him."

The Bull's Eye waved that away. "Some of them are pretty thick, sure, but there are some ace investigators. I wouldn't write them off."

I tried not to snort. "The didn't warn you *we're* out there, did they?"

She ignored that and went on. "El Diablo didn't say the link was mystical. He said there were 'causal relationships.' He also said, 'Like may affect like after all.' Similar, but not the same." She waved a finger, as though addressing a class or something, then tapped the finger against her bottom lip while she thought. "I'm no scientist, but he also said 'quantum,' right? We're talking about a physicist here. There are certainly physicists who take note of the mysterious correspondences in life and wonder if they're connected."

"Synchronicities," I said.

She went on. "He might be, I don't know, way off the deep end of that line of thinking and believe if he hurts people or himself while wearing the old mascot uniform he'll harm the University through some quantum connection."

"Still sounds mystical to me," I said. "I don't see the distinction."

She wobbled a hand in the air. "It goes back to Clarke's third law: any sufficiently advanced technology is indistinguishable from magic."

I sighed and fluttered my lips. "I'm too old for this. I don't need the world to get more complicated just as I was getting a handle on things." I shrugged it off. "The people who sent me here said he was probably a technopagan but so far I haven't seen anyone who looks like him. Have I met everybody?"

The Bull's Eye nodded.

"Maybe he's just a scientist who got there on his own," I said. "What are the odds these chuckleheads are being honest when they say they really have no idea who he could be? Maybe they've run across him somewhere, even if he isn't one of them."

"The ones I've met are above board," she said. "There's something about them." The Bull's Eye hesitated. "It's hard to describe. There's some kind of naïve darkness about them. It's like they think the good guys are more badass than the bad guys or something. They know they're weird and they like it. It's empowering for them." She smiled a little.

So did I. "That's something we're all familiar with," I said. "Jennifer found herself in the thick of a life-threatening problem – more than once – and was able to think her way out of it. You dress in black and walk around your neighborhood at night looking for trouble to unmake. Being smart and showing initiative are both weird these days but we're all proud of ourselves for it."

"And you dress in black and walk around... doing what, exactly?"

"Counting angels on the heads of pins." Why bother being subtly evasive when I could be obviously so? I went on. "So, what are you going to do about El Diablo?"

The Bull's Eye smirked. "I need more intelligence," she said. "You found him twice by happenstance – you say – but I've had no such luck. It sounds like you're closer to cracking that nut than I am."

I waved it off. "I don't want that on my plate. It isn't my situation to resolve. We need to swap problems here."

"You fight the battle you can with the resources you have," she said to me. "We don't get to pick and choose. I'm fighting that vampire. You're fighting El Diablo. Roll out."

I opened my mouth to say something, then stopped and took a different tack entirely. "I'm going to guess you would have been career military but it got cut short due to some unforeseen circumstance." I said it out of the blue, as it occurred to me.

"We're not here to talk about that," she said.

Ah: an exposed nerve. I filed it away. "If you say so." I shrugged. "If we can't swap problems then let's work together. I don't want to fight El Diablo. I want to go after the vampire you saw. If the ticket to that is helping you put away El Diablo, working as a team, so be it." I sighed. "Your turn to sing. What happened when you met the other vampire?"

"There isn't much to tell," she said.

"I doubt that very much. All indications are there's more than enough to tell."

"We are not discussing it." She tensed all over in defense.

I caught her eye for just a second and the force of my own will balled itself up in a fist by reflex. If she had been anyone else I would have lashed out with the hoodoo and simply taken the story from her.

This one time, I did not.

She stared me right in the eye and we both knew something had passed between us: an opportunity missed, a risk redeemed, I didn't know exactly what. I held her gaze but she looked away a moment later. I would have paid a fortune to know what she was thinking but for reasons I could not comprehend I had failed to find out the easy way.

I went back to fiddling with my fingernails and a file. A corpse's nails don't really grow, but a vampire's do. I've always wondered why. "Okay," I said. "You're not ready to talk about it. Let's go back to El Diablo. It's my understanding a big school pisses people off all the time."

"So do medium-sized schools, and little ones." Jennifer tried not to sound bitter as she said it, stepping onto the balcony to join us with Roderick right behind her. I felt a pang of sympathy: I liked Jennifer. I hadn't seen her in a long while but had thought about her plenty of times. She was the friend I hadn't allowed to happen. Now that Roderick had me pointed in the direction of being more sociable I wished I had. On the other hand, smart humans who like to solve puzzles are just about the worst possible choice to be a vampire's pal.

Roderick dug around in the pockets of his white pleather jacket for a stick of gum. I was trying to teach him to be a little more normal and an obsession with a particular flavor of gum seemed harmless enough. "There can't be many young, athletic, good-looking physicists with a chip on their superhuman shoulder," he said.

I nodded. "He thinks Duke ruined him. If they cut his funding or something he could take his work elsewhere and keep going but he isn't trying to do that. Either he lost everything or he thinks he did."

"Something big enough to destroy him would wind up in the paper," Jennifer said. "Or it would be completely covered up and forgotten." She cleared her throat. "Or both: a cover story in the paper while the real deal is buried."

I thought again of Jennifer's experience with the Steeplechasers: saving her school from the walking dead only to be fired for it. Everything had been swept under the rug. The world knew the dead had walked – for one night, in just a few places – but it had been denied the stories of at least one real hero.

I tried to keep us on-task. "Since then, he's turned into something smarter, faster and stronger than humans and he thinks he has nothing left to lose."

The Bull's Eye pursed her lips just a little. "You don't think of yourself as human." It was an observation, not a question.

"No. I don't," I admitted. It bothered me to hear Roderick say 'them' but the truth was I hadn't thought of myself as one of them in a very long time. "I think of myself as being *among* humans, and I try to live that way, to stay connected. Retreating into a walled off existence is a recipe for winding up an insane anachronism who sees people as nothing more than cattle." I favored Roderick with a quick glance and he gave me the most fleeting of encouraging smiles. Gods, but the irony was almost too much to bear, being schooled by Roderick on how to make friends. I looked back at The Bull's Eye. "But I am not one of you and I never will be."

The Bull's Eye coiled up the corners of her mouth for a second but didn't say anything. It felt dismissive, but I didn't have time to say anything.

Jennifer cocked one eyebrow at me. "You don't believe in walling yourself off?"

I sighed a little. "I…" I wasn't sure how to apologize.

She saw it coming and shook her head. "*C'est la guerre.*"

Both The Bull's Eye and I looked intrigued by that remark, and Roderick looked as passive as a clock's face. I narrowed my eyes. I wanted very badly to know what they had been discussing while they were inside.

Jennifer went on. "We all lose people, one way or another. No hard feelings."

I thought of the boyfriend she told me about, the guy who'd drifted off as she became more and more obsessed with the zombies she'd had to fight in a tiny town. I nodded and turned back to The Bull's Eye. "I think you know what it feels like to be outside looking in," I said. "And you know what Jennifer's talking about, too. You were in the military. Bad stuff happened. You saw too much, or knew too much, or something along those lines. Now you're back home and you do this. Why? Because you don't feel like you're one of them, either." I gestured out at the night, at the trees, at the unseen suburban houses full of hidden sleeping souls. "It explains how you were able to get into a tussle with a vampire and survive. You're good at this stuff, so it's what you do." I pointed up and down, at the costume, at the stance, at everything, "Maybe it's your job, maybe you're bored, maybe you want revenge for something. I don't know, but my money says a little of all three."

"I'm here and I have skills. I choose to use them. That's what matters." The Bull's Eye didn't quite look at me.

"You don't like long conversation. Me, I can talk all night long. I've got nothing but time. You're not so big on frittering it away like that. The only time you get so distracted you start forming complex sentences is when you're thinking about a problem that needs to be solved."

Jennifer cleared her throat softly. She thought it was time for me to leave it be, but I've always been terrible at that. I kept addressing The Bull's Eye. "You retreat into terse fragments when you're confronted with yourself, your history. My kind are good at finding weak spots in the armor. If you find yourself facing off again with the vampire you met before, keep that in mind. Don't let him talk. Don't look him in the eye. Just hurt him. Don't let him draw you into anything more complicated than that. Don't let him position you, physically or psychologically. We are like spiders with elaborate webs." I drew a breath. "We capture people so we can drain them; and we love it when our designs are so clever the prey gets hurt. You've earned better than that."

There was a long moment of silence. I glanced at Roderick and his eyes shined over a strange smile.

The Bull's Eye looked down as she spoke. "He wasn't interested in talking." She bit down on the memory and found it bitter. I knew the look of someone who'd stared death in the eye: I'd seen it on Jennifer's face one Thanksgiving night some number of years ago. To my surprise, The Bull's Eye told us the story at last. I thought I'd probably pushed too hard, but I hadn't been able to stop.

When The Bull's Eye finished, I fluttered my lips. "He might be chattier next time. You got lucky."

"Yeah."

Jennifer hadn't reacted at all: she'd heard it before. Somewhat to my surprise, Roderick was absolutely still. His eyes were on The Bull's Eye and he was listening like his life depended on it.

"It sounds to me," I said, trying to move away from the attack on her, "Like he's farming these twins. The rare human who's really turned on by being fed on is also usually pretty ashamed. I mean, they're basically being molested, right? There's a serious power differential going on and that, plus intimacy of some sort, usually means someone is being used." My own voice caught as I thought of that guy from Power Company, the one I'd left passed out in the bathroom. I was sure he had a name, but damned if I could remember it now. At least I hadn't taken over his life. He would remember me as nothing more than some guy who made out with him at the club. I wasn't going to show up night after night until his mind cracked like a raw egg from the pressure of all the hoodoo and abuse. That had to mean something, right? And anyway, a guy's got to eat. "It certainly sounds like one of them enjoys some aspects of it."

The Bull's Eye looked surprised and a little revolted and a little not-so-surprised-after-all. "Humans – we – get off on it sometimes?"

I hesitated. "Not commonly, but there are definitely humans who get into it. They like being so thoroughly dominated and, I don't know, *owned* by someone else. It's a form of retreat, a way of giving up and letting someone else do all the thinking for a while. It's what they have in common with drunks and religious fundamentalists and people with multiple personalities: with *anybody* else who finds a hole to climb inside and pull shut after them." I waved a hand around. "Some vampires have a few regulars, sure, but nobody in his right mind would feed off of the same person or two all the time. I mean, eventually someone notices that kind of thing. The kids in your neighborhood, for instance."

"It's not really my neighborhood, it's just one I patrol."

"Then it's yours," I said. "Ownership is more than paperwork."

The Bull's Eye dismissed that with a gesture. She was not interested in entertaining the notion she asserted stewardship over anyone. It too easily resembled the sort of uninvited dominion the interloper had claimed over the twins. "So what do I do about them?"

I shook my head. "You don't do squat. It's my job. If I can't do it, someone else should be the boss anyway."

The Bull's Eye smirked a little. "How old are you?"

"Ninety, give or take." I chuckled. I wondered why I'd answered so honestly.

"Crosses? Holy water?"

It was my turn to twist up the corners of my mouth. "I brush my teeth in it every night."

She laughed once, high and sharp and honest.

"So we're a team now." Jennifer stood a little straighter as she spoke, dragging us back on-task. "There's a lot going on: stuff you don't know about. Stuff is happening out in the countryside, out on the coast, all over the place. Vampires are popping up in places they aren't supposed to be. They're in places the Bobs thought were clean and so *you* think are clean."

I turned my head slowly and blinked. "How do you know about the Bobs?" I didn't even consider asking about all the other things she had just said. I have spent years, ever since, wondering why I did not.

"I do my research." Jennifer shrugged a little. "That's all I can say."

I turned my gaze to Roderick.

"Oh, Cousin," he sighed. "They're *dead*. It doesn't hurt to tell her just the teensy-tiniest bit, does it? We have to work together. Trust me on this. She had just about everything figured out already anyway."

I narrowed my eyes. "No. This team thing is not happening. I'll go to the ballet with my…" I waved both hands around for a second. "Friends? Sure, why not? I'll go to the ballet with my *friends*, but we are not a team. I am not on any team. This is my problem and I am fixing it. El Diablo is your problem and you are fixing it." Suddenly the whole notion of having worked with anyone else on this seemed stupid: stupidly idealistic, stupidly shortsighted, stupidly useless. It seemed a hindrance more than a help.

"Delta Force." The Bull's Eye blurted it out. "So was my husband. That's how Delta Force works a lot of the time."

I paused and looked at her. We all waited for her to go on.

"When your spouse dies, in Delta Force, they let you go. They cut me loose: pension, honorable discharge, cover story, the usual, but all the handshakes and memorial flags in the world can't make that life come back."

I wondered if she meant her husband's life or her own.

She finished simply: "I couldn't find much of a job so I made one."

"This economy can't be easy to come home to," Jennifer said.

The Bull's Eye shrugged. "It was a long time ago."

"Less than the span of memory." Jennifer met her eyes and nodded. Some kinship of common experience – as women, as victims, as those burdened with survivor's guilt – passed between them and I knew I would never understand it.

The Bull's Eye considered things for a moment. "Life's a bitch." She turned to me again. "You don't have a choice, Withrow."

"I always have a choice."

"Okay," she said, shrugging at me with a little exasperation. "You have a choice: we do this together or you're not involved."

I glanced at Roderick and he offered no help. I twisted up my mouth in obvious bitterness, but as I did so I ran through all the scenarios in my head and they all boiled down to my cousin working with a bunch of people – to whom he referred as *them*, for gods' sakes – while I ran around duplicating some small portion of their efforts and getting nowhere. I hated this, hated having my hands tied, hated feeling like I was again being told what to do in my own town by someone who hadn't earned the right, but I didn't immediately see a way out of it. I finally nodded. "Fine. We're a team." I held up a finger. "For this one thing, this one time."

"Good." The Bull's Eye stood away from the balcony railing. "Let's go find out if these magic computer guys can help us or not."

We all walked downstairs to the main floor and came around into the living room. Sheila, Ramon, Chang, Xi and Dan were sitting with laptops open; Bob was watching Craig Ferguson do his opening routine. "Hey, guys," he said, like we were the other four housemates who were there all the time. I blinked, looked at The Bull's Eye, shrugged.

"Bob," Jennifer said, "Can you tell us about any physicists Duke might have pissed off recently?"

Bob paused the playback and looked at us. He rubbed his eyes. "Lots of them," he said. We waited for him to elaborate, and eventually he made a little "o" with his mouth and realized we were all ears. "They had some major cuts in their Physics department at the beginning of the semester. Something about misappropriated funds or something."

"It was a cover for a scandal," Dan drawled. He didn't bother to look up from his laptop. "They caught a physics student working on a project involving human subjects but it wasn't approved and blah blah blah." Dan waved a hand around. "So he got booted."

"Can you tell us his name?"

Dan thought for a second, then went back to typing. "Sure. They said his name in the papers, but that's boring. Let me crack the Duke HR file server. It should just take a second."

"Wait," Xi said, holding up a hand. "We should take this as an opportunity to say our invocations."

Bob paused the TV, Chang looked up, Ramon continued to stare intently at the screen. Sheila tossed something at him – a hacky sack, it looked like – and he started and looked around.

"Invocations!" Ramon sounded like someone had caught him sleeping in church. "Right! I'll go get the glow sticks."

They ringed up in a circle around Dan as he typed, chanting what at first didn't really resolve as language for me but I eventually realized was mystical verse in computer speak:

10 WE CALL ON THE GUARDIANS OF THE WATCHTOWERS
20 WE CALL ON THE EAST, INTELLECT
30 WE CALL ON THE SOUTH, PASSION
40 WE CALL ON THE WEST, NURTURING CARE
50 WE CALL ON THE NORTH, GOOD JUDGEMENT

60 WE CALL ON THE GODS AND GODDESSES OF MIND AND OF WILL
70 WE CALL MERCURY, WHO ESTABLISHES THE SESSION
80 WE CALL KOIOS, THE QUERANT, THE INQUISITIVE MIND
90 WE CALL ATHENA, GREATEST OF INTELLECTS
100 WE CALL THOTH, WISE MEDIATOR
110 WE CALL SET, PROTECTOR OF MYSTERIES
120 GOTO 10, THE CIRCLE IS CAST

They chanted this in unison, three times, each of them calling one of the gods and snapping his glow stick so that it gave off a weird, neon light then passing the sticks to the left, clockwise, as they did second and third iterations. Then the four who formed the circle around Dan closed their eyes and started producing a low, continuous hum as he hunched over the laptop and typed.

"That's not even valid BASIC." Jennifer looked a little offended.

"Maybe not for computers," I whispered, "But for the universe?"

Five minutes later, paper came gliding out of one of the printers in the dining room. I walked over and took it out, looked at the driver's-license-esque photo and then nodded. "Yep, that's him. Joffrey Hammerton IV. *Joffrey.*" I slowly sounded it out. "Christ. He might as well be named Cracker McFoxHunt. No wonder he's an asshole."

The Bull's Eye cocked one eyebrow at me. "This from a white guy named 'Withrow'?"

I frowned. "Which one first? El Diablo or the vampire?"

"The vampire?" Dan squeaked in surprise.

"The vampire." The Bull's Eye said it, nodding at me. "I owe him one."

Jennifer agreed.

Roderick nodded. "He is my primary concern. Anything else is a bonus."

"Fine," I sighed. "The vampire."

Chapter 12

ight shopping is the best kind of shopping in the whole wide world.

The night after we had met with the technopagans I found myself wandering the aisles of an ÜberBargains out on the edge of town. It was part of a solid three miles of strip malls and cheap apartments running between downtown and suburbia like a defensive trench. Smiles was with me, his Service Animal In Training vest around his mid-section. A kid at the front of the store tried to pet him but I shooed it off with a growl. Hellhounds are not play-toys for curious tweens.

When I told the others I would pick up a few things useful against vampires, Jennifer offered to come with me to use her employee discount. I forbade it. I wasn't ready to manufacture chitchat like nothing ever happened and I wasn't ready to talk about the things that had. I wondered if that's what it's like in families or between friends after they're driven apart by one thing or another only to meet again after the fact: uncomfortable silences crowding in with all the other elephants in the room.

I was dressed in anonymous blacks and grays, my trusty trench coat on despite the stifling heat of the store. The high ceilings and open floor plans make them impossible to climate-control evenly. The store always cranks up the thermostat and hopes for the best. One will be a meat locker and the next a barbecue. That night the ÜberBargains down from Southland Mall & Multiplex was turned precisely to Self-Basting Slow-Roasted. I kept the coat on anyway because I don't see much point in living forever if I can't do it in the wardrobe of my choice. If Roderick could spend eternity balanced on the knife's edge between plastic-clad go-go boy and off-hours drag queen I could sure as hell spend it looking like a goth beatnik.

Times like that – prepping to deal with gods-knew-what from a vampire and a self-declared supervillain – always make me wish I knew a more reliable arms dealer. The Internet can get you anything, sure, but it can't beat browsing a store with real shelves and letting inspiration strike. I bought all kinds of things when I went up against Bob in the '90s but I spent the better part of two years prepping and I got it all face-to-face or through a handful of trusted middlemen. I have yet to find the weapon equivalent of Amazon. Roderick has gotten me as far as using email and a few websites but I know a lot more happens in the Internet's darkest corners than I can imagine or usefully find.

Hell, more happens on simple classified ad sites than you'd think. Humanity specializes in conducting its shadiest business as close to out in the open as it can manage. Just ask the nosiest neighbor you've got. The people next door are not as good at hiding their transgressions as they think they are and, quite frankly, neither are you.

Sporting Goods is always a popular choice for weaponry. I picked up a couple of baseball bats, a headlamp for jogging at night and something called a "kettlebell". Apparently it's the thing gym bunnies use instead of ordinary dumbbells. My interest was mostly from the fact it was a big, heavy weight with a handle. I imagined punching someone with that would hurt like hell.

I'd also taken some inspiration from The Bull's Eye and picked up a few more items of plain black clothing and a plain black baseball cap. I like to stay anonymous when I'm going to do violence but at the same time I like my victims to know who put them down. I wanted the interloper to see my face but I wanted to leave open the possibility anyone else who might wander into the scene would see The Bull's Eye. I had nothing but respect for her, but I was also willing to take advantage of her reputation.

The rest of my haul consisted of a few odds and ends from all over the place: a big tin of lighter fluid; a box of strike-anywhere matches; a roll of braided twine; two packs of plain white undershirts for men; a pack of tube socks; a hatchet; an electric camping lantern with a long-life LED (what will they think of next?); one of those disposable wet-mop things; and a thirty-foot roll of telephone wire. Hardly anybody has a land line anymore, to hear tell, but let me assure you phone cable has its uses. Rubber-sheathed twisted copper cabling is a hell of a lot harder to break free of in an escape attempt than a zip-tie or novelty handcuffs and it is way easier to tie in a knot than a garden hose. I also grabbed a couple of rolls of Halloween-themed duct tape just in case. Abductions and murders always go better with duct tape.

With those various things I had all the makings of blunt weaponry, a nasty garrote suitable for turning into an apparent suicide, a handy clean-up tool, a combination weapon and disposal implement, shaped fire (stuff a sock with an undershirt and newspapers soaked in lighter fluid, insert in bound enemy's mouth, make s'mores) and a light to see by while burying the bodies. I already had a shovel, of course. Every vampire worth her salt carries a shovel in the trunk.

The next time you wander through an ÜberBargains and wonder why the strung-out kid with the bloodshot eyes and the long nails is pushing a cart full of half the hardware and camping sections, ask yourself if it's a good idea to judge a person who might be on their way to murder some guy.

I was strolling along with a pair of headphones on – Depeche Mode in the tape player in my pocket – when I felt someone tap me on the shoulder. I turned around, holding one earpiece away so I could send scampering whoever was about to ask to pet my dog, but I stopped short.

Ross was standing there petting Smiles. The demon stood up straighter and smirked at the shopping cart. "Getting your Christmas list taken care of early?"

"I haven't found the most desperate person in all of Durham yet," I replied. My guard was instantly up. Roderick had me scared and I was as surprised by my own reaction as I was by Ross' appearance in this place. It occurred to me, of course, that his being there meant he always knew where I was and what I was doing. He had chosen that moment to manifest, when I was alone and in public and couldn't do anything too crazy. "So, I'm a little surprised to see you here."

Ross smiled, ducked his head like a kid caught with his hand in the cookie jar, and laughed. "I confess I couldn't stay away." He rolled one perfect shoulder under a tee shirt depicting some cartoon I didn't recognize. "I…" He licked his lips and my fangs started to descend of their own accord. Those spoiled-amber eyes flirted with me from under a blue iridescent brow and he went on. "I find myself intrigued by you, Withrow. I think I may have a small crush."

The thing about vampires is, we are not exactly good at saying no to temptation. After all, that's how most of us got here. Offered a shot at the ultimate transgression – shuffling off mortality itself rather than just this mortal coil – we went all-in. Some of us may have tried to pretend they had to think about it before leaping at the chance but they're the minority. We are people who said *yes* to crazy ideas or we wouldn't be here in the first place.

Long seconds of silence passed between us as Ross – whatever his real name might be, he was "Ross" to me – waited for me to say something and I waited for something to say.

I looked back across my whole life and I saw nothing but one iteration after another of times I've gone out of my way to be a bastard to someone so they'd leave me alone in future. I thought of Mary-Lou Reinholdt on my front step that first time, blinking in the bright lights and trying to tell me about the neighborhood association and my dog. I thought of when I later pointed out to Mary-Lou the single worn spot on my couch to make the point I did not want or need other people in my life and would never be able to have them anyway. I thought of when I stood in the back room of a store just like this one trying to decide whether to kill Jennifer for knowing too much. I thought of the biological family I let my maker dispose of so I wouldn't have to deal with them again; of my trip to Seattle; of meeting Roderick for the first time; and of the shock I felt when I realized the vampires in Seattle actually gave a damn about one another. When I witnessed vampires holding hands in a room full of other vampires I thought I had seen it all *and* the opening act.

I had pushed others away from myself so many times, and so thoroughly, my own psychopath cousin was on me to make friends.

A part of me – relegated to the back of my mind, pushed so far into a corner it could be heard by no one but its own self – knew it was not normal for me to think like this. I knew I did not normally give a damn about any of these things. That part of me also knew with a certainty it found deeply unsettling (and liberating in its own way) that I was not thinking about these things because I *wanted* to. Ross was a demon, a devil, maybe an imp: whatever one might want to call a living spirit of temptation itself. I've already said I don't know if there are gods or heavens but I know there are hells. I didn't know if Ross literally came from one of those but he was clearly something supernatural, something strange, and he had the power to summon up within me those longings I'd most deeply buried beneath nearly seven decades of empty social calendars. If he could do this – if he could find me whenever he wanted and make me feel what I didn't want to feel – then fine, he could have me and it wasn't really my fault if I gave in.

In fact, it might be educational to find out what happened if I did.

Fangs descending, wordlessly barking like an animal, I shot forward at a speed surprising even to me. I locked lips with Ross and pushed in close, shoving him backwards, right up against a big plastic display of googly-eyed jack o' lantern faces made of waxed cardboard and cheap paint. The display tore free of the shelf supporting it, showering us in goofy grins and slow-motion spinning eyes. I'd jumped into super-speed without even realizing it when I kissed Ross and he was only now starting to realize what was happening.

His eyes were open, and so were mine, but his slid closed with deathly slowness and by the time our tongues met I'd slammed him into the next row (Thanksgiving table settings), dragged him around its end-cap display (bundles of split firewood in plastic bags), shoved him into the next (various black-painted candelabras for Halloween parties) and then knocked over a display of bulbs for autumn planting. By the time they were spilling out around our feet, Ross had caught up and we were full-on making out in the middle of an ÜberBargains on a Wednesday night.

People were starting to notice.

His hands twisted around the lapels of my trench coat, pulling me closer than seemed readily possible. My hands slid down the back of his tee shirt to grab both cheeks of his ass and squeeze like I was kneading bread. He made a sound of encouragement, and so did I. I opened my eyes for a second to see where Smiles had gone but he was sitting beside the cart, eyes alert, ears up, seemingly happy to stay right where he was.

I spun us again and Ross and I burst through one of those sets of big, swinging doors into the warehouse area in the back. I thought again of the last time I'd walked through just such a set of doors: behind them I had found the offer of Jennifer's friendship. I had turned that down.

This time I would not be saying *no*.

A pimply kid who didn't look big enough around to hold a whole set of organs produced an awkward guffaw as Ross and I spun and tumbled past him, locked in an increasingly complicated embrace: hands here and there, arms, twisting around one another, palms pressed against one another's flesh. I was not a virgin the night Agatha took from me the problem of my mortal life but neither was I terribly experienced. Affection between two men had not been seen in public and I hadn't seen a whole lot in private, either. Now two men could kiss in public and have random passersby think it amusing rather than revolting.

The back room of a store like ÜberBargains is mostly row after row of floor to ceiling shelves with metal cages around some and open shelving units on others. There are pallets of regular consumer goods in industrial-sized cardboard containers, stacked one atop each other. Ross and I careened off one, then another, playing lusty pinball across the vast space to which "guests" of the store are not normally invited. His hands were all over me, with no regard to what I thought was a pretty unattractive physique, and I was just as eager to explore his. The scales of his flesh were smooth to the touch, with no seam I could detect. I wondered if they were purely some cosmetic magic. It felt like warm flesh to my vampire's hands, not the armored hide of some reptile from infernal realms. As we shifted and twisted in our eagerness to touch every part of one another I could feel his muscles ripple at each caress: tendons stretched, joints popped, his tongue at my neck. I realized in a far-off, distant way someone was trying to talk to us but it didn't matter.

I shoved Ross up against a stack of dog food bags as high as a basketball player could jump, leaned back just enough to let him see my teeth, and snarled. He nodded, hand on the back of my head to pull me in, and I struck. My fangs pierced the silver-blue skin of his throat as easily as that of any mortal and fire spilled out of the wound. I pressed my lips to that perfectly shaped throat and those impossible, imperceptible scales and drank deep of what was, I guessed, the demonic equivalent of blood.

Human blood, or rather the experience of consuming it when it is literally everything one needs to live, is very difficult to describe. It's like trying to describe an orgasm or to describe the sensation of tasting something for the first time. You may say something tastes like an apple, for instance, but like what does an apple taste? You can say an apple tastes sweet and a little sour, crunchy or crisp with a softness underneath, but how do you explain "sweet" to a space alien who's never tasted Earthly sugar before? This is the dilemma I face in trying to describe what it's like to drink human blood. I can't describe the sensation to you other than to say it is hot and salty and for just a little while it will silence the wild animal in the pit of every vampire's guts. It also tastes like memories and sadness and sometimes, when we're very lucky, it tastes like desire or perhaps like surrender. It tastes like all the things that make humankind enjoyable, even admirable. It carries both the nobility of human spirit and the detestable anguish of human carelessness and fear.

Ross' blood didn't taste like that. It tasted like *need*. It tasted like holding a Molotov cocktail in one hand and matches in the other. It tasted like the sensation of holding a handgun for the first time: that moment when you realize guns were made to be shot and the only thing in the world to do with the thing in your hands is to *fire it*. It tasted like suffering and it tasted like wanting to make another suffer. If human blood tastes like vulnerability and good intentions, this stuff tasted like swaggering malice. It was all the best of the bad ideas a mind could fathom and more besides. It wanted me to drink it, deep and forever, and never stop, never be satisfied, never again let out that little sigh of relief when the growling animal inside finally falls into sated sleep.

I wondered what terrible things I would learn if I drank him dry, right there: what unearthly horrors would my Last Gasp make available to me?

I didn't get to find out. He had twisted up his fingers in my hair as I drank, at first, but then he mustered unquestionably supernatural strength and used it to pull me just an inch away but no further. My fangs ached to sink back into that flesh but my brain was starting to unknot itself and I could hear someone – an employee, I guessed – lambasting us for having tumbled backwards into forbidden territory. I started to lick the wound to close it up but Ross or some quality of his own supernatural condition beat me to it: the flesh simply sealed over and the excess blood dried, crumbled and fell away like desiccated ash. I quickly licked my own lips to clean them up but all I could taste was salt and something bitter and powdery. I reached up and pushed my hand across my own mouth out of habit but it came away with just a couple of flecks of that same crusted, sandy residue.

Devils. Weird.

I stood straight, cleared my throat and turned around to look at whoever was accosting us for having wound up back there in the first place.

It was a guy in jeans, a hoodie and a decorative walkie-talkie in his left hand.

"Just pay for your purchases and leave," he was saying to Ross, "And we'll all forget any of this happened."

I smacked my lips for a moment and reached down to straighten out the tee shirt I had tucked into my black jeans. "What's the matter, bucko," I grumbled. "Never seen two fellas engaged in a little heavy petting?" I reached out and put one fingertip in the center of his chest, tapping it once. "Run along and play cops and robbers somewhere else. We ain't breakin' any laws."

The rent-a-cop looked shocked at me, his eyes on the finger I'd used to invade his personal space. I didn't give a good goddamn what he thought. He was a pipsqueak. The whole world was made of pipsqueaks. As far as I was concerned they could all go squeak themselves right to hell and back: I had met a boy who would *kiss me*.

Ross stepped around and tried to pull the focus of the conversation back towards sanity. "Please ignore my friend. We're leaving. I'm very sorry."

I looked at Ross, eyes wide, brow twisted up into a topo map of parallel canyons. "Sorry? Sorry! You just apologized to this guy? What in the hell is the point of being what we are if we're going to go around kowtowing one second and bending over backwards the next so none of these bastards get offended for one fleeting, precious second?"

I mean, Christ, Ross had blue and silver skin. I wondered who in hell this kid thought he was to be standing up to the reptile before him.

Ross didn't even look at me. Instead, he pushed me towards the door. "We are leaving," he said, very firmly, voice very serious. "We are leaving right now."

He motored me out that way, his hands against my chest while my own were busy flipping off the store's security guard with both hands and giving him a raspberry at the same time.

"That was nice," Ross said in something of a rushing, perfunctory manner as he steered me towards my cart and towards Smiles. "Now pay for your things and leave. I'll catch up with you later."

I started to say something, but he pressed a cool finger to my lips.

He deposited me back at the cart, where a couple of employees and one little old lady wearing a whole heap of furs were gawping at us from the other end of the aisle.

"I like a floor show," the lady said to no one in particular. She balled up one claw and tapped it against the arm of an employee, then came out with a ridiculous little hen's cackle before saying, "Hoo!" She sounded like an enthusiastic owl.

Smiles walked over and started licking my hand. That sort of snapped me out of it, and I blinked a few times. "Yes," I said to Ross without looking around at him. "That was... nice." I cleared my throat. (The little old lady cackled again.) "Just, maybe next time, could you, I don't know, call first?"

I turned to address him directly but he was gone. I stuck my head around the end of the row – dodging the jack o' lanterns we'd spilled before – but he was gone. I wondered if there was angry yellow smoke being sucked into a ventilator somewhere.

I felt a little dejected at his exit, but that was quickly replaced by a thundering realization: the thing I had said to the rent-a-cop.

"What in the hell is the point of being what we are," I'd said. I shuddered suddenly, with fear and shock and a bone-deep chill. That's the sort of talk I don't let other vampires use around mortals and I'd gone and used it myself. I could have just hoodooed that security guard into submission on the spot, no problem, but I hadn't. Instead I'd simply tried to assert my superiority over him.

One shot of demon blood and all I wanted was to lord my power over something weaker than myself.

"Your friend's a looker, sonny." The little old lady had tottered over to me while I pondered the awfulness of what I'd just done; not awful in a guilty, morals-y way, but awful in the purely pragmatic sense of preferring stealth over domination as the way to survive in the mortal world.

I glanced down at her, draped in foxes whose eyes were closed forever. "Was he?"

"Sure," she said. "He looked just like my Charlie. Tsk." She shook her head. "Tall men were always my weakness. Of course, every guy was tall next to me." She tittered again and favored me with one of her apparently signature arm-taps. Her hand was covered in age spots, the skin drawn as tight around her knuckles as a tarp on an old boat stored for winter; thin a mattress cover one size too small. Time had used her flesh to shrink-wrap her bones.

The urge to say something cruel sprang from nowhere, deep within me, and I opened my mouth to manufacture some insult she had done nothing to deserve. I felt the flesh of my face twist up even as the rest of me started processing the fact she had not, in fact, seen the same apparent physical form I was seeing whenever I looked at Ross. I wondered if being a supernatural myself gave me some ability to perceive not possessed by mortalkind.

The breath within me paused, poised as it was to say something shockingly cruel, but what passed my lips instead was this:

"I bet Charlie was a really nice guy."

The little old lady looked to the heavens for a moment and clucked her tongue. "He was the best," she said. "He was just the best." She patted me on the arm once, then a second time, and her hand stayed there, her twisted fingers at my elbow for a moment longer than modern sensibilities would normally permit. I allowed it because I am not modern and neither was she. "If you find one that good, hang onto him," she said. "And if you don't, well, have a little fun with the ones you find."

I smiled, we parted, I paid for everything in my cart and on the way out I called my cousin and told him all about it.

"Mm," he said after a moment. "Well then, let's conclude our current business as quickly as we possibly can. We need to kill the interloper and anyone in his thrall."

I didn't really understand why that would be his reaction, but he'd already hung up. Turning my mind towards eliminating the interloper was a welcome distraction, I had to admit. Concentrating on a necessary murder is always a good way to focus the mind.

Chapter 13

The Bull's Eye and I rode up the twins' street, one after the other, around 10:00 the next night. We had hours before the bogeyman-interloper's usual appearance. We were in my beat-up old '77 Firebird, black with beige vinyl interior. I've driven it since I bought it new for cash at one of those "midnight madness" inventory clearance sales. Hard to believe that was nearly forty years ago. It carried us past The House so we could park around the corner. No winding up in a foot chase against someone in a car without having our own nearby.

We took up posts on either side of the street and just watched for a little while, maybe ten minutes, but everything seemed exactly as it had been. The Bull's Eye made a small hand gesture I figured was some sort of Delta Force sign language: some habit she'd picked up and probably lapsed into without thinking. I nodded and we both stepped out and started approaching, staying across from one another, scanning the houses on our respective sides of the street.

Here and there I could see little faces watching us: eyes wide and bodies crouched to peek over windowpanes or hide in shadowed corners. There was the occasional string of purple lights or a jack-o-lantern around and the kids' fear blended in like just another Halloween decoration. *Very seasonal*, I thought to myself. So the kids in this neighborhood *had* seen the interloper and really had started sitting up to watch in terrified fascination. I tried not to whistle in wonderment. I hoped none of them got any ideas like The Bull's Eye had done when she'd finally seen too much. I did not need a dozen vigilantes to deal with in ten or fifteen years.

The air was perfectly still and I could smell no sign of the stranger. I knew he'd be able to smell me, too, but that was part of the plan. I wanted him worried someone had found where he squirreled away a couple of nuts for the winter. I wanted him to rush in full of emotion. My own scent was the bait in the trap.

Every now and then I would lock eyes with one of the children tucked away in their houses. They didn't recoil from me but I knew they could tell I was Other. Children often can. In the dark of this one little place, on this one little night, with mortal minds turning to cartoon bats and princess outfits in search of a little fantastical fun, these kids listened to the part of themselves that hadn't yet been ground down by the world: the part which knew there was something about to go down, something important to the rest of their time in this place. They did not nod or wave or otherwise encourage me but they knew I was there to do something and somehow they knew it was important to witness.

The Bull's Eye and I walked back past The House, double-checked that end of the block, then turned and swapped sides of the street. I stopped in front of it, strode through the gate and stepped onto the front porch without a sound. I may be a big guy, and I may stomp around a lot, but I'm still a vampire. A delicate entrance and exit are our strongest play ninety nine percent of the time.

I could feel the eyes of a dozen children staring at me: kids who knew their homes were a haven but not *safe*.

I raised my fist and rapped with my pudgy knuckles three times on the front door to The House, just as I did for the Book People. I'm from way up the mountains, where we all know Death knocks thrice.

I was surprised at how little time it took for the door to open. I did some figurative math: two nights since The Bull's Eye had been here, right? I guessed the kid who was so into it he loaded his shorts when the vampire pulled out was the one on-call tonight and thus probably the one in a big hurry to get to the door.

The young man on the other side was tall, very thin, filthy blond, glasses-wearing, bookish and extremely hot. A part of me wanted to make him a sandwich but a part of me was busy constructing all sorts of scenarios involving two of him because that would mean twice as many of that beautiful body containing twice as much of his incredibly appetizing *blood*. He took a look at me and opened his mouth to say something, then stopped. His blank, emotionless expression twisted in an instant to something of hate and disgust. "Get out," he said, voice a normal volume but his intonation a hoarse growl. It was a cry from somewhere deep instead of a high, shrill shriek.

We both blinked at it – he and I, even though he said it – and then he said it again. "GET OUT." He started to slam the door but I have rarely let that stop me. I stuck my boot just over the threshold and the door stopped short.

"My name is Withrow," I said, very steadily and evenly, hands in the pockets of my trench coat. "We need to talk."

It didn't surprise me he was hostile. What surprised me was when he tried so hard to close the door he made it split at the point where it touched the toe of my boot. He wasn't as strong as me but he was sure as hell stronger than the door.

"I said," I *said*, but he produced this guttural peal of shock and maybe something not unlike fear as he bared his teeth at me. He, a human being, bared his teeth at me, a vampire. The door ripped and a chunk of it came off with the doorknob in his hand.

"GO AWAY." His voice was loud – really loud, neighbor-waking loud – so I sighed and put my hand in the middle of his chest.

"Inside," I said, and I shoved him bodily backwards. What I noticed when I did was that he tried to hold his ground – tried. Though he failed, he did so with more strength than I would have expected from someone with his frame or his vital signs, which is to say any at all. He was a lot stronger than a human. He looked strung out but he had something more than junkie strength.

Baring my fangs at him, I hissed as hard as I could. That tended to bring humans to heel in a hurry and I wanted to get this over with. I did not like this developing trend of mortals almost as strong as a vampire.

The Bull's Eye slipped across the street, up the steps and through the door around us before I'd even had time to look. I kept pushing and walked the guy into his own house, then looked at the mostly-broken door and said, "Do you got any of that Wild Glue or whatever it is?"

There was a double of Angry Twin sitting much more calmly on the love seat in the living room. He sighed a little. "Yeah. Lots." He was watching TV, legs folded up under him, a game of Solitaire abandoned on the coffee table.

He hadn't even looked up at all the commotion. "Don't worry," he said as he stood and walked into the kitchen. "He gets like that. He'll calm down."

I stood there holding Angry Twin at arm's length while he glared at me with vaguely wild eyes and made noises of increasing complexity. I could feel him struggling with something inside. He could have reached up and hit me or pushed me or something – his arms were longer than mine – but something was holding that in check. He was practically foaming at the mouth as he fought with himself.

Ah, I thought. *The other vampire.* He'd hoodooed them not to fight back against our kind. It was smart to do that to a repeat victim. In the old days it was said vampires would do that to the whole village or the whole town, one poor sap at a time. I imagined it was incredibly cruel, especially if he didn't also wipe their memories of what was happening to them to warrant it in the first place. The Bull's Eye was standing there in the front hall looking it up and down, swiveling and bobbing a little to check every corner and angle without actually moving. I was about to ask her to take Angry Twin off my hands when a cement block flew past my head and exploded on the wall behind me.

"Now, Scott!" It was the kid in the kitchen shouting. "Fight now!"

Scott's eyes rolled back and his hands came up. Even as I was flipping the internal switch that slows time, I realized this kid, too, was faster than a human being should be and his brother was stronger and they both smelled... delicious.

Just like El Diablo, of course.

The fight itself didn't take long but to me it took *forever.*

Scott – Angry Twin, the one I'd pushed back inside – put his hands on my face and was trying to find my eyes by feel since his own eyes seemed to have rolled back into his head. One of his knees came up to go for my groin. I dodged him easily enough and put my hands on his wrists, from underneath, to push him up and away. I had to exert effort to do it, though, whereas most humans are basically rag dolls compared to a vampire. You have to do your share of fighting to find that out, of course. Most vampires spend a long time unaware of how strong they really are.

I'd learned it decades ago.

I was surprised at how much I had to work to get his hands away from me but once I did I pulled him in close by one forearm, swiveled my torso and jabbed the other elbow directly into the middle of the kid's chest. As he started to fall backwards I kept my grip, lifted a foot and put one of my black poseur motorcycle boots in the middle of his stomach in a kick. Usually that would knock his feet out from under him, maybe pop one shoulder out of joint, but this time all it did was make us look like we were doing the stupidest dance ever invented.

I dropped my foot, let go of his arm and delivered a wound-up punch I had plenty of time to aim at his jaw.

One second.

That snapped his head back and spun him halfway around but he responded by following the momentum and twisting a full three sixty around to kick me in the side of the head. He was fast, too, so fast that I didn't see it coming. Either I had turned off the slow-mo or he had turned his *on*. Not okay. Not okay at all.

Just like that, we had dropped the choreographed bullshit and were on each other in a brawl. I bear-hugged him around the waist and lifted him off the ground, over one shoulder. I was trying to drop him on his head behind me; he was trying to beat me to death by pummeling my back and spine. His fists were landing like bowling balls made out of something *way* down the periodic table. It actually hurt, and I cried out in shock and frustration.

From under his right armpit I could see the other guy and The Bull's Eye launching themselves at each other at glacial speeds.

Scott finally hit me so hard I heard something snap and I buckled a bit but that turned out to be okay – when I dropped to one knee he pitched forward and banged his own forehead on the floor. I knit my broken bone or tendon, whatever it was, as I rolled out from under him and leapt like a cat to land on his back.

My instinct was to drop my fangs and go to town right there. I wanted to drain him dry and see how his brother might taste. The Bull's Eye was in the room, though, and that made feeding *not an option*. Sometimes I think that's all civilization boils down to: the persistent presence of others we'd rather not have watch as we express our most basic whims.

Instead, I grabbed Scott's arms and twisted them back behind him, got my knees on him with my three hundred fifty pounds behind them for emphasis, and I donkey punched him once at the base of the skull. I tried to pull my punch so I wouldn't just pulverize his head but I would have been just fine with a mild concussion. He took the blow and buckled, but he fought getting knocked out. He struggled and strained even as he started to go limp, so I did it again. That kind of thing is extremely risky – the brain is a marvel of delicacy and you can very easily fuck someone up for good that way – but it was what I had. This kid was as almost as strong as me and almost as fast, and he knew what he was doing in a fight. I had to get him neutralized in a hurry.

Two seconds had passed.

When his face smacked the hardwood floor – cheap, worn by time, in bad need of refinishing – I noticed blood shoot in either direction and I let time drop back to normal. Behind me, The Bull's Eye and the other guy, Adam, the other twin, finally got to each other. I guessed they had seen a kind of blur and screeching and then it was over, but they were just getting started.

I confess I did not act as quickly as I could have because I wanted to see what The Bull's Eye was capable of. It turned out she was capable of plenty. When the United States Army trains someone for Delta Force they train that person in *everything*. They are probably the most highly trained, most capable human individuals on the planet. The kid that came at her was strong and fast and extremely agile, more agile than his brother, more agile than almost any human being I could imagine, but all that did was help him try to close the gap between his raw abilities and her finely-honed skills. She blocked every attack, bounced on her feet, stayed in motion and dodged several wild swings, then delivered a precision punch to the middle of his chest that had the kid on the floor and gasping for breath in the next second. She hopped backwards, ready to keep going if he stood back up, but he stayed down.

I left my fangs out to keep their attention and said, low, "Now, tell me what the hell is going on with you and your favorite bloodsucker."

Adam looked at me, at my teeth, and started crying big, heaving, sincerity-soaked sobs. I could have said a bless-his-heart right then and there. The Bull's Eye shut what was left of the door. Now the brothers would talk. We both knew it, and we were both glad to have gotten them to that point without having to kill one of them to prove we meant business. Neither of us said anything, but the way we were avoiding looking at one another said it plainly enough: violence is a kind of nudity for the worst, most brutal parts of a soul. To have another see that can be shaming. The part of me that was once a man and not a monster – and the part of me who chooses to manage others like myself – thinks that is exactly how it still should be.

I pulled out my phone and texted the all clear to Roderick and Jennifer. Time for phases two and three.

Scott slept it off in a back room. I mentioned to his brother – Adam – that there was a risk of a concussion but he gave me a derisive snort. I couldn't tell whether he didn't care or whether he thought that wasn't possible for one of them to suffer from that.

The three of us sat down in the living room to talk like civilized people because that's what you do when you're done fighting someone half to death: you treat them like a person to try to get them on your side. The Bull's Eye sat at the other end of their couch from Adam. It had a worn old plaid print on a synthetic fiber of some sort. It looked like it came from the dumpster behind a secondhand store, and maybe it did. I sat in a wingback chair upholstered in orange vinyl. Neither of us were physically restraining or threatening him, but Adam couldn't have gone anywhere without going past one of us to get there.

"It started three months ago," he said. He was staring at the floor, not at us, and his eyes were focused on something much farther away than anything in the room. "It started when we were being worked on by a doctor." He paused. "Well, by this guy who called himself a doctor? He wasn't, I guess, but he said he was. We figured he was a medical student or a resident or something at the hospital. He had a Duke ID, he had a facility on campus and he had equipment with Duke University property tags on them. It all seemed more or less legit." He smiled a little. "And we knew it wasn't."

"How so?" I leaned forward a little in the chair. "What were you doing?"

"Scott answered an ad he saw online. It was asking for volunteer subjects in a study of the effect of vitamin injections on muscle mass. Scott and I are almost identical, physically, but he's always been the smarter one and I've always had better coordination. I played soccer in high school. He played chess. I think he's always been jealous that he and I could have effectively identical bodies but I beat him in sports. I never cared about him beating me at trivia. It's just, you know, the way things are. Every game has a loser." He didn't look up, but he paused.

"You were the one winning the games that were socially acceptable and encouraged," I said. "You were the popular one."

"We were both popular. Twins are viewed as a unit. We were seen as the perfect man with two bodies." He smiled very faintly, like he'd just recalled a fond memory of a dead relation. "Sometimes that's more popular than you might expect."

Neither The Bull's Eye nor I looked surprised or scandalized. He was right, shit happens and people get into weird stuff. That wasn't the weirdest thing I'd heard that week. It wasn't the weirdest thing I'd *done* that week.

The Bull's Eye tried to bring him back on track. "Tell us about the study."

"They weren't injecting us with vitamins." He said it almost completely flatly, as though we hadn't figured that part out yet. "They were something else. They affected our metabolism. Our appetites shot through the roof and kept going. At first, with just a couple of injections, we were eating a fourth meal, maybe a fifth, or we were eating *really* big at the normal three. We were never breakfast people but we found ourselves waking up earlier and earlier to make full breakfasts. Then we started eating bigger breakfasts, then snacks, then two lunches, on and on, and we weren't gaining anything. I assumed he was giving us steroids or human growth hormone or something but we didn't change shape. We stayed the same dimensions rather than bulking up. We just kept getting stronger and faster. We started..."

He laughed a little, suddenly, and then looked sad. "We started playing ping-pong again. We played when we were kids. We'd play against each other, always, and never anyone else, and I would always win. We started playing ping-pong at the student union and we noticed if we pushed we could get faster and faster and we could maintain a volley for minutes at a time. The ball would bounce back and forth so fast I could barely see it. Someone said we sounded like popcorn in a microwave. It started attracting attention. I said we should stop playing in public because people were a little freaked out if they watched us long enough. Eventually we could go so fast I couldn't see his hands and he couldn't see mine. If I tried to look for long it all fell apart, but if I just let myself go, if I let my hands do their own thing, we could play and play and play. It was like I could turn off the conscious part of myself and exceed all those boundaries I'd always pushed against as an athlete. Scott was experiencing the same thing. For the first time he could push against those boundaries and get past them." He sighed slightly. "We loved it."

"So you, what, bought a ping pong table and moved across the freeway to the sketchy part of suburbia?" I gestured at the world outside.

"Not right away." He looked up and at me for the first time, but only briefly. He knew not to look a vampire in the eye. "We were roommates on campus. We would do things like play patty-cake – two grown men playing patty-cake in their dorm room at night – or we would go to the gym in the middle of the night and take turns trying to see how much weight we could dead lift. We were like kids again: anything fast and dexterous, any sort of physical task like that, we would compete at it. It was like in a racing game, when you can play against your own ghost? Like in Mario Kart?"

I had zero clue what the hell he was talking about, but The Bull's Eye seemed to get it. She smiled a little and they shared a glance of understanding. She spoke. "But then something went wrong." All business, all the time: I wondered if she'd always been like that.

"Yeah. Sometimes bad things would happen. I was in a soccer game and I got my feet tangled up with another player. I broke both his ankles. I didn't mean to. I didn't know my own strength anymore. I was an athlete in a body that had outpaced my control over it. I couldn't trust myself on the field. What was worse, everyone thought I had done it on purpose and they *liked* that. Sometimes soccer is a dirty sport. It's the price of playing a game that thinks it's still competing with football for attention. Sometimes players are dirty because they have a chip on their shoulder about that kind of thing, but it wasn't what drew me to the game and it wasn't what I wanted. I told Scott we should quit the trial. He didn't want any part of that, and I was scared of how much he still enjoyed it." His eyes moistened for a moment. It was almost touching, except I wasn't sure I should believe a word of this. "I was scared of what would happen to him if he didn't have someone there to watch out for him, watching his back." The kid wiped his nose on the sleeve of his long t-shirt, like a little boy. "He loved everything about it. Now he had, like, superpowers. He felt he had gained…" He searched for a word, and I provided it:

"Abilities."

He nodded after a moment. "Yeah. To him, it was an additive experience. To me, it was subtractive. I had lost something from it when I lost soccer. The truth, though, was he lost something, too. Once we were *extra* – that's what we call it – he stopped trying all the stuff he had done before. He quit the Strategy Games League on campus and dropped out of College Bowl and basically just sat around doing things like shuffling cards really fast and putting his fist through scrap wood. He's been so happy with himself for being able to do stupid little stuff like that. He didn't want to quit. I think if the guy had offered us more injections, he would have taken it."

"So what broke up this happy arrangement?" I tried not to sound too sarcastic.

"The Duke Athletics people thought I had juiced. They were afraid the guy whose ankles I broke would sue them, or whatever. They asked me to take a drug test and when I did it came back with something they had never seen before. They said there weren't any of the, you know, banned substances, but there were 'anomalies.' They wanted to know what I was shooting and I told them all I'd done was get vitamin injections."

I snorted. "Yeah, you and Lance Armstrong. How hard did the Duke Athletics people laugh?"

The Bull's Eye gave me something like a glare but I ignored it.

Adam's face grew haunted for a moment. "They didn't. They asked where I'd gotten the shots. I mean, they couldn't accuse me of anything without some proof, right? That's what an investigation is. So they asked me where I got them and I told them about the ad and about my brother and me going to this lab in the Physics Department."

The Bull's Eye and I shared a quick glance. "Physics?"

Adam nodded. "'Bioengineering.' That's the term. Scott read up on it. He said it was 'constructionist' in that it tried to come up with new ways to modify living things, usually people, for health-related purposes. That's what this guy was doing. He was trying to invent..." He didn't laugh, more like he caught his breath for a second before going on. "It was like in Captain America. He was trying to invent super-serum. The Duke Athletics people got all that when they went there. They called in the campus cops and interrogated the guy and asked to look at his records. He refused, so they got the Department to seize his records and in the long run it turned out he had been working on us without..." He waved a hand vaguely, slowly. "Approval or something. He was supposed to go before some board or something and he didn't and that meant it wasn't okay for him to have human test subjects and here we were, human test subjects."

"All because you broke some kid's ankles." I clucked my tongue.

"It was an accident. It was the first game of the season. I'd been on the field maybe five minutes." He smiled a little. "That was months ago. The paper never quite got it right, y'know, but they reported something was happening in the Physics Department and someone had gotten defunded and had his graduate project shut down and booted out of school. I was kind of relieved, but Scott got an email from the guy two weeks later, just when I thought maybe things would go back to normal. The shots were starting to wear off. We weren't so 'extra' anymore. Scott was angry but I figured it would blow over. Once he got that email, it was all back on. I couldn't send him by himself, now that I knew what kind of situation we were in." He licked his lips. "I guess maybe I didn't want to give it up, either, so I said yes, and we kept going. We go every week. The guy gives us injections and has us do some tests for a while and then we go grocery shopping and come back home. We've been living like that ever since. We couldn't take the weird vibe people were reflecting back at us in the dorms so we found a cheap rental in a neighborhood where we thought nobody would care and we moved in and kept to ourselves. We haven't been to class in weeks. Mom is going to *kill* us. We haven't told her yet."

I grimaced a little. All that crazy shit to deal with and he was still worried about his mom? He was a kid, just a kid, and some other kid had shot him full of gods knew what.

And, of course, used it on himself.

"Was the guy named Joffrey Hammerton? Blond, slim, good-looking?" I tried to describe how he was dressed the first time I'd seen him, before he stripped down and put on the El Diablo costume. I left off what else I thought: smooth as marble and defined like a dictionary.

"Yeah." He smiled a little. "Joffrey. He had us call him 'Doc Hammer,' like the guy who writes *Venture Brothers*? It was weird, but it made it easier to trust him with a needle in his hand." Adam hesitated. "And he was really, really cute."

I smiled for a moment.

"What vitamins did he tell you he was using?" The Bull's Eye's attention was fully on the kid for his answer. Delta Force get trained in the sciences, medicine, everything. Apparently it takes years. Some vampires pass the time by sitting around reading encyclopedias, cover to cover, whole sets one after the other, and they do things like that: turn out to know a ton about some unexpected subject or show a reasonable working knowledge of countless disciplines. It's sort of amusing in a bloodsucker. It's kind of freaky in a human.

"B-12. I know: we were stupid."

"Where do you meet him? Where do you go for the injections now?"

"This building next to Duke. It's... well, it's kind of hard to describe how to get there. It's in the woods. Sort of."

Damn, I was impressed: El Diablo was not only still working, he was doing it from a building right next to campus. Hell, with all those woods around, the thing might be *on* campus. I thought of the dormant old houses past which I'd walked the night I'd seen him: offices and other spaces waiting for the University to find something to do with them.

"You can show us on a Google map or something. Now, the real reason we're here: tell us about the vampire who visits you every night." I leaned forward to give that some emphasis, but the kid's eyes went wide for a moment and then shut like he had fallen asleep. He just sat there, frozen. The Bull's Eye looked at me for a second and I shook my head. I knew what that was, and this wouldn't be the first time I had broken it. I reached over, put my hands on the sides of the kid's jaw, swiveled his head towards me and said, with all the mystical oomph I could pack, all the hoodoo, everything, "*Tell me about the vampire who drinks from you.*"

All the lights in the room dimmed for just a second. Outside, the night got just a smidgen darker and one of the streetlights down the block popped and went out. I hoped the neighborhood kids stayed up for this once we went into the house itself. I'd hate for them to miss a show.

I could feel him resisting – a reflex, something he didn't even know he was doing and was only doing because he had been trained by the interloper – so I pushed again. "*That vampire has no hold over you. Speak as a free man. We are your only hope for survival.*" Again the lights dimmed, flickering off for a few moments though that hardly affected me. The Bull's Eye had stopped staring at Adam long enough to glance around at the special effects, then turned her attention to me for a long second. Deep in his mind, somewhere near whatever it is that holds the seat of who we are, I felt another rebound as my command bounced off yet more preprogramming. I hated to do it, but I went for the first emotional switch that came to mind. "*If you do not tell us, he will take your brother and you will be alone.*"

Adam ground his teeth together for a few seconds and then the dam broke.

"His name is Dmitri and we are his favorites." Adam's voice came from somewhere high in his throat, straining, something barely surviving the trip up from his diaphragm. "He owns the house and rents it out. He says sometimes he cons someone into thinking they've bought the place, but the paperwork is all fake. He used to drain whoever lived here and rent it out again but he says he's going to keep us here forever. He says we taste the best. He says we make him stronger."

There was more in there; he just didn't want to say whatever it was. I leaned in. "*Keep talking.*" This time I just needed to encourage; I hadn't needed to break down the mental blocks like before. Shadows writhed in the corners of the room, but it was a lot less intense this time. I felt his inhibitions drop much more easily. I let go of his head and sat back a little. I realized abruptly that The Bull's Eye had been holding her breath and now she let it out very slowly.

Adam spoke in a drone. "He says he's lived in the Triangle for nearly a year but he owned the house longer than that." The kid shuddered suddenly, blinked a few tears away and then looked from me to The Bull's Eye. He was empty of information and my commands were already losing their grip. The preprogramming the interloper – Dmitri – had done was starting to reassert itself after only seconds. He was powerful.

It occurred to me he was probably very old.

Adam finished, looking me in the eye, with, "You can't let him take my brother away."

"We won't," The Bull's Eye said. I absolutely believed her, and so did Adam.

"Is your brother..." I cleared my throat. "Is your brother, well, *into* it?" If I'd had a heartbeat I would have blushed.

Adam looked down for a few seconds.

I went on. "There's nothing necessarily wrong with that.

"Scott likes it." Adam licked his lips, looking very pale.

I cleared my throat and tried to sound gentle. "I'm not trying to pry, I'm just saying neither of you did anything wrong. Hell of a way to come out of the closet, yeah, but it's not your fault you're being taken advantage of. He's doing something we're not supposed to do." I stopped and drew a breath. "The things we do, some of them feed the person and some of them feed the *monster* we've all got deep down inside, and what he's doing is the kind of thing the monster likes. It likes to debase a human: to shame them and torture them and make them suffer. Feed it enough of what it wants and it takes over. We're not all psychopaths and it isn't your fault you happened to get caught up in the craziness of someone who is. It's not your fault you're victims, and it's not your fault if you or he like it sometimes. It's never too late to say no, to stand up for yourself, and I will absolutely put a stop to this."

"'We'." Adam's voice was very dead, but he almost met my eyes. "You burst into our home and attacked us and you want me to believe you're the 'nice' one."

I shrugged. I had no good answer. We do what we have to do in order to survive. It's all relative. "Does he warn you before he gets here or does he just show up?"

Adam's gaze wandered back to the floor. "He doesn't have to call. We know his approach." He mumbled the last, finally falling silent and still. His chest rose, but almost like he was asleep.

The Bull's Eye looked over and mouthed, silently and slowly, "Mild shock."

I sighed. By my watch, Dmitri was due to show up in roughly a couple of hours. We had to kill him the very moment he arrived.

had wanted to put Scott and Adam safely away in the attic. I could hoodoo them both asleep so deeply they'd snooze right through any craziness that might happen while the rest of us did our work and, just maybe, I wouldn't be able to smell them from there. No dice: Adam snapped out of it eventually and after that he wouldn't hear of it. He wanted to help. He said he would rather fight for their freedom and I respected him for that. It did occur to me they might be useful combatants given they were now "extra" but I had no idea for how many scenarios Dmitri had accounted in his programming. For all I knew, the kids would switch sides in the middle of the fight. The Bull's Eye came up with our eventual compromise: Scott and Adam would be chained to a structural support pillar in the middle of the kitchen. They wouldn't be able to break free – we hoped – but they could warn us of Dmitri's approach.

We brought Scott into the living room, where I slapped him awake so he and I could go at it for a while inside his head. He wasn't as willing to let go of the experiences he'd had with Dmitri and I knew there had been a point when he had stopped considering himself victimized and started considering himself a willing, consenting participant. I don't claim to understand the complicated boundaries of the ethics of desire, so I didn't take away from him the parts of his Dmitri programming he clearly wanted to keep. Stockholm Syndrome, maybe, but who am I to decide what a body is allowed to like? It was tricky, but I had to try to build in him a sense of the larger context: he was going to be killed by this, sooner or later, and in the meantime it was driving his brother mad. That was what worked, in the end: that sense of having a responsibility to someone other than himself. It was slow-going and it took me the better part of thirty minutes. The things we can do to a human mind are usually imprecise and hurried. There's a lot of "forget I was here" or "remember that we had a great time making out before I left" or maybe "drive home and remember only that you stopped to help someone on the side of the road". We don't get a lot of chances to practice subtle manipulations or memory engineering. That stuff is delicate work and it's never truly permanent. Lots of people turn up every year with what's called "missing time": an hour or three that's just gone from their memory. Often as not, they decide aliens abducted them. We vampires are perfectly happy to leave them be.

Once Scott was allowed to remember what it had been like at first – the horrific pain of having one's neck literally torn open, healed with a clammy lick when the vampire got done with him; the hangover that wouldn't go away; the shame of being assaulted and getting off on it; the humiliation he felt when Dmitri callously turned that shame against him and used it to demand silence, to demand access to his brother, to demand loyalty – then he was willing to sign up to help. After that we let them spend a few minutes in the kitchen just sitting beside each other in silence. They had a lot to work out, the way I figured it.

Plus, it gave me a chance to talk to The Bull's Eye alone while Roderick and Jennifer and Smiles and Dog waited outside.

"So," I said, "There is something we need to talk about."

"Just one something?" The Bull's Eye was so damned hard to read. The training to mask everything must be good. I knew some vampires who could have used that.

"Probably not, but there's something that's just come up."

She nodded, made a little *mm* sound that seemed to indicate to go on.

"It's... well, it's hard to explain. I've been mucking around in these kids' heads and something isn't right in there, something beyond the obvious 'no shit, Sherlock' kind of stuff they've got going on." I drew a breath. "Whenever we fiddle with someone's mind, it's like..." I was grasping at straws. I'd never had to explain this to anyone. Vampires who can do it just *know*, like a baby knows crying. "It's like trying to mash the buttons on an ATM that's buried a foot deep in oatmeal. No, it's not that simple. It's like trying to work a light switch under a foot of oatmeal. We kind of have to dip into this weird place, stick our hand in, feel around in a hurry, flick the switch the right way and go. There isn't a lot of time to look around and take notice, but that's okay because more immediate memories are the things we're usually trying to block – don't look at me like that, the truth is the truth – and they're new and firm and fresh. They're right there on top. They're as distinguishable from their surroundings as the metal faceplate of an electrical switch is from oatmeal."

The Bull's Eye didn't say anything for a moment, so I started to take another breath before she cut me off. "If you ever do that to me I'll kill you."

"I have no doubt of that. Wouldn't dream of it, scout's honor."

"You were not a boy scout."

"You're right, but I am absolutely sincere."

She considered for a moment then said, "Go on."

"So, these kids? The…" I searched around. "The faceplates are falling apart and the oatmeal is going bad." I worked my jaw and then finally said, "It's not this Dmitri guy fucking with them, either. I know what it feels like when a human mind has been rearranged too many times by one of us. It starts to go sort of blank and smooth. It's hard to describe, but it's not *this*. These feel like it feels when dementia is setting in. If I were doing this blind, I'd say they were late-stage Alzheimer's patients. Everything sort of starts to turn into undifferentiated mush." I shrugged at her. "I'm sorry, I don't have a metaphor. It would be like trying to explain how to hear sounds. Just trust me, we know this stuff – *I* know this stuff – and there's something bad wrong with these kids' brains."

"Is it going to get worse?"

"I have no idea. I'm sure as hell no neurosurgeon." I sighed a little. "I should put that on my door: Withrow, comma, No Neurosurgeon For Nearly One Hundred Years." I smiled. She didn't.

"Duly noted," she said, "And now, for the attack plan?"

"I figure we're in the living room, you behind the door, me just inside it? He walks up, smells me and bursts in – or he doesn't, and he just rings the doorbell – and in either case we attack as soon as he's inside. Jennifer and Roderick come in with the hounds."

She made a snorfle noise, exhaling something that was half laugh and half sigh of pity. "No. I take a position in the trees outside, high up, so he won't notice me. You take a position in a back bedroom. If he can detect you, don't let him detect you on the other side of the door. The kids are in the kitchen.

We leave the door unlocked. He will knock, get no answer, get curious and come inside."

"That would make me too wary. I think I'd just leave."

"You don't feel a sense of ownership over both the place and its occupants." She waved a finger, instructive in tone and body language. "He'll be wary, but he'll be lured inside. I begin my approach to the house, blocking his retreat. You attack from the front, I attack from the rear, and Jennifer and Roderick come in from either side. We box him in, flanked on all sides, easy takedown."

I said I liked it. She didn't smile in reply, but she did say, in a sharp way that made me think she was pissed at me until I realized it's probably how she said it in the service, "Thanks."

"If we do that, it's going to be easier for you to stake him," I said. She blinked at me, but I went on. "If you're coming at him from behind, he's got fewer ways to stop you. He can't grab it and aim it away or take it in the shoulder or something."

"We have to... like, with a wooden *stake?*"

"Then we finish him off."

"How are you going to do that?"

"The rest of us are going to beat the hell out of him to distract him, at first, but as soon as he's got the stake in him it's easy: I drain him of everything he's got."

"Cannibalism?"

"Self-defense." I left off that it would also be a form of research. "We tend to be our own best auto-immune system," I said. "Let us kill our own the way we know works."

She thought about that for a second before nodding, but her expression said she hated having to accept that. "Will it traumatize the boys?"

I waved that off. "Nah. Once he's dead his hold over them will break." In truth I expected it to be rougher than that made it sound, but now was not the time for unkind eventualities.

The great danger we present to ourselves – vampires, I mean – is that we are creatures of habit. I'm sure Dmitri was wary for a night or two after his

173

first run-in with The Bull's Eye but he probably got comfortable again as soon as Scott creamed his shorts on command. People fall back into bad habits like they're getting paid time and a half. The worse the habit, the easier it is to backslide.

Around one in the morning, Scott and Adam started moaning, low, from the kitchen. Thirty minutes later, they cried out in wordless agony: so much for subtlety. Their master had arrived.

Dmitri strolled right up the gate – hidden in a back room, I could hear him on the front steps – and even though he stopped at the door and sniffed audibly, he walked inside. He didn't bother with the doorbell, and I had figured he wouldn't. He could smell me, and he knew the jig was up.

Dmitri was confident enough to stroll inside with his hands in his pockets. "I know you are here," he called out.

I decided to match his casual stance, emerging from the bedroom slinging a yo-yo up and down its string, casual as the cat in a canary store.

Scott and Adam stopped wailing and started grunting like pigs in a field full of truffles.

"I smelled you a block away," Dmitri said. His voice was gravelly. He was pissed. He sounded like in life maybe he'd hit the whiskey and the smokes a little too hard, but it was emphasized by his emotional state. I was the intruder, now, and who the fuck was I, anyway? I could read all that, right on the surface, right away. Hell, that was probably half of why the kids up and down the street had noticed him at all: not a lot of sheet-white guys walked down their street acting like they owned the place.

I am also a creature of habit, which meant there were formalities to observe. I had to give him one chance. I spoke, and as I did I could see The Bull's Eye drop from a tree in the front yard in utter silence. I didn't hear her at all, so there was a decent chance Dmitri didn't, either. "My name is Withrow Surrett," I said, voice even and quiet. "I am the boss of these parts, and you've been here for a year without identifying yourself to me. I consider that a crime in my territory. Are you willing to submit to my authority and the behavioral requirements that come with it?"

He smiled. I could see only a silhouette of his face but from the movement of one cheek muscle I could tell he had, more accurately, sneered. He seemed to be dressed in a collared shirt and jeans and loafers. No jacket, and it was getting cold enough as time hurtled towards Halloween that he was pushing his luck just by being visibly unusual. I hated things like that, the little stuff stupid vampires do when they think what they *want* is to get noticed so they can blow off some steam killing whoever asks too many questions.

"I'll take that as a no," I said. "*Go!*"

Time slowed to a crawl, like everything had just dived into a bowl of gelatin, and Jennifer and Roderick burst out of the rooms on either side as Dmitri and I met in the middle. I could see The Bull's Eye bounding up the front walk with the sharpened tip of a broom handle in her hands like a javelin thrower in an instant replay. I guessed she was four steps away from being broom handle length from Dmitri, and at the speed he, Roderick and I were moving it would take me, everything we had to keep Dmitri busy that long.

Jennifer and Roderick came in swinging, her fists angling in slow motion, as did Roderick's. Dmitri dodged it effortlessly, but he didn't realize Roderick was feigning. His other hand came up at proper vampire speed to slam home an upper-cut and shove Dmitri back into the path of Jennifer's thrown punch. I saw pain on their faces as the blows landed, which is to be expected. Punching someone really does hurt if you don't do it just right. I twisted on one foot, the other coming up to plant a boot heel sharply in Dmitri's stomach. That was supposed to knock his feet out from under him but just like Scott he was too strong for me. Each arm shot straight out by his sides to hammer Jennifer and Roderick in the chest and then he grabbed my foot and twisted so that I was lifted into the air and spun like a tree trunk at a log roll.

I went up, bounced off the ceiling and came back down on my face. I didn't let myself take a moment to hesitate, though, rolling against the momentum so that I spun backwards across the floor. Dmitri's boot came down where I would have been if I'd just let physics splay me out on the ground. I bounced up and dove, hands out, but he slapped my hands away much more easily than I would have expected. Jennifer was flying back against the end of the couch and Roderick was trying to recover from the punch to the sternum he'd taken. I stepped around to where Jennifer had been and drove my elbow hard into Dmitri's shoulder as Roderick, bounded forward, dropped to one knee and planted a fist in Dmitri's opposite hip. That was enough to knock the bastard sideways and tip him so I swung around to bring up a knee under the side of his head. He rebounded and Roderick gave everything he had to stand again in time to bring a knee of his own under the other side of Dmitri's head.

Ultimately, that's what vampire fights come down to: trying to addle the other one so hard you get time to debilitate him in some more permanent fashion.

The Bull's Eye had made it one and a half running steps closer to us by that point, so I raised my fist and brought it down on Dmitri's nose, as hard as I could, before he had a chance to get his balance back. It hurt me like hell but blood shot out from the middle of Dmitri's face and my fangs dropped as a reflex action. I raised my first again and brought it down again to the sound of a sick wet crunch. More blood, but all over my hand this time. Roderick joined in, kicking Dmitri in the gut over and over as I punched him five more times.

Jennifer had bounced off the end of the couch in slow motion and with human gracelessness rebounded towards us, hands out. She wasn't moving fast and she wasn't accustomed to precision work when it came to fist fights but she was able to get her hands in Dmitri's face, jabbing at his eyes and clawing at his skin. I tried to say something, to warn her, but I couldn't get the words out slowly enough for a human to understand. Dmitri's fangs tore into her flesh and blood arced out in bright crimson: across his face, across the floor, but luckily also into his eyes.

Jennifer, moving at a molasses pace, bore a look of determination I had never seen on a human's face. The Bull's Eye did this because she was protecting people but Jennifer, I suddenly realized, did this to kill a vampire. The two are very different and I knew in my heart of hearts this meant trouble down the road. No time to speak or think or deal with such things, though. Instead, taking inspiration from Jennifer, I reared back and jabbed Dmitri in the eyes just like an old Marx Brothers routine.

The Bull's Eye had taken that last couple of steps at long last. She kicked the door shut behind her, spun for momentum, aimed and drove the broom handle into the left side of Dmitri's back. He was already trying to stand and somehow had a knife. One of them shot out to stick in my left thigh and it hurt like hell. The other blade missed Roderick, who saw it in time and practically floated backwards out of its path. In the dim light I saw something light up for a moment around Roderick's neck: a cross on a chain, of all the things in the world to see at a time like this on a neck as sinful as his.

The attempted staking seemed to be taking for damn ever and I was worried Dmitri would move before The Bull's Eye could finish planting it. She grimaced with crawling effort before the broom broke the skin, then snagged again, but she had her full weight behind it, her face twisted with furious effort. It occurred to me this might not be the first time she had impaled someone on a broom handle because she certainly seemed to know how much the body tends to push back against that sort of thing. I heard a snap as a rib gave way and then, like a light going off, Dmitri's frantic scrabble to find a way to resist stopped and he dropped into the same molasses speed as The Bull's Eye.

One hilariously slowed-down thump later, The Bull's Eye stood over Dmitri's body with a broom handle connecting her hands with the region right under his left shoulder blade.

Scott and Adam fell into total silence. Everything was suddenly quiet.

I dropped into normal speed, mouth open to ask Roderick what exactly he was doing with a magic necklace – especially given I had gone out of my way not to tell him about that particular aspect of our time in Asheville together the year before – but instead I fell to one knee, myself. The knife blade in my other leg burned like fire. I yanked it out and threw it across the room.

"Alright," The Bull's Eye said to me. "Do your thing. Do it now. The three of you were a blur when I ran up here but you're panting and you got stabbed? I guess? So let's finish this and patch you up."

I checked myself. I was in fact panting. I don't have to breathe, but the muscle memory is strong. I bent over my own traumatized thigh. "*Fuck* but this hurts," I groaned.

Roderick pulled his sleeves down and straightened his shirt. "It is enchanted," he said. "Anti-vampire magic."

I growled at him, "How do you know about magic shit?"

He smiled a little. "There is plenty of it up in the mountains if you know where to look." His words were as coy as his expression. I didn't like this at all, and I wasn't even sure why and I couldn't think properly because my leg hurt so much. Roderick nodded at Dmitri's form. "You are going to need blood to heal that, Cousin." He nodded at Jennifer, "And you need first aid."

I looked down at Dmitri, then back up at everyone else. "Anybody who doesn't want to watch had better turn around," I said, then I snapped the broom handle in two with one hand and hoisted Dmitri into the air by hooking the other under one armpit. Old or new, we all only weigh as much as our collected flesh.

There was a knock at the door —three small raps – and we all fell silent.

The Bull's Eye, without making a sound, leaned against the peephole. Her jaw clenched as there was another knock at the door: three more small, almost apologetic raps of knuckles against wood with a pause between each just about the length of the average human heartbeat.

I looked at Roderick, whose eyes were closed and his hands out and open by his sides: he was pushing his senses out across the yard to try to figure out what the hell was going on. Jennifer was clutching her ripped-up hand to her chest, keeping it elevated, but she didn't give away anything like pain or discomfort.

The Bull's Eye turned and mouthed in silence, her index finger twirling in a circle to indicate a perimeter, "Surrounded."

I heard something heavy smash a window in the front as a foot – no bigger than a child's, and wearing the kind of shoes kids liked last year – kicked out the section of door we'd damaged when The Bull's Eye and I first arrived. Every window exploded inward, almost in unison, and I saw all manner of children in anonymous gray hooded sweatshirts reaching up, gripping jagged glass in bare hands. Their enormous eyes were as black as the new moon and they seemed impervious to pain as they sliced themselves to pieces, hauling their tiny bodies through the windows in a mass of rage.

Roderick and I both flipped on the super-speed and all those angry young bodies, their grasping, blood-smeared, tattered fingers, seemed to freeze in mid-air.

As they poured into the house in ultra-slow-motion I dragged Dmitri into the kitchen and leaning him against the counter in front of the kitchen sink. Adam and Scott strained at their chains in near-frozen tableau. Their eyes rolled with incomprehension and their voices were like bellowing low brass. The parts of them screaming and sobbing were not the thinking, talking parts: they were the blood and the veins and the bodies from which Dmitri had stolen so many times they'd gotten used to it.

A black-eyed kid was pushing her own pale forehead through the window over the sink, one millimeter at a time. In the percentage of a fraction of a second I considered her, one word sprang to mind: Steeplechasers. *Zombies.* These were not the zombies I had put down by the dozen in my neighborhood all those years ago and they were not the all-consuming hive mind constructed from collective *id* Jennifer and I had faced after that, but neither was this girl a human being. Her teeth, bared in rage, were those of a mortal but her eyes were sharp shards of obsidian staring out at a world that did not interest her. If the first zombies embodied chaos and the second type were hunger, these were calculated, calibrated rage. They might not all be the exact same kind of thing in a textbook sense but the way she pursued some violent and alien agenda encrypted against normal comprehension was exactly the same.

I guessed I had less than a second of "normal" time to spare.

I bared my fangs, did the classic vampire hiss – some things we do because we just have to do them when there's an audience present – and said, "Dmitri, I do not know your origin but I do know your end. May you be a lesson to the rest of my domain." The security light in the back yard crackled and went out. I wasn't just saying it to sound good; I was saying it because I think saying that sort of thing aloud really might do *something*: something mystical, I guess. I don't know what, or how to explain why I think that. There was also a more practical reason. It might sound melodramatic in the moment, yes, but there are some things we must say to remind ourselves of why we do things and why we *don't.* Protocols have to be observed in our greetings and in our final partings, too.

I sank my teeth into pale, papery flesh and Dmitri's life filled me up like light in a dark room.

Blood is full of a lot of things. Besides the chemical properties, the things we can taste right away – vegetarian; not a vegetarian; diabetic – we also get a part of who they are. I'm not big on the mystical-istical hoo-hah kind of stuff, in terms of laying it all out and putting together complicated and specific beliefs about the metaphysics of how it works. It's enough for me to know when we drink someone's blood we get some of what they've experienced: emotions, memories, what they're thinking at that moment. This guy was mostly thinking a variety pack containing different flavors of *oh shit this cannot be happening* and as his life passed before his eyes it did mine, as well until, like the last dregs of wine from a bottle, the final spark of whatever had been Dmitri passed into me, activating my own Last Gasp power.

Everything in the little kitchen went dark and the life of Dmitri Chabon Miasnik Miledok, born 1637 in a village on the Ukrainian Steppe, exploded in my vision like a firework of ice.

In such moments, I have the opportunity to pick one topic from my victim's life and learn everything there is to know about it: everything known to them and sometimes, unpredictably, things known by others but *not* to them. It's a way to crack open a volume of truth on one topic and consume it all at once. I have no control after I pick the topic: I have a moment to choose and then I simply get taken for a ride.

Floating before me – for lack of a better way to describe it – were the countless topics contained in any life. I could get a sense of any of them if I lingered too long but all this happens in the space between two seconds and I have only the barest ability to comprehend what I see. I had a brief flash of an absurdly beautiful woman, way out of his league, approaching him at something like a bar: a lot of working men in a dark room with a fire and a couple of candles and mugs of booze to keep them warm in some endless winter night. The men all knew who she was – she was the wife of some local warlord – but she went straight to Dmitri to make him an offer.

She said Dmitri would live forever and be rich, but instead he was lonely and more or less permanently enslaved. She turned him into a vampire so he could be her pet thug, not some equal or lover or even really to pay him a compliment. He was a brute and she wanted a brute so she took him. No less a serf than before, he had killed her two years after she turned him. It had been messy and taken forever and he had hated it so much that he set out to kill a *lot* to try to get himself used to it and to vent the hatred he felt for everyone who was alive, everyone still able to go out in the sun. Dmitri had never had much in the way of aspiration but now he longed for the thrill of seeing such hopes shudder and fade in the dark eyes of a dying victim.

That's what's hardest for many of us: the simple eternity of self. There are a lot of vampiric failures, a lot of people who decide to watch just one more extremely warm sunrise at some point in their first decade. They get stuck being who they were when they were turned and they didn't actually like being that person in the first place. I mean, a desire to escape is why they took the Big Flush, right? As I said, people are creatures of habit and we undead, theoretically immortal, are creatures of habit times a million. We turn into anachronisms all too quickly in the twentieth – sorry, the twenty-first – century. The first time prey looks at one of us oddly because of our dated slang or the unfashionable clothes we wear to hunt, whatever gives us away as not being from the *now*, all too often there's this little internal clock that starts silently counting down to the night when that one of us just can't take it anymore. It's a make or break moment in the gamble for eternity. We feel it when it happens whether we survive it or not.

For me, it was the 1960's. At first I just couldn't handle hippies. I figured it was them or me, basically, but my maker told me if I simply let time pass – and who has more time than a vampire, anyway – it would, in fact, be *me* who won out. She told me they were a fashion that would wane. Hippies aren't gone, of course, and I don't feel the need to kill them on sight – they can be perfectly nice people taken one at a time – but the whole psychedelia thing did turn out to be a phase, another step in a cycle of fads that come and go. With patience I was able to wait for something new to come along and see if I liked it better.

I haven't loved any particular era that's come since then but I have loved being here for them. That's the important thing. I feel like I made it over that hurdle into being more or less capable of keeping up. Now I plan to be the vampire who finds out whether immortality is for real. If I have my way, the day the sun finally fries this planet to a crisp I intend to be halfway around the world, in the middle of wherever it's night at the time, drinking the blood of the last human being.

This guy, though? His unlife hadn't been nearly as interesting as I planned mine to be and he hadn't been nearly as patient. Dmitri was unhappy and he took what small pleasure he could find in turning people into pets and torturing them to death. He thought of it as more than simple feeding: this was cultivation. Rather than the simple pursuit of sustenance, he played feeding like a game of anguish he would always win. The suffering he inflicted had been cold leftovers compared to the warmth of being alive but it had been enough because he could imagine no better alternative. He spent his life as a man in a society that offered no options, no upgrades, and his mind was not up to the task of envisioning something better than that. There was the life he knew or there was death. There was no coloring outside those lines.

Dmitri settled into that dreary, one-way street of a life, drifting along in a society of vampires who mostly interacted with him to assert their higher station. For his part, he sought and found opportunities to demonstrate his own superiority over the herd of seemingly endless humanity. He spent centuries moving from one place to another, eventually chased away by turmoil or the boredom of triumph. This did not mark him as a failure as a vampire the way it would now. Rather, by the standards of the ones who were alive already when he was turned, he was a complete success. His capacity to stave off boredom through the obsessive, repetitive pursuit of one or another mortal life was not a coping mechanism. It was the *point*. He may have found himself no more capable of altering his relative social station as a vampire than he was as a man, but at least he was no longer the lowest rung on the total social ladder. He was taught to fear vampires older than he but at least there were people – humans – who in turn would fear him.

Little changed for him until the nineteenth century drew to a close.

That was what caught the attention of my soul's eye. I realized inherently, in some silent and unknowable way afforded by the Last Gasp, the specific topic of what had happened to him a dozen decades ago was also intricately tied to whatever was going on now. In a strange, innate sense I knew whatever had brought him here was directly connected to Jennifer and to Roderick and to me. I had to know that, and as I observed the dissolution of the rest of the pathetic diagram of pain and pleasure he had called a life, I fell forward into that bright, shining star in the galaxy of his life.

Chapter 15

In 1893, vampires rebelled against their masters.

Dmitri didn't have particulars as to why, but he knew the elders whom he served for centuries, patiently sycophantic in hopes they would one night allow him to sit at the grownups' table, were almost entirely wiped out in a matter of months by their youngest, weakest spawn. That year was a big year: the Colombian Exposition, rebellions, assassinations and popular uprisings all over the world. Dmitri loathed the weakness of humankind and he equally abhorred the ingratitude – the uppitiness, I'd call it – of unworthy young vampires choosing to eliminate their betters so they could steal the night for themselves.

Of course, he was also a bully and all bullies are cowards. Dmitri sucked up to his bosses by killing a few young vampires to show some team spirit but by the standards of time as perceived by most of the really old bastards, the war was over before it started. Elders had been reduced to a hidden remnant in the blink of an eye. Accustomed to isolation and unchallenged authority over their own precious little fiefdoms, they were driven to unite in the end. None of them could win the war on their own and by the time they were talking to one another they couldn't manage to win it together, either. Desperate for an exit plan other than death, the elders huddled up and started brainstorming. In the end, they went with the one idea they liked least: a deal with an actual self-described devil. He told them he couldn't win them the war but he could give them the power to survive it.

It beat nothing, so in 1909 they signed the dotted line.

The demon didn't want much: just an agreement. The agreement didn't even specify they had to do it favors. It just wanted them to *agree*. Dmitri didn't understand why it would want so little, but Dmitri was not an imaginative man. I wondered if the entity with whom they cut these deals had simply gotten its kicks on making a bunch of ancient horrors kiss its proverbial pinky ring or if things were more complicated: maybe it was offering them survival in hopes they would try to bargain up to victory, for instance? I couldn't find that out because Dmitri didn't know it and it wasn't one of those flashes of insight my Last Gasp delivers from beyond the ken of my actual victim.

Uncertain and concealing their nervousness behind a curtain of overt cruelty towards those sad little lapdogs still left to them – such as Dmitri – the elders convened an overwrought, fright-fest ritual straight out of the imaginations of every Satanic Panic picture of the 1980's: human sacrifice, intoned Latin-ish, the works. Everything the devil they knew suggested to them, they did. When they were done, he appeared in a puff of angry yellow smoke and made them a smiling deal: they could be forgotten, raise new minions and escape their certain defeat. He would introduce on those ancient vampires' behalf just enough circumstantial evidence and whispered rumors to get the kids to settle into a complacent sense of victory. This particular devil would cover their tracks, throw still-hunting rebels off the scent and anything else necessary to let his clients retreat into the mists of memory and terrible lore. He assured them the world, changing more rapidly than they could comprehend into one you or I might recognize as modern, was not devoid of places for them.

Even electric light casts a shadow, the demon said to them.

Dmitri loved a cheesy line like that. He loved the way the demon appealed to the worst parts of him. Dmitri loved the play-acted cruelty, the parade of suffering dished out to screaming mortals. The ancients and the spawn still loyal to them gathered one more round of victims and props in some abandoned country church bereft of mortal attention, dressed it up like an after-Halloween clearance sale and let 'er rip. Dmitri joined in with abandon. At the climax of it all, the demon told them his services required only one more tiny thing he'd failed to mention: they had to drink *his* blood.

Vampires had been using blood to lord themselves over victims as far back as anyone could remember. Some loved this idea of upgrading to demon blood for a night. Others feared it would enthrall them the way they – and I – could make dogs into hellhounds by feeding them a little blood at a time until they had been changed into something else, something perceptibly obedient and vicious but more or less still the same in appearance. The demon won over those who hesitated by offering a bonus to sweeten the deal: new powers beyond what their state or the Last Gasp already gave them. Always calculating, always playing the margins, the doubters were convinced they could eventually wrest some victory over the young in future nights. A couple of new tricks, a little breathing room and enough time for the victors to grow confident, they figured, and they could come roaring back when the kids least expected it.

The elders all lined up, drank deep and plunged backwards into the still, dark waters of forgotten threats. Dmitri found the new powers he received were something less than he had hoped for, but useful all the same. His Last Gasp had always allowed him to command for one night the corpus of a victim he killed. After signing and taking a sip of a devil's blood, those bodies would stay active for months at a time and he could have several of them. They weren't enough to form an army but they were plenty to make a gang and he liked that idea. They were just like Steeplechase zombies with one important exception: he could tell them what to do and they only looked a little bit dead instead of all the way.

The demon arranging all this was, of course, the one who introduced himself to me as Ross.

Over time, most of the elders who survived were hunted down despite the demon's assurances and all those papier-mâché atrocities. Several members of the youthful rebellion stayed active, obsessed with eliminating all the ones they remembered. Some elders survived, however, so they ultimately saw the reduction of their own competition as a net gain. Vampires make the best selfish bastards. If you think some entirely mortal and mundane adherent of Ayn Rand decked out in driving moccasins and a club tie is good at ginning up justifications for their own privilege, let me assure you: you ain't seen nothin'.

The survivors worried, though. The world changed ever faster. They became worse and worse at adapting to it. The youthful vampires who rebelled against them were not themselves so young anymore but they still had much greater capacity to cope with modernity. Even if all the elders were forever forgotten, how could they be sure they would also persist in that obscurity? For that matter, why should persistence be enough? Those with wide vicious streaks and short memories – such as Dmitri – eventually found themselves wondering if the demon could help them restart the war at some future date.

To really put up a fight, they knew, they would need to balance the numbers: make more of themselves or eliminate some of the kids. New vampires they made themselves tended to pull on the leash too hard, too early. Human society had lost its penchant for obsequiousness. Recent mortals were unsuited to service. The elders were hesitant to take on the young: they predated the notion of surgical strikes and they lacked the skills to perform their own assassinations. They were accustomed to command, not to having to do the heavy lifting on their own. Some elders wanted to recruit young vampires to their cause, but that never went anywhere, either. They picked up a few promising prospects in the 1950's and 1980's, but they were babies compared to the vampires they would have to face.

Then someone asked Ross what seemed impossible: could they ever bring *back* any of the vampires the rebellion had destroyed?

Ross was only too happy to answer in the semi-affirmative. Gathered together again and dressed for a performance of the Satanic Tabernacle Choir, Ross led them through the magical "logic" such as it was: vampires were already familiar with the basic magic of blood, the act of stealing it to sustain themselves. In that scenario, the life of mortals sustained and preserved the life of the vampire. When vampires were made, the ritual called for the death of the candidate and their restoration to life through a vampire's own blood.

If the goal were to sustain the dead, to reach into the mechanism of time and mortality and bring back something not alive, they would need to think along the same lines. If a sacrificed life could be transmuted into endless life, they might achieve endless death by sacrificing the dead. It hadn't made sense to the vampires who asked, but the demon refused to explain more. He simply insisted that with the right rituals and sacrifices – oh, so very many sacrifices – they could bring back one of their own. It wouldn't matter that one or another of their ungrateful spawn had shoved that dead elder out the airlock of this immortal coil.

Life, Ross had said to them, *Has a kind of power. You feel it when you drink their blood. It sustains you now. Trust me when I say death generates a reflection of that. Life and death are simply perpendicular threads in the tapestry of energies.* All the vampires had to do to get access to that kind of magic was promise to do Ross a few favors at some later date. He didn't specify what those might be.

The elders were too desperate to ask. Instead, they did what he said. The ancients, silly though they felt, gathered in some Southern countryside near the place where one of their own had been destroyed some years before. There they made the right noises to go with the prescribed desecrations and debased acts. They wanted one of their biggest, baddest guns: a vampire who had been one of the most terrifying and the most powerful. They had already mortgaged their fates to a demon, made one promise after another, and gotten what seemed like jack squat for it. They might as well get back an ancient vampire likely to assert her authority over them. In the best-case scenario that would get them a powerhouse combatant and commander stuck holding the check on all this diabolical jazz.

Oh, Ross asked later, *Did I mention there might be side effects? Hard to predict in advance what those might be. There's really only one way to find out.* The vampires all thought the other shoe had finally dropped when Ross asked them for "favors" but they were wrong. The dark threat of owing favors to an unpredictable, deceitful and alien entity couldn't just be enough for them, could it? Even the strings came with strings attached.

The vampires distracted themselves from this new reason to worry by focusing on the fact the ritual worked. Well, it *technically* worked and I suspect that's how it is with most things involving deals with the devil. The vampire they wanted brought back was returned to physical form but mindless. It was all appetite, no smarts. I told you once that vampires are the ultimate preservation of self: the concentrated experience of an individual preserved in a shell they hope is permanent. It appeared all that comprehension and perspective and the shell containing them were not necessarily inherently linked because the elders seemed to have gotten one without the other: an enormously powerful and ravenous vampire who couldn't so much as count its own toes. On the plus side, she was strong as all hell and could take down just about anything they threw in front of her. Like trying to buy a pistol and being handed a Davy Crockett M-28 tactical nuke gun instead, the elders knew they had something they could use to eliminate plenty of their hated enemies if they could just figure out how to aim the damned thing.

While they were trying to keep a lid on their newest reacquisition, Jennifer McCordy and I were dealing with the side effect Ross had so casually mentioned. Resurrecting one dead thing created echoes. That mystical spillover effect was more pronounced the more powerful and ancient their target. Call up a dead flunky and get one night of *Pet Sematary*. Call up an ancient horror of unimaginable power and you trigger a Steeplechase Event just like the ones Jennifer and I fought in our respective towns: the dead rise and start stumbling around the neighborhood until someone sufficiently brave or foolish has to stop them.

Calling out to one spectacular example of the dead had simply rung a great big mystical dinner bell for every dead thing within the supernatural equivalent of earshot.

A cabal of ancient vampires, faithful remnant of a world itself long thought dead and buried, had created zombies by accident, then kept their heads down while everyone else tried to clean up their mess. Upon consideration, what did they care if people suffered and died? As far as they were concerned, collateral damage and an increased air of fearful superstition were just so many sprinkles on top of their return-to-power sundae. What mattered most was to remain undetected by their own subsequent generations of vampires: the youth who overthrew them and the offspring of those rebels.

I marveled again at the ancients' inability to grasp the world of the living. In their arrogant certainty they had assumed humanity would be cowed by the supernatural rearing its head in their lives. They weren't checked in enough to figure out humanity had turned the world of lurking monsters and shadow-draped old manses into a game they could play with their kids on Halloween. People were surprised to see the real thing show up on their doorstep, sure, but they were over it within a day. In their infinite capacity to adjust to new circumstances, humanity legislated around the problem and went about their blissfully ignorant business.

If the world's failure to cower over-long had surprised Dmitri, he'd been even more surprised by the arrival of a clue a few years later. At the end of a complex trail of breadcrumbs and half-rumors, he learned a champion of the young lived in Raleigh, North Carolina, and might make a good target if Dmitri wanted to score a few points with his superiors or thumb his nose at the rebels. Dmitri planned straight away to set up a little base and start gathering information. The demon with which he'd done dealings was only too happy to help. Ross recommended the Bull City. He was certain Dmitri would find something interesting there.

Three things stood out to me in all of this.

First, this – El Diablo and Dmitri and the wonder twin Duke kids, the whole shebang – was too much to be coincidence. Ross must have been behind El Diablo, too.

Second, I wondered if this explained Roderick's lust for destroying demons. Was he aware of the rebellion? How had he found out? Was the camaraderie and closeness enjoyed by the vampires of Seattle such that their offspring were in on the secret?

Third, I was just as certain as could be, way down in the pit of my stomach, that I had seen Seth, my infinitely wise and patient second-in-command, among the glimpses of ancient vampires Dmitri had encountered in his time among the establishment.

As always, the world went dark when the book of Dmitri's life closed on the topic I had chosen and my eyes snapped open on reality. Time was still crawling as I drew out the last, panicked part of Dmitri, psychically kicking and screaming in the face of his own death. Half a dozen kids in identical gray hoodies were smashing through exploding windows at a snail's pace all around us as Dmitri exploded into ash, the broom handle clattering to the floor, and my heft fell forward against the counter.

I turned and spat a mouthful of blood onto the floor, unwilling to consume the dregs of that monster. Like an apple washed in pesticides its whole life, I was not about to let whatever dark energy may have infested him get a chance to do the same to me. That last spatter of him slapped the floor with a wet smack and hissed away to ash and smoke with the rest of all that was left. There's a difference between food and trash. I don't eat the latter when I can avoid it.

The Last Gasp usually knocks me out cold for a second after it ends so, struggling to stand upright I turned to Roderick and, shouting, slurring, managed to get out, "There's a war. Christ in a Cadillac, there's a war and we don't even know. The old vampires are coming back. These kids are Dmitri's

Last Gasp. They're what happens to the people he eats. The old guys made zombies happen in the first place."

That wasn't all his blood had held, though. Coursing through it like a different shade of stone in a block of marble or like copper wire through the wall of a home, electric and invisible and powerful beyond belief, there was this *thing*. I knew it had to be whatever El Diablo had been shooting the kids with. It was like fire. It was like lava moving through the earth. I felt so *alive*. I felt power like I had never known before: I don't mean an expansion of the strength I knew, but rather a different quality of power. This was color and light and ambition. It was everything it means to be alive and vibrant and to have hopes and dreams. It was everything it means to be a human being: want, desire, need, lust, energy, restlessness, exhaustion, warmth and hate. No wonder Dmitri had farmed these twin super-kids. The pairing of his endless thirst for the end of others' ambition and the deep well of ambitious life they offered him was too perfect to be coincidence.

Rather than black out with the end of the Last Gasp, I bounced onto my feet. I was alert and awake and more capable of energetic violence than I'd ever been in my entire life. Roderick eyed me up and down as the kids in hoodies made it another half-inch through the windows and the shattering front door – The Bull's Eye and Jennifer were moving just as slowly, only now starting to react – but it wasn't enough to me just to fight them and win and be done. Roderick smirked at something he saw in my expression and said, "Let's do this the old-fashioned way. It'll be more fun."

We both shut off our super-speed at once. Shattering glass sprayed through the air all around us as Adam and Scott's voices dropped from low brass to high-pitched wailing. The kids in the hoodies roared in horrible unison. The Bull's Eye and Jennifer and Roderick and I set to work, the former two hesitating for a moment while Roderick and I dove into the fight with abandon.

The kids – no, the *revenants* – were more skilled combatants than teens and tweens should have been, sure, but they were still kids. On their own they would have been no match for someone who knew what they were doing. Their strength was the way they fought in unison. They had us surrounded and, mouths gaping, voices keening one long, unbroken minor chord, hands up and clenched like claws, they scampered into position and began a dreadfully slow advance. The four of us stood back to back. I heard Roderick crack all the knuckles in his hands and it spread around the other three of us like a social disease.

"Are we really about to fight a bunch of kids?" Jennifer's voice didn't shake, but she was bothered. This was not the sort of fight she'd had in mind. Her wrist was still torn open from Dmitri's bite. She was holding it high, pressed against her opposite shoulder, but she had a lamp in her good hand to swing like a club.

"No, we're going to put them back in their graves." I growled it out between my fangs, which descended by reflex.

The Bull's Eye and Roderick were both totally silent as we and the kids turned in opposed circles, sizing each other up.

"Zombies?" That was apparently all Jennifer's mind needed to register. Lightning fast, she lunged with the lamp, the kids in front of her dove forward and the rest of us set on anything that moved.

I put my fist through the forehead of one walking dead in front of me while another latched onto the sleeve of my jacket with its teeth. I twisted, putting one foot in its gut and punting it so it smashed through the ceiling. Roderick grabbed one by the belt loops, spun it and brought it down to drive its head through the floorboards, or maybe to drive the floorboards through its head. Jennifer put the light bulb of the lamp through the chest of one, snapped the stem with a twist and stabbed another through the neck.

That left one, whom The Bull's Eye had not (re-)killed. Instead, she was holding it in a headlock. She had it off the ground, its throat caught in her elbow. Its leaden eyes were unblinking as its jaw worked and it hissed what would probably have been a scream if she hadn't already crushed its windpipe. It wasn't destroyed, though, and neither could it kick her hard enough to make her let go. She stood there, panting, having spun it and disabled it with the muscle memory of years of training, and her own eyes were in a far away place: somewhere I'd never go because I'd never been there once already.

I thought of that look in Jennifer's eyes when the "zombies" happened on Thanksgiving night, when she waded into a vast melee with nothing but an aluminum bat and a bad case of shell shock.

Roderick tossed aside the corpse of his opponent and straightened his jacket, dusting it off. Jennifer, breathing hard, hefted the lamp back to take a stab at the one in The Bull's Eye's hands.

I stopped and made a fist, ready to finish it off for her.

The Bull's Eye didn't look at us – not at me, certainly not at Roderick and, though she hesitated, not at Jennifer. Instead, she closed her eyes, staring at a landscape from long ago. "Is there any way to save it," she said. She phrased it as a question but her voice was flat: she already knew the answer.

Dmitri's last pet zombie continued to struggle. Adam and Scott had stopped screaming, their voices finally exhausted. Silence fell all around us except for the clack of a dead child's teeth banging against one another as it tried, furiously, to find something it could grind between them.

"You never fought a Steeplechase, did you?" I tried to ask it gently, but I was still humming with the last of Dmitri's blood, drenched as it was in super-serum. I sounded excited and impatient.

"I've seen – " but there The Bull's Eye interrupted herself. "No," she said, answering the question. "No, I have not."

"But you have seen children die," Roderick purred. He said it in a low, almost hypnotic voice. My vampire ears could detect harmonies in his tone I wouldn't have expected of him: something deep and stirring and soothing all at once. "You have fought in wars both official and not. You have seen enough screaming innocents shot in pursuit of one or another kind of silence: literal, political, social. You do not want to become that person. You do not want to kill what you do not have to kill. You want to solve the problems of the world, not silence them."

The Bull's Eye's grip slacked just a little bit but I was staring at Roderick. I had watched him fail to use the hoodoo on people; hell, he didn't even know what it was. This wasn't exactly that power to compel a mortal to act or to misremember, though. This was something I hadn't seen: persuasion rather than command. For all he struck me as kind of being a murderous robot wearing the skin of someone I pretended to know, this power he was exhibiting was surprisingly effective. I could feel it working on me, just a little bit, and I saw Jennifer's dilated eyes start to relax just a little as she returned to the here and the now.

"There is so much death," The Bull's Eye said. It came out slow and deep, sagging, like a murdered ideal slipping from the chair in which it died. "Can't there be a little life?"

"Give it to me," Roderick said. His voice was soft and sweet and I would have done anything he asked, had he.

The Bull's Eye handed over the struggling little death-child like a poorly wrapped package. Roderick carried it out of the room, into the kitchen. I heard the tearing of flesh, the dropping of a fifty-pound burden on the old linoleum floor and the clap of two hands dusting each other off.

Adam and Scott, having just witnessed up close the horror of Roderick's efficient work, started screaming again. That only lasted a couple of seconds before they stopped all at once. Roderick backed out of the kitchen, into the living room, with one finger pressed to his lips. Winking at them, he turned back to us.

"There," he said. "All done."

I stepped up so I could see in, suddenly afraid Roderick had simply snapped their necks, but they were both unconscious. I figure now, with a little time to reflect, that when the last of Dmitri's super-zombies died it was also the last of his power leaving the world. All sorts of ways he influenced reality must have come tumbling down at once, including the stuff he'd done to screw with the brothers' heads. For all I knew, they'd be asleep through next week but they were breathing.

I sagged against the counter, abruptly overwhelmed by everything: by the fight, by the abrupt departure from my system of the last of the super-serum I'd picked up, by learning there was a war going on and my maker hadn't told me, of seeing Seth there from its beginnings and on the wrong side. I slipped on the greasy ash that had been Dmitri and slid down the cabinets to sit in a heap on the floor, utterly dumbfounded.

"Are you okay?" The Bull's Eye was just ignoring the previous thirty seconds.

"Ten seconds ago I could've walked through a wall of diamond. I could've sliced air in two with my pinky finger." I drew a ragged breath and felt my chest. My heart may not beat anymore unless I tell it to, but the body language largely stays the same. Even though the strength had left me – the bouncing urgency – I could feel something still there, some ethereal connection. The phrase that came to mind was *the connection between all living things*. I had never been much of one for religion or spirituality or mysticism or whatever but I felt like I could almost hear everything *else* in the world having tuned into some frequency no longer available to me. No wonder Dmitri had loved this stuff. No wonder El Diablo had smelled so incredible to me whenever we met.

I sat there, silent, for thirty seconds. I could count them in the quiet heartbeat tick of every bird and bug and stray cat and howling dog for blocks. I could time myself in the rustle of the dying leaves landing atop discouraged autumn grass.

"We have to kill El Diablo," I said, gasping for breath. "We can't let this exist. We can't let..." I waved vaguely at the kids. "There can't be people running around with this in their veins. We'd all go crazy. I would go crazy. Every vampire in the world would go mad."

"Tell me what's happening." Jennifer crouched, eight or ten feet away, and I swiveled mad eyes around to look at her. "Is something wrong?"

"It's this stuff the kids were shooting up. It isn't just a drug. It's *life*." I tried to explain it to her, but it came out like metaphor salad, like a word jumble for English majors. "Imagine everyone in the world were methadone addicts and someone invented heroin. Imagine everyone were alcoholics in a world that only knew beer and someone invented moonshine; a starving world that invents filet mignon; a fish that invents water." I clutched my arms across my chest to hold in the last its of the fading sensation. "I feel so good I think it's making me sick."

The Bull's Eye slowly nodded. She'd seen the world. She had witnessed the chaos people created in pursuit of all-consuming and irresistible hunger or avarice or need. "I think we should capture El Diablo and turn him over to the police," she said, very evenly.

"Yes," Jennifer said. "I like the sound of that."

Roderick was silent for a long moment, then said, "This is my cousin's territory. I accept his decision."

"We have to kill him," I gasped. "But we can fight about this later. Give me five minutes, I think I'm going to pass out."

Then I did.

I came back around after ten minutes, not five. The twins were in their room, not talking but sitting beside one another. The Bull's Eye was watching out the shadowed, blood-soaked windows, prowling the walls to peek through narrow gaps. I was still in the middle of the kitchen floor, covered in Dmitri's ashy remains. Roderick and Jennifer were wondering why the police had never arrived but The Bull's Eye shrugged it off. "Nobody in this neighborhood is calling the cops about this house," she said. "If we set it on fire no one would call 911 until it could be seen from a mile away. They fear this place. They've all been holding their breath for years waiting for something like this to happen."

I stood up without a word and walked into the twins' room. They both snapped their heads up. They were scared. Good things had never happened to them when a vampire was in their house. That's true for most folks, I suppose.

"I need to know where you go to get your injections," I said. "You are not coming with us. You're done with all this. You'll never go back for another shot." Scott opened his mouth but I held out a finger and pointed it at him like an angry parent. "Do not make me break your mind open like a cherry cordial, kid. You're done with that shit. I don't know if what you've already got in you will wear off, but if it doesn't, stay away from me. Stay away from anyone who seems too pretty or too handsome. Stay away from anyone who ever says anything about immortality. All dates are *lunch* dates from now on. I will not be watching you, but she will." I hitched a thumb over my shoulder because The Bull's Eye and Jennifer had walked into the entryway at the front of the house. I didn't distinguish between them because I wanted Scott and Adam to assume I meant whichever one scared them most. "You will never, ever let a vampire feed from you. If one does, kill them. The how doesn't have to be complicated. Cutting off their head will do nicely, as with most things. Is that clear?"

They sat in silence. The Bull's Eye answered from behind me. "Yes. They've got it, or at least they will soon enough." She cleared her throat. "Now, boys, like he said: where did you go for the injections?"

After long seconds staring at each other, they gave us a street address. I didn't know it, but The Bull's Eye wrinkled her brow. "I didn't even know there was anything down that street."

"Nobody does," Adam said. "That's probably the point."

She nodded at him and turned to the rest of us. "Let's go."

CHAPTER 16

In the Morehead Hill neighborhood of downtown Durham are a million little dead-end residential streets. They all look like great shortcuts to get to Duke University but instead they all end at a sagging old porch, a wall of trees or the carcass of some green grocer storefront from a version of Durham long dead but unburied.

One of these streets abruptly turns into someone's gravel driveway and disappears around a gentle curve. At least, that's what it seems to be. If you keep going, you drive past the house at the end of it and find there's more single-track dirt lane beckoning you to follow it into comfortably anonymous darkness: the shadowed cavern of foliage tucked away in an oft-avoided corner of many a neighborhood here and there. Yours probably has one. You may never have even noticed it. In this case, the tree line was clearly where urbanite Durham pressed against the edge of Duke Forest and the Duke campus within, each side of that border huddled under a blanket of kudzu for fear of the other.

We parked Roderick's Cadillac and my Firebird – Jennifer complimented its design, earning her a million friend points – and set off on foot down that gravel road into those ill-advised woods. At the end, impossible for most mortals to see in the dark, was a low, long, yellow-beige building. Duke University had stopped using it for some industrial purpose in the distant past and promptly forgotten. All the way around the property's perimeter there was a chain link fence with rounds of razor wire along the top. Next to the building there were gigantic shelves that held lengths of rusted pipe many feet long. They looked like something one might lay underground, some thin and some big enough for a man to crawl through.

In front there was the usual royal blue Duke University property sign but it was effectively blank. The name of whatever this was had been almost scrubbed off by time and weather. There were only the ghosts of letters left to make words no one needs to know anymore.

Much to my surprise, there were lights on. The old bulbs on the outside of the building burned just bright enough to discourage stupid teenagers who might think razor wire looked like fun. The gate across the entrance to the parking lot was a massive steel affair on rollers. It could have slid out of the way if vines hadn't grown all up both sides. I pitied the guy they would have to send out here to patch up the place once I was done with it.

It turned out this place was pretty close to the technopagan house, also in Morehead Hill. I had wanted to stop in there to ask them about this building but The Bull's Eye was eager to get things over with and all their lights were out anyway. "Maybe they had an omen," I said with a dark little smile, but she didn't think that was terribly funny.

I looked over at her, standing at the gate. "Rip it open?"

"Be my guest." She was cracking her knuckles under her gloves – knife Kevlar, she told me – and I started popping the metal wires of the fence between my fingers like bubble wrap. Roderick was filing his nails in the background, Smiles on one side of him and Dog on the other. Jennifer winced when I started popping the fence apart with my hands. It wasn't terribly quiet, but I didn't much care.

We walked through the hole I made and stuck to the shadows, prowling around the edges of the lot. At the back we saw a door hanging open. There were dim lights coming from inside and I nodded. "We can sneak up that way."

"It's too bright," The Bull's Eye said, shaking her head, but we didn't have other options. I shrugged, she shrugged, and we all set off across tall grass that had been ignored for at least one growing season. In the perfect silence, its crunch was like gunshots. I still didn't care. I stepped up to the door and inside I could hear the clink and clatter of metal against metal.

I figured El Diablo must be in there and it sounded like he was working on something. An abandoned building in the most remote possible corner of Duke University's campus; I had to smile at it. He had set up a secret lair and his greatest enemy – the university that made him – was footing the bill. He might be a hopped-up crazy shooting super-steroids into chess champions in violation of scientific ethics but I had to admire his sense of irony.

Again, the Bull's Eye made some complicated hand signal and I nodded as though I understood. Roderick was standing on his toes, ready to spring. Jennifer was clenching and unclenching her fists, her wounded arm bandaged up by The Bull's Eye on our way over here. I held up one finger in the universal sign of "give me just a second here," then turned the corner of the doorway and walked inside with Smiles trailing happily behind.

"Evening," I said aloud.

El Diablo looked up at me and smiled.

El Diablo's outfit was in worse shape than ever: some of the stitching had started to give way, exposing one leg and a curved shoulder. The smell of him washed over me, a hundred times stronger than before. My fangs dropped right away. Between that physique and the blood inside it, I had a month's worth of wank fantasies at once.

I hated to think what Roderick would do when he smelled this guy.

El Diablo was busy bolting something to something else, what kind of looked like a big metal box, in a way that seemed a little clumsy but done with tremendous strength. When he would tighten a bolt I would hear metal squeal and I realized the wrench in his hand had been slightly bent out of shape. He was capable of bending steel with his bare hands.

I recognized what he was building: it's a kind of improvised bomb that has an armored back and sides to direct the blast. The Olympic bomber, that motherfucker in Atlanta, used one like it in '96. It's worse than a simple explosive. It's a device you'd only use on someone you really hated, someone you really wanted to hurt. I didn't know where or when he planned to deploy it but it would do a hell of a lot of damage when he did. I couldn't believe he had superhuman strength and still relied on bombs. It seemed so *complicated* compared to what he could do with his fists.

The wrench took another twist as he spun it around. He was *really* strong: stronger than Adam and Scott, perhaps stronger than both of them combined.

I already knew he had been sampling the product but I hadn't expected *this*.

"Ah," he said, voice flat in a way that clashed with the sick sneer he was wearing. "The Bull's Eye comes to my lair at long last."

"Yeah." She was behind me, looking annoyed and speaking around my right side. "She does."

El Diablo shifted his gaze, very slowly, and his eyes were completely mad: bugged, not totally focused. He was still beautiful. I couldn't help thinking that. He smelled delicious, too. I had to shut this down immediately. "So, if you don't mind my asking, who the hell is he?" He waved the wrench vaguely in my direction. "Your sidekick?" He smirked as Jennifer and Roderick stepped in behind us. "Oh, brought the whole Scooby Doo crew?"

I cracked my knuckles.

"This one's the guy who wants to kill you to put you out of business." The Bull's Eye shrugged a little, as if to say: you know, like y'do.

Roderick cleared his throat delicately. "As do I."

El Diablo smirked at The Bull's Eye. "And what do you want?"

"I want to turn you over to the authorities so you can repay society for your crimes." She spread her hands. "Nice, clean and easy, and nobody has to die."

He pursed his lips in an expression of mild surprise, perhaps even scandal. "Really? That's terribly quaint, isn't it?"

Ugh. Privileged son of a bitch. The dripping sarcasm coming off a hottie like that said *I get what I want* in tall neon signage. Some of the letters blinked to get your attention.

"No, it's how things work in the real world," she said. "I suspect you're going to cause enough trouble for them that the cops end up shooting you during an escape attempt, to be honest, but I don't get to decide that. You do. Now put down the wrench, step away from the improvised explosive device and get down on the ground with your hands on your head."

El Diablo smiled and in a flash the wrench was flying through the air. I dropped into slow-mo and saw that The Bull's Eye had started dodging before he had started throwing. She knew the whole time how this was going to go but she had to do her thing. She had to let him make his choice for himself. Some things we do because we have to, even when we know they won't work.

El Diablo had started moving as he threw the wrench – it was just a distraction – and he was going about as fast as I could. The last time we'd met, he'd only been *almost* as fast as I am. Very bad, but between Roderick and me I was sure we could take him out. The Bull's Eye and Jennifer would barely get a moment to realize what was happening, again. It wasn't sporting, but I figured it was probably better that way.

As I thought that, at least a dozen college kids in elaborately defaced Duke University paraphernalia surged forward out of the shadows. Athletic gear in hand – basketballs, baseball bats, oars and whatnot – they looked like a sporting goods store under evacuation orders.

They were all moving at super-speed, too.

Of course, on later reflection, I figured it all stood to reason. El Diablo wasn't *only* experimenting on Adam and Scott. He had lots of clients on campus. Once the athletics program got tipped to one kid on a new performance-enhancing drug they tested everybody and found the others. They'd all been kicked off their teams, just the way Dmitri's pet had been, but they were still addicted to El Diablo's happy juice. They could be turned to his purposes if they wanted more.

Now his personal revenge corps, they wore their old gear still but they'd painted over the face of the school mascot or they'd added a leg to the "D" such that their backs now read PUKE UNIVERSITY. It was all adolescent nonsense like that. I thought of how Adam and Scott, top performers in their areas of expertise throughout their lives, had basically run and hidden as soon as there was trouble. They were like little kids caught breaking the rules. I thought of El Diablo's furious lashing out at the university by blowing up part of one of its most prized possessions, like a child throwing a tantrum. If regular old steroids make people rage out, what did El Diablo's super-serum make them do? All indications were it turned them into children in superhuman bodies.

I realized now the hammering on the bomb casing had been another feint on El Diablo's part: something loud enough to mask the heartbeats and quiet breathing of all those human metabolisms so Roderick and I wouldn't hear. El Diablo had been warned – by Ross, I guessed, because there was no way he wasn't a part of this – and had called in his posse of loyal addicts to defend the castle.

Now they came at us, a dozen different representations of the school's entire sports program wielding the implements of their pastimes like weapons of war.

There was a young woman with wild eyes and a track and field javelin who threw it so hard the handle cracked in her hand before she let go. I ducked and rolled out of the way so it sailed on, aimed at The Bull's Eye. Roderick leapt toward it, hands outstretched to catch it. His hands clamped down and pulled it in as he somersaulted, came to a standing stop and threw it back in one smooth motion. The woman who'd thrown it caught it, but not with her hands.

One down.

Blood shot from the wound and Roderick's fangs jutted out. He made some kind of low moan, something seventy years ago I would have considered distinctly sexual. Without hesitation, he launched himself teeth-first at the woman, bringing her down before she could finish falling. Dead blood doesn't normally interest us but the line between dead and fresh gets fuzzy when they haven't quite hit the ground in slow-motion.

I twisted to face our other attackers, grabbed the nearest one by the thigh (lacrosse player or something like it: fancy net on a stick) and used his knee to shatter the jaw of a basketball player coming in from the other side. I grabbed the basketball player by the neck and used his forehead to break the nose of the lacrosse player, in turn. All that fancy stuff left me open to the basketball the player had thrown: it hit me square in the face, popping one of my eyes clean out of its socket and shattering the bone of my skull on that side of my face. It hurt like hell. The basketball exploded like a burst balloon from the force with which he'd thrown it.

I planted one fat hand in the middle of each of their chests, braced myself and pushed hard so they took off through the air across the room. I turned to face Roderick and watched him drain the last of the blood from the woman with the javelin. He stood, wiping delicately at the corners of his mouth with his fingertips. My vision was all crazy: two angles, one straight ahead and one the floor in front of me. Roderick pointed at my dangling eye and laughed.

Vampires are static creatures, bodies locked into the same shape for as long as they can stand, and my form was already trying to assert itself: the bones drew together and my eye retracted on the optic nerve like the winch on my

Firebird's front bumper. All the little shattered pieces settled back into the state they held on the night Agatha turned me into what I am now.

It didn't even hurt.

I mimicked Roderick's taunting jab with my own finger and smirked. "Two to one, Cousin. Try to keep up We've got nine more to deal with here." It was something to distract me from the terrifying realization I could already feel myself forgetting the woman who'd been his first victim of the fight. Whereas the Last Gasp lets me learn everything there is to know about one aspect of a victim's life, Roderick erases his prey from collective memory when he drains the life completely from them. It's a horrifying thing to know exists and we've only spoken of it briefly. I mean, for real, I'm not even sure I remember how I found out he can do it in the first place.

"What is going on with these people?" Roderick looked around at the tableau in which we stood as he spoke. All around us the remaining nine or ten college athletes were still roaring towards us but we were moving even faster than they – so insanely fast, faster than ever, I figured it had to be the blood I'd taken from Dmitri and Roderick had consumed just now. Smiles and Dog hadn't even had time to get involved: they were just now starting to approach where we were. They could move faster than people but not as fast as we did on the super-blood.

"I don't know," I said, "Just fight. We can figure it out later. Stopping it is a higher priority than comprehending the science."

"Gosh," Roderick sneered. "A license for ultraviolence? It's a bit early for Christmas, Cousin."

We launched ourselves in opposite directions, wading in with fists and fangs, and didn't say another word until we were done.

Two dumbbells came flying at me, but I kicked them back into the face of the weightlifting monster who threw them at me from across the room.

Three.

Some country club recruit with a golf club in each hand tried to come after me but I took one away from him and used the other to choke him half to death. My teeth did the rest.

That put me at four of eleven.

A baseball player and a softball player took me by surprise as soon as the golf kid was unconscious: each of them swung for the fences at the same time, clocking me on both sides of my head at once. That almost knocked me out for a second but Dmitri's blood was like electricity in my veins. No, it was like sparks: occasional and unpredictable. I could feel the effects fading but every time I got that burst of something special – something extra, as Adam and Scott had called it – I used it to full effect. I didn't know if it was time or the fact it had been filtered through Dmitri first, but no wonder he'd been drawing from that well every night. I probably would have, too.

The baseball and softball players put me at six out of nine so far.

My last two opponents were a guy in a martial arts outfit kind of thing and a wrestler. I liked the wrestler's body but I didn't like his odds: he was a brute and he didn't know how to fight somebody who wasn't waiting for a referee to tell them to engage. He got his arms around me and squeezed real hard but that just put his neck all the closer. I bit down, white hot fire flooding into my mouth, and when the new karate kid came at me I spun to use my victim as a shield while I drank.

That knocked the wrestler loose, though, so the martial artist and I squared off: pacing around each other in a circle to size each other up.

"I am the only one here," he calmly stated, "Who is trained to fight rather than to play a game."

"I know," I said. "I'm kind of flattered you're fighting me rather than him." I hitched a thumb in a random direction, indicating Roderick. I had no idea where my cousin had gone or what he was doing.

El Diablo and The Bull's Eye and Jennifer were fighting on their own in the middle of the room but it was going at a snail's pace compared to us and neither side seemed especially about to win. El Diablo was much faster and stronger than a human being but The Bull's Eye was a professional soldier and Jennifer had that mad look in her eye, wounded arm and everything. They came to fight and they were not going to be easy to beat.

"You look easier to take," the kid said with a smirk. "Big fat guy like you?"

"I prefer to think of it as marshmallow armor," I said, and took a swing. Banter makes a great thing you can use to conceal a sucker punch.

The guy stepped aside and grabbed my wrist, pulling me closer so he could plant an elbow in my face and knock me back again. It stung like crazy and I staggered a little, completely surprised by the move. As soon as I had my balance back, I lunged at him with a growl. I was annoyed and a little embarrassed and planned to take it out on him. Much to my surprise, he dropped and rolled me right over top of himself, down the back of one of his shoulders, and was standing, facing me, before I'd even had time to clamber back to my feet.

"Try to hit me again," the martial artist said to me. He was smiling beatifically, always moving, all his limbs in motion as he did.

"It would be my pleasure," Roderick said from behind him before punching the kid in the back of the skull. I heard something like a cracker snapping in two: vertebrae, maybe, or the thick bones of the skull. The guy staggered forward just in time for Dog and Smiles to arc slowly through the air and land against his torso. With the burst of energy from the wrestler's super-blood I spun to plant the toe of one boot in the guy's cheek, sending him flying. He clattered into a pile of unidentifiable old equipment.

I drew a deep breath and waggled a finger at Roderick. "Cousin," I scolded. "I took out all eight of them. What on earth have you been doing?"

"Oh, Cousin," Roderick said, lips pursed and his head sadly shaking, his cheeks flush with what I took to be some combination of embarrassment both sincere and posed, "What can I say? I'm a delicate little thing."

Dog and Smiles landed on their feet and, molasses slow, spun towards El Diablo.

Roderick and I both dropped out of warp speed so that the low, droning groans of the fight going on between El Diablo and Jennifer and The Bull's Eye turned into human voices of effort and agony. El Diablo had punched Jennifer right in her wound, an opportunistic strike I might have taken myself in similar circumstances. Jennifer fell to one side as The Bull's Eye landed a kick in El Diablo's back. Smiles ran in and planted his teeth around El Diablo's left wrist, a cruel mirror of the wound he'd just taken advantage of when he hit Jennifer's arm, and Dog impacted El Diablo in the knees, making him drop to one hand and one foot.

Seeing us begin to walk forward, knuckles cracking, only a handful of rejected Duke athletes in view and all of them out of commission, El Diablo did the smart thing: he leapt to his feet and ran for it.

There was an open, oversized trap door in the floor, like a metal door over a mechanic's bay, and he tumbled neatly down it by executing a straight-up somersault and then disappearing over the edge. I heard pounding footsteps as he ran. He was wearing jogging shoes under that get-up and I figured he had finished his share of 5K's with legs like that.

I swung around to The Bull's Eye to say I would go after him, that she should see to Jennifer, but The Bull's Eye was already halfway in the hole. She didn't even look at me. She took off running after him, her boots pounding on concrete in heavy mimicry of his. She was slower, but she looked determined as all hell.

I turned to Roderick. "You and the pups go after him. I need to make sure Jennifer is OK." I looked at her: blood coming out of the wound in her arm and her eyes starting to roll back. The pain and the blood loss were starting to win out over the adrenaline. She was on the verge of passing out but gods almighty had she held her own by being in it this long.

Roderick arched an eyebrow and glanced between Jennifer and me before he shook his head. "Oh no, Cousin," he said. "I would not dare to fight your fights for you."

"That isn't even my fight," I said, waggling my head. "Go help The Bull's Eye."

"Not without you," Roderick said.

I wrinkled up my face in a scowl. I knew what he really wanted. He didn't want me alone with Jennifer and I couldn't even begin to choose from all the reasons why: picking her brain about the conversation he and she had at the technopagans house; finding out why she had used that particular catchphrase of his, *c'est la guerre*, so interesting to me now I knew there was some sort of war going on; or maybe he worried I would try to turn her and screw it up. Hell, maybe he worried I'd drain her dry to silence her on all the stuff she'd seen now that she was running around with vampires, seeing us doing our thing, though the compassion angle didn't really seem to fit. There was a lot about Roderick I'd grown to like, perhaps even admire, but random acts of kindness had yet to appear on that list.

I looked back at Jennifer. "We probably need to call her an ambulance," I said to Roderick. "She's losing blood and not even half conscious."

"She will recover." Roderick stated it as a fact rather than a supposition or an assurance.

I narrowed my eyes at him. "Wait. Have *you* fed her or something? You know what that does to people." What it does to people is make them nuts. I did it to a bunch of people on one occasion while under extreme duress and everyone made it out alive but that was a calculated risk and I only fed each of them once. If I'd kept doing it, they'd all be insane by now. Every time I hear of someone going on a violent spree I wonder if they have any dead friends who like to mix them drinks.

Roderick laughed once, a sharp chirp. "No, Cousin," he said. "But can you not feel the life in her?" He nodded in her direction. "Do you not sense the way her body rises to the occasion? She already works to compensate for the injury. She struggles to wake. Jennifer may be slower and weaker than we but she is immeasurably more alive."

I furrowed my brow. "What in tarnation are you talking about?"

Roderick looked equally confused, and then the light went on. "The Jedi mind trick," he said, and he clapped his hands together. "This is my Jedi mind trick." I opened my mouth to say something smart but he waved me silent again. "No," he said, "Remember? In the bar? In Asheville? You were surprised I could not do what you call 'the hoodoo'. I suppose now it is my turn. I can feel the life in them." He gestured at Jennifer as but one of the many Others: *them*. "It sounds like a song inside my head. Their health, their weakness, their will to live? Their aliveness? No, not that: their *mortality*. I feel that, deep down, as though something inside me resonates with a sympathetic chord." He looked at me again, eyes widening briefly. "My goodness. How do you hunt?"

I started to ask him about his crazy Last Gasp power, about the chords of subtle persuasion I'd heard in his voice before, about all the little things he seemed able to do but I'd never heard of in another vampire, but I didn't. It wasn't the time to get petty and jealous about who was more powerful than whom.

Smiles leaned down and started licking Jennifer's face while Dog panted happily by Roderick's side. That was just enough: Jennifer's eyes fluttered back to normal and she sat up slowly with a low groan.

"Jesus fucking Christ," she said. Rubbing her forehead with her good hand, she blinked and looked around. "They went down there, right?" She nodded at the gaping metal door into whatever had swallowed El Diablo and The Bull's Eye. "Why are we sitting around?"

I helped her stand, but she let go of my hand as soon as she was on her own two feet. I nodded. Roderick smiled. We both waited while she had the honor of being first to climb into darkness.

CHAPTER 17

The ladder led down into a long, dark, narrow sewer tunnel that ran right up under this building. I imagined some earlier era – perhaps the prior century – in which big machines had been trundled into the building above us. The people working with them probably drained whatever horrifying chemicals coursed through those machines directly into the city sewers: countless tons of used oil and other spent fluids coursing away into someone else's water supply. Out of sight, out of mind. If you ever want to meet an environmentalist, meet a vampire. We've got to live with this stuff forever.

Roderick and I dropped down, each of us with an impossibly large dog under one arm, as soon as Jennifer had descended and moved aside. If Roderick and I were capable of super-speed, and El Diablo and his erstwhile clientele had been faster than a human could believably be, and The Bull's Eye was merely extraordinarily gifted but sufficiently trained to compensate while moving at a normal speed, then Jennifer was dragging along like molasses in the middle of a hard freeze. She made it down the ladder and she could walk but running was out of the question. Smiles was sticking more closely to me than to her because the nature of our bond left him no choice. I could sense, however, a part of him – the part of him once a dog rather than a hellhound – wanted to stay with her and protect her. He knew the fight wasn't over and he sensed a wounded ally in need of support.

"I don't guess you guys pack flashlights, huh?" Jennifer said it with a little smirk.

"Of course not," Roderick replied. "We and our servants need very little light."

"Always the human in a party full of elves," Jennifer sighed.

I laughed. "Another D&D joke." She'd made one the very first time we met.

Jennifer smiled more naturally. "Oh yeah," she said. "You played it. I forgot."

I shrugged. "Anything to pass the decades."

Roderick cleared his throat and I nodded at him. "Jennifer," I said as I turned back to her, "It doesn't seem like you're moving real fast."

She waved it off. "Go on ahead. I'll catch up. I just need to get my breath."

Roderick clicked his cheeks at Dog and the two of them took up positions on either side of her: the hellhound in back and Roderick in front. "I will stay with her, Cousin," he said to me.

I looked at him for a moment. "There's something we need to talk about," I said to him. "When I took down Dmitri I saw some things that made me real curious."

Roderick waved both hands at me. "Cousin. Not now. Go."

I grimaced. "Just tell me if you know something special about Seth I might need to hear."

Roderick looked genuinely puzzled. "Your second in command?"

I allowed myself one tiny moment of relief and I wasn't even sure from what. "We'll talk more later," I said. "But if things go totally south, start with Seth. He's older than he lets on." I paused. "And I think I know why you hate demons so much."

Roderick arched one eyebrow. "So noted," he said with a look of dark significance.

I turned and took off pounding down the tunnel, boots stamping the old concrete and dry dust underneath me as Smiles ran alongside.

I could hear both of them – El Diablo and The Bull's Eye – running in the distance. The former could go insanely faster than the latter if there were light around, sure, but down in the dark of the sewers he was constrained to the same speeds as anybody else who didn't fancy smacking into a wall. Creatures of the night don't have that problem. It was pitch dark except for the occasional storm grate and whatever starlight the sky saw fit to sprinkle through but I could see just fine.

Smiles and I surged ahead with only a couple of false turns along the way: the sound of running footsteps echoed wildly around us but his hearing and my eyes let us stay on the right path more often than not. Before long I saw The Bull's Eye disappear around a corner in her pursuit of El Diablo. I saw her flinch as a brick flew past her and exploded against the wall to one side. She was lucky it hadn't hit her, lucky he couldn't see well enough to take proper aim.

As I got closer I started calling out navigation, shouting when it sounded like he'd taken a turn or when I saw some obstacle in her path. There were rats running like crazy away from all this commotion, way up ahead, and I wondered if El Diablo would stumble on them. No such luck. He flew helter-skelter through one potential disaster after another: empty drums and crates here, a pile of equipment there. The Bull's Eye dodged much more expertly, hurdling over sawhorses and spinning in a tight three-sixty to avoid a stack of shovels leaned against the wall. Eventually we came out into a much larger tunnel on a long, straight path. An easy forty or fifty yards ahead, he took a sharp turn in a direction that, on my mental map, had him headed somewhere towards the center of downtown: the very area I'd prowled the first time I smelled Dmitri. Barely pausing to crouch, El Diablo leapt and shot through a manhole, blowing the cover off when he hit it. I could hear him running across pavement in the open air.

"Up," I called, and though I took a few extra long strides to catch up to her so I could hoist The Bull's Eye myself if she needed it, she was already gone, up the ladder, faster than I could have imagined a normal human being could go. I wondered how many combatants in places with funny names had been caught off-guard when she burst in on them like that.

Smiles jumped so I could catch him and haul myself up with just one yank on the ladder using my free hand. We popped out on Chapel Hill Street, running down the middle of the abandoned late-night pavement. El Diablo dogged left, down Duke Street, towards Brightleaf Square. He vaulted a wrought iron fence to land on top of a car – alarm immediately blaring – and took off running across all of them in that row, not touching the ground but instead leaping from hood to hood. Every single car started blaring and lights started flashing. It was damned unsubtle, but I knew that was a part of his game: throw us both off the chase – whichever of us was actually The Bull's Eye – by getting the cops' attention.

Jumping the fence at the other end of the row, El Diablo landed on his feet and pounded asphalt right down the middle of Duke Street towards Main, where a bag lady had just stepped into the crosswalk. He shot through, shoving her out of his way. At the same moment, a ridiculously huge sport utility vehicle with a big blue DUKE UNIVERSITY sticker on the back shot through the intersection between us and them.

When it was gone, the old woman lay dazed on the pavement and El Diablo was racing up the sidewalk towards the cluster of disused tobacco factory buildings past which I'd walked a couple of weeks before. The SUV would have killed that homeless old lady, I realized. El Diablo had saved someone's life by accident. I smiled as I ran: the best hunts are all about little moments of the unexpected.

El Diablo turned and sprinted across the street again, zigzagging with the rest of us in hot pursuit. He was able to put a little pepper on it now he could see where he was going but he was running crazy, hither and yon, with no particular plan. The Bull's Eye worked efficiently at catching up to him. She was able to cut corners, draw direct lines of approach and otherwise do the complex calculus of chasing down someone who didn't seem to know where he was going other than *away*. Smiles and I simply followed her lead. My dog and I were no strangers to hunting frightened prey, of course, but El Diablo was faster than the average truck stop crank fiend.

El Diablo shot through a door that had been, up to that moment, chained and padlocked shut with a big DO NOT ENTER sign taped to its front. He disappeared into darkness but I could hear the sound of footsteps rapidly ascending a staircase. El Diablo didn't hesitate to plunge in after him, so neither did Smiles nor I. The steps were covered in broken tiles and old wood that had started to crumble and it all smelled like old paint. The place was covered in dust and decaying plaster. El Diablo was taking the stairs two at a time, as was The Bull's Eye. I had to turn on the super-speed a little bit just to keep up.

The stairs ended after four floors. El Diablo hit the doors at the top and they fell apart at a touch. We all exited the stairs onto a mostly open, refuse-strewn cement floor where cigarettes were once hustled along on their way to ancient storefronts. The industrial ambience bothered me for a moment: my final confrontation with the Transylvanian had taken place in an abandoned manufacturing setting just like this. It was disorienting in its proximity to déjà vu. I skidded to a halt, Smiles in front of me. El Diablo, facing us, crouched and beckoned to The Bull's Eye with one hand. He wore a mad smile.

Without a single word, they fell on one another and were fighting. He was trying to punch her but he didn't know his own enhanced abilities as well as she practiced her long-trained skills. The Bull's Eye knew exactly how to take down a bigger, stronger opponent. She was bobbing and weaving and staying just out of range or just an inch to the right, almost dancing in and out of the brawl. It looked to me like she was waiting on him to wear himself out or make a mistake so she could take the opportunity that would afford her.

The Bull's Eye had fought men three times her weight in caves in Afghanistan and jungles in Central America. She had killed two bodyguards of a fleeing Asian drug lord who skipped bail on US soil. She had dropped out of trees to garrote her targets, punched their tracheas closed and kicked people so hard in the kneecap that their legs had nearly snapped off. She was a swift, targeted combatant and while he swung wildly she slowly — very slowly, *maddeningly* slowly — was filing him down. She punched him in the upper arm to weaken his swings or kicked him in the shin to hobble his sense of balance. They were flying at and around each other like two angry lions. Not unlike the performance of *Dracula*, this was in its way beautiful and I took a moment to appreciate it.

I realized, as I did so, that Smiles had started growling and switching his view from side to side. We weren't alone. There was another way in, I guessed, because there were a handful of squatters blinking at this ridiculous melee from the perimeter of the room. The space we were in had a few grime-encrusted windows and a set of gaping bay doors hanging open four floors over some gods-forsaken half-decayed alleyway forgotten by time. Between them, plenty of light got in for a few old drunkards to watch what was going on.

I nearly let that stop me from trying to help, but in the end who's going to believe a wino? Anybody with sense would write off anything they said as being brought on by the shakes, right? I cracked my knuckles and stepped forward but The Bull's Eye sternly warned me off.

"No! Call 911," she panted at me. "I can keep him busy until then."

I knew that tone. I'd used it before. *Leave this to me*, it said. *This is my fight.* On the one hand, I was surprised. She hadn't spared him a thought until two nights before. On the other hand, here was the guy at the root of the biggest, baddest problem she had found in all those long, dark "meditation walks" she'd turned into patrols. She dealt with purse snatchers and carjackers and guys busting up convenience stores because they kept her busy and kept her mind off the past. It scratched an itch for justice – no, for fairness – she'd started feeling the first time she was ordered to take down someone she wasn't sure had been targeted on entirely fair terms. It was a sense of unfairness in general that climaxed in the unfair, unfixable death of the love of her life. Solving the problems unsolvable by residents of the neighborhoods she patrolled had been meaningful because it solved a lot of problems of her own: who am I, what do I do now and for whom do I do it? Then, just as soon as she felt settled into that routine, along came a problem she couldn't crack: the bogeyman of the suburbs. He'd nearly done her in – her, after all those cold winds and fierce fights and mountain passes – and in the end she hadn't been strong enough to take him down. She'd needed the help of others despite swearing off all others a long time ago.

I knew exactly how she felt.

I put up my hands in a gesture of acquiescence and stepped away. If she didn't want help, I wouldn't force it on her. She looked to be winning anyway.

I drifted backwards into the stairwell. Smiles didn't want to come with me but my hold over him won out, as I knew it would. The two of us withdrew from the fight. In the deep shadows I drew from my pocket the phone El Diablo had used to set off his bombs: the one he'd thrown over his shoulder and I had caught. I dialed a number I'd had the foresight to look up ahead of time in case it ever proved useful or necessary. A young woman's voice answered brightly, "Duke *Chronicle* offices."

"I've got a tip on a story," I growled. "The Bull's Eye is about to take out El Diablo downtown and if you run you can watch it happen."

"Ha ha, creeper," the young woman said. I didn't blame her: middle of the night and she was probably just now pasting together the next days' edition. I bet she got crank calls from drunks all the time.

"No joke," I insisted. I can't do the hoodoo over the phone, but damned if I don't wish I could. Instead, I said the only thing I could think to convince her. "Ask your photographer who was at the scene of the Duke Chapel bombing. I was the big guy in black. I'm not The Bull's Eye, but I've been on her trail. He'll remember me. Tell him the big guy who ran away called it in. He'll know it was really me if you tell him I remember what he was *not* wearing."

The woman hesitated – of course she had heard about me being there. The kid thought I was The Bull's Eye, too, probably, just like everyone else on the scene. I hoped that one little detail of him showing up in boxers and flip-flops would be the authentication I needed to put my call over the edge into credibility.

"Tell him to hurry," I said. "They're fighting right now, and it won't last much longer."

I hung up and hit a few other buttons. With only a couple of false starts I managed to find the camera in it and start taking pictures of my own.

I heard a smack and a crack, and one of The Bull's Eye's gloved hands skittered off El Diablo's jaw as a tooth flew in a stark white arc across the room; then another. She had started to get the best of him, finally, with a million billion tiny punches. He had managed to connect with her a time or two, too, and I could tell from the way she moved her left arm that it might be mildly fractured or at least sprained at the shoulder. I didn't know how he had managed that, but she was wounded. One more punch sent him spinning away.

He smacked against the wall, his back rebounding on the bricks. She leapt towards him to deliver the knockout, and his hand came up with a hunk of rebar. She impaled herself on it before she even knew it was there. Blood shot backwards in the starlight and The Bull's Eye took two steps back, the wet metal slipping slickly from El Diablo's grip.

It was the sort of gut wound a person dies from. Anybody who's seen one knows it.

The Bull's Eye staggered. Smiles and I both ran forward but she wasn't down yet. Even as I stepped up to try to catch her, The Bull's Eye spun and planted a roundhouse kick right in the side of El Diablo's neck. I heard bones snap, big ones, and the light went out of his eyes. He collapsed against the cement floor with a sound like meat. He was dead in an instant, whether she meant him to be or not. Perhaps five seconds before, less than mortally wounded, she might have had more precision. Not now, not anymore. Perhaps she knew what that rebar in her gut meant and she decided to take El Diablo with her.

I wondered what Roderick would see now, if he were here: how much of El Diablo's life was left, and how much of The Bull's Eye's?

She sagged to her knees as I got there.

"Let me call 911," I said. I fumbled with El Diablo's burner phone, bobbling it as I tried to mash the right buttons. All of a sudden I felt like a clumsy old fool. A moment before, she'd been winning this. She'd had this fight in the bag. Now she was probably dying, and I could have helped her even if she said not to. Between us, we could have finished this the right way.

The Bull's Eye drew a panting breath and shook her head. "Let... me... assess..." She was very lightly touching her own abdomen, feeling around, wincing, eyes fluttering as she did so, then she shook her head. Clouds swept across the sky and moonlight shone in. Blood was flowing out all over, smelling like you wouldn't believe. I knew for sure she was dying when I saw all that life everywhere. El Diablo had torn a gaping wound all the way through the core of her body and the Bull's Eye was fading fast.

She took as deep a breath as she could manage, which wasn't very deep, and tried to focus her eyes on me. "Could you save me now?" Blood swelled again from The Bull's Eye's gut. "If you turned me, would I live?"

I told you once I've never asked to learn the ritual used to make one of us, and that was true, but a part of me wanted to try. A part of me wondered how much of that ritual was playacting and how much was the pseudo-science of our semi-mystical state. I *could* try to turn her right there. I knew the motions if not the words or the why's. If it worked, she could pull out the rebar and the wound would close right up. She'd probably have to drain every homeless guy in here, but it would work. She'd come out of it just like Old Shoe: waking up every night with half her torso missing. She'd be a wreck, but she'd be alive.

The Bull's Eye repeated the question. "Would it work?" Her voice was a thin reed.

"Yes," I said. "Maybe." I hesitated to say more. I didn't know what to say. We see death all the time, all around us, but we rarely give a damn. This time, I gave a damn and I didn't know for sure I could stop it: stop the death or stop giving a damn. Roderick had done a number on me all right. He'd made me care about people again.

"Imagine what I could do." The Bull's Eye blinked. Her eyes were going dim: only seconds now. She turned her face towards me, but not her eyes. Her eyes were elsewhere, looking out the gaping bay door with rain-soaked particleboard half over it. She was looking at the night and the moon and the stars and the pretty little skyline of her pretty little city. "Will you live forever?"

"That's the plan," I said.

Smiles had stood silent guard over both of us, but he leaned in and sniffed her face, then whined loudly.

"Imagine what I would be capable of." She could only whisper.

I cleared my throat. "I already have," I said. "That's why I won't try to turn you. I know exactly how formidable you would become."

She smiled one last time. "I didn't want you to," she exhaled. "I just wanted to know if you would."

Then the Bull's Eye shuddered, a convulsion that traveled all up and down her body, and her eyes stayed open only because she wasn't there anymore to close them. Her body started to fall over but I reached out and caught it so that I could ease her onto the floor. El Diablo might have deserved to die with a hard thud against cold concrete, but she didn't.

Smiles, tied for eternity to my own emotional state, threw his head back and howled.

I could have still tried to turn her, even then, but like she said: imagine what she could do. The Bull's Eye was a noble and brave soul who fought for what she believed in and took seriously this obsession she'd turned into a second job. She had a city full of defenseless persons to protect and she had done so one bungled burglary, weird suburban house and self-made super villain at a time. She was a hero, a real and true one. I could respect her for it; I could even like her for it; but I didn't have any room for that kind of thing in my operation, especially now I knew there was something even bigger going on: a war unfinished but largely forgotten. When animals fight, people are better off getting out of the way. She was people. We were animals. It was that simple.

I maybe could have bitten her at the last second and taken in that final spark out of greed for some aspect of her life story, but her death had been her own and I had too much respect for the life she'd lived to impose myself on how she left it.

I closed her eyes and reached gingerly into her pockets until I found her phone. Then I twisted her neck all the way around, fast as I could, to make sure she wouldn't be the one in a million who rose again as a Steeplechase zombie the next time an elder vampire decided to call back some ancient from the dead. That whole topic was a huge, vast silhouette on the horizon of my mind: the problem I knew I would deal with next, but not the problem in the room with me right that second.

That done, I turned around. The bums were still watching. "She was The Bull's Eye," I said aloud. Then, faster than they could see me move, I stepped up to each of them in turn. *"You will forget that I was here."* I drove into each of their minds with all the force I could muster in silent fury, *"But you will remember her."*

I walked out as they glazed over, their brains working to process the orders they'd been given. At the top of the staircase I dug out El Diablo's phone. It was still recording video of nothing. I couldn't have that laying around, not now I'd sat there and chit-chatted with her while she died. I picked it up, crushed it into pieces with one flex of my thick fingers, and poured it out in a pile in the corner. At least I'd called the *Chronicle*. At least someone might find her. At least they might remember her as one of the good guys.

No, I had to make sure. Flipping open The Bull's Eye's phone, I put it in the hands of one of the winos, a scraggly old guy who looked like a pad of steel wool. *"Call 911,"* I said to him, *"Then set the phone next to her head."* She deserved certainty. The kid from the *Chronicle* might not come here and I couldn't bear the thought of her laying there until the building fell down.

Then I left, simple as that: back down the stairs at a run with Smiles by my side.

The papers got everything wrong in the end, but that's the way things go. *C'est la guerre.*

Chapter 18

Go and look for the dejected, once proud
--Bauhaus, "God in an Alcove"

Jennifer, Roderick and Dog were just coming up the street when Smiles and I emerged from the factory building and slipped through shadows onto the sidewalk in a dark, forgotten stretch of Main Street. Roderick was walking with his hands in his pocket. Jennifer held her bandaged arm in her opposite hand. She looked slowed but nowhere near beaten. Dog, nose down, was leading them towards us one sniff and snuffle at a time.

Jennifer jumped right to the obvious question when she saw Smiles and me were alone. "Is she dead?" Her voice was almost totally flat, but there was a flicker of hope in there.

"They killed each other," I said. I didn't hesitate or hem and haw over wording. I wanted her to know it was true so I just said it straight.

That made her stop for just a second, but then she nodded. She was no stranger to death in circumstances such as these, either.

"You said you had learned something," Roderick murmured. "That we are in a war." He said it so quietly only Jennifer and I could hear it. I figured that meant he knew and he had talked to her about it. He would never have brought it up in front of her if he didn't know already what he might hear in response and if he hadn't discussed it with her. Of course, at the time it never even occurred to me she might have heard me say it back at the House.

"Dmitri thought so, anyway." I shrugged one shoulder at him. "He'd been around a long time and he was still just a flunky for the *really* old bastards. There was a rebellion in the 1890's. The old guys were nearly wiped out. A demon came along and offered to help. Sound familiar?"

Roderick nodded. "Yes. In Seattle it was much the same: a vampire from the city's founding days. Emily told me he was a relic of another time. She wanted us to forget about it: sweep it under the rug and pretend it had ever happened. I could get no further information from her, so I set out on my own." He shrugged.

I nodded. That explained his willingness to pull up stakes and move across the country to take over Asheville for me – and to entertain Agatha's offer of employment. "It makes me wonder about Agatha," I said. "She's never said how old she is. I've always assumed she was around a buck-fifty, maybe two. That puts her just the right age to be on either side."

"You and she have always been close." Roderick's voice was lilting: other emotions ran under those words, ones I did not and would not understand. He was an orphan, after all. No one knew who had made him or why and he had suffered for it ever since. Agatha had offered to adopt him and he had turned her down to work for me; at least, that's what he said. "I wonder why she never told you?"

"None of them did," I replied. "I got the sense of there having been a kind of vow of silence after the rebellion was over." I paused. "Of course, there's still the question of why *you* didn't tell me."

Roderick smirked just a little. "Cousin," he purred, "Would you have believed me?"

Well, he had me there. I would have written it off as the beginning of some crazy spiral.

Jennifer looked to one side, cocking her ear, and cleared her throat. "I hear sirens. We need to go."

I nodded, and the three of us made our wending way back to our cars in total silence. Roderick said a solemn good night and got behind the wheel of his Cadillac. Jennifer paused before climbing into the passenger-side door of his car. She nodded at me. "Roderick has my number," she said. "I want to talk."

Roderick pulled into my driveway – my real driveway, at my house in Raleigh – an hour later. He had taken Jennifer back to her apartment complex, or one she said was hers. I wouldn't have blamed her if she'd lied. If I were human again, and as aware as she was of all the things that go bump in the night, I'd have lied to us, too.

Roderick put out Dog's food, filled his water dish and left him and Smiles curled up in the living room to join me on the back deck. We were deep into the small hours before sunrise. Those are often my favorite time of night. The world is still asleep but it's started to stir in its slumber. For the last few minutes before dawn I can almost feel like I'm in the world of the living.

"So," Roderick said as he scooted his chair forward and put his go-go boots up on the deck rail. "Demons."

"Demons," I said. I told him everything I had seen in Dmitri's head. He sat in patient silence while I talked. When I was done, I added, "Where from?"

Roderick smirked. "You are really asking if there is a Hell," he said. "And, by extension, a Heaven."

I opened my mouth and worked my jaw for a little bit. "I suppose so," I said, "But not because I'm in some all-fired hurry to get there."

Roderick laughed once, a single noise of something that wasn't quite amusement. "Good."

"But still," I said, "Doesn't the existence of one – no, two, counting the one in Seattle – doesn't that raise a lot of questions?"

"Only if you insist they must have a source other than this world," Roderick replied.

I frowned at him and his coy mannerisms. "Okay, cousin," I said. "Out with it. Impress me with your very best theory."

Roderick allowed himself a prideful smile for a moment. "Have you heard of the Buddhist concept of the tulpa?" He folded his delicate little hands together against the back of his head. I shook a no with my own and he went on. "It is a spiritual practice by which a practitioner or, better, a group of practitioners focus their thoughts and energies on the manifestation of a thoughtform: an independent entity of purely psychic qualities."

I scratched the little diamond of facial hair under my lower lip and said, simply, "Huh?"

"They *will* a helpful spirit into being," Roderick said.

"Sounds damned useful around the house."

Roderick nodded. "Indeed it is, or at least until such time as it has been invested with enough power to become independent. At that point it ceases to be a helpful entity and becomes something between a trickster and a poltergeist. It escapes the control of its maker or makers and must be put down. It is not unlike stories of the golem or of Frankenstein's monster or even of Rumplestiltskin: that which solves our problems for us requires a price higher than we might wish to pay. Therefore, it's best to solve your own problems."

"There's no such thing as a free lunch?"

Roderick nodded professorially. "Exactly. According to the Tibetans, a tulpa requires study and effort. But let us say it does not, or perhaps that one or more of the elder vampires was aware of the practice and capable of completing it. A tulpa is, we are told, akin in nature to the motivations of those who bring it forth. Who is to say a gang of ancient vampires, terrified for their lives and eager for an easy 'out' may not have summoned up, consciously or unconsciously, a tulpa resembling a demon because that's what they actually wanted?" Roderick spread his hands like a lawyer making a point in a courtroom drama. "They may have created something eager to help them but unable to win the war on their behalf because ultimately they wanted to believe they could win it themselves. Perhaps they think themselves damned in a moralistic religious sense. Perhaps they liked the idea of 'binding' it after having watched their own offspring use their free will to stage a revolt. Perhaps they simply like the aesthetic. You observed them adopting the garb and ambience with abandon, did you not?"

I considered it, then considered him, then shook my head. "So, what, it happened more than once? Two bunches of ancients summoned up some manufactured entity to help them in their time of need and they just happened to get the same thing? It happened here and it happened in Seattle, just by coincidence?"

"Perhaps it happened many times," Roderick said. "Perhaps it happens even now. Clearly the elders who survive are working in concert. What is successful for one may be shared with others. I would consider it too great a coincidence that it happen by chance; and we have no special reason to believe coincidence is required."

"Wouldn't that kind of be the ultimate ironic pain in the ass, though? To find out demons had been all in their head the whole time?" I clucked my tongue at the idea.

"Not in their heads, Cousin," Roderick corrected me with a waggle of one snow-white finger. "Distinctly outside their heads. That is the point. The tulpa becomes its own being. If this 'Ross' is a tulpa, the one who summoned him up may have long since seen the sun. It would not matter. They may be something we manifest but, invested with enough intent, given enough attention, believed in with sufficient fervor, they are their own entity." Roderick shrugged again. "I find it fascinating to consider them in light of other phenomena with significant overlap: the fair folk, alien abduction, Sasquatch and so on. There are cases of each, some more than others, in which the experience is essentially transactional in nature and the experiencers or witnesses left to believe themselves lucky to have escaped to tell the tale. The fair folk may lay a *geas* on those who wander into their circles; it is claimed extraterrestrial entities require their victims to carry implanted devices in return for their freedom; large hominids intimidate witnesses with loud roars and other harassment climaxing in chasing them from the woods altogether. Each of these has in common the condition of a more powerful entity essentially choosing to allow their victims to go free. Why? I believe it is so the witness-victim will report their experience to others and thus spread the notion of their existence. If these are all creatures sustained by belief perhaps they need us to further that belief for them. What if 'tulpa' and 'fairy' and 'alien' and 'bigfoot' and 'demon' are all merely arbitrary terms for a purely memetic entity reliant on us for reproduction and migration? What if the so-called 'ultraterrestrials' of John Keel are simply a form of life, conjured perhaps from the collective unconscious, gaining sustenance from ongoing belief in their objective truth?"

I blinked at him for a few moments. "Where in the hell do you hear about stuff like this?" I held out my hands and then clapped them against my legs in frustration. "I mean, what does 'memetic' even mean? What's an ultraterrestrial? What in the hell made you bone up on Tibetan thoughtforms in the first place?"

"Podcasts, mostly." Roderick shrugged. "And e-books. We live in the information age."

I snorted and shook my head. "Whatever. So maybe demons aren't from an actual h-e-double-hockey-sticks with a devil and everything. So what?"

"But they do appear to those who want something so badly their desire and desperation attract the attention of the being." Roderick scooted just a little closer. "Two examples come to mind, of course."

"El Diablo," I said. "So desperate to get back at the school that drove him out of his work, so seething with rage, that a demon showed up and started offering ideas."

"And then used the resources it found laying about – such as El Diablo's addicted research subjects – to keep the interest and engagement of Dmitri. If the demon-tulpa is a being of psychic energy summoned into existence by the attention and intention of those who create it and requiring more of those energies over time to sustain it, perhaps it is driven to strike bargains and impress 'normal' material beings with its abilities so that they will thank it, ask for its assistance or otherwise go on needing something it can offer."

I nodded. "Okay," I said. I liked the way it tied things together just enough for me to forget. I didn't want to sit around and stew about cosmology. I had too much on the stove already.

"The other example which comes to mind," Roderick continued, "Is you."

I blinked and stared at him like a horseshoe had just fallen out of his mouth. "What? I didn't summon up any goddamn thoughtforms."

"No, Cousin, you did not." Roderick nodded serenely, calm as the surface of the Dead Sea. "But the tulpa took an interest in you. You have desires to offer it. You have a need it thinks it could fulfill. It flattered you. It tried to distract you while its other clients caused havoc under your nose. It would have harmed you if doing so would make its other patrons stronger; it would have aided you had it supposed that to be been better for it in the end. The demon or devil or tulpa is an inherently untrustworthy being. It makes bargains to maintain relationships but will flit from one to another as its opinion changes regarding which is best. Remember this, Cousin, no matter what it makes you feel."

If I'd been alive, I would have blushed. I would have turned pink and then red and then downright purple with embarrassment. I'd been entirely if only temporarily consumed by a desire for Ross, inexplicably drawn to him in a way I'd assumed was lost to me forever. He'd awakened something deep-seated for which I had not been prepared and that lack of readiness was what had opened me up to him in the first place. Now, reflecting on it, I was almost as angry as I was embarrassed.

In the long run, though, it all paled in comparison to my sense of loss and frustration and unease. What were my bruised little feelings when there was a war going on and a new kind of critter with which to contend? Zombies and vampires and mortals had been more than enough, but now there were pseudo-devils, too? "Well," I said, "That's just great."

"Aloneness is very attractive to them," Roderick said with something proximate to kindness. "Remember that."

I cleared my throat. "Anyway, none of that is nearly so important to me as seeing Seth among the elders back in the day."

"Worrisome, yes," Roderick agreed. "You should ask him about it."

"What, just walk up and say, 'Hey, big guy, kind of saw a glimpse of you in the past. Looked like you'd joined the all-singing, all-dancing Satanic revue'?" I fluttered my lips. "Sure."

"Seth strikes me as trustworthy," Roderick shrugged. "If his aim were to eliminate you, he would have done so long ago. Asking him will either settle your mind or catch him off-guard. I see no disadvantage to either."

I harrumphed. We both turned to stare at what stars we could see in the sky over suburbia.

We were silent for a few minutes before Roderick spoke again. "In truth," he said, "What concerns me most is how Dmitri found out this would be a good place to go. A young champion of the rebels? That must surely be you. This suggests Agatha was on the side of the rebels, which is what I would assume: she likes control of her things but she is willing to grant freedom to those who serve her best, as she did you."

"I asserted my own freedom in my own way," I said. "I was not granted anything. She respected me."

"I do not doubt that is a part of it, Cousin," he said with a sly smile, "But your maker also enjoys scheming. I recommend you ask yourself who might have sent Dmitri here and why. Perhaps Dmitri was not ready for the showdown. I would consider the possibility someone who is aware of the war has fed Dmitri to you, both to eliminate him and to whet your appetite for war."

I blinked at him, surprised. "Why would they do that? Why make everything so complicated? Why not just ask me to join up?"

"Because they know the war was never truly over," Roderick said. "Our makers schemed together to destroy those who made them. They have already demonstrated a preference – and a talent – for conspiracy. There are many reasons someone might not approach you with an open offer of recruitment to some jingoistic cause. You have no special love for authority other than your own." I opened my mouth but he put up one hand to stop whatever sass was about to bubble up. "You do not welcome being told what to do."

I shook my head at that. The things my cousin could say, like it was all a big game and he was the guy giving color commentary during halftime. Unfortunately, he had a point.

I walked into the downtown bar managed by Seth less than ninety minutes after sunset the following night. Roderick had been right: if Seth was on the wrong side of a war I'd suddenly found myself in, I wanted to find out sooner rather than later and I wanted him to have no chance to prepare.

It's a little joint with a polished wooden bar, a long mirrored wall opposite it and a couple of bathrooms at the back of a forest of tall cocktail tables. There are chairs with long legs and high backs but they, like everything else in there, had seen better days. It was all painted black and blue and gray and there were lights under the bar, out of sight, so that Seth and the butch lesbian who helped him out sometimes were lighted from below like co-hosts of some UHF station's late night horror show.

Seth looked up and started to say something but stopped. I had never been to this bar before. I'd never once intruded on what Seth and I both considered to be his sacred space. We all have our own little patches of turf, after all, and even if I claim dominion over most of the state I recognize the wisdom – the humane necessity – of giving other people their space and demonstrating respect for it.

There were only a couple of other people in the bar, early patrons who show up for happy hour and tie one on in hopes they can forget something. They didn't even register my entrance. Seth nodded at me eventually as my boots clacked up to the bar. "You here to see that thing?" The way he asked it suggested I'd come to buy a car or maybe a brick of heroin. It was in no way subtle, nor was it especially meant to be: he was telling me he knew I was here to have some sort of serious talk and he really didn't want to have it in front of tonight's custom.

I nodded. "Sure thing. Let's go take a look."

Seth nodded at the big metal door in the back with EMERGENCY EXIT ONLY scrawled on it in magic marker. "Right this way." He put down the glass he was polishing for lack of anything better to do and walked around to go out. I could see and smell an alleyway beyond. It was almost entirely pitch black. That suited me just fine.

As soon as the door slammed shut behind us and the sounds of early night in a small city settled in, I spoke. "I know about Dmitri," I said. My voice was low and I tried to keep it even and devoid of any judgment. I needed to let Seth's response tell me something about Seth, not about how I'd approached him. "I know you are one of the elder vampires or were at least associated with them at one point in the past. I know about the rebellion."

Seth stood like the taciturn little '80s punk he'd always appeared to be: slumped against the wall, one booted foot lifted to rest a heel against the cement blocks, slouching just so with one hand in a pocket and the other shoving a cigarillo with a plastic filter on the end into his mouth. He hesitated for a second, lit the cigarillo and puffed it three times before blowing a long stream of smoke at the ground. "Just because I'm old doesn't mean I'm one of them." His voice was very quiet and he wouldn't meet my eyes but it sounded like the truth. The very first reaction he'd had to the subject was to try to put some distance between him and his peers.

"I didn't say you were, but I saw you there."

Seth looked up with confusion on his brow. "Saw me where?"

"One of their rituals, a long time ago. One of the big rituals involving the demon they summoned up to try and win the war." I shrugged. "My Last Gasp tells me things from a victim's life. I see visions of truth about them."

Seth pondered for a moment, returning his gaze to the ground and to the glow of the cigarillo tip. The smoke was cloyingly sweet, like he was toking on a joint stuffed with marshmallows. "Hindsight," he said.

"That's what my cousin called it." I nodded. "It's useful."

"But not so useful you use it all the time," Seth replied. He looked up and met my eye. "You don't go out and murder random people to get some voyeuristic thrill as you rewind through their life."

"No." I shook my head. "I do not."

Seth nodded. "That's the difference between you and them," he said. "Or maybe I mean 'us'. I dunno." He gave me a jerky little shrug with his shoulders, eyes on the ground. Seth has always been serene and wise in the face of problems: slow to act or to assume. He was treating me with the same kid gloves he used on any other problem. "Those assholes pulled out the Necronomicons and the ritual knives as soon as they knew they were in trouble. Just like that, they started spilling blood left and right: mortals, other vampires, anybody who was handy. They sliced apart one life after another in hopes the devil would eventually give them what they wanted. It was wrong. It was a nightmare." Seth looked up at me again. "I left after they started that stuff. I had never sympathized with them in the first place, but that didn't much matter to the rebels. Anyone old enough to be anything other than the lowest rung on the organizational ladder was to be considered their enemy." He drew a slow breath. "Even those of us who agreed with them in principle."

"No offense," I said, remembering seeing Seth robed up with the others at one of their ritual events, "But it seemed like maybe it took you some time to reach that conclusion."

He chuckled a couple of times: low panting breaths. "I needed something from the demon, too," he said through smoke. "I needed the ability to escape my… *allies*, I guess. I needed to be forgotten by them."

"So you stuck around long enough to cut a deal on the side?" I cleared my throat and eased my weight against an old crate.

"Pretty much." Seth didn't sound proud of himself. To him, this was an act of confession. "I wanted out and I wanted them not to remember I'd ever been there. The demon faked something up to make them think I was dead and I ran for it. I changed my name, started adopting the contemporary styles and aimed to be under the radar in Raleigh after that."

"Being second in command isn't exactly keeping a low profile." I rested one elbow on its corresponding knee.

"It beats being in charge," Seth finally said. He'd gone back to staring at the ground but spoke again through one great long gust of smoke, "And it keeps the boss off your back."

I nodded. "So," I finally said, "If the old guys were to show back up tomorrow, if the war were all of a sudden hot again, on whose side would you be?"

"My own." Seth looked up and his eyes met mine. "No one's but my own."

I nodded at him. He was telling the truth. "Fair enough," I said.

We sat in silence for a long time. I stared at his aquiline nose and narrow face in half-dark silhouette as he finished the Swisher Sweet. Finally, he spoke. "So, what now?"

"Did Dmitri know you were here? Is that why he came here?"

Seth shook his head. "If he knew I was here he would have just tried to kill me. He wouldn't have been doing anything else with his time. You didn't answer the question."

I sighed. "I don't know the answer."

"There are only two answers," Seth said. He ground the plastic filter of the cigarillo against the heel of the boot he'd had propped against the wall. "Either you're going to try to put an end to me right now or you're going to say my age doesn't matter as long as I'm on your side. If you choose the former, I'm just going to run away. I have no interest in a fight. If you choose the latter, everything stays the way it has been."

"And if they show up again, you're just going to run off?"

Seth paused at that. "Probably."

"That's a hell of a way to spend eternity," I said. My voice was soft and I hoped I sounded sympathetic. I didn't blame him, but neither did I think I could just go off and spend forever with my tail between my legs.

"I've got plenty of time," Seth said. "I've got more time than I'll ever use."

"That sounds like it's more meaningful than it seems at first listen." I cleared my throat.

Seth shrugged that off without looking at me.

"OK, I'm choosing the latter of your two options, but I ask one thing of you as a demonstration of…" I licked my lips. "Not loyalty, not fealty, but of, I don't know, of the absence of ill intent."

Seth looked at me again. His gaze was steady, revealing nothing.

"What's your Last Gasp?" I asked it point-blank, rude as possible in vampire circles. "We don't normally talk a lot about that. Tell me yours. Show me one of the cards up your sleeve. Give me a reason to feel like you're speaking honestly with me."

Seth smiled and looked back down. "I call it 'borrowed time'," he said. I made a noise of incomprehension and he went on. "When I drain the last of someone, I take all the time that would have been left to them if they'd lived out the rest of their normal life." He cleared his throat. "Let's say I drain someone at age 16. If they otherwise would have lived to 80, for instance, that gives me 64 years of time to burn off."

"So, that's 64 years of being you? Or something?" I didn't understand. "You're not immortal like the rest of us?"

Seth chuckled. "No one is. That isn't what I mean, though. I mean I can freeze time. I can step between seconds. You have hindsight: usually that means you experience what you experience between two instants of perceived time. You spend a long time learning stuff but when you snap out of it no time has passed, right?"

I nodded.

"Imagine you could instead press pause on the flow of time like that and walk off into the world as it stands, perfectly frozen, practically uninhabited, for as long as you wish. When you press play, time starts moving again. The time I perceive as passing for me when I do that – when I freeze time – is that surplus of borrowed time being burned off as I move about."

"And the paused time available to you is finite." I humphed with surprise.

"In purely mathematical terms, yes." Seth nodded at me. "But I collected so much time when I was young, before I knew the deal, I don't know if I'll ever run out." He shrugged. "I have millennia of borrowed time to draw on."

I blinked. "How old are you, Seth?"

He smiled at me. "Sorry, man," Seth said. "You asked for one thing, and I gave it to you. Some secrets I keep for myself."

I furrowed my brow. "Prove it."

"The watch," Seth said. "You needed a watch to impress that guy at Power Company, so I stepped out of time, went and got a watch and brought it back to you."

"The noise," I said. "The weird metallic sound when you blipped for a second."

Seth twisted up the corners of his mouth. "Exactly. I don't know how or why it does that, but it does."

I asked the obvious question before I could talk myself out of it. "Why haven't you used this to murder all your old compatriots?" I let my mouth hang open for a second as my brain churned. "It just seems like the easiest way to make sure no one would come after you: step out of time, kill your old peers and then step back in."

"That was the price of being forgotten," Seth said with a small, sad smile. "Ross said I had to give up certainty in order to be forgotten. It had to be a gamble, he told me, or what was the point? So, I swore not to go after my old colleagues and he promised to make them forget me. I thought I was getting the good end of the bargain, right? Who's going to hunt down a vampire they can't remember? But now I shake my head and appreciate how wrong I was. Everyone else may have forgotten me, forgotten who I was or why I may have mattered to them, but I haven't." He chewed a fingernail for a moment. "I still remember it all. I still have to be afraid of who I was."

Roderick set up a meeting with Jennifer for me. I asked him to give her my number and let her know the old prohibition on being found or followed was over. Any concerns I'd once had about discretion were now well and truly water under the bridge. Jennifer called me a few days later and we met for coffee at a little place in Durham not too far from my "abandoned" cabin crash pad: a quiet little shop in a strip mall, with friendly staff and good candy. We sat and split a piece of cake in silence for a while.

"Do you still work at ÜberBargains?" I asked it casually, trying to ease my way into the conversation.

"No." Jennifer shook her head at me. "I quit a few months after, well, that night. You know."

I nodded. "Our own private zombie apocalypse, part two."

She smiled a little. "I couldn't just go to work and pretend nothing had happened. Not again. Not twice. That time was too much. The world was too unlike what I thought I understood about it. I couldn't just put on the blinders and punch the clock."

I wiped my mouth on a napkin and pushed back from the table. "I'm sorry that happened to you."

She looked at me with piercing eyes. "Don't apologize. It wasn't your fault."

Technically, it sort of had been, but that wasn't the point. I waved it off. "I'm sorry because mortals shouldn't have to deal with crap like that."

Jennifer arched one eyebrow at me, a little insulted.

"It sounded a lot less condescending in my head," I murmured. "I'm sorry. You are not an ordinary mortal. I knew that the first time we met."

Jennifer pondered that for a few seconds. "Thanks. I think."

I nodded. "It is intended as a compliment."

"I'm not part of the herd but I'm not a vampire. So what now?" She put her fork down.

I blinked. "Are you asking to be made a vampire?"

She chuckled, low and rueful. "No," she said. "I most certainly am not."

I breathed an obvious sigh of relief. "Good."

"But I don't know what I am," she went on. "I know too much, but you let me live. This time around I was on the team. Sort of." She produced a bitter smirk. "I get the impression from talking to Roderick that you guys don't often make friends."

I blinked. "You talk to Roderick?"

She shrugged. "I have talked to him a couple of times, sure."

"Look," I said, "Just for your information, my cousin Roderick is…"

"Crazy as a soup sandwich." Jennifer smiled for a split second: just a hint of humor at the corners of her mouth. Her eyes softened a little. She was starting to relax.

I relaxed a little. "As you say."

Jennifer nodded. "I know, but I feel like he treats me as a peer. I have trouble finding those with my own kind." She said the last three words as though they tasted bad, and I guessed they did. I hated saying them, too, sometimes.

"Listen," I finally said, my hands falling into my lap. "I cut you off after the ÜberBargains debacle because…" I started to say it was because mortals who get wrapped up in vampire affairs tend not to live very long. That was true, but it wasn't the truth of why I'd mandated she stay away from me and from vampires in general. "Because you're dangerous."

She arched both eyebrows at me over the rim of her cup of coffee.

"You're curious, Jennifer. Curiosity is bad. It's bad for my kind because by necessity we hide from the world. We mostly just want to be left alone. You weren't someone who would just leave things alone. If you were, you never would have been fighting the hive mind alongside me in the first place. I couldn't run the risk of knowing you."

"So what's changed?"

I shrugged. "Roderick got to me. Roderick made me start thinking friends might be more of an asset than a liability."

"That's not true," Jennifer said. She ran a hand through her frizzy hair. "Well, maybe it is, but the truth is you're scared. You need allies but you can't admit it to yourself. There's something big going on and you don't know *exactly* what but you think you need friends to get through it." She looked me in the eye. "Tell me I'm wrong."

I looked away.

"I was up in the mountains, you know." She said it as casually as she could.

I looked back and blinked at her.

"The murder of that old cop? I don't know what went down, but I suspect he was a friend of yours. I talked to the locals. I investigated it to the best of my ability."

"All that business with Clyde and with the Transyl – " I cut myself off.

Wheels turned in Jennifer's head, capturing and recording every atom of meaning I might give away. After a moment of awkward silence she went on. "Clyde, yes, and whoever else. I was there with my team." She produced a business card for NORTH CAROLINA PARA-SCIENCE. "I was looking for signs of vampire attacks and there was a bloodless corpse. I checked it out. We couldn't find out much. It turned out dousing and 'sensitives' and my own moxie didn't get me very far." She shrugged. "I disbanded the group eventually. Groups like that never last very long anyway. They're drama magnets. The point is, I've been doing what I could and I'm going to keep doing whatever I can to learn the way the world really works. Maybe you don't want to be bothered with a human. Maybe you think I want to be your sidekick or something. Maybe you think I'm a security risk. You're wrong, but that's your problem. I'm already involved in this world of yours, Withrow, and I'm not going to be told to go home and act like a good girl. Neither am I going to be an on-demand social acquaintance." She gave me a look that was not entirely unkind. "But I am open to being friends if you are." She paused. "The truth is, you're not the only one who needs a friend who gets this shit. I need one, too."

I let a long-held breath go at last. "Maybe this was a mistake," I said. "I need friends, yes. I need…" I waved my hands around. How could I describe to her the way it felt to be so connected to the world for just a few seconds after I drained Dmitri? How could I describe what it was like to spend the better part of seven decades cut off from the world and to realize, all at once, how terrible that was? "I need a connection to the world of the living. I do not need to get that connection killed, though. I don't need to screw up in my responsibilities to the rest of my kind by bringing smart mortals into things when we're all trying to be as…" I searched my vocabulary. "As discreet as possible."

"Okay," Jennifer was all business. "Turn down an offer to become allies if you like. It's your funeral."

She stood up, and so did I. After a moment, we shook hands, our eyes locked, and she stepped backwards after holding the shake for a moment at the end.

"Jennifer," I said, fishing for some way to express the truth of how vampires see humans, "I have a lot of respect for you. You are a formidable mortal. You're going to do something amazing. I can feel that. I knew that right away, the first time we met."

"I know I am," she said. Jennifer smiled, really smiled, at long last. We weren't going to walk away best buddies, but we were going to walk away liking each other even if we didn't see eye to eye. For me, that was a big deal. It was more than I got the vast majority of the time. "I just hope you're there for it."

I didn't know what to say to that, so I said nothing.

Jennifer turned, but stopped and turned back. "You could have saved her."

"She wouldn't have wanted to be one of us." I shrugged.

"No, I don't mean that. I mean you could have joined the fight she was having." Jennifer held my gaze. She hadn't been there and I had crushed the phone to pieces so she couldn't have watched the video footage I was filming at the time. Jennifer didn't have any facts to go on, but she knew it, deep down, and I knew she was right. "The two of you were alone with El Diablo. The *two* of you could have taken him. I'll never know why you let her die but I know you must have allowed it to happen, to one degree or another. I'm willing to forgive that because I wasn't there and because this is, apparently, a war. Maybe you weren't able to help her; maybe one or another person dying stops meaning very much after you've seen it happen enough times over decades or centuries. I'm not saying all this to make you feel guilty. I'm saying all this so you'll know the quality of friendship you're passing over. Maybe next time you'll choose to save someone or you'll choose to make a friend." She looked away for a moment. "Not everyone gets to live forever, Withrow. We don't all get to be choosy. We don't have the luxury of turning friendship away. We never know when or how or why those friends will be taken from us. We only know they *will*." She looked back at me. "Goodbye." With that, she walked out of the coffee shop.

I finished off the cake and wiped the staff of any memory of our having been there.

I do hate leaving loose ends.

At the end of that week, Roderick and I paid another visit to the technopagans. We coaxed them over to El Diablo's lair, where we found notebooks full of hand-written figures and a laptop running software neither of us could have understood or used. We paid the technopagans to tell us what everything was. Roderick and one of the technopagans went out into the woods and took care of the bombs El Diablo had been building while the others worked. It took several nights but eventually they made sense of El Diablo's research.

El Diablo had come up with a cocktail of steroids, stem cells and chemicals of his own making designed to send a human's metabolism through the roof.

It had crystal meth in it, too. That was part of what made its users so strong and so addicted. Meth turns off the part of the brain responsible for telling you to stop straining a muscle before you damage it. That's where meth strength comes from. The kids taking it were destroying a little more of their bodies every time they performed some feat of might.

The technopagans were able to turn up one more important thing about El Diablo's work: the stuff destroyed brains. I don't mean it merely made its users crazy: it did something to the actual gray matter. The twins' minds were mushy when I used the hoodoo because of severe brain damage they had suffered. It would never correct itself. The technopagans were pretty sure it would keep getting worse. On the plus side, the physical enhancements would fade in time. I made a point of stopping in to check on Scott and Adam and, sure enough, within a month the twins were borderline mental vegetables and had reverted back to their normal physical capabilities. They didn't really recognize me. Their memories were completely shot. I wondered what their mother would think now. I didn't call anyone, though. It was an act of cruelty, but one I felt necessary. I'd called enough cops for one lifetime and their situation was not, ultimately, my problem.

The technopagans also tracked down The Bull's Eye's mundane identity faster than the cops could. I went to her house and spent hours boxing up everything I found that was hand-written. I left her medals alone out of respect but I took her journals, years' worth, and studied them in detail. She was a meticulous diarist. It made piecing together how she got in this situation possible, and I was intensely grateful. I thought about burning them, but I ended up putting them in the attic of my house in Raleigh. Vampires do that a lot: we're big on mementos.

Real estate records turned up three other houses owned by Dmitri, all of them with high turnover rates. Rent checks started going uncashed and tenants never seemed to complain. I didn't blame them. It would be a while before the county noticed anything.

My state was mine again: yet another intruder was gone and so was a hero I didn't want to ever have to put down myself. A part of me was jealous of The Bull's Eye, to be honest. A vampire is a survivor, ultimately defined by self-interest. That tends to make us the villain of the story rather than the hero no matter what wacky fantasies Roderick might have. I was okay with that. He could continue to struggle with it in his own way all he damn well wanted.

I thought a lot about what Jennifer had said: her determination to understand the world vampires occupied. I had no intention of trying to stop her. The truth was, I was finding out I didn't really understand it, either. I kind of hoped she got what she wanted and kind of hoped she hit nothing but dead ends. If Jennifer were successful in her quest it might be useful to know whatever she discovered and I had plenty of ways to find that out. As for what could have been the friendship between us, she had been right about me allowing The Bull's Eye to die but she wasn't there. She didn't understand the circumstances. She would have to make her own peace with that. I couldn't talk her around to my way of thinking. She was too smart to be persuaded like that anyway.

For now, I chose to go back home, scratch my dog behind the ears and wait to see if anyone else reacted to Dmitri's death. That's one of the advantages of trying to live forever: we just need to have a little more patience than our enemies. The demon Ross, the elder vampires, the whole kit and kaboodle could wait until they got tired of hiding and presented themselves in some helpful fashion. I had some ideas of things to do to investigate, but I needed to let them stew a while. In the meantime, I'd acted to defend my turf from whatever bizarre machinations they'd cooked up. I hoped it would provoke some sort of revealing response. I could think things over until they broke cover.

I had all the time in the world.

Epilogue

The most desperate person in Durham, it turned out, was a cashier at Jennifer's old ÜberBargains. Roderick found him via the technopagans: he paid them handsomely and they had asked few questions. When they gave him an address, he went to it and studied it over the course of several nights.

The man who lived there was middle-aged and had a nice house in the suburbs. It was big and expensive and Roderick wondered how he could possibly afford it on a few dollars an hour for thirty five hours per week. Observation filled in the details: a divorce, a layoff, depleted savings. Now the man worked as hard as he could at two part-time jobs. He just barely failed to make ends meet for as long as he possibly could cover the gap between his expenses and his income. He was at the end of his rope and he didn't know what to do. The man had pondered turning to crime, of course, as many before him had done, but he lacked the temperament for it. He was essentially an honest man and Roderick knew the world would eat him sooner rather than later. There were lots of these people: the suburban poor, subsisting in homes too big for their reduced incomes. They were a phenomenon about which Roderick had read on the Internet. Roderick decided to spare everyone the trouble of hoping for the best. He would end the man's life himself. Roderick very carefully set his intention, visualizing himself doing the man in for a specific ritual purpose: a summoning.

Ross appeared when Roderick put his gloved hand on the latch of the man's garage door.

"I didn't expect you to be the one who summoned me in this way," he said. The devil had a glint in his yellow eyes and a wicked smile. He looked like he very much wanted to have sex with something virtuous.

Roderick took his hand from the door. "Just confirming a theory," he said. "I do not wish anything from you."

Ross arched an eyebrow. "That's not true."

Roderick smirked. "Then allow me a small correction. I do not wish you to give me anything or do me any favors. What I want is for you to understand that I will destroy you." Roderick leaned closer to speak. It was an intimate whisper, like suggestions being passed between lovers. "I want you to know that you will suffer and be destroyed. The mechanism driving your continued existence will be disrupted and I will remain after you are banished."

Ross chuckled low in his chest and returned the gesture, leaning close enough to tickle Roderick's ear. "Roderick," he sneered, "I had no idea you cared so deeply about me."

Roderick leaned even closer, his breath cold against Ross' neck. "It is not that I *care* so strongly as to find you contemptible," he murmured. "You have a desire to survive and appetites to sate. I understand that. I am much the same way. I simply cannot stand the competition. The world can only bear so much anguish and I want it all for myself."

"How do you plan to destroy me? I'm a creature of thought, aren't I? That's your theory, anyway." His tone was teasing, on the taunting end of flirtatious.

Roderick let a little breath of laughter escape before he pulled back and looked Ross in the eye. "This is not, as they say, my first rodeo. I destroy. I remove things from the world. It is my calling. It is my art. Where others create, I create *absence*. I have done it many times and once – just once – it was to a creature such as you are. I intend to do so again."

Ross tried not to look concerned as he replied but Roderick could sense just a little fear behind his words. "So why aren't you doing it right now? Why all the big talk?"

"Because half the pleasure is in the cultivation," Roderick murmured. "Ask any gardener, dear boy, and they will tell you the same."

Then Roderick went inside and murdered a frightened little man whose mortgage payment was overdue. By sunrise the next morning the neighbors wondered just how long that house had been abandoned.

Jennifer knocked at the door of the green house on Morehead Hill. The lines running from the telephone pole to the technopagans' home were humming with electromagnetic feedback. She smirked. A younger version of her would have considered a house like this to be heaven.

When the door opened it was Xi. "Ah," he said to her. "Can we help you?"

"Yes," Jennifer said. "I need to talk to your group." She paused then went on. "All of the group. At once."

Xi got out of the way and invited her in. He made some audible bird-like call with his voice, something wordless between a hoot and a holler, and then led her into the living room. The little queen from Duke was sitting there playing a videogame. The rest of the house filed into the small living room in a rush. Apparently the call Xi used meant there was serious business to discuss. Jennifer wasted no time addressing them.

"I need to join your group," she said. They looked at her, and she at them, and she went on. "The world is full of monsters: ghosts, vampires, demons, zombies, black-eyed kids. I need some advantage in order to fight them. Right now I'm just a normal mortal and that isn't good enough. I took out one vampire, one time, but he was already injured and I took him by surprise. He was young, too. The ones I need to help deal with are old and that means I need..." She glanced at the TV and the paused game on its screen. "I need a power-up."

Sheila from Durham Tech shook her head at Jennifer. "We destroyed everything El Diablo manufactured," she said. "We don't have any more and, trust me, you don't want it anyway."

Jennifer smiled a little. "I don't mean that shit. I mean I need magic." She looked around at them. "I was a systems administrator for a while. It feels like a lifetime ago, but I know the tech side. I've never been comfortable with the mystical woo-woo stuff. You seem to have figured out how to blend the way you think about technology with the way you think about magic. I think I can wrap my head around that. So, I'm volunteering."

The group looked around at one another. They didn't seem to have a formal high priest or priestess. Jennifer recognized the look of well-I'm-certainly-not-in-charge on every face. It was all too common in collective living arrangements. Finally the Duke kid said, "*Just* when I thought I'd convinced myself they didn't really say 'vampires' last time."

"Steeplechase zombies aren't the only big bad critter in the world," Jennifer said.

"Not everyone even believes those really happened." He looked a little smug.

"Not everyone thinks 9/11 really happened, either," Jennifer said, "Because some people just can't accept a world too big for them to understand. I can. I've been living in that world ever since Z-Day." She paused. She hadn't actually had this conversation with anyone; not ever. She hadn't even had it with Tim, and that was probably why they weren't in each other's lives any longer. She'd sort of had it with Withrow, but he was a fellow witness. She'd never tried to convince anyone who wasn't. "I was there. I saved a *town*. They don't hand out medals for that, though. Instead, they look at you like you've still got zombie on your hands because they can't face the fears you've already bested: they can't face the world that gave them zombies and they can't face that they had to be saved when it happened. Fine, then. I'm someone who can do those things. I can save my friends, save the town; maybe now I need to save the world. If what's going on between vampires is as bad as it seems to be, we're all in danger and we can't just leave the vampires to clean it all up for us. I knew there was something going on before, but now I know a lot more. Some of them *want* us to be at their mercy, and I say fuck that. I say fight. Now that I've tried doing it I know I need to be…" Jennifer paused and thought of Adam and Scott. She licked her lips. "Extra."

"And you want us to give you that edge?" The kid from Durham Tech, the young one, looked scared as hell when he asked.

"No," Jennifer said. "I want you to teach me what you know and then join me in the war. Here's my offer: you initiate me into your group, teach me everything you know, and I'll become your leader. You need one, and some of you already know that." She drew a quick circle in the air with one finger to indicate the house, the people in it, the whole shebang. "Really, the choice here is whether *you* are going to be the ones to join *me*. I'm doing this one way or another, with one group or another. If you sign on with me, you will get to be there when we crack reality wide open and see its insides. You're already curious about the world around you or you wouldn't be here, in this house. You've approached magic like it's a laboratory and become experts. Now the question is, are you willing to step out of the lab and into the field?"

They were silent for a long time. Finally, Xi spoke up. "We would need some time to talk about it and take a vote."

"You have five minutes," Jennifer said. "I'll be on the back porch."

Ten minutes later they started an initiation ritual they had to make up on the fly.

Roderick walked into the bar, heeled boots clacking like stilettos on the old tile floor. There were a bunch of drunks drinking their dinner. The college crowd hadn't started to filter in yet. The bar had seen better days, of course, but it had also seen worse. Roderick liked it for its simple appeal as a place to get drunk. It was not fancy. It did not have pretenses. It knew what it could offer and it sought opportunities to do so.

Rather like himself, he felt.

Roderick gave Seth what he considered a winning smile: lips pulled back and lots of perfect white teeth.

Seth spoke in a professional tone. "What are you having?"

"You," Roderick said. "For my team. Now."

The man's eyebrows went up, and though he didn't let his gaze wander across the patrons rowed up around them it was clear to Roderick that Seth's concern was for the possibility the mortals in the room might hear them.

"These persons," Roderick said openly, without regard for being overheard, "Do not give a damn what we say as long as you continue to serve them." He waved with one limp-wristed hand, a dandy in a white pleather suit like he'd just stepped out of a time machine. "Do you accept my offer?"

"I'm not on anybody's team," Seth said. "I just look out for myself."

"Not anymore. My cousin is willing to tolerate a free agent because he thinks himself one as well. This is not so. There is a very long game being played and we are all on the field whether we like it or not. I cannot tolerate those who do not accept this."

"Does your cousin know you're here?" Seth's voice was low.

"No," Roderick said. He smiled again. "Neither will you tell him."

"Says who?"

"Says I," Roderick replied. He reached for an empty glass, abandoned by an early patron, and swirled the ice in it for just a moment. "A year ago my cousin thought himself the gun and me the bullet: he could aim and fire me at a problem. He agreed to let me stay in his domain in return for removing the vermin from one particular corner of it. My cousin does not realize just how great a problem he has, however. I do. It is a problem we all share. I intend to solve that problem and I intend to use my cousin to do it." Roderick offered Seth a much tighter expression: lips closed, corners curled up. It was not a joyous expression. "He shall be my bullet, and I, the gun. You wish to be on my side in this endeavor because I will leave you to your own devices once the fight is won."

Seth studied the glass for a moment. "You brought Dmitri here, didn't you?"

This time Roderick smiled with something like real joy.

About the Author

Michael G. Williams is a native of the mountains of western North Carolina. He is a brother in St. Anthony Hall and Mu Beta Psi and believes strongly in the power of found families. Michael lives in Durham with his two cats and more and better friends than he probably deserves.

Michael earned a BA in Performance Studies at UNC Chapel Hill and works as an engineer. He has been a successful participant in National Novel Writing Month for many years and encourages anyone interested in writing to jump headlong into the deep end of insanity for thirty days. More information can be found at www.nanowrimo.org.

For more information on this work and others by Michael G. Williams, visit www.michaelgwilliams-author.com. For information on Michael's open-source marketing, visit The Perishables Project at www.theperishablesproject.com.

Also by Michael G. Williams

Perishables (The Withrow Chronicles #1)
Tooth & Nail (The Withrow Chronicles #2)
"COMPLICATIONS"
"The Several Monsters of Sainte-Sara-La-Noire"
(Theme-Thology: Invasion)
"Daddy Used to Drink Too Much"
(Wrapped in Red: Thirteen Tales of Vampiric Horror)

Connect with Michael via the following sites:

The *Perishables* Project
Twitter
Facebook
Google+
Amazon Author Central
GoodReads
Roderick's Tumblr
Withrow's Tumblr